An Edition of
The Early Writings of Charlotte Brontë
1826–1832

Frontispiece Three issues of the *Young Men's Magazine* for 1830, written by Charlotte Brontë at the age of fourteen, and the untitled booklet 'There was once a little girl', Charlotte Brontë's earliest extant manuscript written at about the age of ten, showing the exact size

An Edition of
The Early Writings
of
CHARLOTTE
BRONTË

VOLUME I
The Glass Town Saga
1826–1832

Edited by
Christine Alexander

Published for the Shakespeare Head Press
by Basil Blackwell

Copyright © Basil Blackwell Ltd 1987

First published 1987

Basil Blackwell Ltd
108 Cowley Road, Oxford OX4 1JF, UK

Basil Blackwell Inc.
432 Park Avenue South, Suite 1503,
New York, NY 10016, USA

British Library Cataloguing in Publication Data

Brontë, Charlotte
An edition of the early writings of Charlotte
Brontë, 1826–1832.
1. Title II. Alexander, Christine
828'.809   PR4165

ISBN 0–631–12988–X

Library of Congress Cataloging in Publication Data

Brontë, Charlotte, 1816–1855.
An edition of the early writings of Charlotte
Brontë, 1826–1832.
Bibliography: p.
Includes index.
I. Alexander, Christine. II. Title.
PR4166.A44 1986 823'.8 86–1103
ISBN 0–631–12988–X

Typeset in 10½ on 12pt Ehrhardt by Columns of Reading
Printed in Great Britain by T. J. Press Ltd, Padstow

To Peter,
Rebecca and Roland

CONTENTS

List of Illustrations	ix
Acknowledgements	x
General Introduction	xiii
Textual Introduction	xx
Abbreviations	xxiv

The Early Writings of Charlotte Brontë 1826–1832

1826–8

'There was once a little girl and her name was Anne'*	3

1829

The History of the Year	4
'The origin of the O'Deans'	6
'The origin of the Islanders'*	6
Two Romantic Tales:	
A Romantic Tale (or The Twelve Adventurers)	7
An Adventure in Ireland	18
Tales of the Islanders, volume I*	21
The Enfant*	34
The Keep of the Bridge*	36
'Sir – it is well known that the Genii'	39
A Fragment, August the 7, 1829*	40
Fragment, August the 8, 1829*	41
The Search After Happiness	42
Blackwood's Young Men's Magazine, August 1829*	54
Blackwood's Young Men's Magazine, September 1829*	62
Blackwood's Young Men's Magazine, October 1829*	70
Blackwood's Young Men's Magazine, November 1829*	78
Anecdotes of the Duke of Wellington*	88
Blackwood's Young Men's Magazine, December (first issue) 1829*	91
Tales of the Islanders, volume II*	99
Blackwood's Young Men's Magazine, December (second issue) 1829*	113

* Published for the first time.

Contents

Characters of the Celebrated Men of the Present Time   123

1830

Description of the Duke of Wellington's Small Palace Situated
on the Banks of the Indiva*   130
The Adventures of Mon Edouard de Crack*   133
Tales of the Islanders, volume III*   140
The Adventures of Ernest Alembert   154
An Interesting Passage in the Lives of Some Eminent Men of
the Present Time   169
'The following strange occurrence'   177
Leisure Hours*   178
The Poetaster, volume I   179
The Poetaster, volume II   187
Tales of the Islanders, volume IV*   196
Catalogue of my Books*   211
Young Men's Magazine, August 1830*   215
Young Men's Magazine, September 1830*   227
Young Men's Magazine, October 1830*   228
Young Men's Magazine, November 1830*   241
Young Men's Magazine, December (first issue) 1830   255
Young Men's Magazine, December (second issue) 1830*   267
Campbell Castle*   281
Albion and Marina   285
Visits in Verreopolis, volume I*   297
Visits in Verreopolis, volume II*   316

1831

A Fragment, 'Overcome with that delightful sensation of
lassitude'*   327
'About 9 months after my arrival at the Glass Town'   333

1832

The Bridal   335

Appendix 1   A Visit to the Duke of Wellington's Small Palace
Situated on the Banks of the Indiva   349
Appendix 2   Poems written by Charlotte Brontë during the years
1829 to 1832 and not included in this volume   352

Textual Notes   354
Index of First Lines and Titles   379

ILLUSTRATIONS

Frontispiece   Three issues of the *Young Men's Magazine* for   ii
1830, written by Charlotte Brontë at the age of fourteen, and
the untitled booklet 'There was once a little girl', Charlotte
Brontë's earliest extant manuscript written at about the age of
ten, showing the exact size. By courtesy of the Brontë Society,
Haworth, copyright © Brontë Society.

1   A page from *Tales of the Islanders*, volume I, chapter 4, written   31
by Charlotte Brontë at the age of thirteen. By courtesy of the
Berg Collection, New York Public Library.

2   *The Keep of the Bridge*, written and illustrated by Charlotte   37
Brontë at the age of thirteen. By courtesy of the Berg
Collection, New York Public Library.

3   Pages from *Blackwood's Young Men's Magazine*, first issue for   98
December 1829, written by Charlotte Brontë at the age of
thirteen. By courtesy of the Brontë Society, Haworth,
copyright © Brontë Society.

4   The initial pages of *The Poetaster*, volume II, a drama written   189
by Charlotte Brontë at the age of fourteen. By courtesy of the
Pierpont Morgan Library, New York.

5   Title-page, preface and first page of *Albion and Marina*,   284
written by Charlotte Brontë at the age of fourteen. By courtesy
of the English Poetry Collection, Wellesley College Library,
USA.

6   The first and last pages of *A Fragment*, written by Charlotte   328
Brontë at the age of fifteen. By courtesy of the Brontë Society,
Haworth, copyright © Brontë Society.

ACKNOWLEDGEMENTS

The greater part of the labour of this volume was the transcription of the original manuscripts in order to produce a text to be edited for publication. This involved not only working with microfilms and photocopies but also travelling to the various repositories of Brontë manuscripts, repositories which are distributed almost equally between Britain and the United States. Because of the tiny size of Charlotte Brontë's early manuscripts and her minuscule script, it was impossible to rely solely on photographic copies of her works. A New Zealand Postgraduate Scholarship and a New Zealand University Women's Fellowship enabled me to carry out the initial work on the unpublished manuscripts in Britain. The Brontë Society, my college Clare Hall, Cambridge, and the Sir Ernest Cassel Trust all kindly assisted me to travel to the United States to work on the manuscripts there. More recently, a grant from the University of New South Wales helped with the purchase of microfilms and photocopies; and a generous award from the British Council gave me the opportunity to return to Britain to complete work on the manuscripts and to confer with colleagues and publishers on editorial matters.

I wish to thank the family of the late Mr C. K. Shorter for permission to publish the juvenile manuscripts of Charlotte Brontë. I am also grateful to the following for permission to use manuscript material in their possession for publication: the Henry W. and Albert A. Berg Collection, New York Public Library, Astor, Lenox and Tilden Foundations; the British Library Board; the Harry Ransom Humanities Research Center, the University of Texas at Austin; the Houghton Library, Harvard; the Huntington Library, San Marino, California; the Walpole Collection, King's School, Canterbury; Special Collections, University of Missouri-Columbia Libraries; the Carl and Lily Pforzheimer Foundation, Inc., on behalf of the Carl H. Pforzheimer Library; the Pierpont Morgan Library; the Robert H. Taylor Collection, Princeton, New Jersey; and the English Poetry Collection, Wellesley College Library. I am grateful to my publishers, Basil Blackwell, for permission to reproduce the texts of six stories from *The*

Acknowledgements

Miscellaneous and Unpublished Writings of Charlotte and Patrick Branwell Brontë (Oxford: Basil Blackwell for The Shakespeare Head Press), vols I (1936) and II (1938); and to the Brontë Society for permission to reproduce four transcriptions by Mr Davidson Cook and Mr C. W. Hatfield of manuscripts no longer in existence.

To the staff of the Brontë Parsonage Museum I owe a special tribute of thanks. Successive librarians, in particular Miss Amy G. Foster, Mrs Sally Stonehouse and Dr Juliet R. V. Barker, have been particularly patient in answering my constant queries over the last ten years and have always made my visits to the parsonage both rewarding and pleasurable. I am grateful especially to the members of the Brontë Society Council, past and present, not only for their kind permission to publish the Brontë juvenilia, but for their constant support and for their willingness to assist Brontë scholarship.

I am grateful for the courtesy and help of the staff of the various libraries in which I worked; they helped to transform what was often a painstaking and tedious task into a pleasure, and they have patiently answered many further queries since my visits. My thanks are therefore due to the following institutions and especially to those staff members mentioned in brackets: the British Library (Mr T. A. J. Burnett); the Brotherton Library (Mr C. D. W. Sheppard); the Ellis Library, University of Missouri-Columbia (Ms Margaret A. Howell); the Harry Ransom Humanities Research Center, University of Texas at Austin (Ms Ellen S. Dunlap and Ms Cathy Henderson); Harvard College Library (Mr Rodney G. Dennis and Ms Susan Halpert); the Huntington Library (Miss Jean F. Preston, Mrs Virginia Rust, Mr William Ingoldsby and Miss Sara S. Hodson); The King's School, Canterbury (Mr D. S. Goodes); the Manchester Public Libraries; the Newberry Library; New York Public Library (Mrs Lola L. Szladits and Mr David Pankow); the Carl H. Pforzheimer Library (Mr Mihai H. Handrea and Ms Rosannah Cole); the Pierpont Morgan Library (Mr Herbert Cahoon and Ms Pamela White); Princeton University Library (Mrs Nany N. Coffin and Mr Alexander P. Clark); Rutgers University Library; the John Rylands University Library of Manchester (Miss Glenise A. Matheson); the Poetry/Rare Books Collection of the University Libraries, State University of New York at Buffalo (Mr Robert J. Bertholf); the Victoria and Albert Museum; Wellesley College Library (Ms Anne Anninger and Ms Susan Barbarossa); and Yale University Library (Miss Marjorie G. Wynne). Thanks are also due to the staff of the Cambridge University Library and of the Social Sciences and Humanities Library of the University of New South Wales for their assistance in tracing secondary material.

Acknowledgements

The following private collectors have generously given me photocopies and detailed descriptions of manuscripts in their possession: Mr Roger W. Barrett, Mr Arthur A. Houghton, Jr, Mr William Self, Mr James W. Symington, and Mr Robert H. Taylor.

Others who have provided advice and assistance in various ways include: Mrs Leslie Barnett, Professor Mary Chan, Professor Mildred G. Christian, Dr Enid L. Duthie, Mr and Mrs S. Edwards, Dr Kate Frost, Dr Philip Gaskell, Mr Joseph R. Geer, Mrs Winifred Gérin, Mr Donald Hopewell, Miss Margaret Lane, Mr Charles Lemon, Mrs Barbara Lloyd-Evans, Miss Hilda Marsden, Professor B. K. Martin, Dr Melodie Monahan, Mr W. T. Oliver, Mr A. H. Preston, Mr N. Raistrick, Professor Derek Roper, Professor Herbert Rosengarten, Dr Mark R. D. Seaward, Mrs Edith M. Wier, and Mr G. A. Yablon. I am also grateful for the expert typing assistance of Mrs Shirley Chuck, Mrs Hazel Hedge and Mrs Ursula Raetze; for the editorial advice of Miss Meryl Potter; and for the photographic skills of Mrs Catherine Marciniak.

My sincere thanks are due to Mrs Margaret Smith and to Dr Tom Winnifrith for their valuable advice and generous hospitality. To Professor Ian Jack of Pembroke College, Cambridge, I owe a special debt of gratitude for introducing me to the Brontë juvenilia, and for his invaluable guidance and encouragement of my work.

Special acknowledgements are due to my family: to my parents for their early support; to my children for tolerating the rival demands of Charlotte Brontë; and especially to my husband and colleague for his constant advice and support.

C.A.

GENERAL INTRODUCTION

The stories and poems in this volume (with the exception of the first tiny manuscript of about 1826) were written during the years 1829 to 1832 when Charlotte Brontë was between thirteen and sixteen years old. By this time Charlotte, her younger brother, Branwell, and her two younger sisters, Emily and Anne, were at home under the care and tutelage of their father the Reverend Patrick Brontë, and their maiden aunt Elizabeth Branwell. Their mother had died in 1821 when Charlotte was five, and their two older sisters had both died of consumption in 1825. The four Brontë children lived in the relatively remote village of Haworth in Yorkshire, and they were further isolated socially as the children of the local Anglican parish priest. This isolation and their obvious need for emotional security in the face of what probably seemed an irrationally hostile world encouraged the children to form 'a little society amongst themselves'. Their father later told Mrs Gaskell, Charlotte's first biographer, how, with Charlotte and Branwell as leaders, they

> composed and acted their little plays . . . Sometimes, also, they wrote little works of fiction they call'd miniature novels. All these things they did of their own accord – and evidently took great pleasure in their enjoyment. (*Brontë Society Transactions*, vol. 8, 1932, p. 94)

In *The History of the Year*, which she wrote on 12 March 1829, Charlotte Brontë describes the 'three great plays' that form the basis of the Glass Town Saga, the tale of an imaginary African kingdom which is revealed in a series of related stories and poems written by Charlotte and her brother Branwell. No manuscripts by Emily and Anne Brontë relating to these early years survive; the first reference made by them to any 'play' is in a diary note by Emily dated 24 November 1834, referring to their later Gondal Saga. Initially the three sets of 'plays' contributing to the Glass Town Saga were distinct: the 'Young Men's Play' was inspired by a set of twelve wooden toy soldiers given to Branwell by Mr Brontë on his return from a clerical conference in

Leeds on 5 June 1826; 'Our Fellows' Play' was derived from Aesop's Fables; and 'The Islanders' Play' was based on current political events. 'Our Fellows' was short lived: Charlotte's only surviving literary contribution to this play, which appears to have been mainly Branwell's invention, is the early fragment 'The origin of the O'Deans'. 'The Islanders' Play' is described in the four volumes of *Tales of the Islanders*, written during 1829 and early 1830; and the remaining manuscripts of the years 1829 to 1830 belong chiefly to the 'Young Men's Play'. Gradually, however, the 'Young Men's Play' and 'The Islanders' merged: the main characters of the two plays were always essentially the same, and after *Albion and Marina*, in which the Duke of Wellington and his two sons travel to Africa, it is possible to speak of a single saga based on the imaginative world of Glass Town.

In the earliest manuscripts, the new land, founded by the 'Twelve Adventurers' or 'Young Men' from Britain, on the delta of the River Niger in West Africa, was ruled by Charlotte's favourite hero, the Duke of Wellington. But the boundaries were soon expanded to include kingdoms for all the children's favourite characters: Wellington's Land (Charlotte), Sneaky's Land (Branwell), Parry's Land (Emily), and Ross's Land (Anne). The Great Glass Town (later called first Verreopolis and then Verdopolis) became the centre of this con-federation of states, and each state had its own particular Glass Town modelled on the capital, which was controlled by all four rulers. Two islands to the south-west of the African coast were given to Stumps and Monkey, two of the twelve adventurers, and a third island was settled by the French, with its capital (modelled on Paris) forming the scene of several stories and 'magazine articles' in this volume.

By the end of 1830, the Great Glass Town had become a hive of commercial and cultural activity. Characters had proliferated and society had become more sophisticated. The footnotes to this edition are intended to guide the reader through the changing myriad of characters and places in the early manuscripts. Charlotte's writing centres first on the Duke of Wellington and then on his two sons, Arthur, Marquis of Douro, and Lord Charles Wellesley (based on the historical duke and his sons). Branwell's early writing concentrates on recording the early battles against the Ashantee natives, on providing the increasing population with magazines and newspapers, and on describing the developing Glass Town underworld.

As the plays became an exclusively literary venture, the children increasingly adopted their favourite characters as pseudonyms, vying with each other for status among the Glass Town literati. Branwell wrote first as Captain John Bud, the historian, and then as Young

Soult, 'the Rhymer'. Charlotte initially adopted Captain Tree, the renowned prose writer, but gradually replaced him with his cynical young rival Lord Charles Wellesley. As a poet, she wrote chiefly as the 'Marquis of Douro', who later dropped his literary role and became Charlotte's hero, the Duke of Zamorna and King of Angria. The contrasting natures of her pseudonyms allowed Charlotte to develop different sides of her literary personality. The Marquis of Douro, an accomplished young nobleman and Captain of the Royal Regiment of Horse Guards, produces serious love poems that are mocked by the ironical tone of Lord Charles Wellesley's anti-romanticism. Lord Charles's delight in scandal makes him an excellent mouthpiece for Charlotte Brontë's stories about his elder brother's love affairs. This role increases in the later manuscripts when Lord Charles ceases to play an active part in the saga and, as 'Charles Townshend', becomes the chief reporter of political and romantic intrigue. In the stories of this volume, however, he plays the often contradictory role of younger brother and cynical narrator.

Lord Charles Wellesley is also the chief contributor to Charlotte's miniature magazine, which is modelled on the pages of her father's *Blackwood's Edinburgh Magazine*. The idea of a magazine for the Young Men, to be written in script so small as to be proportionate to their size as toy soldiers, originated with Branwell. He produced the first issue of *Branwell's Blackwood's Magazine* in January 1829. When Charlotte became editor in August 1829, she changed the name first to *Blackwood's Young Men's Magazine* and then to *Young Men's Magazine* when she began the second series in August 1830. She confided to Mary Taylor, a school-friend, that her habit of writing in tiny characters had been formed by producing this magazine. She said that she and her brother and two sisters 'brought out a "magazine" once a month, and wished it to look as like print as possible' (Mrs Gaskell, *The Life of Charlotte Brontë*, 3rd edn, London: Smith, Elder, 1857, vol. 1, p. 113). The habit of producing little hand-sewn volumes, however, had actually begun much earlier with Charlotte's first little manuscript for her sister Anne, perhaps as early as 1826. These carefully crafted volumes, complete with title pages, prefaces and lists of contents, constitute most of her early surviving work and suggest not only an early awareness of her role as a writer, but also Charlotte's obvious intention to preserve her manuscripts.

The four Brontë children were both creators of and characters in their plays. When the 'Twelves' first arrived in Africa they were protected by the four Chief Genii, the Brontës themselves: Tallii, Branii, Emmii and Annii; and when the Glass Town expanded the

Chief Genii became responsible for the kingdoms of their particular characters. In 'The Islanders' Play' the Brontës also controlled the course of events and participated in the action as 'Little King and Queens', who appeared and disappeared at crucial moments in the stories, conveying vital messages and raising characters from the dead. Gradually, the supernatural role of the young authors was reduced as the characters themselves asserted their independence and as the interests of the four children diverged. By the second half of 1830, the four kingdoms were developing very different characteristics, as we see in 'A Day at Parry's Palace' (*Young Men's Magazine* for October 1830). Whereas Branwell clung to the old scenario of battles and political intrigue, and Charlotte concentrated on her romantic fairytale settings, Emily and Anne preferred the realistic world of Haworth and the Yorkshire moors. Their less glamorous characters Parry and Ross had always been relegated to secondary roles and scorned by Charlotte's grandees. It is hardly surprising that Emily and Anne eventually broke away from the Glass Town Saga to form their own play of Gondal. They took as their cue Charlotte's departure for boarding school at Roe Head in January 1831, and the dissolution of the four Chief Genii is recorded in Charlotte's poem 'The trumpet hath sounded', written during the next Christmas holidays.

Charlotte spent almost a year and a half at Roe Head school, returning home in May 1832. This accounts for the lack of manuscripts during the years 1831 and 1832: throughout her juvenilia a paucity of manuscripts corresponds to periods away from the security and companionship of home. She was homesick at school and her writing ceased, but not her interest in the Glass Town Saga. She found relief in daydreams. These she committed to paper almost immediately on her return home. She ignored the earlier 'destruction' of Glass Town and began a period of intense literary partnership with Branwell that dissolved only when her brother took to alcohol and opium in 1837 or 1838, and when her own maturing moral awareness exposed his limitations. Branwell's influence on Charlotte and the relationship of his manuscripts to her writing are noted where relevant in the footnotes of this edition and are fully discussed in the present editor's *The Early Writings of Charlotte Brontë* (Oxford: Basil Blackwell, 1983). Most of his published writings can be found in the original Shakespeare Head edition of *The Miscellaneous and Unpublished Writings of Charlotte and Patrick Branwell Brontë*, edited by Thomas James Wise and John Alexander Symington (Oxford: Basil Blackwell for The Shakespeare Head Press, vols I, 1836, and II, 1838).

The early manuscripts of 1829 to 1832, however, display a healthy rivalry between the aspiring authors. Both wrote about Glass Town, but their interests and their attitudes to their subjects were very different. Their characters are constantly carping at each other or being misrepresented by their rival creators. In *The Poetaster* and in *Visits in Verreopolis*, for example, Lord Charles (Charlotte's pseudonym) mocks the poetic pretensions of Branwell's 'Young Soult, the Rhymer'; and in the earlier *An Interesting Passage in the Lives of Some Eminent Men of the Present Time* Lord Charles involves Captain John Bud (Branwell's prose pseudonym) in a library theft. Bud responds in Branwell's *The Liar Unmasked*, 19 June 1830 (unpublished manuscript, Brontë Parsonage Museum: B139), denying the theft and lambasting Lord Charles who, he says, 'vomited forth a dose of scandal and self-importance in the shape of an octavo volume'. The manuscript is fit, we are told, only for Charlotte's 'Miss M. Hume, or any of her hysterical and delicate crew'. To Branwell, Charlotte's stories are the flimsy and inconsequential gossip of Glass Town society.

This interchange between brother and sister underlines the difference between their conceptions of their imaginary world, and it explains why it is possible to read Charlotte's manuscripts alone without losing the coherence of the saga. To some extent we are reading only half the story in the following pages, but Charlotte concentrated almost exclusively on the gradual development of her particular characters within the expanding Glass Town world, and it is her version that is important to any study of the later novels. From the time she assumed the editorship of the *Young Men's Magazine* from Branwell in August 1829, Charlotte began to assert her independence from her brother. While still co-operating with him on matters of plot, she increasingly wrote about the social and cultural scene, while he retained his passion for military and political affairs. The final story in this volume, *The Bridal*, is both the culmination of a gradual process in the writings leading up to 1832 and a forerunner of the manuscripts for 1833 to 1835, which deal almost exclusively with the Marquis of Douro and his increasingly complicated *affaires*. In this story, Charlotte takes account of Branwell's latest battles and of his new creation of Rogue who, as the demagogue Alexander Percy, is to rival the Marquis of Douro as protagonist of the later Glass Town Saga. As the title implies, however, it is the love between Douro and Marian Hume that occupies Charlotte's interest. Romantic love is the chief theme developed in the fairytale world of Charlotte Brontë's early manuscripts and it continues to inform the two later periods of her early writing.

In the later manuscripts of 1833 to 1835 and 1836 to 1839, the action of Charlotte's stories moves to the new Kingdom of Angria, won from the Ashantee natives by the Marquis of Douro (now Zamorna) and bestowed on him by Parliament as a reward. The drama now centres on the relationship of Douro with his mentor/rival Alexander Percy, and especially on the complications this rivalry creates for Douro's new marriage to Percy's daughter Mary. But there is no hint yet in the early manuscripts of Mary or of Angria. Volumes 2 and 3 of this edition cover the events of these two later periods in Charlotte's early writing.

Many echoes of the later novels can be found in the juvenilia, and occasionally these are noted in the following footnotes. However, it is more constructive in an edition such as this to record the sources of the early writing rather than its later influences. An attempt has been made to list the relevant sources of Charlotte's juvenilia in the footnotes, although only the most obvious references to the Bible have been noted, since Charlotte's borrowing of biblical phrases is so common as to make complete annotation unacceptably long. The same is true of her pervasive echoes of the Romantic poets.

At seven years old, Charlotte Brontë told her father that the Bible was the best book in the world (*Brontë Society Transactions*, vol. 8, 1932, p. 95). The dramatic historical narrative of the Old Testament and the prophetic visions of the New Testament appealed especially to Charlotte's pictorial imagination, and the influence of the Bible on her style is obvious in the stories of the following pages. Together with the *Arabian Nights* and Charles Morell's *Tales of the Genii*, the Bible is the chief source of the fabulous nature of the early Glass Town and of Charlotte's preoccupation with the supernatural. The many descriptions of Genii palaces studded with precious stones and filled with blinding light, and the Chief Genii themselves, who appear from the clouds with thunder and lightning and trumpet-like voices, derive from Isaiah and the Book of Revelation. The Great Glass Town is known as the 'Babylon' of Africa; the Tower of All Nations is based on the Tower of Babel; and the famous 'Twelves' probably owe their number as much to the twelve apostles as to the original twelve toy soldiers. Several of the tales, such as *Leisure Hours*, have a moral drawn explicitly from the Bible, and other stories are based on current religious controversy. In *Tales of the Islanders*, Charlotte Brontë explicitly prefers her Anglicanism to the 'wickedness' of Roman Catholicism; although we see, too, that she adopted her father's (and the Duke of Wellington's) support for Catholic emancipation. In later manuscripts Charlotte learnt to laugh at the extravagances of Methodism and the wayward clergy of her own denomination.

Charlotte Brontë's early interest in the Bible and religious issues obviously stemmed from her father. Although the tiny manuscript volumes were probably intended to be secret and hidden from prying adult eyes, Mr Brontë was not only aware of their existence but was probably the greatest single influence on his children's early writing. His interests, whether they be in the Classics, in firearms or military campaigns, or in the latest medical remedy, can be noted in the pages of this volume. His passion for literature and his own minor publications (he wrote four volumes of poems and didactic tales, and printed several sermons) provided example and encouragement for the young authors. The *Blackwood's Young Men's Magazine* provides the most obvious example of the children consciously imitating their revered father's adult world. Mr Brontë's bookshelves, full of works by Shakespeare, by seventeenth- and eighteenth-century writers, and especially by Wordsworth, Southey, Scott and Byron, were at the children's disposal. His liberal attitude to his children's education, rare in the nineteenth century, helps to account for the unusually violent content and the romantic penchant of much of Charlotte's early writing. For although her early writing itself is not especially remarkable – many nineteenth-century children wrote juvenile works that have survived (Hartley Coleridge's writings on Ejuxria are an example) – the range of knowledge and the insight into human relations displayed in the pages of her juvenilia are often precocious.

Charlotte Brontë's early writing reveals the formative influences on the later novelist. It allows us to trace her development as a writer and it provides us with important early biographical information. We can note her changing interests – in the English–American commodity trade, in Catholic emancipation, in the French emigrés and Paris, in astrology and supernatural events, in painting and the natural landscape – and her continuing preoccupation with Wellington and his career. We are made aware of a sense of humour and of a tolerance that belies the common biographical assumption that Charlotte's childhood was grim and forbidding. We learn especially that her early writing fulfilled an emotional need, and in the later juvenilia Charlotte describes its hypnotic effect. As we see in volumes 2 and 3 of this edition, she became so intensely involved in the fortunes of her hero and his mistresses that it was not until the age of 23 that she was able to shake off the drug that Glass Town had become. The following pages chronicle the formation of this imaginary world and her increasing commitment to it.

TEXTUAL INTRODUCTION

This is the first volume of a three volume edition of all Charlotte Brontë's early writings. Its production has involved an entirely new transcription of those manuscripts already published, and the transcription for the first time of all other extant manuscripts. The exceptions are six stories of which the original manuscripts no longer exist. Three of these six (*A Romantic Tale, An Adventure in Ireland* and *Characters of the Celebrated Men of the Present Time*) were published in the original Shakespeare Head Brontë which, despite known inaccuracies, is still the most reliable text for these particular manuscripts. The other three (*Young Men's Magazine*, first issue for December 1830, and *Visits in Verreopolis*, volumes I and II) survive in transcriptions made by Davidson Cook and C. W. Hatfield, and I have used these here.

There is only one manuscript for each juvenile work, except in the case of *The Enfant* where the second half of the story is transcribed in Branwell Brontë's script in his magazine of June 1829 (see p. 34 n. 1). He copied Charlotte's story carefully so there are few variants to record.

The contents of Charlotte Brontë's early magazines and manuscript volumes, including poetry and prose, are preserved in this edition in the order in which they appear in manuscript. All poems which are embedded in prose manuscripts are also included; the 33 separate poems written by Charlotte Brontë during the years 1829 to 1832 and not included in this volume are listed in appendix 2. Many of these poems were later revised by Charlotte Brontë and the revisions are generally accepted as part of her mature work. They have therefore been published (with the exception of Charlotte Brontë's translation of Voltaire's *Henriade*) in the new Shakespeare Head edition of her poetry, edited by Tom Winnifrith (Oxford: Basil Blackwell, 1984). But the original drafts of many of these later poems can be found scattered among the stories of this edition of Charlotte Brontë's early writings.

There are special problems in dealing with Brontë manuscripts. Almost all Charlotte Brontë's early works are written in minuscule printed script, which in many cases must be read with a magnifying glass, and the small size of the early manuscripts compounds this difficulty. The first 'magazines' measure 5 by 3.5 centimetres, and often more than a hundred words are crammed onto these tiny scraps of paper. Transcription has therefore been a major task: the text (let alone deletions) is often difficult to read because of the cramped writing and the blotting of ink on poor quality paper. Doubtful readings have been indicated in this edition by a question mark in square brackets. The difficulty of transcribing such minuscule script is a major reason why so much of Charlotte Brontë's juvenilia has not been published before.

As Charlotte matured, the physical size of her manuscript pages increased and her writing is easier to transcribe. The 23-year-old author wrote mainly on scraps of paper torn from notebooks measuring 12 by 18.5 centimetres. Such bibliographical details are recorded in the footnotes and more detailed information, including the provenance of the manuscripts, can be found in *A Bibliography of the Manuscripts of Charlotte Brontë* (Haworth and USA: The Brontë Society in association with Meckler Publishing, 1982) where I have discussed problems of dating and identification. The manuscripts in this edition have been arranged chronologically, and there is only one ('Sir – it is well known that the Genii') that was possibly written by Branwell rather than by Charlotte Brontë (see p. 39, n. 1). Collaborative works in the early magazines are signed 'UT' and 'WT' ('us two' and 'we two'); such contributions are always in Charlotte's script, but the tone, content and signature usually (though not always) indicate that Branwell had a hand in their composition. It is possible, however, if we are to believe General Ramrod in 'Military Conversations' (see p. 74) that 'UT' actually represents the Marquis of Douro and Lord Charles Wellesley (both pseudonyms of Charlotte Brontë). If this is so, then Charlotte may be the author of the eleven juvenile works assumed to be written in collaboration with Branwell.

I have not included in this volume the kind of detailed textual notes one would expect to find in an edition of an author's mature work. It is a moot point whether or not an author's juvenile works merit the same detailed textual attention as the later writings. Certainly a record of all juvenile variants would find a very limited audience. This means that there is still room for a more elaborate edition of the juvenilia that records both the generic text and the clear text, along the lines of the University of Missouri's production of *'The Secret' and 'Lily Hart'*, edited by William Holtz (Columbia: University of Missouri Press, 1978) or the scholarly edition of *Ashworth* by Melodie Monahan, (*Studies in Philology*, 80, 4, 1983). Meanwhile, those readers interested in a full account of Charlotte Brontë's juvenile corrections and deletions can consult my diplomatic edition of 'The Early Prose Writings of Charlotte Brontë', vol. 2 (Ph.D., Cambridge, 1979), where the generic text of all her unpublished prose manuscripts is presented.

I have chosen to record in this edition only those corrections by Charlotte Brontë that substantially alter the meaning of her text and which are decipherable. Many cancelled words are so heavily scored out that they are impossible to read. Alterations of spelling and minor alterations of unsubstantive words (such as the replacement of 'a' by 'the') are not recorded in the notes, although several times I have drawn the reader's attention to Charlotte Brontë's spelling of a particular word. The occasional word unintentionally repeated by Charlotte Brontë (for example, 'have have' and 'room room' in the middle of a sentence) has been silently omitted, and in several cases a word that seems to have been left out of the manuscript has been added in square brackets. Her grammatical errors (such as the occasional use of 'were' for 'was', 'eat' for 'ate', and the unidiomatic use of 'neither . . . or') have not been corrected; and Charlotte Brontë's archaisms (such as 'chuse', 'dreamt', 'clave', and 'courtesied') have also been preserved. Charlotte Brontë often refers to characters and place names by their initials only. For example, in *Tales of the Islanders* she sometimes refers to Orderly-man, Jack-of-all-trades and Gamekeeper by name, sometimes merely by 'OM', 'JOAT' and 'GK'. To avoid confusion, all initials referring to characters and place names have been expanded in this edition, except occasionally where a capital is followed by a dash (for example, 'T—'), reflecting not simply shorthand usage but the nineteenth-century convention of dealing with scandalous material, such as the story of *An Interesting Passage in the Lives of Some Eminent Men of the Present Time*. All other contractions, except those on the title and advertisement pages of the miniature magazines, have also been spelt out in full. It should perhaps be noted here that Charlotte Brontë almost invariably uses ampersands in her early stories, except at the beginning of a sentence when she prefers to use 'And'.

It is well known that Charlotte Brontë's spelling and punctuation were poor, even in her mature work. The early manuscripts abound in such juvenile errors as the confusion between 'their' and 'there', 'where' and 'were', and the use of 'ei' for 'ie'. However, her spelling improved over the years, and this can be seen in the plates to this volume, which illustrate her original manuscripts. Her capitalization is haphazard and inconsistent, and her punctuation is even less reliable. In the early juvenilia, punctuation is often simply absent. In the later juvenilia, Charlotte Brontë usually closes one speech and opens the next with a single inverted comma intended to apply to both sentences. From about

1835, she makes persistent use of the dash, which often replaces both comma and full point. Unfortunately she also uses the dash without reason (often to fill a space at the end of a line), and it is sometimes difficult to distinguish between this and an intended comma or period. To record all these details would require a copious textual apparatus, such as that provided in my edition of Charlotte Brontë's *Something about Arthur* (Austin: Humanities Research Center, University of Texas at Austin, 1981), which includes a complete list of deletions and corrections. In this edition, however, I have merely silently corrected such minor errors and have included photographs of some of the manuscripts to illustrate Charlotte Brontë's idiosyncratic spelling and punctuation.

Many of the early stories have been published previously – often poorly transcribed, in piecemeal, private, limited editions – chiefly by Thomas James Wise, C. K. Shorter or C. W. Hatfield. So inaccurate are some editions, such as *The Adventures of Ernest Alembert: A Fairy Tale*, edited by Thomas James Wise (London: printed for private circulation, 1896), where many phrases and even sentences have been inserted, that one can only conclude that either the editor was working from another manuscript (which is unlikely) or that he chose to 'improve' the original (which in the case of Wise is *not* unlikely).

The aim of this edition is to correct the effects of such tampering with Charlotte Brontë's early writings and to provide an accurate, clear text for the widest audience with a minimum of editorial intervention. Printing costs have made it impossible to preserve original page breaks, or to begin a new manuscript on a new page. However, the end of each manuscript listed in the contents is indicated by a short double rule. Paragraphs have been introduced where necessary to facilitate reading; but the original format of the title-pages, contents pages and advertisements of the miniature magazines and volumes of stories has been preserved. Charlotte Brontë's notation of numbers (she used Arabic numerals or wrote the number out in full, as the mood took her) has also been retained, since there is no real justification for regularizing her style in this regard. The desire for increased clarity and accessibility has been the sole reason for normalizing the text, and it is hoped that those changes that have been made in no way detract from the whimsical nature of what, after all, are 'early writings'. It must be remembered that these stories and poems were never meant for publication; most of them are the result of childhood play and adolescent fantasy. Their quality is uneven, and they are at times embarrassingly crude, but they are worthy of attention, for they represent a unique record of the apprenticeship of a major English writer.

ABBREVIATIONS

BL	British Library
BPM	Brontë Parsonage Museum, Haworth
HCL	Harvard College Library
NYPL	New York Public Library
PML	Pierpont Morgan Library, New York
Poems	*The Poems of Charlotte Brontë*, edited by Tom Winnifrith, Oxford: Basil Blackwell for The Shakespeare Head Press, 1984
SHBCM	*The Miscellaneous and Unpublished Writings of Charlotte and Patrick Branwell Brontë*, edited by Thomas James Wise and John Alexander Symington, 2 vols, Oxford: Basil Blackwell for The Shakespeare Head Press, 1936 and 1938
SHLL	*The Brontës: Their Lives, Friendships and Correspondence*, edited by Thomas James Wise and John Alexander Symington, Oxford: Basil Blackwell for The Shakespeare Head Press, 1932
[ ]	Editorial addition
[?]	Doubtful reading
[?1 word]	Indecipherable word or words
〈 〉	Manuscript deletion (in textual notes)
〈? 〉	Doubtful manuscript deletion (in textual notes)

The Early Writings of
CHARLOTTE BRONTË
1826–1832

'There was once a little girl and her name was Anne'[1]

There was once a little girl and her name was Anne.[2] She was born at a little village named Thornton and by and by she grew a good girl. Her father and mother was very rich. Mr and Mrs Wood were their names and she was their only child, but she was not too much indulged.

Once little Anne and her mother went to see a fine castle near London, about ten miles from it. Anne was very much pleased with it.

Once Anne and her papa and her Mama went to sea in a ship and they had very fine weather all the way, but Anne's Mama was very sick and Anne attended her with so much care. She gave her her medicine.[3]

---

[1]Charlotte Brontë's earliest extant manuscript, written for her younger sister Anne c.1826–8, in BPM: B78; untitled hand-sewn booklet of sixteen pages (5.6 × 3.6 cm) in white, grey and blue spotted wallpaper cover. The story is illustrated by six tiny coloured paintings of a house, a castle, a rowing boat, a sailing boat, a lady walking a dog and the mother's sick room. Untitled manuscripts are referred to, in this edition, by their first line or initial phrase, shown in inverted commas.

[2]The name Anne is variously spelt 'Ane' and 'Ann'.

[3]The story is followed by a small map illustrating the imaginary countries of Taley, Vittoria, Brany and Waiting, and by two pages of geographical notes as follows:

Wellington	*Parry*
Population 11,000,000	Population 11,000,000
Upper Canada	Ireland
England	East Indies
West Indies	Lower Canada
[?Luanfernan Doz]	New Discovered Is
St Catherine	Orkney Isles
Spice Is	Malabar
New Discovered!	Madagascar

3

The History of the Year[1]

Once papa lent my sister Maria[2] a book. It was an old geography and she wrote on its blank leaf, 'Papa lent me this book'. The book is an hundred and twenty years old. It is at this moment lying before me while I write this. I am in the kitchen of the parsonage house, Haworth. Tabby the servant[3] is washing up after breakfast and Anne, my youngest sister (Maria was the eldest), is kneeling on a chair looking at some cakes which Tabby has been baking for us. Emily is in the parlour brushing it. Papa and Branwell are gone[4] to Keighley. Aunt[5] is upstairs in her room and I am sitting by the table writing this in the kitchen.

Keighley is a small town four miles from here. Papa and Branwell are gone for the newspaper, the *Leeds Intelligencer*, a most excellent Tory newspaper edited by Mr Wood [for] the proprietor Mr Henneman. We take 2 and see three newspapers a week. We take the *Leeds Intelligencer*, party Tory, and the *Leeds Mercury*, Whig, edited by Mr Baines and his brother, son-in-law and his 2 sons, Edward and Talbot. We see the *John Bull*; it is a High Tory, very violent. Mr Driver[6] lends us it, as likewise *Blackwood's Magzine*, the most able periodical there is. The editor is Mr Christopher North,[7] an old man, 74 years of age; the 1st of

[1]Four page manuscript, plus one cancelled page (10 × 6 cm) in BPM: B80(11). The following description of the three 'plays' is continued by the next two fragmentary manuscripts.

[2]The eldest of the six Brontë children, who at the age of seven assumed much of the responsibility for the younger children after their mother's death in 1821. It was Maria who first taught the children to act their own little plays, and records exist of her precocious knowledge of current political events. She died of consumption at Lowood School in 1825, followed soon after by her next sister, Elizabeth.

[3]Tabitha Aykroyd, a Methodist widow who worked for the Brontë family from 1824 until just before her death almost 30 years later. She was much loved by the children, who gleaned from her most of their knowledge of fairytales and local lore. Her name is usually spelt 'Taby' in the early manuscripts.

[4]Manuscript page 1 ends here with the date 'March 12 1829'.

[5]Miss Elizabeth Branwell of Penzance, who stayed to help the Brontë family after the death of her sister Mrs Brontë; she remained with them for the rest of her life.

[6]The local doctor, who continued to lend the Brontës newspapers at least until November 1834 (see Emily Brontë's diary note, *SHLL*, vol. 1, p. 124), but who had discontinued *Blackwood's Magazine* by 1831, when Elizabeth Branwell decided to subscribe to *Fraser's Magazine* for her nephew and nieces (see *SHLL*, vol. 1, p. 88).

[7]Pseudonym of John Wilson, editor of *Blackwood's Magazine* and author with John Gibson Lockhart and Dr William Maginn, of the famous 'Noctes Ambrosianae', a series of boisterous imaginary conversations which were held in Ambrose's Tavern, Elysium, and which appeared in *Blackwood's* from 1822 to 1835. Timothy Tickler, Ensign O'Doherty (pseudonym of Maginn), Peter Macrabin, Mordecai Mullion and the 'Ettrick Shepherd' (James Hogg) are interlocutors in the 'Noctes Ambrosianae'.

April is his birthday. His company are Timothy Tickler, Morgan O'Doherty, Macrabin Mordecai, Mullion, Warrell, and James Hogg, a man of most extraordinary genius, a Scottish shepherd.

Our plays were established: *Young Men*, June 1826; *Our Fellows*, July 1827; *Islanders*, December 1827. Those are our three great plays that are not kept secret. Emily's and my bed plays were established the 1st December 1827, the others March 1828. Bed plays mean secret plays; they are very nice ones. All our plays are very strange ones. Their nature I need not write on paper for I think I shall always remember them. The *Young Men* play took its rise from some wooden soldiers Branwell had, *Our Fellows* from Aesop's *Fables*, and the *Islanders* from several events which happened. I will sketch out the origin of our plays more explicitly if I can.

1 Young Men's[8]

Papa bought Branwell some soldiers from Leeds.[9] When Papa came home it was night and we were in bed, so next morning Branwell came to our door with a box of soldiers. Emily and I jumped out of bed and I snatched up one and exclaimed, 'This is the Duke of Wellington! It shall be mine!'[10] When I said this, Emily likewise took one and said it should be hers. When Anne came down she took one also. Mine was the prettiest of the whole and perfect in every part. Emily's was a grave-looking fellow. We called him 'Gravey'. Anne's was a queer little thing, very much like herself. He was called 'Waiting Boy'. Branwell chose 'Bonaparte'.[11]

March 12, 1829

---

[8]This heading occurs at the top of manuscript p. 4, the remainder of which is cancelled (see textual notes), and the description continues on the next page.

[9]See Branwell Brontë's more detailed description, *The History Of The Young Men From Their First Settlement To The Present Time*, 15 December 1830 – 7 May 1831, in *SHCBM*, vol. 1, pp. 63 and 76.

[10]Above and below 'mine' are the mis-spelt words 'Arther' and 'Athur' respectively; Arthur was the Duke of Wellington's Christian name.

[11]As the 'play' moved away from the material beginnings of toy soldiers, the names of Emily's and Anne's favourite characters were changed to those of 'Parry' and 'Ross', based on two famous explorers who are mentioned in the pages of *Blackwood's Magazine*, November 1820 and June 1821. Gravey (later Gravii) survived in the saga as the Glass Town's 'Metropolitan Archbishop'. Napoleon Buonaparte, Wellington's great adversary, had recently died as a prisoner on St Helena in May 1827, but his legendary fame was still equal to that of Charlotte's hero. Branwell, however, soon changed his soldier's name to 'Sneaky', whom he described as 'ingenious, artful, deceitful but courageous' (*SHCBM*, vol. I, p. 66). Later Branwell transferred his allegiance to the imaginary character 'Rogue', who retained many of Napoleon's characteristics (see *The Bridal*, n. 10).

5

'The origin of the O'Deans'[1]

The origin of the O'Deans was as follows: we pretended we had each a large island inhabited by people six miles high. The people we took out of Aesop's *Fables*. Hay Man was my chief man, Boaster Branwell's, Hunter Anne's and Clown Emily's.[2] Our chief men were ten miles high except Emily's who was only four.

March 12, 1829.

═══════

'The origin of the Islanders'[1]

The origin of the Islanders was as follows. It was one wet night in December, we were all sitting round the fire and had been silent some time, and at last I said, 'Suppose we had each an Island of our own'. Branwell chose the Isle of Man, Emily Isle of Arran and Bute Isle, Anne, Jersey, and I chose the Isle of Wight.[2] We then chose who should live in our Islands. The chief of Branwell's were John Bull, Astley Cooper, Leigh Hunt, etc.; Emily's Walter Scott, Mr Lockhart, Johnny Lockhart etc.; Anne's Michael Sadler, Lord Bentinck, Henry Halford, etc.; and I chose Duke of Wellington and son, North and Co.; 30 officers, Mr Abernethy, etc.[3]

March 12, 1829.

═══════

[1] One page manuscript (9.5 × 6.2 cm) in BPM: B80(11).
[2] Only Boaster and Clown can be found in the titles of Aesop's *Fables*; Hay Man and Hunter are not even mentioned in the 1825 edition, translated by Samuel Croxall, which Winifred Gérin suggests the young Brontës used (*Charlotte Brontë: The Evolution of Genius*, Oxford: Clarendon Press, 1967, p. 25). Branwell Brontë signed several of his early tales 'Boaster' but the other names are not found elsewhere in the juvenilia.

[1] One page manuscript (9.5 × 6.2 cm) in NYPL: Berg collection; bound with *Tales of the Islanders*.
[2] Islands off the coast of Britain, each reflecting the children's interests: the Isle of Man is in the Irish Sea; Arran and Bute are off the west coast of Scotland; Jersey is part of the Channel Islands; and the Isle of Wight is just off the south English coast.
[3] The children's chief men were almost all famous men of the time: John Abernethy and Sir Astley Paston Cooper were noted surgeons, the latter being surgeon to George IV and the Duke of Wellington's neurologist; Sir Henry Halford was a well-known physician and doctor

6

TWO ROMANTIC TALES
by Charlotte Bronte
April 28, 1829[1]

A ROMANTIC TALE
[or The Twelve Adventurers][2]
Written April 15, 1829

CHAPTER I
[The Country of the Genii]

There is a tradition that some thousands of years ago twelve men from Britain of a most gigantic size, and twelve men from Gaul, came over to the country of the genii, and while there were continually at war with each other; and, after remaining many years, returned again to Britain and Gaul. And in the inhabited [parts] of the genii country there are now no vestiges of them, though it is said there have been found some colossal skeletons in that wild, barren land, the evil desert.

---

to Mrs Charles Arbuthnot, a close friend of the Duke of Wellington; Michael Thomas Sadler and Lord George Bentinck were members of Parliament, the former a social reformer and the latter a supporter of Catholic emancipation and the Reform Bill and later leader of the Opposition; James Henry Leigh Hunt, Sir Walter Scott, John Gibson Lockhart and John Wilson (the 'Christopher North' of *Blackwood's Magazine*, whose 'Co.' is listed by Charlotte Brontë in *The History of the Year*) were all well-known poets, writers and critics. Lockhart married Scott's daughter and their eldest son was Emily Brontë's favourite, Johnny Lockhart, the suffering 'Hugh Littlejohn' for whom Scott wrote *Tales of a Grandfather* (Edinburgh, 1827–9), owned by the Brontë children (BPM: 4). John Bull was a popular name for England, personifying the bluff frankness and solidity of the English character.

[1]On brown paper cover of hand-sewn booklet, signed (?on title-page) 'Haworth. C. Brontë. April 15th 1829, and April 28th 1829'; manuscript formerly in the Law Collection, now lost. The text of the following story is reprinted from *SHCBM*, vol. 1, pp. 3–13, with some editorial changes. It has been checked for possible mis-readings beside the vastly inferior transcription in *The Twelve Adventurers*, ed. Clement Shorter and C. W. Hatfield (London: Hodder and Stoughton, 1925), pp. 1–18, and beside C. W. Hatfield's transcript in the Brontë Parsonage. Where the texts vary, the editor has chosen the most likely reading, usually from the most reliable version, but there are no major variations between the texts.

[2]The alternative title and the chapter headings were listed by Charlotte Brontë in *Catalogue of my Books*, 3 August 1830; they do not occur in the original manuscript.

But I have read a book called *The Travels of Captain Parnell*, out of which the following is an extract:

About four in the afternoon I saw a dark red cloud arise in the east, which gradually grew larger till it covered the whole sky. As the cloud spread the wind rose and blew a tremendous hurricane. The sand of the desert began to move and rolled like the waves of the sea. As soon as I saw this I threw myself on my face and stopped my breath, for I knew that this was the tornado or whirlwind. I remained in this situation for three minutes; for at the end of that time I ventured to look up. The whirlwind had passed over and had not hurt *me*, but close by lay my poor camel quite dead. At this sight I could not forbear weeping; but my attention was soon diverted by another object. About one hundred yards further off lay an immense skeleton. I immediately ran up to it and examined it closely. While I was gazing at the long ghastly figure which lay stretched upon the sand before me the thought came into my mind that it might be the skeleton of one of those ancient Britons who, tradition tells us, came from their own country to this evil land, and here miserably perished. While I was pursuing this train of meditation, I observed that it was bound with a long chain of rusty iron. Suddenly the iron clanked and the bones strove to rise, but a huge mountain of sand overwhelmed the skeleton with a tremendous crash, and when the dust which had hid the sun and enveloped every[thing] in darkness cleared away, not a mark could be distinguished to show the future traveller where the bones had lain.

Now, if this account be true – and I see no reason why we should suppose it is not – I think [we] may fairly conclude that these skeletons are evil genii chained in these deserts by the fairy Maimoune.[3]

There are several other traditions, but they are all so obscure that no reliance is to be placed on them.

CHAPTER II

[The Voyage of Discovery]

In the year 1793 the *Invincible*, 74 guns, set sail with a fair wind from England; her crew, twelve men, every one healthy and stout and in the best temper. Their names [were] as follows:

---

[3]Maimoune is a fairy, daughter of Damriel, king of a legion of genii in 'The Story of the Amours of Camaralzaman', in the *Arabian Nights*.

Marcus O'Donell,	Ronald Traquair,
Ferdinand Cortez,	Ernest Fortescue,
Felix de Rothsay,	Gustavus Dunally,
Eugene Cameron,	Frederick Brunswick,
Harold Fitzgeorge,	and
Henry Clinton,	Arthur Wellesley.
Francis Stewart,	

Well, as I said before, we set sail with a fair wind from England on the 1st of March 1793. On the 15th we came in sight of Spain. On the 16th we landed, bought a supply of provisions, etc., and set sail again on the 20th. On the 25th, about noon, Henry Clinton, who was in the shrouds, cried out that he saw the Oxeye.[4] In a minute we were all on deck and all eyes gazing eagerly and fearfully towards the mountain over which we saw hanging in the sky the ominous speck. Instantly the sails were furled, the ship tacked about, and the boat was made ready for launching in our last extremity.

Thus having made everything ready we retired to the cabin, and everyone looked as sheepish as possible and noway inclined to meet our fate like men. Some of us began to cry; but we waited a long time and heard no sound of the wind, and the cloud did not increase in size.

At last Marcus O'Donell exclaimed, 'I wish it would either go backward or forward.'

At this Stewart reproved him, and Ferdinand gave him a box on the ear. O'Donell returned the compliment; but just then we heard the sound of the wind, and Ronald shouted out, 'The cloud is as big as me!'

Brunswick pulled Ronald away from the window and ordered him to hold his tongue. Ronald said he would not and began to sing. Felix de Rothsay put his hand over Ronald's mouth. Harold Fitzgeorge got Rothsay behind by the throat. Ernest Fortescue held his fist in O'Donell's face and Marcus floored Ernest. Cameron kicked Clinton to the other end of the cabin, and Stewart shouted so loud for them to be quiet that he made the greatest noise of any.

But suddenly they were all silenced by a fierce flash of lightning and a loud peal of thunder. The wind rose and the planks of our ship creaked. Another flash of lightning, brighter and more terrible than the first, split our mainmast and carried away our foretop-sail; and now the flashes of lightning grew terrific and the thunder roared tremendously.

[4]Sailor's name for a cloudy speck indicating the approach of a storm. Sir Henry Clinton, a British general under Wellington at Waterloo, was aide-de-camp to the Duke of York in 1793, the date of this story.

9

The rain poured down in torrents, and the gusts of wind were most loud and terrible. The hearts of the stoutest men in our company now quailed, and even the chief doctor was afraid.[5]

At last the storm ceased, but we found it had driven us quite out of our course and we knew not where we were.

On the 30th, Gustavus Dunally who was on deck cried out, 'Land!'

At this we were all extremely rejoiced. On the 31st we reached it, and found it was the island of Trinidad. We refitted our ship and got in a store of provisions and water, and set sail once more on the 5th of May.

It would be endless to describe all our adventures in the South Atlantic Ocean. Suffice it to say that after many storms, in which we were driven quite out of our course and knew not in what part of the world we were, we at last discovered land. We sailed along the coast for some time to find a good landing-place. We at last found one.

We landed on the 2nd of June 1793.[6] We moored our battered ship in a small harbour and advanced up into the country. To our great surprise we found it cultivated. Grain of a peculiar sort grew in great abundance, and there were large plantations of palm-trees, and likewise an immense number of almond-trees. There were also many olives and large enclosures of rice. We were greatly surprised at these marks of the land being inhabited. It seemed to be part of an immense continent.

After we had travelled about two miles we saw at a distance twenty men well armed. We immediately prepared for battle, having each of us a pistol, sword and bayonet. We stood still and they came near. When they had come close up to us they likewise stopped. They seemed greatly surprised at us, and we heard one of them say, 'What strange people!'

The Chief then said, 'Who are you?'

Wellesley answered, 'We were cast up on your shores by a storm and request shelter.'

They said, 'You shall not have any.'

Wellesley: 'We will take it then!'

We prepared for battle; they did the same.

It was a very fierce encounter, but we conquered: killed ten, took the Chief prisoner, wounded five, and the remaining four retreated. The Chief was quite black and very tall; he had a fierce countenance and the finest eyes I ever saw. We asked him what his name was, but he would

---

[5]These words are quoted in Branwell Brontë's *History Of The Young Men*, in *SHCBM*, vol. I, p. 66.

[6]1791 in manuscript, an obvious error (noted in *SHCBM*, vol. 1, p. 5).

not speak. We asked him the name of his country, and he said, 'Ashantee'.[7]

Next morning a party of twelve men came to our tents bringing with them a ransom for their Chief, and likewise a proposition of peace from their King. This we accepted, as it was on terms the most advantageous to ourselves.

Immediately after the treaty of peace was concluded we set about building a city. The situation was in the middle of a large plain, bounded on the north by high mountains, on the south by the sea, on the east by gloomy forests, and on the west by evil deserts.[8]

About a month after we had begun our city the following adventure happened to us.

One evening when all were assembled in the great tent and most of us sitting round the fire which blazed in the middle of the pavilion, listening to the storm which raged without our camp, a dead silence prevailed. None of us felt inclined to speak, still less to laugh, and the wine-cups stood upon the round table filled to the brim. In the midst of this silence we heard the sound of a trumpet which seemed to come from the desert. The next moment a peal of thunder rolled through the sky, which seemed to shake the earth to its centre.

By this time we were all on our legs and filled with terror, which was changed to desperation by another blast of the terrible trumpet. We all rushed out of the tent with a shout, not of courage, but fear; and then we saw a sight so terribly grand that even now when I think of it, at the distance of forty years from that dismal night when I saw it, my limbs tremble and my blood is chilled with fear. High in the clouds was a tall and terrible giant. In his right hand he held a trumpet; in his left two darts pointed with fire. On a thunder cloud which rolled before him his

---

[7]Charlotte Brontë would have read of the Ashantee Wars of the 1820s in old newspapers and magazines. The Ashantee tribes of the Glass Town Saga were originally her small ninepins, brought from Leeds by Mr Brontë at the same time as the twelve toy soldiers, the original 'Twelve Adventurers'. Branwell Brontë records in detail the children's imaginary wars between the 'Twelves' and the Ashantees in *The History Of The Young Men*, SHCBM, vol. 1, pp. 62–95. The names of only two of Charlotte's twelve adventurers are duplicated in Branwell's account (Arthur Wellesley and Frederick Brunswick, Duke of York); his adventurers rather than Charlotte's survive throughout the Young Men's Play.

[8]The actual location of Glass Town and its surroundings may have been inspired by the article in *Blackwood's Magazine*, June 1826, entitled 'Geography of Central Africa. Denham and Clapperton's Journals', which included a detailed map of the River Niger delta, showing the Mountains of the Moon (or Jibbel Kumri) to the east and Ashantee to the west (see frontispiece to vol. II of this edition). The area is also described in Goldsmith's *Grammar of General Geography* (London, 1823), used by the young Brontës (BPM: B45), and illustrated in the *Grammar* in a map of Africa which shows such places as the kingdom of Dahomey, mentioned later in this story.

11

shield rested. On his forehead was written 'The Genius of the Storm'. On he strode over the black clouds which rolled beneath his feet and regardless of the fierce lightning which flashed around him. But soon the thunder ceased and the lightning no longer glared so terribly.

The hoarse voice of the storm was hushed, and a gentler light than the fire of the elements spread itself over the face of the now cloudless sky. The calm moon shone forth in the midst of the firmament, and the little stars seemed rejoicing in their brightness. The giant had descended to the earth, and approaching the place where we stood trembling he made three circles in the air with his flaming scimitar, then lifted his hand to strike. Just then we heard a loud voice saying, 'Genius, I command thee to forbear!'

We looked round and saw a figure so tall that the Genius seemed to it but a diminutive dwarf. It cast one joyful glance on us and disappeared.

CHAPTER III

[The Desert]

The building of our city went on prosperously. The Hall of Justice was finished, the fortifications were completed, the Grand Inn was begun, the Great Tower was ended.

One night when we were assembled in the Hall of Justice, Arthur Wellesley, at that time a common trumpeter, suddenly exclaimed, while we were talking of our happiness, 'Does not the King of the Blacks view our prosperity with other eyes than ours? Would not the best way be to send immediately to England, tell them of the new world we have discovered and of the riches that are in it; and do you not think they would send us an army?'

Francis Stewart immediately rose and said, 'Young man, think before you speak! How could we send to England? Who could be found hardy enough to traverse again the Atlantic? Do you not remember the storm which drove us on the shores of Trinidad?'

Arthur Wellesley answered, 'It is with all due deference that I ventured to contradict the opinions of older and more experienced men than I am; and it is after much consideration that I ventured to say what I have said. Well do I remember that storm which forced us to seek refuge among foreigners. I am not so rash as to suppose we of ourselves could cross the ocean in the damaged and leaky vessel we possess, or that we could build another in time enough to avert the danger which I fear is coming. But in what a short time have we built [the city] we now are in! How long has it taken to rear the Grand Hall where we now are? Have not those marble pillars and that solemn dome been built by supernatural power? If you view the city from this Gothic window and see the beams of the morn gilding the battlements of the mighty towers, and the pillars of the splendid palaces which have been reared in a few months, can you doubt that magic has been used in their construction?'

Here he paused. We were all convinced that the genii had helped us to build our town. He went on, 'Now, if the genii have built us our city, will they not likewise help us to call our countrymen to defend what they have built against the assaults of the enemy?'

He stopped again, for the roof shook and the hall was filled with smoke. The ground opened, and we heard a voice saying, 'When the sun appears above the forests of the east be ye all on the border of the evil desert. If ye fail I will crush you to atoms.'

The voice ceased, the ground closed, and the smoke cleared away. There was no time for us to consult; the desert lay ten miles off, and it was now midnight. We immediately set off with the Duke of York at our head. We reached the desert about 4 a.m.; there we stopped. Far off to the east the long black line of gloomy forests skirted the horizon. To the north the Jibbel Kumri or Mountains of the Moon seemed a misty girdle to the plain of Dahomey; to the south the ocean guarded the coasts of Africa; before us to the west lay the desert.

In a few minutes we saw a dense vapour arise from the sands, which gradually collecting took the form of a Genius larger than any of the giants. It advanced towards us and cried with a loud voice, 'Follow me!' We obeyed and entered the desert.

After we had travelled a long time, about noon the Genius told us to look around. We were now about the middle of the desert. Nothing was to be seen far or near but vast plains of sand under a burning sun and cloudless sky. We were dreadfully fatigued and begged the Genius to allow us to stop a little, but he immediately ordered us to proceed. We therefore began our march again and travelled a long way, till the sun went down and the pale moon was rising in the east. Also a few stars might now be dimly seen, but still the sands were burning hot and our feet were very much swollen.

At last the Genius ordered us to halt and lie down. We soon fell asleep. We had slept about an hour when the Genius awoke us and ordered us to proceed.

The moon had now risen and shone brightly in the midst of the sky – brighter far than it ever does in our country. The night-wind had somewhat cooled the sands of the desert, so that we walked with more ease than before; but soon a mist arose which covered the whole plain. Through it we thought we could discern a dim light. We now likewise heard sounds of music at a great distance.

As the mist[9] cleared away the light grew more distinct till it burst upon us in almost insufferable splendour. Out of the barren desert arose a palace of diamond, the pillars of which were ruby and emerald illuminated with lamps too bright to look upon. The Genius led us into a hall of sapphire in which were thrones of gold. On the thrones sat the Princes of the Genii. In the midst of the hall hung a lamp like the sun. Around it stood genii and fairies without, whose robes were of beaten gold sparkling with diamonds. As soon as their chiefs saw us they sprang up from their thrones, and one of them seizing Arthur Wellesley and exclaimed, 'This is the Duke of Wellington!'

Arthur Wellesley asked her why she called him Duke of Wellington.

The Genius answered, 'A prince will arise who shall be as a thorn in the side of England, and the desolator of Europe. Terrible shall be the struggle between that chieftain and you! It will last many years, and the conqueror shall gain eternal honour and glory. So likewise shall the vanquished; and though he shall die in exile his name shall never be remembered by his countrymen but with feelings of enthusiasm. The renown of the victor shall reach to the ends of the earth, kings and emperors shall honour him, and Europe shall rejoice in its deliverer; though in his lifetime fools will envy him, he shall overcome. At his death renown shall cover him, and his name shall be everlasting!'

When the Genius finished speaking we heard the sound of music far off, which drew nearer and nearer till it seemed within the hall. Then all the fairies and genii joined in one grand chorus which rose rolling to the mighty dome and stately pillars of the genii palace, and reached among the vaults and dungeons beneath; then gradually dying away it at last ceased entirely.

As the music went off the palace slowly disappeared, till it vanished and we found ourselves alone in the midst of the desert. The sun had just begun to enlighten the world and the moon might be dimly seen; but all below them was sand as far as our eyes could reach. We knew not which way to go, and we were ready to faint with hunger; but on once more looking round we saw lying on the sands some dates and palm-wine. Of this we made our breakfast, and then began again to think of our journey, when suddenly there appeared a beaten track in the desert, which we followed.

[9]'light' in manuscript, an obvious error.

About noon, when the sun was at its meridian, and we felt weary and faint with the heat, a grove of palm-trees appeared in sight towards which we ran; and after we had reposed awhile under its shade and refreshed ourselves with its fruit, we resumed our march; and that same night to our inexpressible joy we entered the gates of our beautiful city and slept beneath the shadow of its roofs.

CHAPTER IV

[News from Home]

The next morning we were awoke by the sound of trumpets and great war-drums, and on looking towards the mountains we saw descending on the plain an immense army of Ashantees. We were all thrown into the utmost consternation except Arthur Wellesley who advised us to look to the great guns and to man the walls, never doubting that the genii would come to our help if we of ourselves could not beat them off by the help of the cannon and rockets. This advice we immediately followed, while the Ashantees came on like a torrent, sweeping everything, burning the palm-trees, and laying waste the rice-fields.

When they came up to the walls of our city they set up a terrible yell, the meaning of which was that we should be consumed from the face of the earth, and that our city should vanish away; for as it came by magic it should go by the same. Our answer to this insolent speech was a peal of thunder from the mouths of our cannon. Two fell dead, and the rest gave us leg bail setting off towards the mountains with inconceivable swiftness, followed by a triumphant shout from their conquerors.

They came back in the afternoon and in the most submissive terms asked for their dead. We granted their request, and in return they allowed us to witness the funeral.

A few days after, on the 21st of September, Ronald came running into the Hall of Justice where we all were, shouting out that there was a ship from England. The Duke of York immediately sent Arthur Wellesley to ascertain the truth of this.

When he arrived at the seashore he found all the crew, consisting of fifty men, had landed. He then examined the state of the ship and found it was almost a complete wreck. He asked the men a few questions and they seemed greatly surprised to find him here, and asked him how he contrived to live in such a country. He told them to follow him.

When he brought them to the Hall of Justice, the Duke of York ordered them to relate their story.

They cried, 'We were driven on your shore by a storm and request shelter.'

The Duke of York answered, 'Fellow-Englishmen, we rejoice that you were driven on our part of the coast, and you shall have shelter if we can give it.'

Accordingly they remained with us about a fortnight, for at the end of that time the genii had fitted out their ship again, when they set sail for England accompanied by Arthur Wellesley.

For about ten years after this we continued at war with the blacks, and then made peace; after which, for about ten years more, nothing happened worth mentioning.

On the 16th of May 1816, a voice passed through the city saying, 'Set a watch on the tower which looks towards the south, for tomorrow a conqueror shall enter your gates!'

The Duke of York immediately despatched Henry Clinton to the highest tower in the city. About noon Clinton cried out, 'I see something at a great distance upon the Atlantic.'

We all of us ran to the watch-tower, and on looking towards the ocean we could discern a dark object upon the verge of the horizon which as it neared the shore we saw plainly was a fleet. At last it anchored and the crew began to land.

First came 12 regiments of horsemen, next, three of infantry, then several high officers who seemed to be the staff of some great general; and last of all came the general himself, whom several of us asserted had the bearing of Arthur Wellesley.

After he had marshalled the regiments he ordered them to march, and we saw them enter the gates of the city. When they arrived at the tower they stopped, and we heard the general in the tone of Wellesley say, 'Hill,[10] you may stop here with the army while I go to the Palace of Justice, as I suppose they are all there if they be yet in the land of the living. And, Beresford,[11] you must come with me.'

'No, no, we are here, Arthur, almost terrified out of our wits for fear you shall burn the tower and sack the city!' exclaimed the Duke of York as we descend[ed] from our hiding-place.

---

[10]Modelled on General Sir Roland Hill, whom the Duke of Wellington served with in Copenhagen (1807) and again in the Peninsular Wars, and who was commander-in-chief of the British Army while Wellington was prime minister.

[11]Modelled on General William Carr Beresford, friend of Wellington and marshal of the Portuguese army. His reorganization of this army led to its victories under Wellington in the Peninsular Wars.

16

'What! Are you all here, and not one of you slain in battle or dead in the hospital?' said His Grace, as he sprang from his war-horse and we shook hands with him one at a time. 'But come, my brave fellows, let us go to the Grand Inn, and in Ferdinando Hall we will talk of what we have done and suffered since we last met.'

'Please, your Grace, in what part of the town are the army to be quartered?' said one of the staff.

'Oh, never you fear for the army, Murray,[12] we are not among Spaniards. Let them follow me.'

'The army are to follow His Grace the Duke of Wellington,' said Murray.

'His Grace the Duke of Wellington!' we all exclaimed at once in surprise.

'Yes – His Grace the Duke of Wellington,' said another of the staff. 'I don't know who you are, but our most noble general is the conqueror of Bonaparte and the deliverer of Europe.'

'Then the genii don't always tell lies,' said Marcus O'Donell; 'and I am very glad of it for I always thought Duke, you would return to us with more glory than you had [when you] went away from us.'

'Indeed,' said Murray with a sneer.

'Murray,' said His Grace sternly, 'I shall call you to account for this insolence and punish by martial law if you don't make a handsome apology to this gentleman.'

Murray immediately advanced to O'Donell and said, 'Sir, I am very sorry for my foolish insolence and I promise you I will never offend you so again.'

'Very well, Murray, very well indeed,' said the Duke. 'Now shake hands and be friends. I hate civil war.'

By this time we had arrived at the Grand Inn, which was a most superior building and large enough to accommodate 20,000 men. We were soon seated in the hall and listening to Beresford as he related to us how Europe had been set free from the iron chain of a despot, and how the mighty victory had been achieved with which all the civilised world had rung; of the splendid triumphs which had taken place on that glorious occasion; and how all the high sovereigns of Europe had honoured England with their presence on that grand occasion. Longer could we have listened and more could he have told had we not heard

---

[12]Variously spelt 'Murray' and 'Muray' in the early manuscripts, and based, like Hill and Beresford, on an old Peninsular officer of the Duke of Wellington. General Sir George Murray later served in the Duke's Cabinet 1828–30. On 1 February 1830, Charlotte Brontë wrote a poem entitled 'A Wretch in Prison, by Murry' (*Poems*, p. 89), but there is no other reference to Murray's imprisonment in the existing early manuscripts.

the sound of the midnight bell which reminded us that it was time to retire to rest.

Some days after this the Duke of York expressed a wish to return to his own country, and one of the ships with about twenty men were appointed to convey him there.

There were now in the city fifteen thousand men, and we determined to elect a king. Accordingly a council of the whole nation was summoned for the 14th of June 1827. On that day they all assembled in the Palace of Justice. Around the throne sat Marcus O'Donell, Ferdinand Cortez, Henry Clinton, Gustavus Dunally, Harold Fitz-george, and the Duke of Wellington and his staff. An intense anxiety pervaded the council to know who would be proposed as king, for not a man of us knew and no hints had been thrown out. At length the great entrance was closed, and Cortez proclaimed the whole nation to be present. Stewart then rose and said, 'I propose the most noble Field-Marshal Arthur, Duke of Wellington, as a fit and proper person to sit on the throne of these realms.'

Immediately a loud shout burst forth from the multitude, and the hall rang, 'Long live our most noble Duke.' Wellington now rose. Immediately a profound silence pervaded the house.

He said as follows, 'Soldiers, I will defend what you have committed to my care.' Then, bowing to the council, he retired amidst thundering sounds of enthusiastic joy.

C. BRONTË

AN ADVENTURE IN IRELAND[1]

During my travels in the south of Ireland the following adventure happened to me. One evening in the month of August, after a long walk, I was ascending the mountain which overlooks the village of Cahir,[2]

---

[1]Second story in manuscript volume *Two Romantic Tales*, formerly in the Law Collection, now lost. The text is reprinted here from *SHLL*, vol. 1, pp. 78–81. It has been checked beside *The Brontës: Life and Letters*, vol. 1, ed. Clement Shorter (London, 1908), pp. 74–6, and beside *The Twelve Adventurers*, pp. 19–24, which has only a few minor variations.

[2]'Cahin' in all published versions of this manuscript, but this is probably a mis-transcription for 'Cahir', a town in Tipperary, Ireland. The mountains of Killala, which Charlotte Brontë also refers to here, are in Co. Mayo, Ireland.

when I suddenly came in sight of a fine old castle. It was built upon a rock, and behind it was a large wood, and before it was a river. Over the river there was a bridge, which formed the approach to the castle.

When I arrived at the bridge I stood still awhile to enjoy the prospect around me: far below was the wide sheet of still water in which the reflection of the pale moon was not disturbed by the smallest wave; in the valley was the cluster of cabins which is known by the appellation of Cahir; and beyond these were the mountains of Killala. Over all, the grey robe of twilight was now stealing with silent and scarcely perceptible advances. No sound except the hum of the distant village and the sweet song of the nightingales in the wood behind me broke upon the stillness of the scene.

While I was contemplating this beautiful prospect, a gentleman, whom I had not before observed, accosted me with 'Good evening, sir; are you a stranger in these parts?'

I replied that I was. He then asked me where I was going to stop for the night. I answered that I intended to sleep somewhere in the village.

'I am afraid you will find very bad accommodation there,' said the gentleman; 'but if you will take up your quarters with me at the castle, you are welcome.'

I thanked him for his kind offer and accepted it.

When we arrived at the castle I was shown into a large parlour, in which was an old lady sitting in an armchair by the fireside, knitting. On the rug lay a very pretty tortoise-shell cat. As soon as we entered the old lady rose; and when Mr O'Callaghan (for that, I learned, was his name) told her who I was, she said in the most cordial tone that I was welcome, and asked me to sit down.

In the course of conversation I learned that she was Mr O'Callaghan's mother, and that his father had been dead about a year.

We had sat about an hour, when supper was announced, and after supper Mr O'Callaghan asked me if I should like to retire for the night. I answered in the affirmative, and a little boy was commissioned to show me to my apartment. It was a snug, clean, and comfortable little old-fashioned room at the top of the castle. As soon as we had entered, the boy, who appeared to be a shrewd, good-tempered little fellow, said with a shrug of the shoulder, 'If it was going to bed I was, it shouldn't be here that you'd catch me.'

'Why?' said I.

'Because,' replied the boy, 'they say that the ould masther's ghost has been seen sitting on that there chair.'

'And have you seen him?'

'No, but I've heard him washing his hands in that basin often and often.'

'What is your name, my little fellow?'

'Dennis Mulready, please your honour.'

'Well, good-night to you.'

'Good night, masther, and may the saints keep you from all fairies and brownies,' said Dennis as he left the room.

As soon as I had laid down I began to think of what the boy had been telling me, and I confess I felt a strange kind of fear, and once or twice I even thought I could discern something white through the darkness which surrounded me. At length, by the help of reason, I succeeded in mastering these, what some would call idle fancies, and fell asleep.

I had slept about an hour when a strange sound awoke me, and I saw looking through my curtains a skeleton wrapped in a white sheet. I was overcome with terror and tried to scream, but my tongue was paralysed and my whole frame shook with fear. In a deep hollow voice it said to me:

'Arise, that I may show thee this world's wonders,' and in an instant I found myself encompassed with clouds and darkness. But soon the roar of mighty waters fell upon my ear, and I saw some clouds of spray arising from high falls that rolled in awful majesty down tremendous precipices, and then foamed and thundered in the gulf beneath as if they had taken up their unquiet abode in some giant's cauldron.

But soon the scene changed, and I found myself in the mines of Cracone. Here were high pillars and stately arches, whose glittering splendour was never excelled by the brightest fairy palaces. There were not many lamps, only those of a few poor miners, whose homely figures and rough visages formed a striking contrast to the dazzling grandeur which surrounded them. But in the midst of all this magnificence I felt an indescribable sense of fear and terror, for the sea raged above us, and by the awful and tumultuous noises of roaring winds and dashing waves, it seemed as if the storm was violent. And now the mossy pillars groaned beneath the pressure of the ocean, and the glittering arches seemed about to be overwhelmed. When I heard the rushing waters and saw a mighty flood rolling towards me, I gave a loud shriek of terror.

The scene vanished and I found myself in a wide desert full of barren rocks and high mountains. As I was approaching one of the rocks, in which there was a large cave, my foot stumbled and I fell. Just then I heard a deep growl, and saw by the unearthly light of his own fiery eyes a royal lion rousing himself from his kingly slumbers. His terrible eye was fixed upon me, and the desert rang and the rocks echoed with the tremdous roar of fierce delight which he uttered as he sprang towards me.

'Well, masther, it's been a windy night, though it's fine now,' said Dennis, as he drew the window-curtain and let the bright rays of the morning sun into the little old-fashioned room at the top of O'Callaghan Castle.

C. BRONTË,
April 28th, 1829

FIRST VOLUME OF TALES OF THE ISLANDERS JUNE 30 1829[1]

Tales of the Islanders
By Charlotte Brontë

[Chapter 1 An Account of their Origin][2]

The play of the Islanders was formed in December 1827, in the following manner. One night, about the time when the cold sleet and dreary fogs of November are succeeded by the snow storms and high, piercing, night winds of confirmed winter, we were all sitting round the warm, blazing kitchen fire, having just concluded a quarrel with Tabby concerning the propriety of lighting a candle, from which she came off victorious, no candle having been produced. A long pause succeeded which was at last broken by Branwell[3] saying, in a lazy manner, 'I don't

---

[1]Title on brown paper cover of manuscript in NYPL: Berg Collection; formerly a hand-sewn booklet of twenty pages (9.9 × 6.3 cm), the pages have since been separated and bound with volumes II, III, and IV. The following title appears on verso of cover. 'The origin of the Islanders', an earlier version of the opening of this manuscript, occupies page 1.

[2]Titles to the various chapters in each volume were listed by Charlotte Brontë in her prose manuscript *Catalogue of my Books*.

[3]'B' in manuscript. Here, as in other early manuscripts, Charlotte Brontë often uses initials rather than the full name of a well-known character. Almost all proper names in this manuscript, including those of political characters such as Prince Leopold (PL), are abbreviated by Charlotte in capital letters. Where possible, they have been expanded in this edition.

know what to do.' This was re-echoed by Emily and Anne.

Tabby: Wha ya may go t'bed.

Branwell: I'd rather do anything [than] that.

and Charlotte: You're so glum tonight, Tabby. [? Well] suppose we had each an island.

Branwell: If we had, I would choose the Island of Man.

Charlotte: And I would choose Isle of Wight.

Emily: The Isle of Arran for me.

Anne: And mine should be Guernsey.[4]

Charlotte: The Duke of Wellington should be my chief man.

Branwell: Herries[5] should be mine.

Emily: Walter Scott should be mine.

Anne: I should have Bentinck.

Here our conversation was interrupted by [the], to us, dismal sound of the clock striking seven and we were summoned off to bed. The next day we added several others to our list of names, till we had got almost all the chief men in the kingdom.

After this, for a long time, nothing worth noticing occurred.

[Chapter 2 A Description of Vision Island]

In June 1828, we erected a school on a fictitious island, which was to contain a thousand children. The manner of the building was as follows.

The island was fifty miles in circumference and certainly it appeared [more] like the region of enchantment or a beautiful fiction than sober reality, in some parts made terribly sublime by mighty rocks, rushing streams and roaring cataracts, with here and there an oak either scathed by lightning or withered by time and, as if to remind the lonely passenger of what it once was, a green young scion twisting round its old grey trunk. In other parts of the island, there were green [?woods], glittering fountains springing in the flowery meadows or among the pleasant woods where fairies were said to dwell, its borders

[4]See 'The origin of the Islanders', n. 2: in the earlier version Emily also chose Bute Island, and Anne chose Jersey rather than Guernsey, both part of the British Channel Islands off the coast of northern France.

[5]John Charles Herries (1778–1855), statesman. Among other appointments, he was financial secretary to the Treasury under Lord Liverpool in 1823, a colleague of Canning in the House of Commons and chancellor of the Exchequer in Goderich's ministry (1827). Under Wellington, he became master of the Mint (1828–9) and president of the Board of Trade (February–November 1830).

embroidered by the purple violet and the yellow primrose, and the air perfumed by the sweet, wild flowers and ringing with the sound of the cuckoo and turtle dove, or the merry music of the blackbird and thrush, formed the beautiful scenery.

One speciality around the palace school was a fine large park, in which the beautiful undulations of hill and plain variegated the scenery which might otherwise have been monotonous. Shady groves crowned the hills, pure streams wandered through the plains watering the banks with a lovelier verdure, as clear lakes whose borders are overhung by the drooping willow, the elegant larch, the venerable oak, and the evergreen laurel, seemed the crystal, emerald-framed mirrors of some huge giant. Often at times it is said of one of the most beautiful of these lakes, that when all is quiet the music of fairyland may be heard and a tiny barge of red sandalwood, its mast of amber, its sails and cordage of silk, and its oars of fine ivory, may be seen skimming across the lake and, when its small crew have gathered the water-lily plant, back again and, landing on the flowery bank, spread their transparent wings and melt away at the sound of mortal footsteps, like the mists of the morning before [the] splendour of the sun.

From a beautiful grove of winter roses and twining woodbine, towers a magnificent palace of pure white marble, whose elegant and finely wrought pillars and majestic turrets seem the work of mighty genii and not of feeble men. Ascending a flight of marble steps, you come to a grand entrance which leads into a hall surrounded by Corinthian pillars of white marble. In the midst of the hall is a colossal statute holding in each hand a vase of crystal, from which rushes a stream of clear water and breaking into a thousand diamonds and pearls falls into a basin of pure gold, and finally disappearing through an opening rises again in different parts of the park in the form of brilliant fountains, these falling part into numerous rills which, winding through the ground, throw themselves into a river which runs into the sea.[6]

At the upper end of the hall was a grove of orange trees bearing the golden fruit and fragrant blossoms often upon the same branch. From this hall you pass onto another splendid and spacious apartment all hung with rich, deep, crimson velvet; and from the grand dome is suspended a magnificent lustre of fine gold, the drops of [which] are pure crystal. The whole length of the room run long sofas covered also with crimson velvet. At each end are chimney-pieces of dove-coloured Italian marble, the pillars of which are of the Corinthian order, fluted and wreathed with gold. From this we pass into a smaller but very

---

[6]Compare Coleridge's sacred river in 'Kubla Khan'.

elegant room, the sofas of which are covered with light blue, velvet flowers with silver and surrounds with small, white marble columns.

And now from fine halls, splendid drawing-rooms, I must begin to describe scenes of a very different nature. In the Hall of the Fountain, behind a statue, is a small door, over which is drawn a curtain of white silk. This door, when opened,[7] discovers a small apartment at the farther end of which is a very large, iron door, which leads to a long, dark passage, at the end of which is a flight of steps leading to a subterranean dungeon, which I shall now endeavour to describe.

It has the appearance of a wide vault, dimly lighted by a lamp [?of asphalt], which casts a strange, death-like lustre over part of the dungeon and leaves the rest in the gloom and darkness of midnight. In the middle is a slab of black marble, supported by four pillars of the same. At the head of it stands a throne of iron. In several parts of the vault are instruments of torture, for this place is the dreadful hall where wicked cockneys[8] are judged by that most unjust of judges, Colonel Naughty,[9] and his gang STOD[10] and the rest.

At the end of this dungeon is the entrance to the cells, which are appropriated to the private and particular use of Hal B. Stunt, the cockneys and the naughty school children.[11] These cells are dark, vaulted, arched and so far down in the earth that the loudest shriek could not be heard by any inhabitant of the upper world; and in these, as well as the dungeons, the most unjust torturing might go on without any fear of detection, if it was not that I keep the key of the dungeon and Emily keeps the key of the cells, and the huge, strong, iron entrances will brave any assault, except with the lawful instruments.

The children which inhabit this magnificent palace are composed only of the young nobles of the land, except such as Johnny Lockhart.[12] The chief governor under us is the Duke of Wellington. This, however, is only an honorary distinction, as when applied to His Grace returned the following answer:

---

[7]Until here, the manuscript is written in Charlotte Brontë's bold cursive hand. From here on she writes in her usual minuscule printing, so increasing the numbers of words she is able to fit on a line.

[8]Probably a reference to 'The Cockney School of Poetry' (Leigh Hunt, Keats, Hazlitt and their London friends) attacked in the Tory *Blackwood's Magazine*.

[9]Young Man Naughty, a notorious Glass Town villain or 'rare lad', known for his body-snatching activities.

[10]Unidentified minor characters.

[11]Here, as elsewhere in the manuscript, the words 'school' and 'guards' are simply indicated by a capital letter ('S' and 'G').

[12]See 'The origin of the Islanders', n. 3.

Little King and Queens (these are our titles),
I am sorry to say my avocations of soldier and statesman will not allow me to comply with your requests that I be governor of some hundreds, not [to say] any thousands, of children, unless the title be merely honorary and I am to have a few scores of subordinates under me. With the request that it may be thus so, I remain your obedient subject,

W.

The request was complied with.

The guards for keeping the children in order and taking them out to walk are the Marquis of Douro and Lord Charles Wellesley,[13] for which they are peculiarly fitted as they lead them into the most wildest and most dangerous parts of the country, leaping rocks, precipices, chasms, etc., and little caring whether the children go before or stop behind, and finally coming home with about a dozen wanting, who are found a few days after in hedges or ditches with legs or head broken, and affording a fine field for Sir A. Hume,[14] Sir A. Cooper and Sir H. Halford to display their different modes of setting and trepanning, etc.

The guards for thrashing the children when they do [wrong] (and sometimes they exercise the privilege when they do not need to) are Colonel O'Shaugnesy and his nephew Fogharty.[15] These are often eminently useful. I forgot to mention that Branwell has a large black club, with which he thumps the children upon occasion and that most unmercifully.

I have now done my notices of the school children for the present.

[Chapter 3 Raton's Attempt][16]

Among our Islanders, there are Baines's three sons, 'T', 'E' and 'T', who go by the separate names of Toltol, Nedned or sometimes 'rr'

[13]Sons of the real Duke of Wellington (see general introduction). This is the first appearance of these major characters in the juvenilia.

[14]Sir Alexander Hume (also Hume Badey) based, like the following two characters, on doctors associated with the Duke of Wellington (see 'The origin of the Islanders', n. 3). Dr John Robert Hume was the Duke's surgeon from the time of the Peninsular Wars (1808).

[15]Unidentified characters.

[16]Northern dialect: a rat (variously spelt ratton, raton, ratten). In this chapter heading, derived from Charlotte Brontë's *Catalogue of my Books*, the word is spelt 'ratten'; but throughout this manuscript 'raton' is used.

[Raton], and Tomtom.[17] These three are the most mischievous trio in existence. Toltol is about two feet long, Nedned is about half the length of his brother, and Tomtom is three-quarters as long as Ned. Tol is dressed in a lawyer's gown and a huge wig, which reaches to his feet and wraps round him. Rat is attired in a coarse piece of sackcloth, tied round the neck and feet with rope and having the appearance of a tail and ears, and Tom is dressed in the dress of a reporter.

About a year ago, as we were wandering in one of the woods which belong to the great domain of Strathfieldsay,[18] we heard a low voice behind us saying, 'There has been a storm today and the now blue and radiant arch of the mighty firmament has been overcast with dark clouds, the gloom of which was only broken by fierce gleams of lightning, which shot across the black vapours, like the word of revenge through the clouds, hatred which obscured the bright dawn of Whiggish intellect! And I was appointed to be their avenger! Yes, this arm (here we saw an arm of little more than a inch long dart through the foliage), this arm shall wreak their spite upon the head of that stern Duke, in whose domains I am. But soon I shall bring his pride down to the dust and make him bow to the sovereign people.'

Then with a rush through the tangled grass (for the spiteful creature did not reach higher than the grass), it reached the park gate. But here, a great obstacle presented itself, for the keeper of the gate is an old veteran, who has followed the Duke through all his wars and attended him in all his battles, and if he had seen the animal he would certainly have taken it for a rat and would have treated it accordingly.

Ned turned round and seeing us, he said, 'Little Queens, will you open that gate?'

As we wished to see the end of this adventure, we took Raton up and threw him over the high wall, and then knocked at the gate. We presently heard a rustling among the trees and the soldier stood before us.

Little Queens: If you please, Orderly-man, will you open that gate for us?

---

[17]Edward Baines, proprietor of the *Leeds Mercury*, had three sons (Mathew Talbot, Edward and Thomas), all of whom worked on the newspaper at various times. The following attempt by Edward ('Ned' or 'Raton'), who became editor of the *Leeds Mercury* in 1818, to poison the Duke of Wellington probably refers to the Whig newspaper's attacks on Wellington as Tory prime minister. The Baineses were also strong advocates of Catholic emancipation, which the Duke opposed at this time.

[18]The estate of Stratfield Saye in Hampshire was presented to the Duke of Wellington by the nation in 1817. Its name is spelt variously by Charlotte, usually as one word, with an 'h' and without the final 'e' (Strathfieldsay); this version has been preserved throughout the edition.

Orderly-man: I must first know who you are.

'We're Little Queens.'

Orderly-man: Oh, you are, are you. Come then.

So saying, he opened the gate and we entered.

Raton ran swiftly up the park and narrowly escaped being trod to death by a deer, which bounded close past him. There was, however, one thing which threatened to stop his progress and that was a river that gently and silently was winding its way through the park. For a while he stood still on its banks and looked around. Behind him was the large wood he had just quitted. It was situated on a high hill and covered to the top with dark, green foliage, interspersed here and there with the lightly waving branches of the purple beech or the pale green of the white poplar. On each side of him lay the extensive and beautiful park, bounded by the wide domains of the great Duke. Before him was the splendid mansion of Strathfieldsay and close to his feet was the river, on the opposite banks of which stood a deer, stooping its head and branching antlers to drink of the pure waters which flowed before it. On the branches of a young oak, which grew close by the stream, sat a nightingale, which was beginning its early song to the silver moon that now appeared like a pale crescent in the clear sky of the east. Over all, the setting sun shed a golden radiance, which invested everything with a splendour that made it appear like burning gold.

For a while Raton seemed moved by the beauty of the scene, but suddenly exclaiming, 'rr, no weakness!', he leaped into the river, and, swimming across, he gained the opposite bank. Then running with inconceivable swiftness up the rest of the park, he reached the house, ran through the hall, the gallery, up the stairs and at last reached the Duke's library.

Nobody was there and upon the table stood a tumbler of water. Into this Raton put something, which, however, did not change its colour. Then leaping from the table, he hid himself behind a large book, which lay on the carpet.

Just then, the sound of footsteps was heard in the gallery. The door opened and a tall man[19] with the air and carriage of a soldier entered, followed by another who was likewise tall but very stout. The first was His Grace the Duke [of] Wellington and the second was Sir Alexander Hume.

As soon as they entered the Duke took from a shelf a volume, and, sitting down, the following conversation ensued.

---

[19]Above these words in the manuscript is a tiny sketch of a face, presumably that of the Duke of Wellington.

Duke of Wellington: What do you think of Walter Scott's *History of Napoleon?*[20]
Hume: Do you mean me to take the fact of it being written by a pekin[21] into consideration, my lord?
Duke: Yes.
Hume: Then I think it is written as well as a pekin is capable of writing.
Duke: Do you think it has any truth in it?
Hume: A great deal, my lord.
Duke: You have given it a high meed of praise.
Hume: Do you think I have praised it too highly?
Duke: Oh, no.
Hume: I would never wish to praise a pekin too much.

After this, a silence of about half an hour ensued and still the Duke did not touch the water. Raton began to be impatient and to fear for the success of his enterprise.

At last His Grace took up the glass and drained its contents. Raton was on the point of giving a shriek through joy but restrained himself.

Just then, Hume said, 'I never thought much good came of drinking cold water,' and a few m[inutes] after he exclaimed, 'My lord, are you well? How pale, how very pale you are! I never saw anybody more so.'

Here Raton shouted out, 'And pale he will always be!'

The Duke fixed his stern eye on him and the creature shrank, shuddering back to his corner.

'My lord, are you dying? Ring the bell to Queens.'

His Grace's features collapsed with agony, the volume fell from his hand, and he sank back into his chair.

Just then, a loud yell rang in our ears, a rushing noise was heard and a Giant of Clouds stood before us. He touched the Duke and new life seemed to be given him. He stood up and in a firm tone demanded the name of the giant. It answered with a voice of thunder, 'Mystery', and then slowly vanished.

His Grace then ordered everyone out of his presence and, a few days after, Raton was found in his father's house at Leeds,[22] pale with horror, trembling and half dead, but how he got there is uncertain. Nor could he ever be induced to give any explanation, and truly a mystery doth the whole affair remain to this day.

---

[20]*The Life of Napoleon Buonaparte*, 9 vols, Edinburgh, 1827.
[21]A civilian. Hume was with Wellington's army at the Battle of Waterloo.
[22]'L' in ms. Edward Baines, Snr, was not made MP for Leeds until 1834, and so he would not have had a London residence at the time this manuscript was written.

[Chapter 4 Lord Charles Wellesley and the
Marquis of Douro's Adventure]

Prince Leopold[23] and Sir George Hill[24] have always entertained a great
dislike to the Marquis of Douro and Lord Charles Wellesley. Prince
Leopold, it is well known, is a very mean sort of personage, with an
appearance of cunning about him that is very disagreeable. Sir George
Hill is frank and brave, somewhat given to gambling and an undue
dislike of pekins. It has been lately surmised that he only pretends to
dislike Arthur and Charles Wellesley for a little amusement, and this is
most likely true.

A little while ago, as Emily and me, one stormy night, were going
through the wood, which leads to school, we saw by the light of the
moon, which just then broke through a cloud, the flashing of some
bright substance. The moon then became obscured and we could
discern nothing more but see very black cloud.

We heard a well-known voice saying, 'Oh Arthur, I wish we had
never come. What will my father say if he ever gets to know of it? And I
am beginning to get very cold, for it rains fast and the wind is high.'

'Wrap your fur cloak closer round you, Charles, and let us lean
against this old tree, for I shall not be able to stand much longer
without some support. The sky is quite covered with dark clouds and
how dismally the wind is moaning among the trees.'

'Arthur, what was that noise I heard? Listen!'

'It is a raven, Charles. I am not much given to superstition but I
remember hearing my grandmother say it is a sign that something bad
is coming to pass.'

'If we were to die here tonight, and remember, Arthur, we came here
by appointment of two of our worst enemies, what would my mother do
and my father?'

Here they both sobbed aloud, and we likewise heard strange and
horrible noises weep through the wood.

'What is the matter with our dogs, Arthur? Are they dying?'

'No, Charles, but that likewise is said to be a sound of death.'

'A sound of death, Arthur! But listen again to the raven. Oh! this is a
dreadful place.'

'Hush, Charles! They are coming.'

[23]Probably modelled on Prince Leopold of Saxe-Coburg, uncle to the future Queen
Victoria and later King of the Belgians.
[24]See *A Romantic Tale*, n. 10.

The glimmering of a lantern appeared through the trees and two men burst upon the path. One of them [was] tall and bony, but he had an expression of pity in his face as he said, 'Poor fellows! Though I don't particularly like you, yet I'm sorry you've had to wait so long in the rain this cold night.'

The other was a mean, despicable wretch and he squinted.

'Prince Leopold and Sir George Hill, we are quite ready to follow you, but go slowly for we cannot possibly walk fast.'

'Come along, then.'

So saying, they set off, and we followed close behind. By the light of the lantern, we could see that the Marquis of Douro and Lord Charles Wellesley had two bloodhounds with them, and, as soon as they emerged from the forest, these two dogs gave a dreadful yell. Prince Leopold shook with terror and Charles patted them, at which they moaned piteously. After this, they were silent for a while and the march proceeded.

After climbing a great many high, steep rocks and leaping many ditches, we entered on the confines of [a] great moor. Just then, the bloodhounds stopped again and gave another horrible cry, which rang all over the wide heath and seemed to be answered from a great distance with a deeper and more dreadful yell.

'Do make your nasty dogs hold their tongues or else I will,' said Sir George.

'If you touch them, Hill, you must take the consequences. They might bite you.'

Prince Leopold [was] panting with fear.

'Come on boys,' shouted Sir George, with a peal of hollow laughter, which was answered by the echoing rocks with tenfold vehemence. Just at that moment, a dull flapping of wings and an ominous croak was heard.

'What in the name of wonder is that?'

'It's a raven!' replied Leopold, almost fainting with cowardice.

'Oh! Do make haste, that we may reach some shelter, for the darkness of the night is increasing, the rain is falling faster and the wind sweeps with more fearful blast over this wild, bleak moor.'

They all moved on, and after a while a light became visible on the verge of the horizon, which, as they approached it, vanished; but by the help of the lantern we could discern a small and seemingly deserted cottage. They entered it and we followed by a door, which was decayed by time and shattered by violence in many places.

'And is this where you intend to take us?' exclaimed the Marquis of Douro.

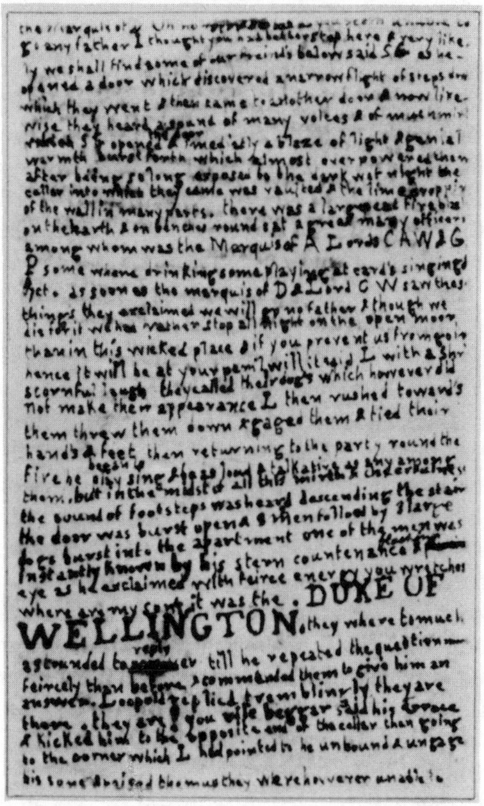

Plate 1 A page from *Tales of the Islanders*, volume 1, chapter 4, written by Charlotte Brontë at the age of thirteen (original size)

'Oh, no, but as you seem unable to go any farther, I thought you had better stop here, and very likely we shall find some of our friends below,' said Sir George, as he opened a door, which discovered a narrow flight of steps, down which they went and then came to another door, and now likewise they heard a sound of many voices and much mirth. Sir George opened the door and immediately a blaze of light and genial warmth burst forth, which almost overpowered them after being so long exposed to the dark, wet night.

The cellar into which they came was vaulted and the lime dropping off the wall in many parts. There was a large, peat fire blazing on the hearth and on benches round sat a great many officers, among whom was the Marquis of A, Lords C, A, W, and GP.[25] Some were drinking, some playing at cards, singing; and yet as soon as the Marquis of Douro and Lord Charles Wellesley saw these things, they exclaimed, 'We will go no farther and though we die for it, we had rather stop all night on the open moor than in this wicked place, and if you prevent us from going hence, it will be at your peril.'

'Will it?' said Leopold, with a shrill, scornful laugh.

They called their dogs, which however did not make their appearance. Leopold then rushed towards them, threw them down and gagged them, and tied their hands and feet. Then returning to the party round the fire, he began to play, sing and be as loud and talkative as any among them.

But in the midst of all this mirth and cheerfulness, the sound of footsteps was heard descending the stairs. The door was burst open and two men, followed by three large dogs, burst into the apartment. One of the men was instantly known by his stern countenance and flashing eye, as he exclaimed with fierce energy, 'You wretches, where are my sons?'

It was the DUKE OF WELLINGTON!

They were too much astounded to reply, till he repeated the question more fiercely than before and commanded them to give him an answer. Leopold replied tremblingly,

'They are there.'

'They are! You vile beggar,' said His Grace, and kicked him to the opposite end of the cellar. Then going to the corner which Leopold had pointed to, he unbound and ungagged his sons and raised them up. They were, however, unable to stand and fell back again. His Grace then turned to the rest and said in a tone of voice which showed he meant to be obeyed, 'I command you all to quit this place, and if ever

[25]Unidentified characters.

you return here again, I shall make you suffer for it and that dreadfully.'

Immediately they flung open the door, rushed up the stair and scampered off as fast as they could.

In the meantime, the other man, who was Doctor Hume, had given Arthur and Charles something which strengthened them so much that they could stand and even walk. The Duke then enquired how they came to that house.

Just at this moment, we issued from our hiding place and related all the circumstances, after which, we asked how His Grace got to know of Charles and Arthur being there. His Grace told us that as he was on his way to school, accompanied by Hume and his great bloodhound, he thought he heard at a distance the yelling of his son's dogs, which was immediately answered by his own, and that after he had gone about a mile farther, he met a country man who told him that he had seen his sons on the Great Moor in the company of George Hill and Prince Leopold; that then, though it was night, he rode towards the moor but was met on his way by his sons' dogs, who led them to the cottage.

As soon as His Grace had finished, he rose to depart and Arthur and Charles followed.

When they had got up the dark, narrow stairs and to the door of the cottage, they were surprised to find the rising sun beaming through the chinks of the door, and when they reached the open air, the scenes which greeted their eyes were truly refreshing. Instead of dark, watery clouds, there was the blue, radiant, dome-like sky, in which the pale moon was yet visible. The glorious sun was rising in the east and making the rain, which had fallen the preceding night, and which still remained on the balmy heath, to sparkle like fine diamonds. A few, little, wild mountain-sheep were to be seen, and as they drew near they [?scurried] away and sprang up the rocks, till they could view us safely at a distance. The lark sprang from his mossy bed at our approach and began to warble its matin song, and the higher it mounted up in the blue heavens, the sweeter did its song become, till it could no longer be heard.

In a short time, they came to the edge of the moor and reached school about nine o'clock, all sound in life and limb. Thus ended the Duke's, Marquis's and Lord's adventure of the cottage.

Charlotte Brontë   June the 31, 1829

The Enfant[1]
by C. Brontë

One fine morning in the month of July,[2] 1829, M. Hanghimself[3] arose from his little bed in a corner of the tavern of which he was the lawful possessor and, opening the door, he looked out into the narrow street [?onto] where the rays of the sun had hardly leave to penetrate by reason of the mouldering and ruined towers of an old castle, which overshadowed this part of the good city of Paris.

Suddenly M. Hanghimself was startled by the sound of wings, and, looking up, he saw a fairy hovering over the castle. She lighted on the highest tower, and fixing her eyes on him, she uttered in a loud and terrible voice some mysterious words, which chilled the heart of M. Hanghimself but which he could not comprehend. Then spreading her large, white wings, she rose majestically above the city and continued her aerial course, till she became only like a dim speck in the clear summer sky to the strained eyes of M. Hanghimself, who knew that this portended that something was to happen to him ere long, whether good or bad he knew not. So after looking steadfastly upwards for some time, he re-entered the tavern and began to tidy the sadly disarranged kitched.

While thus employed, he heard a [?loud knocking] at the door and hastened to open it, but was astounded on perceiving that he had given

---

[1]Two page manuscript (12.5 × 7 cm) in BPM: B80(9); fair copy of an original draft now lost. The first draft of *The Enfant* was copied (with minor variations) by Branwell Brontë into his *Branwell's Blackwood's Magazine* for May and June 1829; the June issue only is extant (HCL: Lowell I(8)). The main differences between Branwell's and Charlotte's texts are in isolated words, for example Branwell writes 'leaping', Charlotte 'jumping'. Branwell's spelling is worse than that of Charlotte and her later version, being a fair copy, is more polished. Whether or not she copied Branwell's version of her earlier draft, she took the opportunity to 'improve' her story; for example, she adds the epithets 'poor little' to 'Enfant' in this later version.

The Enfant is followed by a related poem, beginning 'Highminded Frenchmen love not the Ghost', dated 17 July 1829 and signed by Charlotte Brontë with the additional signature 'Young Soult'. Charlotte is either using Branwell's pseudonym here or transcribing a poem by Branwell, although the number of errors and corrections suggest it is an original draft. The poem refers to Napoleon and reflects the same interests as the story: see *Poems*, p. 259

[2]As suggested above, the story was originally written in May and June 1829. Here Charlotte has altered the month of her story to coincide with the time she made this copy. In later manuscripts, particularly, it was her habit to set her story at the time of writing.

[3]Branwell Brontë's earlier version of *The Enfant* refers to 'Moses Hanghimself', so 'M' may refer to Moses rather than Monsieur.

admittance to no less a personage than the farfamed madman PIGTAIL,[4] who stood before him clothed in the dress and wearing the insignia (that is, brush and soot pack) of a chimney sweeper. He was accompanied by a little, pale, thin Enfant.

'Have you any chimneys to sweep?' said Pigtail wildly.

'I have. You may sweep this,' answered Hanghimself.

'Come then,' muttered the madman taking hold of the Enfant by the hair of its head.

The poor little creature screamed out. Pigtail kicked it and ordered it to go up the chimney. The Enfant obeyed and Hanghimself begged Pigtail not to hurt it any more.

'Hold your tongue you prater,' said Pigtail angrily.

Hanghimself was silent, and taking up a tin can he went out to purchase a little wine for the Enfant, whom he observed to be very weak and tired.

When he came back he saw a flood of water rushing out of the door and beheld Pigtail kicking and trampling on the Enfant, who was quite insensible. Throwing down the can, he ran off as fast as he could towards the house of the Intendant of Police and related to him all the circumstances.

'Poh, poh,' said the Intendant, 'this is much too trivial for me to interfere with. Go about your business and don't come troubling me with such nonsense.'

M. Hanghimself then bent his way towards the Tuilleries[5] and, when he had there arrived, he addressed himself to a little page, who introduced him to the Chamber of Presence. There sat the mighty Emperor, who had made all Europe to tremble before him, surrounded by his great marshals and high officers.

At any other time M. Hanghimself would have been awed by all this state, but he felt a love for the poor little Enfant, for which he could by no means account, and this emboldened him to address the Emperor with some degree of confidence. Therefore throwing himself on his knees at the feet of Napoleon, he recounted the whole affair.

'Soult,'[6] said the Emperor, 'order a party of gendarmes to go

[4]A mad Frenchman, who features mainly in Branwell Brontë's early manuscripts and whose habit it is to steal, exploit and murder children. His history is told by Branwell in *Letters From An Englishman*, vol. II, *SHCBM*, vol. 1, p. 106.

[5]A former palace in Paris, residence for the sovereigns of France.

[6]Marshal Soult was Wellington's opponent in the Peninsular Campaign and again at Waterloo, under Napoleon. Branwell uses his name as a pseudonym in the early juvenilia, and he later becomes the important Angrian character Alphonse Soult, Marquis of Marseilles, Ambassador to Verdopolis and then Duke of Dalmatia.

instantly to this fellow's house, the Tavern of the Castle, and bring hither Pigtail and the Enfant.'

'Your orders shall be obeyed, sire,' replied Soult, as he quitted the apartment.

The Emperor then asked Hanghimself if he had any children.

'I had but it was stolen from me,' answered Hanghimself, and the tears gushed from his eyes as he spoke.

'Well, perhaps this may be yours,' replied the Emperor.

'It may, it may,' shouted Hanghimself, and he began to jump [?high] like a madman for joy.

'Moderate your transports,' said the Emperor. 'Had it any mark by which you may know it?'

'Yes, it had the mark of an adder bite [?on] its left arm,' returned Hanghimself.

Just at this moment, the gendarmes entered with Pigtail and the Enfant. Hanghimself immediately snatched up the Enfant and uncovering its left arm gave a shriek through joy, for there was the identical mark of the adder bite. The Enfant was no less rejoiced when it found that Hanghimself was its father, and the two leaped about as if they were half frantic.

In the meantime, Pigtail took the opportunity of jumping out of the window and so escaped to continue his mysterious wanderings.

At length, when Hanghimself and the Enfant had recovered some degree of composure, the Emperor gave them 200,000 livres, with which Hanghimself purchased a beautiful estate and seat finely situated in the fruitful province of Languedoc, where he now lives with his Enfant, two of the happiest and most contented people in all France.

July 13, 1829

The Keep of the Bridge[1]

This keep or round tower is celebrated in tradition as being the abode of the fairy Ebon.[2] It is situated on a small acclivity. Before it flows a broad stream of water and behind it there is a large wood or rather forest, which covers a very high hill, said to be the identical hill on

[1]Single page manuscript (9 × 5.5 cm) in NYPL: Berg Collection; accompanied by two pages of pencil sketches: the first entitled 'The Keep of the Bridge', dated 'CB 1829'; and the second entitled 'the ruins of [?Corrantugals] Palace', dated 'CB May 20 1829'.

[2]Charlotte Brontë is possibly transforming the nickname 'Ebony', given to Blackwood in the 'Noctes Ambrosianae' of *Blackwood's Magazine*.

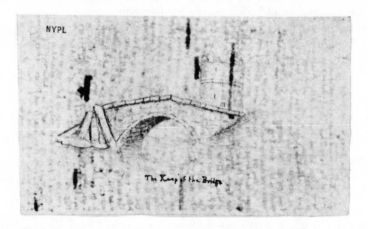

Plate 2 *The Keep of the Bridge*, written and illustrated by Charlotte Brontë at the age of thirteen

which the magician of the sea lost his life for presuming to release Gambia[3] from the horrible dungeon, in which the fairy had confined him.

When I saw the keep it was night and the moon was shedding her mild glory on all around, illuminating the topmost branches of the gloomy forest, whose shade was too dense for the light to penetrate farther, and gilding the ivy which clung to the grey walls of the keep, so as to make them appear as if they were embroidered with silver; while in the clear, still waters of the river, the whole arch of the firmament, with bright moon hanging in the midst and the sparkling stars spangling the sky, were reflected so truly as to seem almost as magnificent as the glorious original.

After contemplating this beautiful prospect for some time, I entered the tower, and, passing through the dreary hall, lighted only by a ray of moonlight which found its way through an arched and grated window, I opened the massive iron door which leads to Gambia's dungeon; and then, descending the long, narrow stairs, I reached the dreadful apartment. And dreadful indeed it was. There was still burning the torch of the magician, which cast a bloody, unearthly light around the place, and, as I entered the huge door closed after me, though no living creature appeared.

I was alone – it was night – I could not open the door, though I tried with all my strength. I thought, how dreadful it would be to die in such a place; yet this, I knew, must be the inevitable consequence of my temerity. I threw myself on the ground in despair and remained motionless and stupid with horror for some time.

At last, I saw a thin, misty form rise out of the earth. It beckoned to me: I arose; the door opened; I found myself outside the castle. I immediately quitted the haunted tower and returned to it no more.

CB   July 13, 1829

---

[3]This name is possibly derived from the River Gambia in West Africa, mentioned in the Brontës' early geography book and in *Blackwood's Magazine* (see *A Romantic Tale*, n. 8); in the Glass Town Saga the river becomes a central feature of Wellington's Land, which is later called Senegambia.

'Sir – it is well known that the Genii'[1]

Sir – it is well known that the Genii have declared that unless they[2] 'perform certain arduous duties every year, of a mysterious nature, all the worlds in the firmament will be burnt up and gathered together in one mighty globe, which will roll in lonely grandeur through the vast wilderness of space, inhabited only by the four high Princes of the Genii, till time shall be succeeded by eternity'. The impudence of this is only to be paralleled by another of their assertions, namely, 'that by their magic might they can reduce the world to a desert, the rivers to streams of livid poison and the clearest lakes to stagnant waters, the pestilential vapours of which shall slay all living creatures, except the blood-thirsty beast of the forest and the ravenous bird of the rock. But that in the midst of this desolation the Palace of the Chief Genii shall rise sparkling in the wilderness, and the horrible howl of their war-cry shall spread over the land at morning, at noontide and night; but that they shall have their annual feast over the bones of the dead and shall yearly rejoice with the joy of victors.' I think, sir, that the horrible wickedness of this needs no remark, and therefore I haste to subscribe myself, yours etc.,

UT

July 14, 1829

---

[1]Single page manuscript (8.2 × 6.5 cm) in BPM: B79; probably intended as a letter to the editor of the *Young Men's Magazine*. The original signature has been erased and replaced by 'UT' ('us two'), implying that Branwell contributed to its composition (see general introduction). It is possible that this manuscript was written solely by Branwell and copied by Charlotte, since the tone and subject reflect his early writing rather than that of Charlotte. The early Glass Town was subject to the tyranny of the four Chief Genii (the Brontë children themselves), a role disliked by Branwell, who provoked a Young Men's rebellion against their tyranny. The four Chief Genii were formally expelled from the saga in Charlotte's poem 'The trumpet hath sounded', 11 December 1831, and although Branwell surprisingly tried to resurrect them (in 'Ode on the Celebration of the Great African Games', 26 June 1832, and 'A Few Words to the Chief Genii', 27 March 1833), the Chief Genii appear in a minor role in only two of Charlotte's later manuscripts, *The Foundling*, 31 May – 27 June 1833, and *The Green Dwarf*, 2 September 1833.

[2]The Young Men.

A Fragment, August the 7, 1829[1]

One cold, dreary night in the month of December, the Marquis and Marchioness of Wellesley and their children, who were all grown up,[2] were sitting in the private parlour round a blazing, cheerful fire. They appeared quite comfortable in all outward things and yet they kept sighing and fidgeting and yawning, as if some great trouble oppressed them.

At last Lady Wellesley rose up from her seat, and, going to the window, she drew aside the splendid curtain and looked out into the dark, stormy night. After gazing for some time, she returned to the fire, saying in a despairing tone, 'When will little Arthur come?'

'I wonder what he is like now,' exclaimed Lord Wellesley.

'Oh Arthur, Arthur, do come,' said the Honourable and Reverend Doctor Wellesley.

'I don't know what I shall do if he does not come soon,' returned Lord Cowley.

'It's quite miserable without him,' answered Lord Maryborough.

'When we last saw him he was a pretty little baby,' said the Marquis of Wellesley.

'Sweet, little creature,' ejaculated the Marchioness.

Just at this moment, the door opened and a tall, handsome young man appeared. They all started up joyfully, exclaiming, 'That's Arthur!' and, running towards him, almost smothered him with kisses and caresses, while he in return did the same to them. After the exuberance of their joy had a little subsided, they gathered round the fire once more, but now perfectly happy as little Arthur was there.

After a short time, the Marquis of Wellesley said, 'Now my dear son, tell us all that you have done and suffered since I placed you in the arms of your orderly-man, to be conveyed on board the ship, which was to take you to Eton College.'[3]

'Yes, do, Arthur,' exclaimed the rest.

Arthur consented and began as follows.

C. Brontë   August the 8, 1829

---

[1]Single page manuscript (9.8 × 6.2 cm) in BPM: B80(12).
[2]Wellesley was the real Duke of Wellington's family name. His parents and brothers – Marquis of Wellesley (Jnr), Lord Maryborough, Lord Cowley and Dr Wellesley – all feature in this manuscript; the ages of the brothers have been distorted by Charlotte Brontë to make the Duke appear the youngest and the darling of the family. He was, in fact, neglected and not particularly liked by his family when young.
[3]School of the real Duke of Wellington and his two sons.

Fragment, August the 8, 1829[1]

On the third day I came to a wide plain, in the middle of which was a mound of earth and over it, suspended in the air, there was a very bright light, which illuminated the mound with a radiant splendour, more glorious than the sun at noonday. On all the plain, the shadow of mystery and desolation rested, and the light over the mound was very wonderful.

As I was wishing to know the reason of it, my attention was directed to the figure of an old man, sitting on a grey stone and clad in white garments. I approached him and asked the cause of that light in the air. He rose and as he held up his head, I could see that his countenance had not the expression of a human being, but something of a superior nature.

'That mound,' said he, 'is the grave which contains the remains of Arthur, Duke of Wellington, and I am the guardian of his narrow house.[2] Over his tomb you see no monument of human erection, but there the light of his glory stands fixed in the heavens; and it shall eternally illuminate the small spot of earth where lie the bones of that mighty one. And look up, do you not see his name in the celestial arch, there in its radiance? It shall everlastingly remain and shall make the silver moon, the sparkling stars and even the golden sun itself appear dim and lustreless to it.'

The being then stopped, but as it was speaking its countenance had changed, its statute had dilated, its white garments had disappeared, and it stood before me a mighty and majestic spirit, wearing on its head a crown of emeralds, clothed in robe of green, holding in its right hand a flaming spear and in its left a shield of adamant. For a moment it stood thus and then rose in terrible grandeur through the air, its wings making a noise like thunder, till it vanished from my sight.

C. Brontë   August the 8, 1829

---

[1]Single page manuscript (9.8 × 6.5 cm) in BPM: B80(10).
[2]The historical Duke of Wellington did not die until 1852, only three years before Charlotte Brontë herself.

41

The Search After Happiness
A Tale by C.
Brontë
August the seventeenth, 1829[1]

THE SEARCH AFTER
HAPPINESS[2]
A TALE BY
CHARLOTTE
BRONTË
PRINTED BY HERSELF
AND
SOLD BY
NOBODY ETC., ETC.
AUGUST
THE
SEVENTEENTH
EIGHTEEN HUNDRED
AND
TWENTY-NINE

PREFACE

The persons meant by the Chief of the City and his sons are the Duke
of Wellington, the Marquis of Douro and Lord Wellesley. The city is

---

[1]On grey paper cover of manuscript in BL: Ashley 156; hand-sewn booklet of fifteen pages
(8.9 × 5.6 cm). The title-page follows, with preface on verso.
[2]'HAPINESS' in manuscript; the word is spelt incorrectly only on this title-page.

the Glass Town. Henry O'Donell[3] and Alexander Delancy[4] are Captain Tarry-not-at-home and Monsieur Like-to-live-in-lonely-places.

CHARLOTTE BRONTË
August the 17
1829

A TALE BY CB
July 28, 1829
The Search After Happiness

CHAPTER I

Not many years ago there lived in a certain city a person of the name of Henry O'Donell. In figure he was tall, of a dark complexion and searching black eye. His mind was strong and unbending, his disposition unsociable, and, though respected by many, he was loved by few.

The city where he resided was very great and magnificent. It was governed by a warrior, a mighty man of valour, whose deeds had resounded to the ends of the earth. This soldier had two sons, who were at that time of the separate ages of six and seven years.

Henry O'Donell was a nobleman of great consequence in the city and a peculiar favourite with the governor, before whose glance his stern mind would bow, and at his command O'Donell's self-will would be overcome; and while playing with the young princes he would forget his usual sullenness of demeanour. The days of his childhood returned upon him and he would be as merry as the youngest, who was gay indeed.

One day at Court, a quarrel ensued between him and another noble. Words came to blows, and O'Donell struck his opponent a violent blow on the left cheek. At this the military King started up and commanded O'Donell to apologize. This he immediately did, but from that hour a

---

[3]Compare Marcus O'Donell in *A Romantic Tale*.
[4]Variously spelt throughout the manuscript 'Delancy' and 'De Lancy'. The name was probably suggested by that of Sir William de Lancey, a Peninsular colleague of the Duke of Wellington, who was mortally wounded fighting near the Duke at the Battle of Waterloo, 1815.

spell of discontent seemed to have been cast over him and he resolved to quit the city.

The evening before he put this resolution into practice, he had an interview with the King and returned quite an altered man. Before, he seemed stern and intractable; now, he was only meditative and sorrowful. As he was passing the inner court of the palace, he perceived the two young princes at play. He called them and they came running to him.

'I am going far from this city and shall, most likely, never see you again,' said O'Donell.

'Where are you going?'

'I cannot tell.'

'Then why do you go away from us? Why do you go from your own house and lands, from this great and splendid city, to you know not where?'

'Because I am not happy here.'

'And if you are not happy here, where you have everything for which you can wish, do you expect to be happy when you are dying of hunger or thirst in a desert, or longing for the society of men when you are thousands of miles from any human being?'

'How do you know that that will be my case?'

'It is very likely that it will.'

'And if it was I am determined to go.'

'Take this then, that you may sometimes remember us when you dwell with only the wild beasts of the desert or the great eagle of the mountain,' said they, as they each gave him a curling lock of their hair.

'Yes, I will take it, my princes, and I shall remember you and the mighty warrior King, your father, even when the Angel of Death has stretched forth his bony arm against me and I am within the confines of his dreary kingdom, the cold, damp grave,' replied O'Donell, as the tears rushed to his eyes, and he once more embraced the little princes, and then quitted them, it might be, for ever.

CHAPTER THE II

The dawn of the next morning found O'Donell on the summit of a high mountain which overlooked the city. He had stopped to take a farewell view of the place of his nativity. All along the eastern horizon there was a rich glowing light, which, as it rose, gradually melted into the pale blue of the sky, in which, just over the light, there was still visible the silver crescent of the moon. In a short time the sun began to rise in golden glory, casting his splendid radiance over all the face of nature, and illuminating the magnificent city, in the midst of which, towering in silent grandeur, there appeared the palace where dwelt the mighty Prince of that great and beautiful city, all around the brazen gates and massive walls of which there flowed the majestic stream of the Guadima,[5] whose banks were bordered by splendid palaces and magnificent gardens. Behind these, stretching for many a league, were fruitful plains and forests, whose shade seemed almost impenetrable to a single ray of light; while in the distance, blue mountains were seen raising their heads to the sky and forming a misty girdle to the plains of Dahomey. On the whole of this grand and beautiful prospect, O'Donell's gaze was long and fixed; but his last look was to the palace of the King, and a tear stood in his eye as he said earnestly, 'May he be preserved from all evil! May good attend him, and may the Chief Genii spread their broad shield of protection over him all the time of his sojourn in this wearisome world!'

Then, turning round, he began to descend the mountain. He pursued his way till the sun began to wax hot, when he stopped, and, sitting down, he took out some provisions which he had brought with him and which consisted of a few biscuits and dates.

While he was eating, a tall man came up and accosted him. O'Donell requested him to sit beside him and offered him a biscuit. This he refused, and taking one out of a small bag which he carried, he sat down and they began to talk. In the course of conversation, O'Donell learned that this man's name was Alexander Delancy, that he was a native of France and that he was engaged in the same pursuit with himself, i.e. the search of happiness.[6] They talked for a long time and at last agreed to travel together. Then, rising, they pursued their journey.

Towards nightfall they lay down in the open air, and slept soundly till morning, when they again set off; and thus they continued till the third day, when, about two hours after noon, they approached an old castle, which they entered; and, as they were examining it, they discovered a subterraneous passage which they could not see the end of.

'Let us follow where this passage leads us and perhaps we may find happiness here,' said O'Donell.

[5]Spelt 'Guadiana' in later manuscripts; it flows over the plains of Dahomey and surrounds the Glass Town. The name was probably suggested by the River Guadiana in southern Spain, which brings relief to a desert area. It was the scene of much action during the Peninsular Wars and was mentioned by Wellington in dispatches.

[6]This story was probably influenced by Johnson's *Rasselas*, although there is no definite evidence that Charlotte Brontë read the work.

Delancy agreed. The two stepped into the opening. Immediately a great stone was rolled to the mouth of the passage, with a noise like thunder, which shut out all but a single ray [of] daylight.

'What is that?' exclaimed O'Donell.

'I cannot tell,' replied Delancy, 'but never mind, I suppose it is only some Genius playing tricks.'

'Well, it may be so,' returned O'Donell, and they proceeded on their way.

After travelling for a long time – as near as they could reckon about two days – they perceived a silvery streak of light on the walls of the passage, something like the light of the moon. In a short time they came to the end of the passage and, leaping out of the opening which formed it, they entered a new world.

They were at first so much bewildered by the different objects which struck their senses that they almost fainted, but, at length recovering, they had time to see everything around them. They were upon the top of a rock which was more than a thousand fathoms high. All beneath them was liquid mountains tossed to and fro with horrible confusion, roaring and raging with a tremendous noise and crowned with waves of foam. All above them was a mighty firmament, in one part covered with black clouds from which darted huge and terrible sheets of lightning. In another part an immense globe of light, like silver, was hanging in the sky and several smaller globes, which sparkled exceedingly, surrounded it.

In a short time, the tempest, which was dreadful beyond description, ceased; the large black clouds cleared away; the silver globes vanished; and another globe, whose light was of a gold colour, appeared. It was far larger than the former and, in a little time, it became so intensely bright, that they could no longer gaze on it. So after looking around them for some time, they rose and pursued their journey.

They had travelled a long way when they came [to] an immense forest, the trees of which bore a large fruit of a deep purple colour, of which they tasted and found that it was fit for food. They journeyed in this forest for three days, and on the third day they entered a valley, or rather a deep glen, surrounded on each side by tremendous rocks whose tops were lost in the clouds. In this glen they continued for some time and at last came in sight of a mountain, which rose so high that they could not see the summit, though the sky was quite clear. At the foot of the mountain there flowed a river of pure water, bordered by trees which had flowers of a beautiful rose colour. Except these trees, nothing was to be seen but black forests and huge rocks rising out of a wilderness, which bore the terrible aspect of devastation and which stretched as far as the eye could reach. In this desolate land no sound was to be heard, not even [the] cry of the eagle or the scream of the curlew, but a silence, like the silence of the grave, reigned over all the face of nature, unbroken except by the murmur of the river as it slowly wound its course through the desert.

CHAPTER THE III

After they had contemplated this scene for some time, O'Donell exclaimed, 'Alexander, let us abide here. What need have we to travel farther? Let us make this our place of rest.'

'We will,' replied Delancy. 'And this shall be our abode,' added he, pointing to a cave at the foot of the mountains.

'It shall,' returned O'Donell, as they entered it.

In this country they remained for many long years, and passed their time in a manner which made them completely happy. Sometimes they would sit upon a high rock and listen to the hoarse thunder rolling through the sky and making the mountains to echo and the deserts to ring with its awful voice. Sometimes they would watch the lightning darting across black clouds and shivering huge fragments of rock in its terrible passage. Sometimes they would witness the great, glorious orb of gold sink behind the far distant mountains which girded the horizon, and then watch the advance of grey twilight, and the little stars coming forth in beauty, and the silver moon rising in her splendour, till the cold dews of night began to fall. And then they would retire to their bed in the cave with hearts full of joy and thankfulness.

One evening they were seated in this cave by a large, blazing fire of turf, which cast its lurid light to the high arched roof and illuminated the tall and stately pillars, cut by the hand of nature out [of] the stony rock, with a red and cheerful glare that appeared strange in this desolate land, which no fires had ever before visited, except those fierce flames of death which flash from the heavens when robed in the dreadful majesty of thunder. They were seated in this cave then, listening to the howling night-wind as it swept in mournful cadences through the trees of the forest, which encircled the foot of the mountain and bordered the stream which flowed round it. They were quite silent, and their thoughts were occupied by those that were afar off and whom it was their fate most likely never more to behold.

O'Donell was thinking of his noble master and his young princes, of the thousands of miles which intervened between him and them, and the sad, silent tear gushed forth as he ruminated on the happiness of those times, when his master frowned not, when the gloom of care gave place to the smile of friendship, when he would talk to him and laugh with him and be to him, not as a brother – no, no – but as a mighty warrior, who, relaxing from his haughtiness, would now and then converse with his high officers in a strain of vivacity and playful humour not to be equalled. Next he viewed him in his mind's eye at the head of his army. He heard, in the ears of his imagination, the buzz of expectation, of hope and supposition which hummed round him as his penetrating eye, with a still keenness of expression, was fixed on the distant ranks of the enemy. Then he heard his authoritative voice exclaim, 'Onward, brave sons of freedom! Onward to the battle!' And, lastly, his parting words to him: 'In prosperity or in misery, in sorrow or in joy, in populous cities or in desolate wildernesses, my prayer shall go with you!' darted across his mind with such painful distinctness, that he at length gave way to his uncontrollable grief at the thought that he should never behold his beloved and mighty commander more, and burst into a flood of tears.

'What is the matter, Henry?' exclaimed Delancy.

'Oh, nothing, nothing,' was the reply, and they were resuming their tacit thinking, when a voice was heard outside the cavern, which broke strangely upon the desolate silence of that land which for thousands of years had heard no sound save the howling of the wind through the forest, the echoing of the thunder among mountains or the solitary murmuring of the river, if we except the presence of O'Donell and Delancy.

'Listen!' cried Alexander. 'Listen! What is that?'

'It is the sound of a man's voice,' replied Henry, and then snatching up a burning torch he rushed to the mouth of the cave, followed by Delancy. When they had got there, they saw the figure of a very old man sitting on the damp, wet ground, moaning and complaining bitterly. They went up to him. At their approach he rose and said, 'Are you human or supernatural beings?'

They assured him that they were human. He went on: 'Then why have you taken up your abode in this land of the grave?'

O'Donell answered that he would relate to him all the particulars if he would take shelter for the night with them. The old man consented and, when they were all assembled round the cheerful fire, O'Donell fulfilled his promise and then requested the old man to tell them how he came to be travelling there. He complied and began as follows.

CHAPTER THE IV

I was the son of a respectable merchant in Moussoul.[7] My father intended to bring me up to his own trade, but I was idle and did not like it. One day, as I was playing in the street, a very old man came up to me and asked me if I would go with him. I asked him where he was going. He replied that if I would go with him he would show me very wonderful things. This raised my curiosity and I consented. He immediately took me by the hand and hurried me out of the city of Moussoul so quickly that my breath was almost stopped and it seemed as if we glided along in the air, for I could hear no sound of our footsteps.

We continued on our course for a long time, till we came to [a] glen surrounded by very high mountains. How we passed over these mountains I could never tell. In the middle of the glen there was a small fountain of very clear water. My conductor directed me to drink of it. This I did and immediately I found myself in a palace, the glory of which far exceeds any description which I can give. The tall, stately pillars, reaching from heaven to earth, were formed of the finest, purest diamonds; the pavement sparkling with gold and precious stones; and the mighty dome, made solemn and awful by its stupendous magnitude, was of one single emerald. In the midst of this grand and magnificent palace was a lamp like the sun, the radiance of which made all the palace to flash and glitter with an almost fearful grandeur. The ruby sent forth a stream of crimson light, the topaz gold, the sapphire intensest purple and the dome poured a flood of deep, clear splendour, which overcame all the other gaudy lights by its mild, trimphant glory.

In this palace were thousands and tens of thousands of fairies and genii, some of whom flitted lightly among the blazing lamps to the sound of unearthly music, which died and swelled in a strain of wild grandeur, suited to the words they sung:

> In this fairy land of light
> No mortal e'er has been,
> And the dreadful grandeur of this sight
> By them hath not been seen.

---

[7]Probably Mosul, a leading city in northern Iraq, formerly associated with the Ottoman Empire. From 1818 to 1826 Britain held mandatory power for Iraq and negotiated a boundary settlement between Turkey and Iraq; hence, Mosul would have been in the news at this time.

T'would strike them shuddering to the earth
Like the flash from a thundercloud;
It would quench their light and joyous mirth
And fit them for the shroud.

The rising of our palaces
Like visions of the deep,
And the glory of their structure
No mortal voice can speak.

The music of our songs
And our mighty trumpets' swell,
And the sounding of our silver harps
No mortal tongue can tell.

Of us they know but little,
Save when the storm doth rise
And the mighty waves are tossing
Against the arched skies.

Then oft they see us striding
O'er the billow's snow-white foam,
Or hear us speak in thunder
When we stand in grandeur lone,

On the darkest of the mighty clouds
Which veil the pearly moon,
Around us lightning flashing,
Night's blackness to illume.

The music of our songs
And our mighty trumpets' swell
And the sounding of our silver harps
No mortal tongue can tell.

When they had finished there was a dead silence for about half an hour; and then the palace began slowly and gradually to vanish, till it disappeared entirely and I found myself in the glen surrounded by high mountains, the fountain – illuminated by the cold light of the moon – springing up in the middle of the valley; and standing close by was the old man who had conducted me to this enchanted place. He turned round and I could see that his countenance had an expression of strange severity which I had not before observed.

'Follow me,' he said.

I obeyed and we began to ascend the mountain. It would be needless to trouble you with a repetition of all my adventures. Suffice it to say that after two months time we arrived at a large temple. We entered it. The interior, as well as the outside, had a very gloomy and ominous aspect, being entirely built of black marble. The old man suddenly seized me and dragged me to an altar at the upper end of the temple; then, forcing me down on my knees, he made me swear that I would be his servant for ever. This promise I faithfully kept, notwithstanding the dreadful scenes of magic of which every day of my life I was forced to be a witness.

One day he told me that he would discharge me from the oath I had taken and commanded me to leave his service. I obeyed, and after wandering about the world for many years, I one evening laid myself down on a little bank by the roadside, intending to pass the night there. Suddenly I found myself raised in the air by invisible hands. In a short time I lost sight of the earth and continued on my course through the clouds till I became insensible, and when I recovered from my swoon I found myself lying outside this cave. What may be my future destiny I know not.

CHAPTER THE V

When the old man had finished his tale, O'Donell and Delancy thanked him for the relation, adding at the same time that they had never heard anything half so wonderful. Then, as it was very late, they all retired to rest. Next morning O'Donell awoke very early, and looking round the cave, he perceived the bed of leaves on which the old man had lain to be empty. Then rising he went out of the cave.

The sky was covered with red, fiery clouds, except those in the east whose edges were tinged with the bright rays of the morning sun as they strove to hide its glory with their dark veil of vapours, now all beauty and radiance by the golden line of light which streaked their gloomy surface beneath this storm-portending sky; and far off to the westward, rose two tremendous rocks whose summits were enveloped with black clouds rolling one above another with an awful magnificence well-suited to the land of wilderness and mountain which they canopied.

Gliding along in the air between these two rocks was a chariot of light, and in the chariot sat a figure, the expression of whose countenance was that of the old man, armed with the majesty and might of a spirit.

O'Donell stood at the mouth of the cave watching it till it vanished, and then, calling Delancy, he related the circumstance to him.

51

Some years after this, Alexander went out one morning in search of the fruit on which they subsisted. Noon came and he had not returned; evening, and still no tidings of him. O'Donell began to be alarmed and set out in search of him but could nowhere find him. One whole day he spent in wandering about the rocks and mountains, and in the evening he came back to his cave weary and faint with hunger and thirst. Days, weeks, months, passed away and no Delancy appeared. O'Donell might now be said to be truly miserable. He would sit on a rock for hours together and cry out, 'Alexander! Alexander!' but receive no answer except the distant echoing of his voice among the rocks. Sometimes he fancied it was another person answering him and he would listen earnestly till it died away. Then, sinking into utter despair again, he would sit till the dews of night began to fall, when he would retire to his cave to pass the night in unquiet, broken slumbers or in thinking of his beloved commander whom he could never see more.

In one of these dreadful intervals he took up a small parcel and, opening it, he saw lying before him two locks of soft, curly hair, shining like burnished gold. He gazed on them for a little time and thought of the words of those who gave them to him.

'Take this then, that you may remember us when you dwell with only the wild beast of the desert and the great eagle of the mountain.'

He burst into a flood of tears. He wrung his hands in sorrow, and, in the anguish of the moment, he wished that he could once more see them and the mighty warrior King, their father, if it cost him his life.

Just at that instant a loud clap of thunder shook the roof of the cave. A sound like the rushing of wind was heard and a mighty Genius stood before him.

'I know thy wish,' cried he with a loud and terrible voice, 'and I will grant it. In two months time thou returnest to the castle, whence thou camest hither, and surrenderest thyself into my power!'

O'Donell promised that he would, and instantly he found himself at the door of the old castle and in the land of his birth.

He pursued his journey for three days, and on the third day he arrived at the mountain which overlooked the city. It was a beautiful evening in the month of September and the full moon was shedding her tranquil light on all the face of nature. The city was lying in its splendour and magnificence surrounded by the broad stream of the Guadima. The palace was majestically towering in the midst of it, and all its pillars and battlements seemed in the calm light of the moon as if they were transformed into silver by the touch of a fairy's wand.

O'Donell stayed not long to contemplate this beautiful scene but, descending the mountain, he soon crossed the fertile plain which led to the city, and, entering the gates, he quickly arrived at the palace. Without speaking to any one, he entered the inner court of the palace by a secret way with which he was acquainted, and then going up a flight of steps and crossing a long gallery, he arrived at the King's private apartment.The door was half open. He looked in and beheld two very handsome young men sitting together and reading. He instantly recognized them and was going to step forward, when the door opened and the great Duke entered. O'Donell could contain himself no longer, but rushing in, he threw himself at the feet of His Grace.

'O'Donell! Is it you?' exclaimed the Duke.

'It is, my most noble master!' answered O'Donell, almost choking with joy. The young princes instantly embraced him, while he almost smothered them with caresses.

After a while they became tranquil, and then O'Donell, at the request of the Duke, related all his adventures since he parted with them, not omitting the condition on which he was now in the palace. When he had ended, a loud voice was heard saying that he was free from his promise and might spend the rest of his days in his native city.

Some time after this, as O'Donell was walking in the streets, he met a gentleman who he thought he had seen before, but could not recollect where or under what circumstances. After a little conversation, he discovered that he was Alexander Delancy, that he was now a rich merchant in the city of Paris and high in favour with the Emperor Napoleon. As may be supposed they both were equally delighted at the discovery. They ever after lived happily in their separate cities; and so ends my little tale.

C. Brontë   August the 17, 1829

Contents

Chap. I   Character of O'Donell. Cause of his travels.

Chap. II   Set out. Meeting Delancy. Coming to the old castle. Entering the new world. Description.

Chap. III   Coming to the cave. Manner of life. Arrival of the old man.

Chap. IV   Old man's tale.

Chap. V   Departure of the old man. Disappearance of Delancy. Transportation of O'Donell. His arrival at the city. His arrival at the palace and his interview with his chief. He finds Delancy. End.

FINIS

AUGUST
1829 – CB[1]

BLACKWOOD'S
YOUNG MEN'S
MAGAZINE
EDITED BY THE
GENIUS
CB
PRINTED BY
CAPTAIN
TREE[2]
AND SOLD BY

CAPTAIN CARY, SERGEANT BLOOD,
CORPORAL LIDELL, ETC., ETC., ETC.[3]

A TRUE STORY
BY CB

In the Palace of Waterloo,[4] there is a secret court of about 500 yards in diameter. It is surrounded by Corinthian pillars of polished white

---

[1] Date on brown paper cover of manuscript, in HCL: Lowell I(6); hand-sewn booklet of twenty pages (5 × 3.4 cm).

[2] Glass Town novelist and rival of Captain Bud, father of Sergeant Bud (hence the second article in this magazine). Also a pseudonym of Charlotte Brontë in the early juvenilia and rival of another of her pseudonyms, Lord Charles Wellesley.

[3] Title-page. Charlotte Brontë's initials are surrounded by a heart-shaped colophon.

[4] Glass Town residence of the Duke of Wellington and his family; named after the Battle of Waterloo, 18 June 1815, the historical Duke's most famous victory.

marble and paved with the same. It is more than 900 feet high and is surmounted by a round dome of white agate, sparkling with stars of gold and rich ornaments of the purple sapphire.

In this court, in the summer of the year —, about that time of the day when the palace begins to cast its shade eastward, stood 2 young men, or rather boys, apparently of about 17 or 18 years of age. They were tall, slender, remarkably handsome, and were so much alike that it would have been difficult to distinguish the one from the other, were it not for a shade of thought which occasionally passed over the features of the elder; and his fine wavy hair was also a little darker than that of the other, whose merry smile, which now and then lighted up his handsome face, and the gaiety with which he would sometimes toss aside his own light, curly hair and the playful manner in which he spoke to his brother when he observed the shade of thought come across his fine features, all betokened a more gay disposition than that which belonged to the elder.

They were slowly pacing to and fro, and occasionally stopping as if to listen, when a secret entrance in the court opened and two figures of the following description entered: not above 3 feet high, their heads very large in proportion to their bodies and covered with a profusion of black, shaggy hair. Their dress was a close garment reaching below the knee and over that, a large mantle wrapped loosely round them.

'Well, so you are come at last,' said the youngest of the 2 boys.

'Yes we are, Lord Charles,' returned the creatures in an unearthly tone of voice, which well accorded with their appearance, 'but young noblemen, we once more most solemnly warn you to consider the step you are about to take.'

'We have considered it over and over and we are more and more determined to see what no mortal has ever yet seen, namely the Feast of the Genii, and this will be the night of the festival, therefore lead on,' replied Arthur.

'If you are discovered, you will pay for it,' muttered the goblins.

'Lead on, lead on,' answered Charles impatiently, as they quitted the secret court.

To be continued.

Review of the *Causes of the Late War*
by the Duke of Wellington[5]

It is now, we should suppose, somewhere about a 100 years since any book of the least consequence has appeared; not excepting the Duke's *History of the Causes of the Late War*, which we are persuaded was written by our own scrivener Sergeant Bud,[6] and this judgement is founded upon half a dozen good reasons:

Firstly, because the margins are uncommonly narrow; secondly, because the style is like that of a rule to show cause why a prosecution for libel should not be tried against some unhappy individual; thirdly, because Bud, at the time when it was writing, was often out of the way when we wanted him and we always found him either going in or coming out of the palace; fourthly and lastly, because we are sure His Grace never would have the patience to write such a long, dry thing.

His Grace's hand is, however, visible in many places where the merry wit sparkles in that barren page, like diamonds in a desert, or the elegant metaphor springs out, [?precepts] like shady palm trees out of burning sand.

Since writing the above, we have administered to our worthy scrivener a dose of tell-truth-stuff[7] and he says that he wrote the whole, except those parts which we have particularized as being excellent and which he got His Grace to do for him, and likewise to have it published in his name that it might sell the better. After this, we gave unto the gentleman a new square cap and cloak, together with a purse of gold, which he now comfortably enjoys and we shall now take leave of the reader to drink a cup of tea, which we see smoking.

[5]'Jonathan Adams' cancelled and replaced by the Duke of Wellington as author of this article. John Quincy Adams appears in an article written by Charlotte Brontë two months later: see 'An American Tale' in *Blackwood's Young Men's Magazine*, November 1829.

[6]A rascal lawyer and sometime publisher and bookseller; son of Captain John Bud, the eminent Glass Town political writer, who, as Branwell's pseudonym, wrote *The History Of The Young Men* which recounts in detail the founding of Glass Town and the Young Men's wars against the Ashantees. Charlotte Brontë seems to be referring to this work: she often ridicules Branwell's pompous style, and her pseudonym, Captain Tree (publisher of this magazine), never misses an opportunity to attack his rival Captain Bud.

[7]A magic medicine administered by the four Chief Genii to jog a' character's memory. Often an expedient *deus ex machina*.

Poetry

O when shall our brave land be free,[8]
When shall our castles rise,
In pure and glorious liberty
Before our joyful eyes?

How long shall tyrants ride in state
Upon the thunder cloud,
The arbiters of England state
And of her nobles proud?

Thou sun of liberty arise
Upon our beauteous land;
Terrible vengeance rend the skies,
Let tyrants feel thy hand.

Let tyrants feel thy hand we cry,
And let them see thy gaze;
For they will shrink beneath thy eye
And we will sing thy praise.

The song of vengeance shall arise,
Before the morning sun
Illuminates the arched skies
Or its high course doth run.

The song of vengeance shall not cease
When midnight cometh on,
When the silver moon shines out in peace,
To light the traveller lone.

July the 24   UT

[8]Referring to the tyranny of the four Chief Genii: see 'Sir – it is well known that the Genii',
n. 1.

57

Military Conversations[9]

Characters
The Duke of Wellington
Marquis of Douro
Lord Wellesley
General Bayonet
General Ramrod
Corporal Spearman
Captain Cannonball
Sir Alexander Hume Badey

A large room hung with tapestry, blazing fire, candles lighted, bottles and glasses on the table, 10 o'clock at night.

Duke of Wellington: Well, my brave fellows, we are assembled together again. It is a long time since we all met.
Sir Alexander Hume Badey: Yes, it is, my lord, but now we meet in good health.
General Ramrod: It wouldn't much matter if we did not, as you are here Badey. By the by, are you in good practice?
Sir Alexander Hume Badey: It does not matter to you.
Duke of Wellington: The first man that quarrels is to be kicked out of the room.
Sir Alexander Hume Badey:
  Shrugging his shoulders.
Hand me the bottle.
General Bayonet: How are the young men, Spearman?
Corporal Spearman: They are very well.
Captain Cannonball: I hope they are coming here tonight. Are they, please Your Grace?
Duke of Wellington: Who?
Captain Cannonball: The Marquis of Douro and Lord Wellesley.
Duke of Wellington: Oh, Arthur and Charles, yes, I believe they are. I don't know, I am sure though.

---

[9]Modelled on the 'Noctes Ambrosianae' of *Blackwood's Edinburgh Magazine*: see *The History of the Year*, n. 7. Charlotte Brontë as 'editor' is following a tradition here begun by Branwell in his magazines; see 'Nights' in *Branwell's Blackwood's Magazine*, June and July 1829 (unpublished manuscript, HCL: Lowell I(7 and 9)).

[10]*General Ramrod*: You should not let them stop too much with old women, my lord.

Duke of Wellington: You are the only old woman they have ever spoken to.

General Ramrod: My lord!

General Bayonet: What clever young men they are. I admired their speech on the subject of the Genii.[11]

Corporal Spearman: So did I, excessively.

Captain Cannonball: There were some fine flashes of eloquence in them, and a noble high spirit was visible throughout.

Corporal Spearman: That spirit is hereditary.

Sir Alexander Hume Badey: Yes, it is, and it has gone on increasing till it has produced that glorious spirit who now rules England. Here's to the health of the Great Duke of Wellington!

Drank with tremendous cheering, 9 times 9.

Duke of Wellington: Thank you.

Rings the bell.

Enter a servant.

Tell the Marquis of Douro and Lord Wellesley to come in.

Exit [servant].

Corporal Spearman: I propose the health of the Marquis of Douro and Lord Wellesley.

Drank with long and loud cheering.

Duke of Wellington:

With animation.

Thank you, thank you my brave fellows.

Enter the Marquis of Douro and Lord Wellesley with three large dogs.

Marquis of Douro: Do you want us, father?

Duke of Wellington: Yes, sit down here by me.

Lord Charles Wellesley: And do you want Blood and Hounds, father? Because if you do, we've brought them with us.

Duke of Wellington: Woo, woo, woo, come here.

At General Ramrod, General Bayonet, Corporal Cannonball and Sir Alexander Hume Badey.

Sts, st.[12]

Omnes: Oh, pray don't, my lord, my lord.

Duke of Wellington: Come back then, Blood and Hounds.

---

[10]There is a pencil sketch of an eagle's head here, above the text at the top of the page.

[11]Possibly the preceding poem, signed 'UT': see textual introduction.

[12]Presumably a hissing sound to encourage the dogs.

Sir Alexander Hume Badey: Sing a song, young man.
Marquis of Douro: Not I.
Sir Alexander Hume Badey: Will you then, Charles?
Lord Wellesley: No.
Sir Alexander Hume Badey: I will then, so here's to begin:

What is more glorious in nature or art,
Than a bottle of brandy clear?
There's nothing I like so well for my part,
It rids you of every fear.

It raises your spirits on stillest night,
It carries you lightly along,
It wings you away from this pitiful [?sight],
And disposes your mind for a song.

For a song like mine it makes you wish
And it keeps your eyes from a doze,
Unless you are dull as a kettle of fish,
Then it sends you off to repose.

I hope, high Duke, that you like my song,
Which for your pleasure I chant,
As it is beautiful and not long
Your approbation grant.

Duke of Wellington: Corporal Spearman, take this drunken fellow to the triangle.[13]
Corporal Spearman: Yes, my Lord.
Sir Alexander Hume Badey: Have pity on me, my lord. My lord!
Duke of Wellington: Take him off.

[Advertisements]

A magnificent painting of
the Chief Genii in Council[14] is

[13]A frame of three halberts (combined spear and battle-axe) joined at top to which a soldier was bound for flogging.
[14]See 'Review of *The Chief Genii in Council* by Edward De Lisle' in *Blackwood's Young Men's Magazine*, December (second issue) 1829.

now to be seen at Captain
Cloven's house. Terms of admittance 3s.

Tales of the Tavern. 2 series,
just published, price 20s.

---

*Tales of Captain Lemuel
Gulliver in Houynhmhm Land*[15]
price 10 shillings 6d.

---

*Adventures in the Glass
Town,* by a young man. In
3 vols, price 2 2s.

Contents

1 A True Story, by CB
2 A Review of the *Causes of the
Late War,* by Duke of Wellington
3 A Song, by UT
4 Military Conversations
5 Advertisements
        August 1829 by
        Charlotte
        Brontë

A copyright of a book containing
5 splendid engravings, crown
octavo, to be sold. Apply to Sergeant
Gloveinhand, Brandy Lane, Glass
Town. NB The engravings
are in mezzotinto style;
nothing but the most absolute
necessity has induced the
advertiser to part with them.

---

[15]Possible evidence that the young Brontës read Swift's *Gulliver's Travels* about this time.

5 silver tankards to be sold
at Monsieur Clearemens[?load's]
tavern. The silver is so much
refined as to appear like
pewter, but it is in reality
the most precious gold.

====

[BLACKWOOD'S YOUNG MEN'S MAGAZINE]
SEPTEMBER
1829 CB[1]

A TRUE STORY
BY CB

When the young nobles had quitted the city and palace, they entered the beautiful plain which surrounds it. It was now evening and the balmy fragrance of the air as it gently stole over was perfumed by the orange groves, the vineyards, the almond trees and the gardens of roses and myrtles; and the ear was delighted by the sweet song of the nightingale, the cooing of the dove and the melody of the blackbird and thrush; while the eye was pleased by the lovely scenery which surrounded them and the view of the radiant heavens, as the mighty sun sank slowly behind the far distant hills and all the west was flaming with the glorious purple clouds which were floating on beautiful blue sky.

'What a delightful evening,' exclaimed Charles.

'It is indeed,' replied Arthur, 'and how magnificent the city looks with all its towers glowing in the crimson light of the setting [sun].'

'Yes,' returned Charles, 'and look, Arthur, at the windows of the palace sparkling like fine rubies among the majestic linden trees.'

Thus they continued in conversation, till they had travelled a long way and were far from the city and all the dwellings of men. There was no sound save of their own footsteps, as they silently ascended a steep mountain. The vermilion clouds had changed into dense masses of

---

[1]Date on brown paper cover of untitled manuscript, in BPM: SG. 95; hand-sewn booklet of sixteen pages (5.2 × 3.1 cm), no title-page.

floating vapours. It was twilight and a few stars began to be dimly seen.

'You have come to your journey's end,' exclaimed one of the figures who had guided them, as they approached a huge iron door in the mountain. When they came near, it opened of itself and discovered a dark, dreary cave, the roof of which was arched. They entered. The 2 figures placed them in a particular part of the cave, told them not to stir from it and they vanished.

They had waited about an hour when a strange bloody light spread itself over all the cave, glittering pillars rose to the roof which sparkled exceedingly, four diamond thrones appeared, sounds of music were heard at a distance, troops of genii and fairies began slowly to glide into the cave till it was full and then a very bright light shone on all, which announced the approach of the Chief Genii.

At last they came, and then all the millions of their slaves broke out with the sound of harp and trumpet and drum in the following words:

Lo our mighty chieftains come,
Clothed in glory infinite,
With the sound of harp and drum,
Loud peeling to their might.

On they march in splendour,
To their adamantine thrones,
And there they sit in grandeur,
While our high melodious tones

Are peeling to the arched roof,
Making the palace ring,
Making the mountains echo,
And the desert wild to sing.

O may they reign eternally,
In the glory of their might;
May their armies be victorious,
While they like stars of light

Illuminate the darksome world,
While their sceptres' might
Changes the present stars of night,
Into a glorious day.

When they had finished, a table appeared spread with bulls, roasted whole, and splendid golden goblets filled with wine. They all sat down and began their feast. When they had ended, each of the Chief Genii

63

rose and blew a tremendous blast with their mighty trumpets, which shook all the palace. Instantly the genii and fairies started up, and approaching their chieftains, who now stood like pyramids of fire, they bowed in succession before them. Then, changing into red lurid flames, they stood in dreadful ranks waiting their commands. The diamond pillars of the palace disappeared, the glittering roof was covered with black clouds and terrible peals of thunder were heard rolling through the darkened air. Thus they continued for a while and then disappeared among the dark clouds, which in a short time cleared away.

'What a terrible scene we have witnessed,' said Arthur.

'We have indeed,' replied Charles.

'How magnificent and yet how awful, and without hurt we have seen what no mortal has ever before seen,' said Arthur.

Here their conversation was interrupted by the arrival of those who had guided them to the cavern. With them they instantly quitted the place and arrived at Waterloo Palace before dawn the next morning.

C. Brontë   August the 20, 1829

Review of the painting of the Spirit of Cawdor Ravine[2]
By Dundee,[3] a private in the 20th

The legend from which this painting is taken is of a very ancient date. The spirit is represented in the form of a large hound and it is impossible not to be struck by the supernatural glare of its eyes,[4] which are fixed on a gigantic figure standing on the summit of a high mountain and formed of clouds. The shadowy right hand is uplifted, the left holds a spear of vapours and its head is crowned with stars. It stands in an attitude of the most sublime majesty and appears as if about to deprive the wicked spirit of its might and power.

The stream running through the ravine is so natural that you fancy you hear the sound of its roaring. The scarred oak, with the green sapling twining round it, is wonderful. The sky covered with dark clouds, the flood rushing from it and the flash of lightning, which almost dazzles your eyes, is sublimely awful and sets both in grand

---

[2]The name 'Cawdor' suggests that Charlotte Brontë is already familiar with Shakespeare's *Macbeth*, although the story of Macbeth is also told by Scott in *The Tales of a Grandfather*; see 'The origin of the Islanders', n. 3.

[3]George Dundee is a popular artist of 'the sublime' in the early Glass Town Saga; he later becomes Sir John Martin Dundee. The early Dundee is modelled on a well-known artist of the time and is later also identified with the historical painter John Martin.

[4]Probably the gitrash; see *Young Men's Magazine*, August 1830, n. 5.

relief: the bright spirit standing on the rock.
On the whole, a more magnificent picture was never painted.

CB   August 21, 1829

Interior of a Pothouse[5]
By Young Soult[6]

The cheerful fire is blazing bright
And casts a ruddy glare,
On beams and rafters all in sight
And on the sanded floor.

The scoured pewter on the shelf
Glitters like silver cups,
And all the ware of stony delf
Doth like to gold allure.

And where this fire so magical
Doth spread its light around,
Sure many scenes most magical
Are acted in that ground.

About that oaken table,
In the middle of the floor,
Are sat those who are able
To play one card or more.

And now behold the stakes are set,
Now watch the anxious faces
Of all who have laid down a bet,
Scarce can they keep their places.

But see the teller holds the card
Above the silent crowd,
Look at his meagre visage hard
And list his accents loud.

---

[5]A small, unpretentious or low public-house (*OED*).
[6]This poem was originally signed 'UT' at the beginning and end, but the signatures were
then cancelled and replaced by 'Young Soult', a pseudonym of Branwell Brontë. The subject
matter also suggests that Branwell was largely responsible for the composition of this poem.
The following poem on the Glass Town, although also signed 'UT', can probably be
attributed to Charlotte, again on internal evidence.

He says the card is number one,
Look at that fellow there,
I think he has his business done,
Behold his ghastly stare.

Now he has drawn his sword
And plunged it in his side;
Look at his dying struggle,
While gushes forth the tide

Of red and streaming blood.
The current of his life,
Pouring a crimson flood,
While all within the strife

Of racking pain of body
And torturing pain of mind,
Doth rend his heart in pieces;
And will no friend most kind,

Wipe from his brow the clammy sweat
And cheer his dying hour,
Promise to aid his orphans dear
With all within his power?

No, there they'll always let him lay
And pass unheeding by,
Unless they find him in their way
When they'll kick him all awry.

Or bearing up a flag
In the neatly sanded floor,
They'll throw him in and leave him there
And think of him no more.

And now I've done my verses,
You may read them if you choose,
Or throw them in the fire,
As I've nought to gain or lose.

Young Soult   August the 21, 1829

The Glass Town
By UT

'Tis sunset and the golden orb
Has sunk behind the mountains far,
And rises now the silver moon
And sparkles bright the evening dew.

But in the west a crimson light
Along the horizon glows,
Tinting all nature with the bright
Gay colour of the rose.

And over all the eastern sky,
The robe of twilight gray
Is heaving up the heavens nigh,
While the pale milky way

Goes clearer still and clearer,
As vanishes the light,
Till it arches all the firmament,
Like a rainbow of the night.

But the sound of [?roaring waters],
From distance far I hear,
Like the rushing of a cataract
It falls upon my ear.

'Tis the roaring of the multitude
Within those mighty walls,
Whose noise is like to raging
Of rushing waterfalls.

'Tis the great and glorious city,
Whose high ruler doth defy
The mightiest of the armies,
Who their strength against [?him try].

May he ever reign in glory,
May his glittering sword be dyed
In the life blood of his enemies,
Though on the clouds they ride.

Charlotte Brontë

May he bring them to the [?city]
With fearful scorn and shame,
May they bow their heads below him
And dread his mighty name.[7]

But now the roaring sound has ceased,
The city is sunk to sleep,
And o'er the world night's curtain folds,
Mid silence still and deep.

But yet the silver moon shines out,
And the sparkling stars
Are wheeling down the firmament
Their shining, pearly rays.

No sound doth break the silence
Save the merry nightingale,
As it pours its sweet warbling
Down the still and lonely vale.

UT   August the 25, 1829

[Advertisements]

Captain Knownothing has on
sale several pots of the best
cinnamon which will be of
great use to any heir.

Sergeant Thumphimself: 30
bushels of the most beautiful
artificial roses. The smell is
delightful and very good for
the health.

Sir Alexander Badey[8] has
discovered a medicine, the
property of which is to cure
people of all diseases.

---

[7]This line is followed by a cancelled signature and date; Charlotte Brontë had originally intended to end her poem here with her usual eulogy on the Duke of Wellington, ruler of the Glass Town.
[8]Sir Alexander Hume Badey (or Bady).

68

The Early Writings 1826–1832

[Contents]

A True Story, by CB 8
Review of a Painting 9
The Pothouse, by UT 10
A Poem, by UT 11
Advertisements 12

Books

The Law, in 50 vols
folio, price 600 guineas;
very closely printed
by Sergeant Bud,
Scrivener to Tally, Chief Genius
Charlotte, Son of Captain
Bud, bencher of the Inner
Temple, member of [?Furnivsh]
Inn and of the honourable society
of Grays Inn, London.

*A Supplement to the
Law*, in 25 vols folio, by the
Same Author.

*The Golden Ball and its
Rulers*, A Tale by UT, in 2 vols octavo.

Tales of Narrow Alleys,
by UT.

*A Guide through the Glass
Town*, by Ned Laury,[9]
one who knows every
corner of that great
city.

A Royal Atlas, 1 vol.
folio, price £10 10s.

———————

[9]A 'rare lad' or Glass Town villain; later, loyal retainer of the Duke of Wellington.

69

Charlotte Brontë

[BLACKWOOD'S YOUNG MEN'S MAGAZINE]
OCTOBER
1829 – CB[1]

THE SILVER CUP
A TALE

In the year 1829, lived Captain Henry Dunally,[2] a man whose possessions in this world bring him in £200,000 a year. He was the owner of a beautiful country seat, about 10 miles from the Glass Town and lived in a style which, though comfortable and happy, was some thousands below his yearly income. His wife, a comely lady in the 30th year of her age, was a person of great management and discretion, and given to use her tongue upon occasion.

They had 3 children, the eldest of whom was 12, the second 10 and the youngest 2 years of age. They went by the separate names of Augusta Cecilia, Henry Fearnothing (the name of a maternal uncle of no great character among the more sober part of mankind and to this class both Dunally and his wife belonged) and Cina Rosalind. These children had, as may be supposed, each a different character. Augusta was given to being rather mystical among the others. Henry was a very wicked, wild boy, and Cina was a pet.

One afternoon, as Lady Dunally was seated in the parlour reading aloud a most beautiful and affecting novel to Augusta and the Captain (who by its influence had fallen asleep, for he had no feeling and his wife had once declared that she had never seen him weep however overpowering the tale she might be reading). Augusta was working and Cina feeding on a piece of cake, which her mother had given her to quiet her. As they were thus employed, the door opened and a servant appeared saying that there was a man at the door with something to sell but she did not know what. Dunally went out and in a short time came back with a beautiful silver cup in his [hand], embossed with the most delicate workmanship.

'What's that?' exclaimed his wife. 'Look what a great ugly thing! You're not going to buy it, I hope?'

---

[1]On grey-brown paper cover of untitled manuscript in HCL: Lowell I(5); hand-sewn booklet of sixteen pages (5.3 × 3.5 cm); no title-page.
[2]Compare Gustavus Dunally in *A Romantic Tale*.

'I have bought it.'
'You have bought it!'
'Yes.'
'And without consulting me?'
'Aye, truly.'
'And what did it cost pray?'
'Guess.'
'20 shillings perhaps, it's not worth more.'
'100 guineas.'
'100 guineas! Am I asleep or awake?'
'You ought to know best yourself.'
'I'll tell you Captain Dunally, I should think you had lost your senses to buy such a thing without consulting me!'
'Law dear, you'd better hold your tongue, wife of mine.'
'I shall not.'

In this way, they went on for some time, till at length Lady Caroline Dunally rushed out of the room in a furious passion, banging the door after her and saying that he might drink wine out of the silver cup when he was measuring his length on a prison floor.

The next morning Lady Dunally made her appearance at breakfast with her anger a little cooled, but after breakfast was over another circumstance occurred which raised it again with tenfold fury. There was in the library a miniature ship composed entirely of glass and made with the utmost skill and ingenuity. This ship was kept in a beautiful rosewood box, inlaid with brass, of which either Captain or Lady Dunally always kept the key; and it was on the 10th of June, 1802, about half-past 10 o'clock ante meridien, that Lady Caroline Dunally entered the aforesaid library and beheld her favourite Cina seated on the rich, Persian carpet and busily engaged with an elegant parasol, now all torn and broken, in smashing the beautiful ship to pieces and about to crack the delicate masts and cordage. [Cina] gave a laugh like an idiot. For a moment the lady stood transfixed with horror at the heart-rending scene, then rushing in she snatched up the child and shaking her furiously threw her down on the floor and wept aloud for some time till she was interrupted by the entrance of Captain Dunally.

'Look there you careless wretch, look there!' exclaimed she. 'That would never have happened if you had kept it locked as you ought to have done.'
'Why, my dear, I'm sure it was your turn to keep the key.'
'It was not, I tell you.'
'But it was, dear.'
'What an untruth. You don't seem to mind what you say.'

'Neither do you, for last night I, with these hands, gave you the key of that box and you put it in your workbag. Augusta, go and see whether it's not there now.'

'Yes, papa,' replied Augusta, as she quitted the room. She returned in a short time with the key in her hand.

'There now, you see, there it is.'

'Well and what of that, people can't always remember everything.'

'Can't they, indeed, but they can keep from telling lies, and as for you Cina, I've a great mind to knock your brains out against the wall (giving her a great slap). Get along about your business, you nasty little thing.'

About a week after this, as Lady Dunally was sitting in the parlour working, the Captain came in and sat down without speaking. She looked at him. He appeared very serious and gloomy.

'What is the matter, my dear?' exclaimed she.

'Why, I fear that a great dishonour is going to be done to our family. This morning as I was walking along the streets of the Glass Town, I saw a placard pasted up against the walls, the purport of which was that this afternoon Sergeant William Fearnothing Danvers was to be hung for murder.' There he stopped, for Lady Dunally had fainted away, as this F. Danvers was no other than her brother.

In a short time, she recovered, but all that day, as may be supposed, she was in a state of the utmost distress, as were all the rest of the family, with the exception of Henry, who appeared to be quite indifferent. He went out of the house, however, and did not return till evening. The excuse he assigned for his absence was that he had been spending the evening with a schoolfellow of his.

Next morning, Lady Isabella Danvers paid a visit to her sister, in order to condole with her on the unfortunate circumstance which had happened. After a little conversation, she remarked, 'Sister, I am greatly surprised that you should allow Henry to witness the execution. It was quite against all the rules of fashionable society.'

Lady Dunally: Why, yes, it certainly would have been if I had allowed [it], but I assure you I did not.

Isabella Danvers: Gravey[3] came to my house immediately after the execution and informed me of it, and in the evening I had an interview with Lady Cordula Silly, who requested me to tell you that, as you had

[3]Edward Gravey (or Gravi), Emily Brontë's original hero (see *History of the Year*) and one of the original twelve Young Men (see Branwell Brontë's *The History Of The Young Men*, *SHCBM*, vol. 1, p. 66); he becomes Arch-Primate of the Glass Town.

72

so grossly offended against all laws and rules, she could have nothing more to do with you. Subsequently to this, the Ladies Serena Surry, Arabella Goodly, Cecila Welldone and Rosalind Kiverlish, godmother to your youngest daughter, visited me and said that they must henceforth give up all intercourse with you. I assure you it is with the greatest pain I inform you of this, but it is to give you an opportunity of clearing yourself if the imputation is untrue, as I believe it is.

Lady Dunally: It is indeed, Isabella, and I beg that you will tell them so.

Isabella Danvers: That I certainly will do, Caroline.

Rising to go.

And now goodbye.

Lady Dunally: Goodbye, sister.

As soon as she was gone, Lady Dunally called Henry to her and, giving him a spoonful of tell-truth-stuff, she asked him if he had gone to see his uncle hung. He replied that he had. At that moment his father came in. She related the circumstances to him and he gave his son a hearty beating for his unfeelingness.

That night he dreamt that the cause of all this work which had lately taken place was the silver cup. In the morning he rose early and, taking the cup, he filled it with odours.[4] Immediately it split in pieces and in a short time vanished. When his wife came down, he told her his dream and what he had done. She was perfectly satisfied. The fashionables in a little while became satisfied of her innocence in the affair of the execution. The glass ship was mended by invisible hands; Cina was no longer a pet; Augusta was no longer mystical and ever after they lived as comfortably and happily as could be.

Captain Tree   September 1, 1829

On Seeing a Beautiful Statue and a Rich Golden Vase full of Wine, lying beside it in the Desert of Sahara

See that golden goblet shine,
Decked with gems so starry bright,
Crowned with the most sparkling wine,
Casting forth a ruby light.

Emerald leaves its brim encircle
With their brilliant green,
And rich grapes of sapphire purple
Twined with these are seen.

---

[4]A substance which, in the Glass Town Saga, dispels unwanted genii and their possessions.

73

Charlotte Brontë

Near a majestic statue
Of purest marble stands,
Rising like a spirit
From the wilderness of sands.

But heark unto that trumpet swell,
Which soundeth long and loud,
Rivalling the music
Of the darkest thunder cloud.

'Tis the signal that from hence,
We both of us must go,
So come my brother dear,
Let it be even so.

UT   Sept. 2, 1829

Military Conversations

Dusk, curtains down, fire blazing brightly, candles unlighted.
Captain Cannonball: It's been a dismal day today.
Sir Alexander Hume Badey: Not it. Hand me a pipe, Marquis of Douro.
Marquis of Douro: I didn't know you smoked, Badey. You once told us that it was unwholesome and that it made our teeth black.
Lord Wellesley: Varnish couldn't make his teeth blacker than they are, so smoke away, old boy!
Duke of Wellington: He eats sweetmeats and pastry of all sorts, I'm told, when he's out of my sight. Do you Badey?
Sir Alexander Hume Badey: No, my lord.
General Ramrod: Oh ha, by the by, do you know, please Your Grace, that it's found out who UT are?
Duke of Wellington: I do not.
General Ramrod: Guess.
Duke of Wellington: I can't. Perhaps Arthur and Charles Wellesley?[5]
General Ramrod: You're right, my lord; what an excellent magician you are.
Duke of Wellington: You know that I could divine things from my youth up,[6] Badey.

[5]Both pseudonyms of Charlotte Brontë. This suggests that 'UT' does not necessarily indicate collaborative efforts by Branwell and Charlotte, and that Branwell may not have contributed as much as has been thought to Charlotte's magazines; see textual introduction.

[6]In her juvenilia, Charlotte Brontë often attributed this quality of prescience to the Duke (see *Anecdotes of the Duke of Wellington*) and later transferred it to the Angrian character Warner Howard Warner.

74

Sir Alexander Hume Badey: I do, my lord.
Marquis of Douro: Father, may the candles be lighted?
Duke of Wellington: No.
General Bayonet: This house looks as if it was haunted.
Duke of Wellington: And don't you know that it is?
General Bayonet: No, my lord. I hope it's not. Is it, my lord?
Duke of Wellington: Oh yes. About 5 years ago, one very dark, cold night, about the middle of winter, I was sitting in this very room. The fire was low as it is now, and the wind was howling in the same mournful cadence as that blast which has just swept past the window. The clock struck twelve. At that moment, I took it into my head that I would go up to one of the garrets which was said to be haunted. I took up the candle and went out of the room. In a short time, I came to the top of the long, dark stairs and proceeded along the passage which led to the garret door. When I reached it, the [?candle] went out and I was left in the dark. I stood still a moment, debating whether I should go backward or forward, when suddenly I saw pale blue light streaming through the openings of the door. I approached it and looking through a crevice I saw a sight which I shall never forget. There were twelve skeletons standing in the middle of the cold, drear garret, clasping each other's bony hands so firmly that it seemed as if they could never be disunited. For a little while they stood still and then they began to grow shadowy. Suddenly a black cloud appeared with a sound as if all the winds of heaven had gathered together in one terrible blast. The cloud veiled the ghosts in its darkness and vanished.
General Bayonet: What a dreadful sight that must have been. Did you ever see anything young men?
Marquis of Douro and Lord Charles Wellesley: Yes, once. About seventeen years ago, when we were very little we, out of bravado, determined to sleep in the haunted garret, notwithstanding that our nurse tried to dissuade us by every means in her power.

Well, the night came and we were safely lodged in bed. For a moment Meg stood by the bedside with the candle in her hand. She looked at us, sighed piteously and then quitted the room, and we now confess that we felt something approaching to regret as the sound of her departing footsteps fell on our ears and the rays of light slowly vanished, till all was silence and darkness, except the pale beams of the winter moon, which stole through the gothic window and showed us the dreary appearance of the garret. At this moment a strange fear and [?shivering] came over us and we hid our faces beneath the bedclothes. We continued so for a short time, and then looked up again when, lo, a form clothed in a shroud sat in the window seat with its ghastly glazed eyes fixed full on us. We trembled fearfully. A faint sickness seized us when slowly it rose, and gliding noiselessly to the bedside it stretched forth one white death-like hand and touched us. Its touch was like the coldest ice, or a drop of that stream which is colder than ice, and thrilled through our frames causing us to shake and tremble exceedingly. Our eyes closed and when we opened them again it was gone.

Exit all in [?appropriate order], except the Duke of Wellington.

Contents

The Silver Cup, A Tale I
The Statue and Goblet in the Desert II
Military Conversations III
Advertisements IV
Contents V

[Advertisements]

An immense crystal ink glass,
to be sold full of exquisite black wine,
by Private Laymenin-after-making-their-beds-comfortable.

To be sold: a large silver cup,
value one hundred pound sterling,
by Monsieur Let-nought-go-
till-he-cannot-hold-it-any-longer.

To be sold: several garlands
and beautiful lilies of large growth,
by Captain Slope.

To be sold: an assortment
of golden cups, goblets, vases,
dinner and dessert services of silver,
tea and coffee services of fine
china, splendid drawing-room
furniture, card tables, 10 packs

of cards, billiard tables, rich Persian, Turkey and Brussels carpets, etc., etc., etc. The whole of the above was lately the property of Colonel Despard Bankrupt. The sale will commence on the 12th of October, 1829, and will be conducted by Private Mannering of the Crimson Owl Tavern, Despair Lane, outside the Glass Town.

To be sold: a carriage and six noble, white horses, together with two fine bay hunters and a pack of hounds, late the property [of] Major Lemar Suicide. Further particulars may be known on application to Private Cassada, White Sun Pothouse, Crack Alley.

Books

A Treatise on the Nature of Clouds, by Captain Snuff

A Book of Utility, by Monsieur Heregos, price 3 halfpence.

A Tavern Tale, by Private Inwithhim, price 5 shillings.

A Book of Politics, by Sergeant UP AND DOWN, price £2 2s.

How to Curl One's Hair, by Monsieur Whats-the-reason.

A Treatise on Perfumery,
by Captain Coxcomb, price 1s.

The Magician. A Wild Romance.[7]
by Captain Tree, price
£1 1 shilling.

[BLACKWOOD'S YOUNG MEN'S MAGAZINE]
NOVEMBER
1829 CB[1]

SCENES ON THE GREAT BRIDGE
By the Genius CB

Early one beautiful morning in the month of August, I[2] set off for Augereau's little cottage. When I reached it, I found that he was gone out. The door was open, however, and I went in. As usual all was peacefulness and cleanliness. On the clear, bright fire was set the kettle, and the cheerful sound of bubbling water saluted me as I entered. On the clean hearth stood a three-legged stool and by it was a small oaken table, covered with a white napkin, and hung up on a peg against the wall was his candle.

I had not waited long when Augereau entered with a can full of new milk.

Me: Well Augereau, I suppose you are going to the city?
Augereau: Yes.
Me: Shall I go with you?
Augereau: If you please, but you must wait till I have saddled my ass.
Me: Very well.

[7]Possibly an early Brontë manuscript, now lost; see *Visits in Verreopolis*, vol. 1, n. 16.

[1]On grey-brown paper cover of untitled manuscript in HCL: Lowell I(4); hand-sewn booklet of sixteen pages (5.3 × 3.5 cm); no title-page.

[2]Chief Genius Talley, that is, Charlotte Brontë. She appears again as the protagonist of her tale in the following story, 'A Scene in my Inn'; here she assumes her favourite role as master of a tavern.

Augereau then went out and in a short time came back saying that he was ready. We immediately set off, along with the ass laden with milk. It was, as I have said, a beautiful morning in the month of August, and, as we passed under the stately trees, which mingled their green branches above us, we sometimes shook their tall, slender stems, causing the glittering dewdrops to shower upon our pathway and bestrew it with precious gems. The air was perfumed with the breath of the dim wood-violet and wild rose, while the little birds began their matin song at our approach and their melody awakened the echoes of the wood, till all the air resounded with sweetest music.

We travelled thus for some time when, emerging from the trees, we entered the high road, and the great and splendid city, with its majestic towers and glorious palaces, burst upon our view; and the running to and fro of its horses and of its chariots, and the noise of its mighty multitude sounded in our ears like the rushing of many waters.

In a short time we came to the great bridge and truly the arches are so high that they are dreadful; and when I stood on it and looked down on the tremendous waters, which were rolling and raging beneath with a noise like distant thunder, I could not help thinking of the intrepidity of those little mortals who had erected the great fabric on which I stood. There is, at each end of the bridge, a beautiful and elegant tower, in which the keepers of the toll reside, and no one is permitted to pass without paying the requisite sum.

When we arrived at the bridge, I observed Augereau to be at a stand. After a little meditation, both he and his ass plunged into the river and would instantly have been swallowed up if I had not stretched out my hand and conveyed them safely over to the other side, where I soon lost sight of them.

I had stood a little while on the bridge when a dashing English captain came galloping up, mounted on a stately warhorse.

'What's to pay, old boy?' exclaimed he to the toll keeper, a fine, venerable-looking old man.

'6d, sir,' replied he. 'In the meantime, I beg that you will be a little more respectful.'

'6d! Who ever heard of such a thing. I'll report you to the Duke, you old rascal. I suppose you keep a good half in your own stupid pouch.'

Old Man: I don't though, and I've a good mind to throw you over the bridge for such a lie.

Captain: I'll not pay you a farthing (he said) at the same time clapping spurs to his horse.

At this instant, he was interrupted by a tall, black man, who came from nobody knew where. He instantly seized the bridle and cried out

with a loud voice, 'If you don't pay, you're a dead man.'
Captain: Well, I won't, you vile blackamoor!
Blackamoor: Won't you, well try. As he said this, his stature dilated and his eyes became like burning coals and 2 immense wings sprung from his shoulders.
Captain: A genius, a blackguard!
Genius: Yes, I am a genius. Now pay or die.

The Captain, at this, seeing there was nothing else for it, threw down the 6d and galloped off.

CB

THE SONG OF THE ANCIENT BRITONS ON LEAVING THE GENII LAND[3]
by UT

Farewell, O thou pleasant land,
Rich are thy fields and fair,
Thy mighty forests they are grand,
But freedom dwells not there.

Thy rugged mountains rise sublime
From the barren desert wild,
And thou wouldst be a pleasant land
If freedom on thee smiled.

Our hearts are sad as we turn from thee
And thy pleasant smiling shore,
To think that not again shall we
Behold thee ever more.

Ere many days are passed away
The sea will between us lie,
And when in freedom's land we dwell,
For thee we'll heave a sigh;

Because that o'er thee triumph
Those tyrants of the air,
Who dwell in halls of thunder
And robes of lightning wear.

[3]See *A Romantic Tale* by Charlotte Brontë and *The History Of The Young Men*, Chapter 1 (*SHCBM*, vol. 1, pp. 64–5) by Branwell Brontë for descriptions of the ancient Britons' habitation of the land of the Genii, namely Guinea or Ashantee in West Africa.

But now we're bound afar off,
To our fathers' land we go,
Swift foaming billows roll us,
And winds of heaven blow.

There rises freedom's palace,
Like a tower of burning gold,
Around it roars the ocean,
With its world of waters rolled.

Up to the glorious castle,
Where mighty freedom dwells,
While round her like a tempest,
Sea music sweetly swells.

But now we're bound afar off,
To our father's land we go,
Swift foaming billows rolling
And winds of heaven blow.

UT   Sept. 1829

A Scene in my Inn

One very cold and dark night, about the middle of December 1829, I was sitting alone by my kitchen fire, which was blazing high and clear. The warmth of the fire soon made me feel sleepy, and I was just dropping into a slumber when a knocking at the inn door aroused me. I got up and went to open it, which, when I had done, I perceived by the light of a lamp, which hung over the doorway, a tall man dressed in uniform.

'What do you want?'
Man: Board and lodging for the night.
'Come in then.'
He walked forward and I led the way to the kitchen. When he was seated, I lighted a candle in order to observe him better. He was, as I have said, tall. His eye was dark but scowling, his nose aquiline and his lips firmly compressed.
'Get me something to eat.'
'Have patience,' said I. 'What will you have?'
'A sandwich or something of that kind.'
I gave him what he desired and then sat down opposite to him.
Me: What is your name?

81

'Barnard Tosser.'
'Where do you live?'
'I'm a waiter at the Blue Cat Tavern.'
Me: Indeed, you have not the appearance of such a one.
At this, he seemed disconcerted but after a short pause answered
quickly, 'I'm reduced.'
'Are you? Humph. How did you get to be reduced?'
'Mind your own business.'
'Tell me the history of your life and I'll befriend you.'
'Will you swear to do so?'
'I will.'
I then gave him a spoonful of tell-truth-stuff and he began as follows.

'I am the only son of Sir William Fitzroy. My father died at the age of
40 and left me the whole of his immense property. I was a very sober
and steady young man till one day, about 5 years ago, as I was passing a
tavern, [a door] opened and my acquaintance came out and asked me to
walk in. I complied. There were a party of 10 persons sitting round a
table gambling. My friend asked me if I would lay a stake. After much
persuasion, I consented and laid a small one. I won, laid another, won
that, and so on, till I found myself in possession of a considerable sum
of money. I was then about to take my leave, when my friend stopped
me with the request that I would take a glass of wine. This I did and
another and another till my head grew giddy, my brain reeled, and I
was carried home in a state of intoxication.

'Next morning, I went to the same tavern where I gambled and was
successful, drank and was intoxicated again; and thus I went on till I
became an experienced drunkard and gamester and had a continual
flow of good luck, when one evening, as I was gaming, I staked my
whole fortune and lost it.

'Then I became desperate. I took the name of Barnard Tosser,[4] set
up a house for murdering people, robbing them and selling their bodies
for dissection.[5] About a year ago, I poisoned a man of great
consequence in the city. I was found out, taken up, tried, found guilty
and sentenced to be hung for it. I, however, found means to escape
from prison and set up for [a] pothouse master.

[4]'Barnaby' in manuscript: a mistake since he has previously been introduced as 'Barnard'.
[5]A common practice of Glass Town villains, probably based on the famous case of the
murderers Hare and Burke, who sold bodies to the surgeon Dr Knox for dissection. Hare
turned king's evidence and Burke was hanged in 1829. See also *An Interesting Passage in the
Lives of Some Eminent Men of the Present Time* and Branwell's *Letters From An Englishman*
(*SHCBM*, vol. 1, p. 102).

'One stormy evening, as [I was] sitting cosily by the fire, a tall, stout man knocked at the door. I told him to come in and asked what he wanted. He answered that he was a stranger in these parts and wanted shelter for the night. I pointed to a bed in the corner. He laid down and soon fell asleep. When I heard him snoring, I went up to him with the candle in my hand. I looked at his face and saw that he was the man who had informed against me on the occasion of the murder which I had committed. I immediately went away from the bedside and began to make a cake of white flour, sugar and cream. When I had finished, I awoke him and told him to eat it as he might be hungry. He thanked me and began to devour it greedily. In a short time he complained of being ill. I said, "Wait a bit and you'll be better soon." After an hour of excruciating torture, he died. I took up a flag in the middle of the floor, laid him in the opening and then covered it up. This murder, like the former, was discovered and I am now fleeing from the officers of justice. You have promised to defend me.'

He had scarcely concluded, when the trampling of horses' feet became audible and a loud knocking was heard at the door. I immediately hastened to open it and three men rushed in.

'We demand the body of Marcellus Fitzroy[6] dead or alive!'

'But you shan't have it,' said I, banging the door in their faces.

After this, I restored to Fitzroy his lost possessions, where he now lives happy and contented.

C. Brontë   Sept. 8, 1829

An American Tale[7]

'The mill-wheel of America is going downwards,'[8] said Scipio Africanus Clarkson,[9] a zealous partisan of John Quincy Adams,[10] as he

---

[6]A minor character of the same name appears in two later manuscripts by Charlotte, *A Day Abroad* (15 June 1834) and *The Spell* (21 June – 21 July 1834). A General Fitzroy also appears briefly in *Tales of the Islanders*, volume III.

[7]Although this manuscript begins as a story, it is intended as a play and occupies the same position in *Blackwood's Young Men's Magazine* as 'Military Conversations', Charlotte's usual monthly play. It has, therefore, been edited in the format of a play with the characters' names and stage directions italicized.

[8]The Brontë children followed the fate of the American colonies and their trade with England in the newspapers and magazines of the time. In *Branwell's Blackwood's Magazine* for June 1829 (HCL: Lowell I(7)), the Americans discuss the wool trade and Andrew Jackson proposes a toast to 'American Liberty'.

[9]Charlotte Brontë probably learnt from Branwell Brontë's ancient history lessons and from J. Lempriere's *Bibliotheca Classica* (London, 1797) on her father's bookshelves (BPM: 212)

read the account of General Andrew Jackson's success in the *Boston Manufacturer*. 'That's as plain to me as that I sold my 30 bags of cotton at a ruinously low price last market day.' As he said this, he was seated upon a single chair with his heels lower than his head (a very unusual custom with him).

'But here's Mr Ricestalk coming, I'll hear what he says about the matter.'

At this moment the door opened and Mr Socrates Ricestalk entered.

'Good morning, Mr Ricestalk.'

'Good morning, sir.'

'Will you take a seat?'

'Thank you,' replied Mr Ricestalk, as he drew 2 chairs to the fire and sat down upon them in a most unseemly fashion.

Clarkson: What think you of the times?

Ricestalk: Why trade's very kedge,[11] I guess.

Clarkson: Is it? This is the first time I ever heard so.

Ricestalk: Indeed! Well, but Jackson's President now I reckon.

Clarkson: I guess he is and sorry I am for it.

Ricestalk: Sorry for it!

Clarkson: Yes.

Ricestalk: And why?

Clarkson: For many reasons. You, Socrates, are a young man and therefore are likely to be dazzled by military successes, but I am old and experienced and I know very well that any soldier, however much he may appear to be devoted to the cause of independence and yet still being accustomed to command, he likes it in his heart and cannot brook disobedience in any shape.[12] Therefore, I believe that in time General

---

that Scipio Africanus was a great Roman general, conqueror of Spain and of Hannibal at the Battle of Zama (202 BC). She and Branwell often use Greek and Roman names in their early manuscripts, most of which can be found in the *Bibliotheca Classica*.

[10]John Quincy Adams, eldest son of President John Adams, was the sixth president of the United States (1825–8). His controversial election over Andrew Jackson and others led to irreconcilable differences between the followers of Adams and those of Jackson. In 1828 Jackson was elected president over Adams, and this is probably the event referred to here.

[11]East Anglian and Yorkshire dialect: brisk, lively; in good spirits (*OED*).

[12]As a military man, Jackson had a history of collision with civil authority and, as president, was inclined to look upon his Cabinet members as inferior officers. He was the first president from the New West – vigorous, brusque, uncouth, relentless and open – and opposed to Old World traditions, supported by Adams and his followers. Jackson was seen as a champion of the masses opposed to the powerful capitalists and hence to tariffs. The fears expressed about Jackson here were also current at the time of Wellington's appointment as prime minister in Britain.

Jackson may by slow degrees work such a change in the patronage of our public offices that he will have it entirely to himself, and, having gained that object, he may corrupt the senate and in short may eventually make himself king or president for life with the right of appointing a successor. What think you of that?

Ricestalk: It would be a bad thing certainly.

Clarkson: Well, and in the second place, look over to England and see who they have for a president there. It's like fastening the rope about their own necks, and I reckon the Duke will make no high scruple about drawing them up and get somebody to pull their legs too, while their idiot King[13] stands by eating a sugar plum mingled with poison and watching his courtiers dance to the sound of military music: the trumpet and the drum, which he little thinks are the joyful heralds of his own downfall!

Ricestalk: They say Jackson's against the tariff.

Clarkson: Is he? Well, if that's thrown aside America is certainly done for. Why, already the best woven cotton sells at 1s. a yard! And the best raw cotton at 3 dollars the bag. Who can stand that, do you think? The great capitalist will give up trade and retire, and the little capitalist will break. If the tariff is repealed, great and little will go together and the whole nation will be bankrupt!

Ricestalk: Nay, I hope not quite so bad as that either.

Clarkson: Your hopes are vain, I can tell you, for if the protecting duty is taken off our cotton, English cotton will find its way to America and then it stands to reason that those who buy foreign goods will not buy home-made.

Ricestalk: Well, but now our cotton is not admitted to the English market, whereas it would be if the tariff was repealed.

Clarkson: Nonsense, the English market is too much overstocked with goods cheaper than we could sell ours to admit American manufactures.

Ricestalk: Well, perhaps it may be so, but now I must bid you goodbye.

Clarkson: Goodbye.

Exit Ricestalk.

CB   Sept. 9, 1829

---

[13]Unlike his father, George IV did not go insane; but by 1828, when Wellington became prime minister, George IV was a worn-out debauchee, indecisive in government and an unpopular sovereign.

Charlotte Brontë

On Seeing the Garden of a Genius
by UT

How pleasant is the world
Where mighty genii dwell;
Like a vision is the beauty
Of wild forest, stream and fell.

Their palaces arise
From the green and flowery ground,
While strains of sweetest music
Are floating all around.

Their castles of bright adamant
All mortal strength defy,
Encircled round with genii
Towering like rocks on high.

And now behold that verdant plain
Spangled with star-like flowers,
Watered by purest silver lakes
And crowned with emerald bowers.

In the midst appears a palace
Of yellow topaz bright,
From which streams forth a glory
Of sunny golden light.

O if the dwellers of this land
Heeded their dreadful name,
How all the mortal world would sing
That bright and quenchless fame.

But now the eye of hatred
Follows where ere they go,
In the sea or in the firmament
It tries to work them woe.

They may robe themselves in darkness,
Themselves with lightning crown;
They wield the sword of vengeance
But to them we'll not bow down.

They may frame in the dark ocean
High palaces of pearl,

Mid the silver orbs of heaven
Their dragon wings unfurl.

And throned on the stars of night
While thunder rolls around,
May bid the earth to wait on them
But vain shall be the sound.

And how pleasant is the world
Where mighty genii dwell;
Like a vision is the beauty
Of wild forest, stream and fell, etc., etc.

UT   Sept. 9, 1829

Contents

Scenes on the Great Bridge   I
Song of the Ancient Britons   II
A Scene in my Inn   III
An American Tale   IV
On Seeing the Garden of a Genius   V
Advertisements   VI
Contents   VII

[Advertisements]

To be sold: 100 pairs of excellent shoes, by Monsieur Let-
him-walk-20-miles-an-hour.

To be sold: a painting of a bull-
fight, 3 feet long and 2 feet wide,
by Private He-shall-limn.

TO BE SOLD BY AUCTION
17 stone of Good White Flour
And
20 loaves of the best white
BREAD
impregnated with Prussian
BUTTER

By Captain Make Thousands
NOT
EAT any more food for
THE
Remainder of their precious
LIVES

TO BE
SOLD: 20 POUNDS
of the essence of white
FLOUR
A NEWLY invented
THING
which is an infallible remedy
for ALL COMPLAINTS
By SIR ALEXANDER HUME
BADEY

A
BOOK AGAINST
All fashions of Limners
and Draughtsmen, by
Captain He-can-handle-a-sword-
but-nothing-
else.

Anecdotes of the Duke of Wellington[1]

I

The Duke invariably reposes on the celebrated small camp bedstead
which formed his couch during the whole of his Peninsular Campaigns.

[1]Two page manuscript (7.9 × 4.5 cm) in BPM: B81. About the same time, Charlotte
Brontë wrote the following sentence on a scrap of paper: 'On September the 25 1829, I put in
the Life of the Duke of Wellington a piece of paper burnt at one end and on it was inscribed –
Charles and Arthur. Charlotte Brontë Sept 25, 1829' (BPM: B108). This suggests that Mr
Brontë owned a biography of the Duke of Wellington from which Charlotte Brontë gleaned
much of her information on her hero.

He always rises at 5 o'clock in the morning and a female domestic is allowed a quarter of an hour to prepare her noble master's morning repast, which he takes in the room which forms his dormitory. His mother, the dowager Countess of Mornington, is yet alive; in the full possession of all her faculties and in the enjoyment of good health at the advanced age of 90 having survived her husband 48 years.[2]

C. Brontë
October 2, 1829

II

Passing along amidst the vast and unknown crowd, I recognize a face of which the glance of a moment awakens a world of proud and glorious recollections. Fourteen years have now rolled away since I last beheld it and then but for an instant, as it shot past me through the blaze of battle and vanished in its storm; but no one who has once seen, can ever forget that of the Duke of Wellington. It is, moreover, but little changed and yet wears the same still smile and calm dignity which never for a moment forsook it, even in the mortal struggle and earthquake shock of battle.

Malcolm's Tales of Flood and Field[3]
CB   Sept 1829

III

In June 1811, when the British army were quartered at Caxilo[4] there was a dinner given by the officers and Lord Wellington was present. As usual, he was the life and soul of the party, and his sparkling wit and playful humour were making the hours dance pleasantly along, when a dispatch arrived from Marshall Beresford.[5] For a moment, an expression

---

[2]Charlotte Brontë was probably working from memory here. The Duke of Wellington's father, Garrett Wellesley, died on 22 May 1781, and his mother, Anne, died 50 years later 'in her ninetieth year on 10 Sept 1831' (*Dictionary of National Biography*).

[3]John Malcolm, *Tales of Field and Flood; with sketches of life at Rome*, Edinburgh: Oliver and Boyd, 1829.

[4]Whether intentional or not, Charlotte Brontë seems to be confusing Cartaxo with Truxillo, where Wellington's army was stationed in July 1829 and August 1829 respectively, during the Peninsular Wars. Again, she appears to be working from memory. She has read or heard her father read *The United Service Journal and Naval and Military Magazine*, July 1829, part 2, which includes a similar account related by Major Stothert, an officer of the Guards.

[5]See *A Romantic Tale*, n. 11.

of deep thought passed over his lordship's fine features and intelligent countenance, but he instantly resumed his vivacity and the conversation, happening to turn on the infallible remedy for gout, he joined in it with his usual warmth and by his great talents made what would otherwise have been dull and uninteresting, lively and droll in the extreme. The party remained till 3 o'clock in the morning and at day-break the whole army were in full pursuit of Massena,[6] for the dispatch contained nothing less than the important intelligence that he had begun to retreat: such is the self-government of the great Duke.

United Service Journal[7]
July 8, 1829   C Brontë

IV

The character of the Duke of Wellington is one of the most wonderful that ever any man had. It is noble, dignified and vigorous in the extreme. He appears to possess the gift of prescience; the past and the future are alike before him. His vision is uncommonly acute and his finely formed frame is so knit and moulded as to be equal to the greatest hardships of the most terrible campaigns; it is light, active, muscular and symmetrical. His mind approaches as nearly to the perfection of greatness and wisdom as human fallibility will allow.

Extracts from Sir Walter Scott's
History of the Emperor Napoleon[8]
Charlotte Brontë
September the 30, 1829

------

[6]General Andre Massena was one of Napoleon's most famous officers. He led the French 'Army of Portugal' against Wellington.

[7]*The United Service Journal*, January 1829 – April 1843; previously called *Naval and Military Magazine*, March 1827–8.

[8]Walter Scott, *Life of Napoleon Buonaparte* (Edinburgh: William Blackwood, Longman, Rees, etc., 1827); discussed three months earlier in Charlotte Brontë's *Tales of the Islanders*, volume I.

[BLACKWOOD'S YOUNG MEN'S MAGAZINE]
DECEMBER
CB 1829[1]

On the Great Bay of the Glass Town

1 'Tis pleasant on some evening fair,
    After a summer's day,
    When still the breeze and calm the air
    And sea-waves gently play,

2 To view the bay o'er whose still breast
    White sails do softly glide;
    How peacefully its waters rest
    Like to a sleeping child.

3 When the blue concave of the sky
    Is clear without a stain,
    And the bright arch of heaven on high
    Imparts to the wide main

4 Its beautiful and sapphire glow,
    While the sun's golden light
    Makes all the western sky to glow
    With streams like ruby bright,

5 Then like fair piles of burnished gold
    Those marble pillows stand,
    Palaces of immortal mould
    And castles tow'ring grand.

6 While murmuring sounds of pomp and mirth
    Rise from the mighty walls
    And wildly mingling sweep forth
    Like thund'ring waterfalls;

7 Till softened into echo's tone
    On the calm sea they die,
    Or rising with the [?east] moan
    On winds of heaven fly

---

[1]On brown paper cover of untitled manuscript, 'first issue' for December 1829, in BPM: 10; hand-sewn booklet of twelve pages (4.9 × 3.6 cm); no title-page.

8　To play with them amid the strings
　　Of harps whose magic voice,
　　Into the long dark forest sings
　　While fairies round rejoice,

9　As through tall trees the wild winds moan
　　And silver moonbeams glance,
　　The harp peals forth with triumph's tone
　　And spirits mirthful dance.

　　　　　　　　　　　　　UT　　November 2, 1829

The Swiss Artist[2]

Many years ago there lived a man of the name of Jean de Valence, who, with his wife Louise, resided in a small hut on one of the high and stormy summits of the Alps. They had but one child, a boy of about [?nine] years of age, who at an early time of life discovered symptoms of a remarkable genius for the sublime art of painting: not, it is true, in that department of it which consists in merely depicting with mechanical skill the stupid lineaments of some portrait customer's countenance; but in the higher art of tracing, with the rough materials he could procure, the bold and rugged mountains which surrounded him; in delighting to depict with a true hand the wild gorgeousness of alpine scenery among which he dwelt, radiant glaciers of the giant Mont Blanc, the grand stream of the Rhône whose source is amid the mighty Appenines, and the dark forests of pine-trees covering with their sombre mantle the white summits of these immense mountains. These were the subjects he delighted to delineate.

　　One stormy evening, as with his father and mother he was sitting by the fire of their little hut, a knock was heard at the door. Louise immediately opened it, and a stranger habited in the dress of a traveller entered. He requested shelter for the night, which was cheerfully granted. In a short time, when his limbs, benumbed with cold, were revived by the warmth of the fire and his craving hunger appeased by the coarse fare which the hospitable cottager spread before him, he began to look around and casting his eyes on the drawings of young

---

[2]This replaces the cancelled title 'The French Artist A Tale', which is followed by three cancelled lines: 'Not many years ago there lived in one of [?three words] places of the South of France there'. Charlotte intended her artist to come from the south of France (hence the mention of Mont Blanc and the Rhône), but she appears to have been undecided about the location of the Alps and so altered her title to 'The Swiss Artist'.

Alexandre, which hung upon the walls of the hut, he expressed his admiration in warm terms and eagerly requested to be informed who was the artist who had produced such excellent specimens of painting with the rough materials he must necessarily have had. When his curiosity was satisfied, his surprise and admiration redoubled, and after highly praising Alexandre he abruptly added that if he would consent to go with him to Paris, he would put him in the way of making his fortune.

At this proposal Alexandre was transported with joy, for he had often heard of the magnificence of that great city, the splendour of the Tuilleries and the grand collection of paintings and statues which adorned the Louvre gallery, taken by Napoleon from the Eternal City and the City of Flowers[3] but since restored to their original places by the mighty Wellington, whose triumphant career was marked by the hand of justice and mercy and not that of oppression and tyranny. The parents of Alexandre were likewise exceedingly delighted at this prospect of their son's aggrandizement for they now learnt that the person who presented it was the Comte de Lausanne.[4] That night they all retired to rest full of joyful anticipations for the morrow, which was fixed on as the day of Alexandre's departure.

All night he lay awake, meditating on the future path which he had chalked out for him and anticipating the results of his proposed journey. At length the light of the approaching sun began to gird the horizon, irradiating the summits of the mountains with his golden reflections and gliding into the darkness of the hoary pine forests by its glowing rays, now every instant increasing in brilliancy. At length the sun rose in eclipsing splendour, and at his presence all nature rejoiced.

After a hasty breakfast and when Alexandre had taken leave of his parents, he set off in company with the Comte. As he passed over the snow-covered mountains and among the dark forests, his reflections on the past served to moderate his joyous anticipations for the future. He thought how often amid those wild regions he had hunted the swift chamois and sometimes, in the middle of the chase, had stopped on the summit of some steep rock to view the grand scene around, above and below him; how on some calm night he had contemplated the dark

---

[3]Charlotte Brontë probably means 'City of Lilies' here; she is referring to Napoleon's plundering of the Italian art works from Rome and Florence respectively. Many of these works, together with other European treasures, were restored to their owners by the Duke of Wellington in 1815, much to the fury of the French.

[4]The name was probably influenced by that of the central character in Branwell Brontë's dramatic poem *Lausanne*, written at the same time, 18–23 December 1829 (unpublished manuscript, BPM: B138).

dome of the sky, hung with its thousand stars and with the white moon shining in the midst like a pearl in the depths of the ocean; then the quiet of his father's hut, which stood like an eagle's nest on cliffs inaccessible except to the bounding hunter, flashed across his mind, and the thought came upon him that he might never more behold it but might die in the, to him, foreign land that he was travelling to.

But these painful reflections did not continue long, for as the day-spring had awakened the glad song of nature and as the kingly sun wheeled his burning chariot along the sapphire pavement of the sky, louder, more joyful and glorious did that song become till Apollo reined for a moment his fiery horses,[5] glowing in clear meridian splendour, the noontide chorus lays from all the nations of the earth pealing in solemn gratitude to the great Creator of all things. In that glad hour it is almost impossible, amid the universal rejoicing of nature, to remain sad and sorrowful, and so the gloom on Alexandre's mind cleared off and gave place to more lightsome and stirring thought of fame and glory hereafter.

It would be tedious to follow them through all the particulars of their journey. Suffice it to say that, after 7 days from the time of their departure, they arrived safely at the great city of Paris.

Nov. 20, 1829   CB

Lines Spoken by a Lawyer[6] on the Occasion of the
Transfer of this Magazine

All soberness is past and gone,
The reign of gravity is done,
Frivolity comes in its place,
Light smiling sits on every face.

Gone is that grave and gorgeous light,
Which every page illumined bright;
A flimsy torch glare in the stead
Of a bright golden sun now fled.

Foolish romances now employ
Each silly, senseless girl and boy;
O for the strong hand of the law
To stop it with its powerful claw.

[5]Helios, the Greek sun-god, often identified with Apollo, climbed the vault of heaven in a chariot drawn by snow-white horses to give light and in the evening descended into the ocean.
[6]Probably Sergeant Bud. This poem is strongly influenced by Branwell, who saw Charlotte's take-over of his magazine as a retrograde step; see general introduction.

At night I lay my weary head
Upon my sofa or my bed;
In the dark watches of the night
Does flash upon my inward sight,[7]

Visions of times now pass'd away,
When dullness did the sceptre sway;
Then to my troubled mind comes peace,
Would those bright dreams did never cease.

Thus sang a lawyer in his cell,
When suddenly the midnight bell
Rang out a peal both loud and deep,
Which told it was the hour of sleep.

WT   Nov. 20, 1829

Lines by One who was Tired of Dullness upon the Same Occasion[8]

Sweep the sounding harp string
All ye winds that blow,
Let it loudly swelling
Make sweet music flow.

Let the thundering drum roll,
Gladness fly around,
Merry bells peal a toll,
Ringing trumpets sound.

Let the mighty organ
Play a peal and swell,
Roll its clouds of sound on
Till echoes every dell.

Sweetly, sweetly breathe flute,
Pour thy gentle strains,

[7]Compare Thompson, 'Sister Songs' ('I had endured through watches of the dark') and *Othello* I, i, 124 ('dull watch o' th' night'); and Wordsworth, 'I wandered lonely as a cloud', ll.19–21.

[8]This is Charlotte Brontë's reply to the previous poem: she expresses her enthusiasm for lighter topics, for the Genii and their gorgeous palaces, rather than the dullness of her brother's writing.

Let thy music rise, lute,
No more Dullness reigns.[9]

Sweep the sounding harp string
All ye winds that blow,
Let it loudly swell and ring,
Make sweet music flow.

In your splendid cloud halls
Princely Genii dance,
Till from the vapour walls
Bloody lightnings glance.

Your music is black thunder,
Therefore let it sound,
Tear the earth asunder,
Shake the sky around.

Fairies of the greenwood
Sing amid the trees,
Pour of joy a bright flood,
Dance upon the breeze.

Drink from the bright flower
Crowned with crystal dew,
[?two words] with the grass
[?one word] of snowy hue.

No longer hid your name is
Ye spirits of the air,
For now your mighty fame is
Set forth in colours fair.

Sweep the sounding harp string
All ye winds that blow,
Let it loudly swelling
Make sweet music flow.

UT
Nov. 21, 1829

---

[9]Charlotte is probably thinking of Pope's *Dunciad*, where authors accused of dullness are held up to ridicule.

96

CONTENTS

On the Great Bay of the Glass Town I
The Swiss Artist II
On the Transfer of this Magazine, by UT III
On the Same, by the Same IV
Contents V
Advertisements VI

Madame Charlotte Brontë
December 1829

ADVERTISEMENTS

TO BE SOLD
1000 HORSES BY
GERALD
Dreadful
at his grandstand, east end of
the Glass Town, between the Tower
of Babylon[10] and the gates of the
first court of the great palace
WATERLOO.[11]
G.D. can say with truth that his
horses are noble animals.

TO BE SOLD
A magnificent painting of
Britannia, Hibernia and Caledonia[12]
personified, under the patronage
of THE DUKE of
WELLINGTON.

TO BE LENT
The unprecedented sum of 6d.
by Private Candlestick who

---

[10]Tower of Babel, later called 'Tower of All Nations': the Glass Town equivalent of its biblical model. Rising in the midst of the city, it was originally inspired by the Tower of Babel in John Martin's painting 'The Fall of Babylon'. See also Charlotte Brontë's poem 'Lines Addressed to the "Tower of All Nations"', written two months earlier on 7 October 1829 (*Poems*, p. 80).

[11]See *Blackwood's Young Men's Magazine*, August 1829, n. 4.

[12]The Roman names for England, Ireland and Scotland, common in poetic usage.

Plate 3 Pages from *Blackwood's Young Men's Magazine,* first issue for December 1829, written by Charlotte Brontë at the age of thirteen

dwells between the gates of [the]
wall of JERICHO and the [wall of]
CHINA.

TO BE PURCHASED
Nothing, by Captain
CRACK-BRAINED

GRAND PROPOSAL by
SERGEANT SHUFFLE which
if carried into effect will
enable men to go to prison
for Nothing.

TO BE SOLD
A reel of thread, by
Corporal Needle of
Sewing Street, Cotton Square.

═══════

SECOND VOL. OF TALES OF THE ISLANDERS[1]

TALES of the ISLANDERS VOLUME II

CHAPTER I
[The School Rebellion][2]

I have before put forth a volume of these tales, in which the subject of
the school was mentioned. In that volume, I laid down the rules by
which the school was governed and likewise the names of the governors
with their several characters, etc. I shall now proceed with this subject.

---

[1]On brown paper cover of manuscript in NYPL: Berg Collection; formerly a hand-sewn
booklet of sixteen pages (9.2 × 5.6 cm), the pages have been separated and bound with vols I,
III and IV.

[2]The chapter titles in brackets are those given by Charlotte Brontë in her *Catalogue of my
Books*.

For some time after it was established, the institution went on very well. All the rules were observed with scrupulous exactness, the governors attended admirably to their duty; the children were absolutely becoming something like civilized beings, to all outward appearance at least: gambling was less frequent among them; their quarrels with each other were less savage; and some little attention was paid by themselves to order and cleanliness. At this time we constantly resided in the magnificent palace of the school, as did all the governors, so that nothing was left entirely to the care of servants and underlings. The great room had become the resort of all the great ministers in their hours of leisure (that is in the evenings) and they, seeing how well [?it]³ were conducted, resolved to uphold the institution with all their might.

This prosperous state of affairs continued for about six months, and then Parliament was opened and the great Catholic Question⁴ was brought forward and the Duke's measures were disclosed and all was slander, violence, party spirit and confusion. Oh, those 3 months, from the time of the King's speech to the end! Nobody could think, speak or write on anything but the Catholic Question and the Duke of Wellington or Mr Peel. I remember the day when the *Intelligence Extraordinary* came with Mr Peel's speech in it, containing the terms on which the Catholics were to be let in. With what eagerness Papa tore off the cover, and how we all gathered round him, and with what breathless anxiety we listened, as one by one they were disclosed and explained and argued upon so ably and so well and, then, when it was all out, how Aunt said she thought it was excellent and that the Catholics [could] do no harm with such good security. I remember also the doubts as to whether it would pass into the House of Lords and the prophecies that it would not. When the paper came which was to decide the question, the anxiety was almost dreadful with which we listened to the whole affair: the opening of the doors, the hush, the royal dukes in their robes and the great Duke in green sash and waistcoat, the rising of all the peeresses when he rose, the reading of his speech, Papa saying that his words were like precious gold and, lastly, the majority one to 4 in favour of the bill. But this is a digression and I must beg my

³Presumably referring to the school; grammar obviously incorrect.
⁴When Wellington formed a Cabinet in January 1828 with Peel as home secretary, Roman Catholics could not sit in Parliament. By June, when O'Connell, a Catholic, defeated Vesey Fitzgerald (a Protestant Irish landlord who favoured Catholic relief and was Wellington's choice for a ministerial position) in his Clare re-election, Wellington and Peel realized that if they did not now support Catholic emancipation they might be faced with an Irish revolt. In April 1829, a Catholic emancipation bill finally passed both houses.

readers to excuse it – to proceed with my subject then.

In consequence of this Catholic Question, the Duke and Mr Peel were of course obliged to be constantly in London and we soon took ourselves off to the same place. O'Shaugnesy and his nephew were away shooting somewhere and the whole management of the school was left to the Marquis of Douro and Lord Charles Wellesley. The upshot will be seen in the next chapter.

CHAPTER II

For some time we heard not a word about the school and never took the trouble to enquire, until at length, one morning as we were sitting at breakfast, in came a letter, the which when we had opened we perceived was from my Lord Wellesley. The purport was as follows:

June 8   Vision Island

Little King and Queens,

I write this letter to inform you of a rebellion, which has broken out in the school, the particulars of which I have not time to relate. All I can say is that I am at present in a little hut built in the open air and – but they are coming and I can say no more –

I remain yours etc.,
Charles W.

PS   Since I wrote the above we have had a battle in which our bloodhounds fought bravely and we have conquered. We are, however, reduced to a great extremity for want of food, and, if you don't make haste and come to our help, we must surrender. Bring my father's great bloodhound with you and Doctor Hume and the gamekeeper likewise.

As soon as we had read this letter, we ordered a balloon, the which when it was brought we got into and then steered our way through the air towards Strathfieldsay. When we had there arrived, we took up Blood and Hounds[5] and the gamekeeper and then went quick-way to the Island.

We alighted in the grounds about the school and, on casting our eyes towards the myrtle grove, we saw the stately palace rising in its magnificence from the green trees which grew thickly around and towering in silent grandeur over that isle, which [was] rightly named a

[5]Wellington's two bloodhounds that feature in 'Military Conversations', *Blackwood's Young Men's Magazine* for August 1829.

101

dream, for never but in the visions of the night has the eye of man beheld such gorgeous beauty, such wild magnificence, as is in this fairy land; and never, but in the imaginings of his heart, has his ear heard such music as that which proceeds from the giant's harp, hid from sight amid those trees. Listen! There is a faint sound, like the voice of a dying swan, but now a stronger breeze sweeps through the strings and the music is rising. Hark how it swells! What grandeur was in that wild note. But the wind roars louder. I now heard the muttering of distant thunder, it is drawing nearer and nearer; and the tunes of the harp and swelling till all at once amidst the roaring of thunder and the howling of the wind, it peals out with such awful wildness, such unearthly grandeur, that you are tempted to believe it is the voice of spirits speaking. This is the storm.

But to proceed with my subject: after we had been in the island about half an hour, we saw Lord Wellesley approaching at a distance. When he came near he accosted us with, 'Well, Little Queens, I am glad you are come. Make haste and follow me, for there is not a moment to be lost.'

As we went along, he, at our request, gave us the following narrative as to the origin of the school rebellion.

'For about 3 days after you were gone, things went on very well, but at the end of that time symptoms of insubordination began to manifest themselves. These we strove to check, but in vain, and, instead of growing better, they grew worse. The school now was divided into 4 parties, each of whom was headed by a chieftain, namely, Prince Polignac, Prince George and Johnny Lockhart and the Princess Vittoria.[6] These 4 were constantly quarrelling and fighting with each other in a most outrageous manner and, after struggling a few weeks with them to no purpose, they all ran off and are now encamped in a very wild part of the island which we shall presently come to. They are well provided with 2 cannons each party and a quantity of powder and shot. Sometimes they all unite against us and then we have a bad chance, I assure you, but now you are come to our assistance, we shall soon do for them.'

[6]Prince Jules de Polignac, French ambassador in London and later chief minister of Charles X; George IV (reigned 29 January 1820 – 26 June 1830); Johnny Lockhart, son of John Gibson Lockhart and grandson of Sir Walter Scott; and Princess Victoria, who became Queen on 20 June 1837 on the death of her uncle William IV, Duke of Clarence. The various factions in the school rebellion probably refer to the different alliances preceding Catholic emancipation. George IV vacillated between his brother Cumberland, who opposed the bill, and Wellington, who now supported it; Polignac, a leader of the 'Cottage Clique' of foreign ambassadors, often caused difficulties for Wellington in his relationship with George IV.

As soon as he had ended, we emerged from the forest in which we had till then been travelling and entered a deep glen, through which rushed an impetuous, brawling river, roaring and foaming amongst the large stones which impeded its course and then, as its channel deepened and widened, it became calm and smooth, flowing silently through the wide, green plain on the right hand, fertilizing and refreshing it as it went. On our left arose rocks, frowning darkly over the glen and blackening it with their mighty shadow. In some parts they were covered with tall pine-trees, through which the wind moaned sadly as it swept among their scathed branches. In other parts, immense fragments of rock looked out from their shaggy covering and hung their grey summits awfully over the vale. No sound but the echo of a distant cannon, which was discharged as we entered the glen, and the scream of the eagle startled from her aerie disturbed the death-like silence.

In a short time, we came to the place where the children were encamped. The tents of the Vittorians were pitched on the summit of a rock; those of the Polignacs, in a deep ravine; and the Georgians had taken up their abode in an open spot of ground and the Lockhartians had entrenched themselves among some trees. The hut of the Marquis of Douro and Lord Wellesley was built beneath the shade of a spreading oak. A tremendous rock rose above it. On one side was a gently swelling hill, on the other a grove of tall trees and before it ran a clear, rippling stream.

When we had entered the humble abode, we beheld the Marquis of Douro lying on a bed of leaves. His face was very pale. His fine features seemed as fixed as a marble statue. His eyes were closed and his glossy, curling hair was in some parts stiffened with blood. As soon as we beheld this sight, Charles rushed forward and, falling on the bed beside his brother, he fainted away. The usual remedies were then applied to him by Doctor Hume, and, after a long time, he recovered. All this while, Arthur had neither spoke nor stirred, and we thought he was dead. The gamekeeper was raving, and even the hardihearted[7] Hume shed some tears and Charles seemed like one demented.

In this emergency, we thought it advisable to send quick-way for the Duke of Wellington. This we accordingly did and, as soon as we saw him coming, one of us went out to meet him. When we had informed him of what had happened, he became as pale as death. His lips quivered, and his whole frame shook with agitation. In a short time, he arrived at the hut and then going up to the bedside he took hold of one lifeless hand and said in a tremulous and scarcely audible voice,

---

[7]Coined by Charlotte Brontë?

'Arthur, my son, speak to me.'

Just then, at the sound of his father's words, Arthur slowly opened his eyes and looked up. When he saw the Duke, he tried to speak but could not. We then, in the plenitude of our goodness and kindness of heart, cured him instantaneously by the application of some fairy remedy, for as soon as we had done so the Duke drew from his finger a diamond ring and presented it to us. This we accepted and thanked him for it.

After these transactions, we informed His Grace of the school rebellion. He immediately went out, without speaking a word, and we followed him. He proceeded up to the place where they were encamped and called out in a loud tone of voice that if they did not surrender they were all dead men, as he had brought several thousand bloodhounds with him, who would tear them to pieces in a moment. This they dreaded more than anything and therefore agreed to surrender, which they did immediately, and for a short time thereafter the school prospered as before; but we, becoming tired of it, sent the children off to their own homes and now only fairies dwell in the Island of a Dream.

C. Brontë   October 6, 1829

CHAPTER THE THIRD
[The Strange Incident in the Duke of Wellington's Life]

About a year after the school rebellion, the following wonderful thing happened in the family of the Duke of Wellington. One pleasant morning in the month of September 1828, the Marquis of Douro and Lord Charles Wellesley went out to follow the sport of shooting. They had promised to return before 8 o'clock but, however, 10 o'clock came and they had not returned; 12 [o'clock] and still no signs of them. Old Man Cockney[8] then ordered the servants to bed and when they had retired and all was quietness, he went into the great hall and sat down by the fire, determined not to go to bed till they came back.

He had sat about half an hour listening anxiously for their arrival, when the inner door gently opened and Lady Wellesley appeared. Old Man [?Cockney] could see by the light of the fire, for he had put out the candle, that she was very pale and much agitated.

'What is the matter, madam?' said he.

Lady Wellesley: 'I was sitting down working when suddenly I saw the

[8]Former veteran of the fictitious Duke of Wellington; now supervisor of his household at Strathfieldsay.

light, cast on my work by the taper, turn blue and death-like, burning phosphorus or asphalt, as I looked up and saw the figures of my sons all bloody and distorted. I gazed on them till they vanished, unable to speak or stir and then I came down here.'

She had scarcely finished the recital of this strange vision when the great door was heard to open with a loud, creaking noise, and the Duke of Wellington entered. He stood still for a moment earnestly looking at Lady Wellesley and the old man and then said, in a distinctly audible but hollow tone of voice, 'Catherine, where are my sons, for I heard while sitting in my study their voices moaning and wailing around me and supplicating me to deliver them from the death they were about to die. Even now, I feel a dreadful foreboding concerning them which I cannot shake off. Catherine, where are they?'

Before Lady Wellesley could answer, the door again opened and we appeared. He immediately addressed us and begged of us to tell him what had become of them. We replied that we did not know, but that, if he liked, we would go in search of them. He thanked us gratefully, adding that he would go with us, and then, after he had taken leave of Lady Wellesley, we immediately set off.

We had gone as near as we could, about 4 miles, when we entered a very wild, barren plain, which none of us had ever seen before. We continued on this plain till we lost sight of everything else and then suddenly perceived the whole aspect of the sky to be changed. It assumed the appearance of large, rolling waves, created with white foam. Also we could hear a thundering sound, like the roaring of the sea at a distance, and the moon seemed a great globe of many miles in diameter.

We were gazing in silent astonishment at this glorious sight, which every minute was growing grander and grander and the noise of thunder was increasing, when suddenly the huge waves parted asunder and a giant clothed in the sun with a crown of 12 stars on his head[9] descended on the plain. For a moment our sight was destroyed by the glory of his apparel and when it was restored to us, we found ourselves in a world the beauty of which exceeds [?beyond] my powers of description. There were trees and bowers of light, waters of liquid crystal flowing over sands of gold with a sound the melody of which far exceeds of music the finest-toned harps or the song of the sweet-voiced nightingales. There were palaces of emerald and of ruby, of diamond, of amethyst and pearl, arches like the rainbow of jasper, agate and sapphire spanning wide seas, whose mighty voices were now hushed

[9]Compare Revelation, xii, 1.

105

into a gentle murmur and sang in sweet unison with the silver streams which flowed through this radiant land; while their glorious song was echoed and re-echoed by high mountains, which rose in the distance and which shone in the glowing light like fine opals set in gold.

We had been here for a short time when the sky blackened, the winds rose, the waves of the ocean began to roar. All beautiful things vanished and were succeeded by tall, dark cypress and fir trees, which swayed to and fro in the wind with a mournful sound like the moans of dying mortals. A huge black rock appeared before us, a wide and dark cavern opened in it, in which we saw Arthur and Charles Wellesley. The giant then came again and, taking them and us in his arms, flew swiftly through the air and landed us all in the great hall of Strathfieldsay.

CHAPTER THE IV
[Tale to his Sons]

It was a beautiful evening in the month of August, when the Duke of Wellington and his sons were seated in a small private parlour at the top of the great, round tower at Strathfieldsay. The sun was just setting and its beams shone through the gothic window, half-veiled by a green, velvet curtain which had fallen from the golden supports and hung in rich festoons, with a glowing brilliance equal to the crimson light which streams from the oriental ruby, but, unlike to that beautiful gem, it was every moment decreasing in splendour, till at length only a faint rose tint remained on the marble pedestal, which stood opposite bearing the statue of William Pitt[10] and which, but a little while ago, had shone with a brightness resembling the lustre [of] burnished gold.

Just as the last ray disappeared, Lord Charles Wellesley exclaimed, 'Father, I wish you would relate to us some of your adventures either in India or Spain.'[11]

'Very well, I will, Charles. Now listen attentively,' replied His Grace. 'Would you like to hear too, Arthur?'

'I should, very much,' answered the Marquis with a gravity and

[10]William Pitt, 'The Younger', English statesman and prime minister (1783–1801) during the outbreak of the French Revolution and again from 1804 to 1806.

[11]Wellington served in India with his regiment from 1796 to 1803, gaining rapid promotion through his ability and the influence of his brother Lord Mornington, later Marquis Wellesley, governor-general of India. In 1808, Wellington was promoted lieutenant-general and placed in command of troops destined to fight against the French in Spain and Portugal in the Peninsular Wars.

calmness which formed a striking contrast to the giddy gaiety that marred the deportment of his younger brother.

His Grace then began as follows: 'In the year and the day of the Battle [of] Salamanca,[12] just as the sun set and the twilight was approaching, I finished my dispatches and walked forth from the convent gates of the Rector of Salamanca in order to enjoy the coolness of a Spanish evening. To this purpose I proceeded through the city till I came to the outside of its walls and then strolled heedlessly along by the clear stream of the Tormes, following as it led, until I found myself far away from the city and on the borders of a great wood, which stretched over many high hills to the verge of the horizon. There was a small pathway cut through this forest, which I entered, striding over the river which had now dwindled into a diminutive rill. Strictly speaking, this was not a prudent step nor one which I should advise you, my sons, if ever you should be in the like circumstances, to take, for the evening was far advanced, and the bright light of the beautiful horizon cast an uncertain glowing glare on everything, which made travelling through a dark wood which I knew nothing of exceeding dangerous. The country was likewise much infested with daring robbers and organized banditti, who dwelt in such lonely situations, but there was a sort of charm upon me which led me on in spite of myself.

'After I had proceeded about a quarter of a mile, I heard a sound like music at a distance which in a short time died away, but when I had got very deep into the forest, it rose again, and then it sounded nearer. I sat down under a large, spreading maple tree, whose massive limbs and foliage were now beginning to be irradiated by the moonlight which pierced into the depths of the forest and highly illumined with its beams the thick darkness.

'I had not sat here long when, suddenly, the music which had till then sounded soft and low like the preluding of a fine musician on a sweet instrument, broke out into a loud, deep strain which resembled the pealing of a full-toned organ when its rich floods of sound are rolling and swelling in the sublime Te Deum and echoing amid the lofty aisles, pealing to [the] [?high] dome of some grand cathedral with a deep, solemn noise like the loud, awful rumbling and terrible thunder; or the sudden burst of that most sublime of all music, martial music, when the ringing trumpet and the rolling drum are sounding together with the fierce onset of a brave and noble army. Then you feel the grandeur of the battle amid the lightning and roar of the cannon, the

---

[12]Salamanca, the famous Spanish university city situated on the River Tormes, was the site of one of Wellington's great victories on 22 July 1812.

glancing of swords and lances, and the thunder of the living cataract of men and horses rushing terribly to Victory, who stands arrayed in their garments with a crown of glory upon her head.

'But to proceed with my story. No sooner had this loud concert sounded than the dark forest vanished like mists of the morning before the sun's brightness and slowly there rose up on my sight a huge mirror, in which were dimly shadowed the forms of clouds and vapours all dense and black, rolling one over the other in dark and stormy grandeur, and among them in letters of lightning I saw the "Futurity".

'By degrees these clouds cleared away, and a fair and beautiful island appeared in their stead, rising out of the midst of a calm and peaceful ocean, and linked to it by a golden chain was another equal in beauty but smaller. In the middle of the largest of these 2 islands was a tall and majesty female seated on a throne of ruby, crowned with roses, bearing in one hand a wreath of oak-leaves and in the other a sword, while over her the tree of liberty flourished, spreading its branches far and wide and casting the perfume of its flowers to the uttermost parts of the earth. [In] the midst of the other island there was likewise a female, who sat on an emerald throne. Her crown was formed of shamrocks, in her right hand she held an harp and her robes were of a crimson hue as if they had been dyed in blood. She was as majestic as the other, but in her countenance was something very sad and sorrowful, as if a terrible evil hung upon her. Over her head were the boughs of a dark cypress, instead of the pleasant tree which shaded the other island, and sometimes she swept the chords of the harp, causing a wild and mournful sound to issue therefrom like a death wail or dirge.

'While I was wondering at her grief, I perceived a tremendous monster rise out of the sea and land on her island. As soon as it touched the shores a lamentable cry burst forth which shook both islands to their centre, and the ocean all round boiled furiously, as if some terrible earthquake had happened. The monster was black and hideous and the sound of his roaring was like thunder. He was clothed in the skin of wild beasts and in his bare head was branded, as with a hot iron, the word "bigotry". In one hand he held a scythe, and, as soon as he entered the land, the work of desolation began. All pleasantness and beauty disappeared from the face of the country and pestilential morasses came in their stead. He seemed to pursue with inveterate fury a horrible, old man who, a voice whispered in my ear, was called the Romish Religion. At first he seemed weak and impotent but as he ran he gathered strength, and the more he was persecuted the stronger he became till at length he began, with a terrible voice, to defy his persecutor and, at the same time, strove to break the golden chain which united the two islands.

'And now I saw the form of a warrior approaching, whose likeness I could by no means discern but over whom a mighty shield was extended from the sky. He came near to the monster whose name was "bigotry" and, taking a dart on which the word "justice" was written in golden characters, he flung it at him with all his might. The dart had struck in the heart and he fell with a loud groan to the earth. As soon as he had fallen, the warrior, whose brow had already many wreaths on it, was crowned by a hand which proceeded from a golden cloud with a fresh one of amaranths interwoven with laurel.[13] At the same time, the two spirits arose from their thrones, and, coming towards him, they cast garlands and crowns of victory at his feet, while they sung[14] his praises in loud and glorious notes. Meantime, the desolated land was again overspread with pleasant pastures and green woods and sunny plains, watered by clear rivers flowing with a gentle sound over green [?rocks], while the wild harp pealed in sweetly swelling tones among the branches of the tree of liberty.

'The sound ceased and lo, I was beneath the maple tree and a nightingale was serenading me with its beautiful song, which caused me to dream of sweet music.'

CB   November 21st

Anno Domini 1829

CHAPTER THE V
[The Marquis of Douro and Lord Charles Wellesley's Tale to his Little King and Queens]

In the year 1772, in the pleasant month of June, four inhabitants of Fairy-land took it into their heads for a treat to pay a visit to the inhabitants of the earth. In order to accomplish this end, they took the form of mortals, but first it was necessary to obtain leave of Oberon and Titania,[15] their king and queen. Accordingly, they demanded an audience of their majesties and were admitted. They stated their wish and petition, which was immediately granted, and they prepared to depart.

Having descended to the earth in a cloud, they alighted in a part of

---

[13]Symbolic of everlasting (amaranth) and victorious peace (laurel).

[14]Throughout the manuscripts of 1826 to 1832, Charlotte Brontë uses 'sung' as the past tense of 'to sing', a practice common in the seventeenth, eighteenth and early nineteenth centuries but now rare.

[15]King and Queen of the Fairies in Shakespeare's *A Midsummer Night's Dream*.

England which was very mountainous and quite uninhabited. They proceeded along for some time till they came to the verge of a rock that looked down into a beautiful vale below. Through it ran a clear and pleasant stream, which followed the vale in all its narrow windings among the high, dark mountains which bordered it and the massive branching trees which grew in thick clumps casting a cool and agreeable shade over all the valley. Through these it meandered with a rippling sound until, when the glen broke from its confinement among them and spread into a wide, green plain all dotted with great, white poplars and stately oaks and spangled with pearly daisies and golden buttercups, among which likewise occasionally peeped out the pale primrose or the purple violet, it also expanded into a broader and deeper current, rolling or rather gliding on with a still murmur that resembled the voice of some water spirit heard from the depths of its coral palaces, when it sings in lonely silence after the sea has ceased to heave and toss in terrible black beauty and night walks in awful majesty on the face of the earth, all clothed in stars, while Luna sheds pale light from her silver lamp to illumine the pathway of the dark and stately queen.

In the midst of this valley, there was a small thatched cottage which had once been the pleasant abode of a flourishing husbandman, who was now dead, and his children one by one had forsaken it and the sweet spot where it stood, each to pursue his own fortune, till it was now entirely deserted and had fallen into a state of ruin and decay. The fairies proceeded down the vale towards the cottage and, when they arrived there, began to examine it. The walls were all grey and moss-grown. Vine tendrils were still visible among the weaths of ivy which clasped around the doorway and one silver star of jasmine peeped out from among the dark leaves. The little garden was all grown over with nettles and rank weed, and no trace remained of its former beauty, except a single rose bush, on which still bloomed a few half-wild roses, and beside it grew a small strawberry plant with two or three scarlet strawberries upon it, forming a fine contrast to the desolation which surrounded them.

In this place the fairies determined to take up their abode, which they accordingly did, and they had not been long there when the following occurrence happened. They were sitting one evening round the fire of their hut (for being now in the form of mortals, they acted like them), listening to the wind which moaned in hollow cadences as it swept along the valley, and its voice was sometimes mingled with strange sounds which they well knew were the voices of spirits rising in the air, invisible to the dull eyes of mortals.

They were sitting, as I said before, around the fire of their hut, when suddenly they heard a low knocking at the door. One of them immediately rose to open it and a man appeared clothed in a traveller's cloak. They enquired what he wanted. He replied that he had lost his way in the glen and that, seeing the light stream across his path from their cottage, he stopped there and now requested shelter till the morning when he might be able to pursue his journey with the advantage of daylight. His request was immediately granted and, as soon as he was seated, they asked what the cause of his travelling was. He replied that if they chose he would relate to them his whole history, as he could perceive that they were persons of no ordinary description and might perhaps be able to assist him in his distress. They consented and he began as follows.

'I am the son of a gentleman of great fortune and estate, who resided in one of the southernmost counties of Ireland. My father and mother were both Roman Catholics and I was brought up in that faith and continued in it until I became convinced of the error of the creed I professed. My father's confessor was a man of strange and unsociable habits, and was thought, by those among whom he dwelt, to have converse with the inhabitants of another world. He had received his education in Spain, and it was supposed that in the country he had learnt the science of necromancy.

'The manner in which I became converted to the Protestant religion was as follows. There lived in our family an old servant who, unknown to my father, was a seceder from the Roman Catholic Church and a member of the Church of England. One day, I unexpectedly entered the room and surprised him reading his Bible. I immediately remonstrated with him on the impropriety of what he was about and desired him to leave off, telling him that it was against the laws of the true church and contrary to the admonitions of our priest. He replied mildly but firmly, quoting many passages of scripture in defence of what he did and arguing in such a manner as to convince me that I was in the wrong. Next day, I paid him a visit at the same hour and found him similarly employed. I had a long conversation with him, the effect of which was to induce me to search the Bible for myself. I did so and there discovered that the doctrines of the Church of England [?were those which] most closely assimilated with the word of God. Those doctrines I accordingly determined to embrace.

'As soon as my conversion became known, my father strove to dissuade [me] from it, but I remained steadfast and [?resolute]. In a short time he ceased to trouble me. But not so with the confessor. He was constantly advancing arguments to induce me to recant; but failing,

111

he made use of the following expedient as a last resource.

'I was standing one evening in the court of my father's house, when suddenly I heard a voice whisper in my ear, "Come this night to the great moor at 12 o'clock." I turned round but could see nobody. I then debated with myself what it could be and whether I should go or not. I at length determined to go and when the clock struck eleven I set off. The moor alluded to lay about four miles off. It was a wide, barren heath stretching three leagues to the northward. In a short time I reached it. The night was very dark. No moon was visible and the stars were only dimly seen through the thin, cloudy vapours that sailed over the sky veiling the dark azure with a sombre robe and casting a melancholy gloom on the [?scene] beneath. All around me was silent, except a little stream flowing unseen among the heather with a sound resembling the hoarse, incessant murmur which the seashell retains of its native caverns where the green billows of the deep are roaring and raging with an eternal thunder.

'I had not waited long when slowly I saw rising around me the dim form of a sacred abbey, the stately pillars, the long drawn sweeping aisles, the echoing dome and the holy altar; all arose in gradual and mysterious order while a solemn and supernatural light stole through the high arched windows and beamed full upon a tomb which stood in the centre and which I knew to be my grandfather's. I was gazing at these things in wrapt and silent astonishment, when suddenly I saw a tall white robed figure standing upon the monument. It beckoned to me with its hand. I approached, and it then addressed me in the following words, "Son, why have you deserted the ancient and holy religion of your ancestors to embrace a strange one which you know not of."

'I was going to reply when, at that moment, I perceived the confessor standing near. I instantly comprehended the whole scheme and exclaimed in a loud voice, "Your wiles are discovered. The faith I profess is true and I well know that this [is] all necromancy."

'When the priest heard this he flew into a terrible rage and, stamping with his foot, a fire sprung out of the ground. He then threw some perfumes on it and said in a voice made tremulous by ungovernable fury, "Depart hence vile heretic!" and immediately I found myself in this valley. You know the rest.'

Here the traveller stopped, and little more is known of the story, except that the fairies restored him to his family, who became devout members of the Church of England. The priest afterwards disappeared in a very unaccountable way and the fairies no longer dwell in that little hut, of which only a mossy remnant now remains; but the tradition still lives in many a peasant's fireside tale when gloomy winter has apparelled the earth in frost and radiant snow.

This tale was related to Little King and Queens, Seringapatan, Old Man Cockney, Gamekeeper, Jack-of-all-trades and Orderly-man[16] by the Marquis [of] Douro and Lord C. Wellesley, as they sat by the fire at the great hall of Strathfieldsay.

C. Brontë   December 2, 1829

====

[BLACKWOOD'S YOUNG MEN'S MAGAZINE] DECEMBER CB 1829[1]

Review of 'The Chief Genii in Council', by Edward De Lisle[2]

It is now many years since any painting of great merit has appeared, if we except the 'Spirit of Cawdor' by George Dundee, which we reviewed in our number for September.

The one which is the subject of our present article almost atones, however, by its excellence for the mediocrity of those which have preceded it. Indeed, the City of Might (as the Glass Town is called by that admirable novelist Captain Tree) appears to be much more famous for writers of eminence than for painters of eminence, for the only artists of merit in the present time are Dundee and De Lisle; but these are of superlative excellence and their glorious works will live from generation to generation (yea, for thousands of years if this sublunary system should last so long), after the stiff, unnatural, colourless portraits of the French limners (we do not mean Le Brun and Vernet

---

[16]Veterans of the fictitious Duke's early campaigns, now his retainers. Apart from Old Man Cockney, who resides at the Hall, they live in soldiers' cottages on the estate of Strathfieldsay and frequent the Horse Guards; see also *Tales of the Islanders*, vol. III.

[1]On brown paper cover of untitled manuscript, 'second issue' for December 1829, in BL: Ashley 157; hand-sewn booklet of twenty pages (5 × 3.3 cm); no title-page.

[2]Edward or Frederick (later Sir Edward) De Lisle, an eminent Glass Town portrait painter patronized first by the Earl St Clair and then by the Marquis of Douro.

and Co.)[3] are dead, buried and forgotten, together with the miserable beings they represent.

But if we recollect rightly, we sat down to review the individual painting of 'The Chief Genii in Council' and not to write a general and voluminous treatise on all the great and little artists who now flourish or decay. So, here's to begin.

The painting above referred to is of large, almost gigantic dimensions, and none the worse is it for that, as gazing at small and exquisitely finished pictures is apt to ruin one's eyesight. The Genii are seated upon thrones of pure and massive gold, in the midst of an immense hall surrounded by pillars of fine and brilliant diamond. The pavement sparkles with amethyst, jasper and sapphire. A large and cloud-like canopy hangs over the heads of the Genii, all studded with bright rubies, from which a red, clear light streams, irradiating all around with its burning glow and forming a fine contrast to the mild flood of glory which pours from the magnificent emerald dome and invests everything with a solemn, shadowy grandeur, which reminds you that you are gazing on the production of a mighty imagination. In the centre hangs a sun-like lamp and you can hardly bring yourself to believe that is not a reality when you see the bright, glittering and flashing of the precious gems occasioned by the glorious reflections of this mighty lamp.

Over the great entrance a very black cloud is hovering, under which, however, a wide expanse of fairy landscape is visible, and it is a relief to turn from the contemplation of the intense and fearful splendour of the hall to view the visionary beauty of this scene: this land of the rose and myrtle tree, all adorned with smiling plains and crystal lakes in which the white water-lily floats and the flowering reed grows stately on its green banks among vines and sweet blossomed laurel trees, while gentle hills rise in the distance, over which a softened haze is floating like the light shed from a company [of] spirits winging their way through the silent air as they come from afar, from the dark habitations of mortals,

---

[3]Charles Le Brun (1619–90), painter to Louis XIV. With Colbert, Le Brun founded the Academy of Painting and Sculpture (1648) and the Academy of France at Rome (1666) and gave a new development to the industrial arts when the Gobelins Tapestry Factory became a royal establishment in 1662. It is possible, however, that Charlotte Brontë may have been referring here instead to Marie Louise Elizabeth Le Brun (née Vigée) (1775–1842), a French portrait painter who had painted Lady Hamilton and who had been helped in her career by Joseph Vernet. Again, the Vernet Charlotte refers to here is difficult to identify, but she is probably referring to Antoine Charles Vernet (1758–1836), the son of Joseph Vernet and a French portrait and landscape painter popular with the king and later with Napoleon. He was famous for his ability to paint animals from nature, which accords with the Vernet Charlotte mentions at the end of *Characters of the Celebrated Men of the Present Time*.

to dwell in palaces of glory. The whole calm, fair and beautiful land is sleeping beneath the light of a full clear moon, shining in the midst of an unclouded heaven. But we must conclude with saying that it is a glorious picture.

C. Brontë   December 9, 1829

HARVEST IN SPAIN

Now all is joy and gladness, the ripe fruits
Of autumn hang on every orchard bough;
The living gold of harvest waves around,
The festooned vine, empurpled with the grape,
Weighed to the ground by clusters rich and bright
As precious amethyst, gives promise fair
Of future plenty. While the almond tree
Springs gracefully from out the verdant earth,
Crowned with its emerald leaves, its pleasant fruit,
And waving in the gentle, fragrant breeze
Which sweeps o'er orange groves mid myrtle bowers
And plays in olive woods, drinking the dew
Which falls like crystal on their tufted leaves,
Hid by luxuriant foliage from the beam
Of the great glorious sun which shines on high
In bright and burning strength, casting its rays
To the far corners of the mighty land,
Enlight'ning and illuminating all,
Making it glow with beauty and with joy,
And raising songs of gladness and of praise
To God, the father and the king of all.

December 9 UT 1829

The Swiss Artist Continued

Soon after the arrival of Alexandre[4] in Paris, the Comte de Lausanne asked him one morning if he should like to see the great Louvre gallery. To this he eagerly replied that nothing would please him more and accordingly they both set out that same afternoon.

When they arrived there, Alexandre was at first so struck by the

---

[4]Spelt 'Alexander' by mistake in this manuscript: see the first part of 'The Swiss Artist', *Blackwood's Young Men's Magazine*, December (first issue) 1829.

multitude of beautiful statues and pictures which surrounded him that he could not utter one word, but, at length recovering in some measure, he proceeded to examine each in detail. There, the vigorous sterness of Michael Angelo, the grace and beauty of Raphael and the glorious colouring of Titian, together with the exquisite finish of Leonardo da Vinci, the living portraits of Vandyke and the sacred sublimity of Fra Bartolommeo[5] all burst upon him in grand and such continued succession that at length he exclaimed, almost in the language of Shakespeare's *Merchant of Venice*, 'These are not men but geni-gods who have imitated the magnificence of nature so truly.'[6]

When he returned to the house of his patron, he immediately commenced a picture, the subject of which was a scene in the Tyrolese Alps. In the course of about a fortnight it was finished, and then, having placed it in the proper light, he called the Count to view it.

The foreground represented a company of hunters attired in the picturesque garb of the Tyrol, reposing beneath the shade of a group of young chestnut trees. On the hunters a breath of sunlight was visible, cast from a bright and brilliant sunset horizon, on which a few purple clouds edged with gold were floating, while higher up in the heavens the lustre of the clouds was softened into a pearly hue, forming a fine contrast to the intense ruby light which glowed in the west. The rich, local tints on the young chestnuts, which stood in deep shadow, strongly resembled those of Titian in his martyr saint,[7] and the high mountains which rose in the distance, partly glittering with ice and partly blackened by huge forests of pine-wood, stood forth in grand relief from a sky of clear and silvery azure.

The Comte stood for some time gazing in wrapt and silent astonishment at this beautiful performance of his young protégé, who watched his countenance with intense and earnest anxiety. At length the Comte broke silence by expressing his admiration of the picture in warm and enthusiastic terms, saying at the same time that he would be an honour to the country who owned him and that in future ages his name should be classed with those of the greatest masters of antiquity.

Some time after this occurrence, and while Alexandre was engaged in painting the portrait of a nobleman of the city of Paris, the Comte

---

[5]Compare Charlotte Brontë's 'List of painters whose works I wish to see', 1829: 'Guido Reni, Julio Romano, Titian, Raphael, Michael Angelo, Coreggio, Annibale Carracci, Leonardo da Vinci, Fra Bartolommeo, Carlo Cignani, Vandyke, Rubens, Bartolomeo Ramerghi' (BPM: B80(13)).

[6]*Merchant of Venice*, III, ii, 136.

[7]Titian's *Martyrdom of St Peter* in SS Giovanni e Paolo in Venice; painted in 1530 but destroyed by fire in 1867. An engraving of the painting was widely known in nineteenth-century England.

entered his apartment with a letter in his hand. Having sat down, he informed him that the letter came from a friend of his in Italy and contained an earnest wish that he would visit that fine country. This wish, the Comte added, he intended to comply with, and, if Alexandre chose, he would take him along with him. Alexandre instantly gave a joyful consent, expressing at the same time his sincere thanks and fervent gratitude to his kind and generous benefactor for thus offering him another opportunity for improving his knowledge of the fine arts.

In a few days everything was prepared and they accordingly set out on their journey. It would be tedious to follow them through all the particulars. Suffice it to say, that after visiting Florence, Genoa, Milan, Venice, the Lake of Garda, the Palace of the Medici in Fiesole, etc., etc., they at length arrived at Rome, the Eternal City, once imperial mistress of all the known world but now a mass of gorgeous and magnificent ruins, domes, pillars, palaces, temples, aqueducts, fountains, and statues, all mingling together in strange and wild confusion and situated in the midst of a barren and desolate campagna, made desolate by the pestilential malaria, whose noisome and destructive [presence] hath laid waste a pleasant and fruitful land.

Here they resided about a year and then, after having seen and examined the whole wilderness of ruins, they returned to Paris.

But my story is becoming very long and I must hasten to the conclusion. 10 summers had rolled away and Alexandre de Valence was now a wealthy and far-famed artist, [?but] he longed to behold his aged parents once more and to revisit the scenes of his early youth. At length his determination was fixed and, after informing the Comte of it, he set off the next day. It was early on a fine, autumnal night when he gained the summit of a steep rock on which his native hut was built. The full, round, harvest moon shone with intense brilliancy in the midst of a sky of unclouded lustre, and the solemn stars looked on all beneath in still [?redness] and serenity, which lent a character of sacred awe to the whole scene that forcibly touched the heart of de Valence and for a time subdued his glad and joyous anticipation into a quiet, calm happiness. But when he at length sprang over the threshold of his father's hut, the full tide of his enthusiasm returned again. But oh, what gladness was in the hearts of his venerable parents when they once more embraced their beloved son, now risen to fame and riches, and found that in the midst of his prosperity he had not forgotten them.

But now I must soon leave off. Alexandre, his parents and his patron lived many long years after this, in the fear of God and the love of their neighbours, full of peace and happiness.

Captain Tree   Dec. 10, 1829

CONVERSATIONS

Night. Captain Tree, Captain Bud, Marquis of Douro and Lord Charles Wellesley.

Captain Bud: Well, this has been a right snowing, blowing winter's day.

Marquis of Douro: Oh, I like such weather, when the snow is drifted up into great curling wreaths like a garland of lilies woven for the coffin of a giant or to crown his head with when he is wrapped in his shroud, when the crystal icicles are hanging from the eaves of the houses and the bushy evergreens are all spangled with snow-flakes, as if it was spring and they were flourishing in full blossom—

Lord Charles Wellesley: When all the old women traverse the streets in real woollen cloaks and clacking iron pattens. When apothecaries are seen rushing about with gargles and tinctures and washes for sprained ankles, chilblains and frost-bitten noses. When you can hardly feel your hands and feet for the cold and are forced to stand shuddering over the fire on pain of being petrified by the frost, how pleasant that is Arthur.

Captain Tree:
    Laughing.
That will do Lord Charles, but do you dislike spring as much as you dislike winter?

Lord Charles Wellesley: Nearly. Only consider of the frosty nights and windy, showery, uncertain days, when you can't stir abroad without an umbrella in your hand and if you unfurl it you are in danger of being lifted over the tops of the houses; or perhaps you may be going over a bridge and in that case nothing but death stares you in the face. Oh, oh, summer and autumn for me.

Marquis of Douro: Yes, yes, I like summer: cornfields green as emeralds, trees with the foliage thick and dark [?in full] woods frowning in shadowy grandeur, all the gardens flowering and blooming and casting a sweet, fragrant smell as you pass by their high, ample walls covered with fruit trees on which the ripe summer or the ripening autumn fruits are hanging in rich gem-like clusters.

Captain Tree: Now, Lord Charles, what do you say to autumn?

Lord Charles Wellesley: The pleasantest season of the year. Up you get at break of day and off with your gun and greyhound, through the fields all hoary with frost, in the cool crispness of an October morning. Presently the horizon becomes illuminated with a faint light, which by degrees grows brighter and brighter till it is of a glowing orange, and, at length, just as you are passing some pleasant rural farm-house, a stately

118

chanticleer[8] breaks out with a long, silver chime. The thin veil of gray mists is suddenly rent asunder, and the glorious, round sun appears in majestic splendour over the tops of the high, blue hills, that are dimly seen among rolling clouds of vapour in the distance.

Marquis of Douro: Well done, Charley. Now let us have a little politics. Captain Bud, what do you think of the state of France?

Captain Bud: I'll tell you what, young man, the French are naturally of a republican disposition, and they will not long bear a monarchical, much less an absolute, government even if the head be their own beloved Napoleon (who, by the by, has lately shown himself of a very tyrannical demeanour: witness the executions of Talleyrand, of [?Designates] and of Maria Louisa). Bernadotte is likewise going on in a very stylish manner.[9]

Captain Tree: They say he's lately got many accessions to the Faction Du Mange.[10] Is that true I wonder?

Captain Bud: Perfectly so. Within the last three weeks, no less than 4 thousand persons have sent in their adherence, including Pigtail, Skeleton and Young Napoleon.[11]

Marquis of Douro: Young Napoleon is behaving in a manner not very becoming his high station.

Captain Tree: It is only a week since he was taken before a magistrate on the charge of stealing 3 rings off the finger of a man, under pretence of telling him his fortune.

Lord Charles Wellesley: The poor wretch is in danger of starving. Last

---

[8]A possible indication that Charlotte Brontë had read Chaucer's *Nun's Priest Tale*. Chanticleer, the cock, also figures in *Reynard the Fox*.

[9]Charlotte Brontë's use of historical characters and events often bears little relation to fact. Napoleon had died in 1821 and been succeeded by Louis XVIII. In 1829, Charles X was on the French throne (since 1824) but was soon to take refuge in England after the French Revolution of the 'July Days', which established Louis Philippe as a constitutional monarch. The executions Charlotte mentions are all fictitious. By 1829, Talleyrand, the famous French diplomatist and statesman under both Napoleon and Louis XVIII, had all but retired, although he later became ambassador to London for Louis Philippe. Prince Bernadotte of Sweden was at this time a candidate for the French throne but lost to Louis Philippe. Maria Louisa, daughter of the defeated Austrian emperor, married Napoleon in April 1810 after he divorced the barren Josephine. In 1811 she bore 'Napoleon II' (who died 1832), but she returned to Austria with her son when Napoleon abdicated in 1814. 'Designates' is unidentified: the word is difficult to decipher.

[10]Probably imaginary; although Charlotte Brontë may be referring to *le parti du manche*, based on the expression *être du côté du manche*, literally 'to be on the right side of the broomstick' (presumably those in power).

[11]'Young Napoleon' is probably based on Louis Napoleon, third son of Napoleon's brother, and later Napoleon III. Napoleon's own son had none of the Napoleonic ambition or 'romance' attached to this cousin. Skeleton is one of Pigtail's murderous band; see *The Enfant* n. 4.

night, as I was standing by the fire of Tally's Inn, a knocking was heard at the door. Somebody opened it and Young Napoleon entered. Tally asked him what he wanted. He replied that he was come a-begging and then walked up to me. I said, 'How do you do, Prince?' He answered that he was very poor and hungry, and his pale, haggard countenance confirmed the truth of what he said. I immediately gave him a guinea and he went away. A short time after he was gone, I had occasion to look what o'clock it was, but behold my watch had vanished, and this morning it was found in his possession.

Captain Bud: What a rogue. But now young men, let us have a song.

Lord Charles Wellesley:

Aside.

Shall we?

Marquis of Douro: I don't mind, except that I'll not sing.

Lord Charles Wellesley: Well, we'll recite then. But what shall be the subject, Bud?

Captain Bud: England.

Marquis of Douro and Lord Charles Wellesley:

Merry England, land of glory,
Plenty on thee fall,
Joy dwell on thy castles hoary,
Gladness in each [?one word] hall.

Might be on thy stately towers,
Beauty in each dell,
In thy blossomed, vernal bowers,
May peace ever dwell.

When war's trumpet fierce is sounding
Britain's Lion roars,
O'er the mighty waters bounding,
To the foes' dark shores.

When in battle, he stands war-like
And his meteor sword
Gleams amid the fight more star-like
Round him blood is poured,

Till his mane is red and gory
And his flashing eye,
As he springs to future glory,
Is of crimson dye.

Now when victory hath assuaged him
Of his thirst for blood,

Neath his oak-tree he hath laid him,
While around the flood

Of the raging, mighty ocean
Guards his own fair land,
Standing mid the wild commotion
All serene and grand.

Marquis of Douro and Lord Charles Wellesley: Now, will that do?
Amidst loud cheering, the curtain falls.

CONTENTS

Review of 'The Chief Genii in Council' I
Harvest In Spain II
Swiss Artist Concluded III
Conversations IV
Advertisements V

December 1829   Number II
We have been obliged to have 2 numbers this month.

ADVERTISEMENTS

GRAND DISCOVERY !!!!
CAPTAIN Brainless has lately discovered a method by which men
may get rid of their money.

TO BE SOLD: the worth of
THREE halfpence and a penny.

TO BE SEEN: A SIGHT

Any gentleman who is tired
of his life may learn a very
easy way to make off with
it, by applying to Colonel Sup.

YOUNG Man Naughty[12]
will instruct
pupils in the elegant
art of assassination.

A General Index to the
MAGAZINES[13]

A True Story 1
Causes of the Late War 2
A Song, by UT 3
Conversations 4
A True Story 5
The Spirit of Cawdor 6
Interior of the Pothouse 7
The Glass Town, A Song [by] UT 8
The Silver Cup 9
The Statue and Vase, by UT 10
Conversations 11
Scene on the Great Bridge 12
Song of the Ancient Britons, by UT 13
A Scene in my Inn 14
An American Tale 15
On Seeing the Garden of a Genius, by UT 18
The Bay of the Glass Town, [by] UT 17
The Swiss Artist 18
On the Transfer of this Magazine, by UT 19
On the Same, by UT 20
The Chief Genii in Council 21
Harvest in Spain, by UT 22
The Swiss Artist 23
Conversations 24

[12]A notorious Glass Town villain, associate of Dr Hume Badey; see *Characters of the Celebrated Men of the Present Time*. In a poem 'Young Man Naughty's Adventure', 14 October 1830(?), (*Poems*, p. 111), Charlotte Brontë describes how he killed the witch of the moor one night while poaching.

[13]The General Index is on manuscript pp. 17 and 18; these and the following two blank pages consist of two folios of a sheet of paper sewn into the end of the booklet at a later date from the time the booklet was made.

We now take leave of our readers.
CHARLOTTE BRONTË[14]

CHARACTERS OF THE CELEBRATED MEN OF THE PRESENT TIME[1]

BY CAPTAIN TREE

CHAPTER THE FIRST
Character and Description of the Duke of Wellington

The first time I saw His Grace was about twenty or 21 years ago. He was then in the 19th year of his age and very much like what the Marquis of Douro[2] is now, except that his countenance was more manly and there was a certain expression of sarcasm about his mouth which showed that he considered many of those with whom he associated much beneath him. The next time is only 3 or 4 years since. He was attired in his field-marshal's uniform and was standing in Cloud Square surrounded by his staff. His appearance came up to my highest notions of what a great general ought to be: the high stern forehead, noble Roman nose, compressed disdainful lip, and in short, the whole contour of his features were exactly what I should have wished for in the hero of Waterloo, conqueror of Buonaparte.

And now for His Grace's character. He is without dispute one of the greatest men that ever lived. In his disposition he is decisive, calm,

---

[14]Followed by a crudely drawn colophon of a flower.

[1]Hand-sewn booklet of sixteen pages (5.1 × 3.3 cm) in yellow paper cover; formerly in the Law Collection, now lost. The text here has been reprinted from *SHCBM*, vol. 1, pp. 37–43, with some editorial changes. It has been checked beside C. W. Hatfield's transcription in the BPM, which unfortunately is simply a copy of an incorrect version of C. K. Shorter; Hatfield never saw the original manuscript. In *Catalogue of my Books*, Charlotte Brontë gives the title of this manuscript as 'Characters of Great Men of the Present Age'.

[2]Spelt 'Duro' throughout this manuscript, but 'Douro' elsewhere. The name is based on the River Duero ('Douro' in Portuguese), associated with Wellington's Peninsular Campaign; Wellington was given the title Marquis of Douro in 1812, which he bestowed on his seven-year-old son, Arthur Richard Wellesley Douro.

courageous and noble-minded. His genius is not confined merely to military affairs. He is equally irresistible in the Cabinet as in the field. The campaigns in the Peninsula prove that the resources of his great mind are inexhaustible. On his bravery and prudence the fortune of all Europe hung for 6 years, and how nobly he returned the trust that was reposed in him is known to every man.

There was no neglect in him, no wavering in his determination. When once a thing was decided it was decided and acted upon. All his conduct was calculated to inspire confidence into the minds of his soldiers and to make them more resolute in the defence of their king and country. And now some dare to say that this man, this great, this mighty man, knows not how to defend England, to save her in her present terrible situation – that he who saved her when the star of destruction cast its livid, wasting beams over all her rolling fields and stately cities cannot now save her when no foreign foe threatens her desolation. Let those who say so remember the time when the haughty Napoleon went on conquering and to conquer, when every general that was sent against him withered and died at the blast of his trumpet, and fled in terror and dismay at every victory, leaving the victor haughtier than before.

When at length the glorious Wellington arose and the joyous heart-gladdening news rang on the ears of a fainting, dying nation that Buonaparte was beaten and vanquished, who was the terrible vanquisher? It was the Immortal Wellington. If he saved England in that hour of tremendous perils, shall he not save her again? I leave the question to be answered by those of my readers who have the mind to comprehend it.

CB   Captain Tree
December 12, 1829

CHAPTER THE 2
CHARACTER OF THE MARQUIS OF DOURO AND LORD C. WELLESLEY

The eldest of these young noblemen, the Marquis of Douro, is now in the 22nd year of his age. In appearance he strongly resembles his noble mother. He has the same tall, slender shape, the same fine and slightly Roman nose. His eyes, however, are large and brown like his father's, and his hair is dark auburn, curly and glossy, much like what his father's was when he was young. His character also resembles the Duchess's, mild and humane but very courageous, grateful for any

124

favour that is done and ready to forgive injuries, kind to others and disinterested in himself.

His mind is of the highest order, elegant and cultivated. His genius is lofty and soaring, but he delights to dwell among pensive thoughts and ideas rather than to roam in the bright regions of fancy. The meditations of a lonely traveller in the wilderness[3] or the mournful song of a solitary exile are the themes in which he most delights and which he chiefly indulges in, though often his songs consist of grand and vivid descriptions of storms and tempests: of the wild roaring of the ocean mingling with the tremendous voice of thunder, when the flashing lightning gleams in unison with the bright lamp of some wicked spirit striding over the face of the troubled waters, or sending forth his cry from the bosom of a black and terrible cloud. Such is the Marquis of Douro. And now for his brother.

Lord Charles Wellesley is in the 19th year. His countenance is striking and handsome. His eye is full of life and vigour. His hair falls in light yellow ringlets over his forehead. All his motions are full of animation, and the expression of his face is so spirited, has so much vivacity in it, as to charm and cheer every beholder. His disposition is in exact keeping with his appearance: lively, gay and elegant. His wit is sharp and piercing, but he often lets it play harmlessly round his opponent, then strikes him fiercely to the heart. His imagination is exceedingly vivid, as the graphic delineation of nature and character is.

Some of his tales prove his genius and mind are naturally high and bright. His songs are exquisitely beautiful and mostly consist of light and airy visions of the supernatural objects, of wild though gentle reveries of the world of immortals; but his spirits are generally the mild and fair beings which haunt the pleasant green wood or the crystal spring, which drink the fragrant dew of heaven from the lily's white blossom or the cowslip's golden cup, which live in the low vale among dim, purple violets or yellow primrose buds; and not the horrible monster which roars aloud in the distant and slays whole armies of men with one wave of his black and silver wing.[4] It is generally supposed that the tale of *The Golden Lily*[5] was written by Lord Charles and that is my opinion, for the gorgeous and lofty though light and airy magnificence of the style do not at all accord with the known disposition of his brother. There are indeed glorious descriptions of

---

[3]See 'A Traveller's Meditations', *Young Men's Magazine*, December (second issue) 1830.

[4]A description of the contrast between Charlotte's (that is, Lord Charles Wellesley's) conception of the genii and that of Branwell Brontë.

[5]Charlotte Brontë often refers to stories that she has written, but there is no trace among her extant manuscripts of *The Golden Lily* or the following *Wandering Exile*.

fairy palaces and bowers and arbours and trees, all seen by the wondering eyes of mortals, depicted on the sky in the solemn stillness of midnight, or hovering in high noon between earth and heaven amid the sounding of mysterious music and the voices of invisible minstrels; but what a difference between that and the *Wandering Exile* by the Marquis of Douro. There are spirits here too but they are shrouded cloudy ghosts who come from the regions of the dead to warn their living relatives of dangers which are near at hand. Here too are sounds, but they are strange, wild, and unearthly, and all unlike the merry music which glows clearly in *The Golden Lily*.

In short, the Marquis of Douro's strains are like the soft reverberations of an æolian harp which, as its notes alternately die and swell, raise the soul to a pitch of wild sublimity or lead it to mournful and solemn thought, and when you rise from the perusal of his works you are prone to meditate without knowing the cause, only you can think of nothing else but the years of your childhood and bright days now fled forever. On the contrary, the songs of Lord Charles resemble the glad sweet music of the dulcimer, and when you have finished reading a book of his you feel light and gay and merry, as if you could tread on air. So there's the difference.

CB   Captain Tree   Dec. 16, 1829

CHAPTER III
CHARACTER OF CAPTAIN BUD[6]

This great politician is now 45 years of age. He is tall, bony and muscular. His countenance is harsh and repulsive. His eye is deep set, glittering and piercing. All his movements are rather slow and lagging. His gait is awkward. One of his shoulders projects beyond the other and, in short, his whole appearance is not of the most pleasing kind. He is, however, the ablest political writer of the present time and his works [?exhibit] a depth of thought and knowledge seldom equalled and never surpassed. They are, however, sometimes too long and dry, which they would be often if it was not for their great ability. Flashes of eloquence are few and far between, but his arguments are sound and conclusive. Some of his apostrophes are high and almost sublime, but others are ridiculous and bombastic. He never condescends to be droll but keeps on in an even course of tiresome gravity, so much so that I have often fallen asleep over his best works and have as often taken shame to myself for it.

[6]Pseudonym of Branwell Brontë; see *Blackwood's Young Men's Magazine*, August 1829, n. 6.

His disposition is nervous, crabbed and irritable, but nevertheless, his integrity is upright and flexible. It is said that he is hypochondriac and that at different times he supposes himself a flame of fire, a stone, an oyster and a crayfish, and that he even sometimes believes himself to be a heatherbell apt to be blown away at every blast of the wind; but that upon such occasions his friends always take care to keep him out of sight. What credit may be put in these assertions I know not, but I believe them to be founded on fact.

Captain Tree   C Brontë
Dec. 17, 1829

CHAPTER IV
CHARACTER OF YOUNG SOULT[7]

This truly great poet is in his 23rd year. He is about the middle size and apparently lives well. His features are regular and his eye is large and expressive. His hair is dark and he wears it frizzed in such a manner as to make one suppose he had lately come out of a furze bush. His apparel is generally torn and he wears it hanging about him in a very careless and untidy manner. His shoes are often slipshod and his stockings full of holes. The expression of his countenance is wild and haggard, and he is eternally twisting his mouth to one side or another. In his disposition he is devilish but humane and good natured. He appears constantly labouring under a state of strong excitement occasioned by excessive drinking and gambling, to which he is unfortunately much addicted. His poems exhibit a fine imagination, but his versification is not good. The ideas and language are beautiful, but they are not arranged so as to run along smoothly, and for this reason I think he should succeed best in blank verse. Indeed I understand that he is about to publish a poem in that metre which is expected to be his best. He is possessed of a true genius which he has cultivatd by great effort. His beginnings were small, but I believe his end will be great and that his name will be found on the pages of history with those of the greatest men of his native country.

CB

Captain Tree   Dec. 17, 1829

---

[7]Pseudonym of Branwell Brontë; see *The Enfant*, n. 6.

CHAPTER V
CHARACTER OF SERGEANT BUD

This person is in his 25th year. He is tall and thin. His profile is handsome but his full face is skinny. His eye is bright and he is altogether tolerably good-looking. He is a clever lawyer and a great liar, a brow-beating counsel and an impudent barrister, a lengthy writer and an able arguer, a crabbed miser and a vile scoundrel, an unsociable fellow and a proud wretch, a real rascal and a dusty book-worm. He is, in fact, his father's own son. Anybody may bribe him, as I know to my cost. He will flatter you before your face like a courtier and slander you behind your back like a blackguard; and it is a downright shame for Tally to patronize him as she does.[8] The men who clapped the ass to his seat did perfectly right, and if I had it in my power I would first duck him in water, next I would give him 70 stripes with a cat-o-nine-tails, then I would make him ride through the Glass Town on a camel with his face turned to the tail, and lastly I would hang him on a gallows 60 feet high. When he was dead, he should be cut down and given to the surgeons for dissection.

CB   Captain Tree   Dec. 17, 1829

CHAPTER THE 6th
CHARACTER OF ROGUE[9]

Rogue is about 47 years of age. He is very tall, rather spare. His countenance is handsome, except that there is something very startling in his fierce, grey eyes and formidable forehead. His manner is rather polished and gentlemanly, but his mind is deceitful, bloody, and cruel. His walk (in which he much prides himself) is stately and soldier-like, and he fancies that it greatly resembles that of the Duke of Wellington. He dances well and plays cards admirably, being skilled in all the sleight-of-hand blackleg tricks of the gaming table. And, to crown all, he is excessively vain of this (what he terms) accomplishment.

CT   Dec. 17, 1829

---

[8]Sergeant Bud is scrivener to Chief Genius Tally (Charlotte Brontë); see *Blackwood's Young Men's Magazine*, August 1829, n. 6. Tally is variously spelt Tally, Talley, Talli and Tallii.
[9]See *The Bridal*, n. 10.

CHAPTER THE 7th
CHARACTER OF YOUNG MAN NAUGHTY

This man is in his 54th year. He is of gigantic stature, very bony, skinny and muscular. His features are large and coarse. His eye is small, grey and restless. His disposition is of the blackest and bloodiest dye. All his actions are marked by cold and assassin-like cruelty. His demeanour is insolent and brutal. His murders are of the most savage kind. He delights to torture his victim before he slays him. In short, no deed is too bad for him.

C. Tree   Dec. 17, 1829

CHAPTER 8th
DOCTOR HUME BADEY[10]

Badey is very tall, stout and tubby. He has as much feeling as a stone but is one of the best surgeons and physicians now alive.

CB   Captain Tree
Dec. 17, 1829

CHAPTER THE 9th
PIGTAIL[11]

Pigtail is 7 feet high. He is as ugly as can well be imagined and tremendously cross to those unhappy mortals who may happen to get into his clutches.

C. Tree   CB   Dec. 17, 1829

CHAPTER THE 10th
CHARACTERS OF DE LISLE, LE BRUN, DUNDEE, and VERNET[12]

These men are all about the middle size and neither very handsome nor very ugly. They are 4 of as good painters as ever lived: De Lisle great in

[10]Variously spelt Badey, Bady, Badry and, later, Badhri; see *Tales of the Islanders*, vol. 1, n. 14.

[11]See *The Enfant*, n. 4.

[12]See *Blackwood's Young Men's Magazine*, September 1829, n. 3, and December (second issue) 1829, n. 2 and 3.

the beautiful, Le Brun in the passions, Dundee in the sublime and Vernet in painting animals.

Charlotte BRONTË

Captain Tree   Dec. 17

1829

CONTENTS

DUKE OF WELLINGTON I
MARQUIS OF DOURO II
LORD CHARLES WELLESLEY III
CAPTAIN BUD IV
YOUNG SOULT V
SERGEANT BUD VI
ROGUE VII
YOUNG MAN NAUGHTY VIII
BADEY 9
PIGTAIL 10
LE BRUN, DE LISLE, DUNDEE, AND VERNET 11

CHARLOTTE BRONTË

Dec. the 17, 1829

CAPTAIN TREE

Description of the Duke of Wellington's Small Palace Situated on the Banks of the Indiva[1]

In the summer of the year 18—, a circumstance of a very urgent and painful nature obliged me to take a journey from the Glass Town northward along the range of the Jibbel Kumri to the city of Gondar[2] in

[1]Two page manuscript in cursive script (18.4 × 11.4 cm) in PML: Bonnell MA 2538. An alternative, published text, entitled *A Visit to the Duke of Wellington's Small Palace Situated on the Banks of the Indiva*, is printed in Appendix 1.

[2]The name, though not the nature, of the place may have influenced Emily Brontë's choice of the word 'Gondal' for the central nation in her imaginary saga; in the 'Vocabulary of Proper Names' at the back of the Brontës' copy of Goldsmith's *Grammar of General Geography* (London: Longman, 1823), Anne Brontë has written immediately above the entry 'Gondar, a capital city of Abyssinia', the following: 'Gondal a large island in the north pacific' (BPM: B45).

Abyssinia, where I continued about a month; and then, all things being settled to my satisfaction, I took my departure by the straight route through the kingdom of Negritia, when I was again forced to alter my course and pass up the River Senegal. From thence I proceeded northward of Timbuctoo and entered the great desert of Sahara; and on the third day of my journeying there I perceived, as the evening was closing in, an object rising out of the sea of sands and just visible on the verge of the west horizon, which I soon recognized to be one of those oases or green spots of the wilderness, which rejoice the heart of the weary traveller as a fair island does that of a despairing mariner after long nights and days of sorrowing toil and tempest on a fathomless and boundless ocean.[3]

On the evening of the fourth day I entered it, but, after walking a little way up the country, I began to be in doubt whether or not I should turn back again, for I had often heard that beings of a supernatural nature (not genii or fairies) reside in parts of these deserts, which they transform from barren and dreary sand into blooming and fragrant paradises. And a paradise indeed did this appear. The whole horizon was bounded by gentle hills covered with groves of plantains and palmettos, intermixed with long slopes of green and pleasant verdure.

In the middle of the island was a palace of the purest white marble, whose simple but most beautiful and noble style of architecture forcibly reminded [me] of many of the great palaces of the Glass Town. Around it lay a wide garden, which stretched over all the country as far as the range of hills. Here the tufted olive, the fragrant myrtle, the stately palm tree, the graceful almond, the rich vine and the queenly rose mingled in sweet and odorous shadiness and bordered the high banks of a clear and murmuring river, over whose waters a fresh breeze swept, which cooled delightfully the burning air of the desert which surrounded [it].

After a little reflection I determined to proceed, and, after I had walked about half an hour, I came to a bower of ranjulas[4] and high genii lilies. Being exceedingly weary, I laid down under its shade and fixed my eyes on the bright heavens, now glowing in the intense

---

[3]Charlotte Brontë is writing this description with Goldsmith's *Grammar* open in front of her. All the place names (except the River Indiva) appear on the map of Africa and the text (p. 74) has the same description of the Sahara as a sea: 'the sands being moved by the winds like waters, and storms on them being more destructive to travellers than the sea to voyagers. They have oases, or fertile spots, like islands, whose inhabitants are separated from the rest of the world'. Several lines on, Charlotte again refers to her oasis as an 'island' and mentions the palmetto, described in detail on p. 59 of Goldsmith's *Grammar*.

[4]An imaginary flower?

131

brilliancy of an eastern sunset. The air was filled with soothing balm and wafted on its light wings the gentle rippling of the pure stream which flowed softly through this wonderful garden.

I had lain thus for I cannot tell how long, until the moon rose slowly into the wide sky and the quiet evening star was shining in the west, when suddenly I heard a young and merry voice, whose sweet tones carried me back to the metropolis of the world and brought to my memory many adventures in which a certain young nobleman was concerned. I arose and listened eagerly as the voice thus proceeded: 'My darling little Tringia and my sweet Trill,[5] I wish you could tell me what and who are the inhabitants of those thousand worlds which roll eternally over your pretty heads. I wonder what were the horrible commotions which split that one star into three, and whether the spirit of the mighty Newton roams in crowned majesty over the glorious plains of the centre of light and life, or whether his disembodied soul soars as far above its sphere as did his sublime and almost superhuman mind above those of the common race of mortals.[6] But now I see my dear Philomel is pluming and decking himself to air my concerto which will soon call Arthur and perhaps my father and mother to witness your graceful dancing. Begin.'

At this moment a gush of rich melody began to flow in unison with the sweet tones [of] a harp-like instrument, and, as I turned the corner of a long green avenue (for I had now risen from the place where I had been sitting), I beheld the figure of an extremely handsome boy, whom I soon recognized as Lord Charles Wellesley, reclining under the shade of an immense chestnut and playing upon a small Spanish guitar, with a nightingale perched upon his shoulder, a beautiful green monkey and a small, silky-haired animal, something like a young kitten, bounding and dancing before him in the brilliant light of the uprisen moon.

In a short time a rustling was heard among the trees, and the Duke of Wellington, Lady Wellington and the Marquis of Douro entered the avenue. They all likewise sat down under the chestnut.

I now stept forward. At first they were greatly surprised at the sight of me, but after I had related to them who I was and the cause of my

[5]Lord Charles Wellesley's pet monkey and kitten respectively. They feature, together with 'Philomel' the nightingale and 'Pol' the parrot, in many manuscripts from 1829 to 1830, including the poem known as 'Homesickness' written only two weeks later than this story; see *Poems*, p. 94.

[6]Sir Isaac Newton (1642–1727), philosopher and astronomer. Published *Optics*, his theory of light and colours, with his mathematical discovery *Method of Fluxions*, in 1704. The first book of his *Philosophiae Naturalis Principia Mathematica*, containing his laws of motion and the idea of universal gravitation, was exhibited at the Royal Society (of which he was later president for 25 years) in 1686, and the whole was published in 1687.

being in that place, His Grace instantly recognized me and gave me a friendly and hearty welcome.

I remained there some days and then took my departure for the Glass Town, at which place I arrived about 3 months afterwards, as well in health as I could possibly expect from a journey of so many leagues in such a country.

Captain Tree   January the 16, Anno Domini 1830

THE ADVENTURES
OF MON
EDOUARD de CRACK
February 22, 1830[1]

The Adventures of Mon
EDOUARD de CRACK
BY
LORD CHARLES
WELLESLEY

PRINTED
FOR
SERGEANT TREE
AND SOLD
BY

[1]On yellow paper cover of manuscript in HCL: Lowell I(3); hand-sewn booklet of 20 pages (5 × 3 cm). A square design in ink fills the whole of the cover between the title and the date at the bottom.

ALL
Booksellers in the Glass Town . . . Paris, etc. etc.

PREFACE

My motive for publishing this book is that people may not forget that I am still alive, though a good way from Ashantee. The personages spoken of will easily be recognized by the reader.

CW   February the 22, 1830

I began this book on the 22 of February 1830 and finished it on the 23 of February 1830, doing 8 pages on the first day and 11 on the second. On the first day I wrote an hour and a half in the morning and an hour and a half in the evening. On the third day I wrote a quarter of an hour in the morning, 2 hours in the afternoon and a quarter of an hour in the evening, making in the whole 5 hours and a half.

CB

CHAP. the I

Edouard de Crack was born in a pleasant vale in one of [the] provinces of sunny France. His father was a vine dresser, a native of Savoy, and his mother was a Pyrenean peasant.

In this vale Edouard passed his childhood and youth until he was about 25 years of age, without having once crossed its boundaries but not without many a fervent wish so to do. All the book-knowledge he possessed was obtained under the tuition of one Jose le Brun, an old man of whom little was known in the hamlet where he resided, except that he was one of the oldest animals in existence and of a very irritable temperament.

Of this Jose, Edouard learnt that there was a famous city called Paris, having thousands of people in it and a church called Notre Dame, almost as high as a mountain. And he so raised his curiosity by the description he gave of a certain wonderful palace in that city, named the Tuilleries, that at length Edouard determined in his own mind that he would either see that city or perish in the attempt, for he imagined that it would be a dangerous and almost impracticable enterprise.

While he was pondering these things in his mind and watching for an opportunity to put his resolution into practice, a fever which then raged in the village seized both his parents, and, in a few days, they sunk under its violence and breathed their last. Their obsequies were performed with due solemnity and Edouard, after disposing of his small patrimony (his father's cottage and vineyard), took a final leave of his native valley, with all his slender fortune on his back and in his pockets to the amount of about 20 pounds English money.

It would be tedious to trouble the reader with a repetition of his adventures during a journey of about 100 miles, nor indeed is that at all necessary, there being nothing uncommon in them or more strange than generally happens to a counry lad on his first setting out a-travelling. Suffice it to say, that in a few days he arrived at PARIS and, after landing on the quay of the Seine and paying for his passage, he proceeded to examine the new and surprising objects which presented themselves to his attention. He was lost in astonishment as he gazed at the lofty houses, magnificent churches, wider streets and the innumerable quantity of horses and equipage, which were constantly rattling to and fro with a confused clamour and din, which for a few moments quite bewildered him.

But what struck him most forcibly was the aspect of the inhabitants of this wonderful city. A lean, haggard race of mortals with sunk eyes, hollow cheeks and yellow, tawny complexions. Some were attired in the most brilliant and flaring colours, some in faded but still gaudy raiment, and others in mere tattered rags through which their blackened, withered skin and, in many instances, bleached bones could be seen peeping ghastily from under the filthy covering; but notwithstanding their squalid misery, even these had some gay coloured article about them, such as a yellow ribbon round the arm or a scarlet patch on the forehead.

The whole of this motley assemblage seemed in a manner deranged. Some were skipping and dancing with various strange antics and gestures. Others were gambling and acting plays in the open street. On one side was a company of showmen performing to the delight of a numerous mob who had gathered round them; on the other, a large awning of crimson cloth, under which was spread a board covered with loaves of very white bread and bottles of rich, thick cream. At the head and foot of it sat two men upon barrels, each with a box by them into which they cast the money of those who came to purchase their merchandise. Down the sides of the board were two long forms upon which men were sitting, eating and drinking the victuals in profound and unbroken silence.

While Edouard was gazing at them with open mouth and staring eyes, a little, thin, haggard and sorry-looking young man brushed by him with a strange hook-like machine in his hand, and passing swiftly up the street vanished through a narrow, low door in the side of a decayed, old house. Edouard watched him till he disappeared, and then turning to the cake vendors asked for a slice of bread. The man demanded six sous and Edouard put his hand in his pocket in order to get them out, but discovered that neither a sous nor a demi-sous remained there. He uttered a loud cry, and immediately all the bystanders set up a wild and haggard laugh, which frightened him excessively.

When he had recovered from the first dreadful shock produced by finding himself in total destitution, he began to look about him for some means of subsistence. While he was in this dilemma, a tall gaunt man[2] came up to him and demanded if he were willing to serve as a waiter in a tavern. He immediately replied that he was, and the man bade him follow him. He complied and they proceeded on their way. When they had gone a few yards, they turned down into a narrow, dark, filthy lane framed by 2 rows of lofty houses, now ruinous and apparently uninhabited. At the entrance lay the white bleached skeleton of a man, and all round there peeped from the mud here and there a human skull or other bone. At sight of this ghastly figure, de Crack stepped back a few paces, but his conductor immediately ordered him to proceed, and, as they passed close by, he stumbled upon the head, which crashed under his weight. At this de Crack gave an involuntary shriek and shudder, but the unfeeling tavern master only kicked aside the carcase with a muttered imprecation and they went on.

In a short time after, they stopped at a low door, which they entered by crawling upon their hands and knees, and in this manner they proceeded along a very narrow and low passage till they came to a small door, which the man opened, and immediately a scene opened upon the view which the bewildered eyes of De Crack had never before beheld the likeness of. Six living anatomies were sitting upon the damp floor of a cellar. The naked walls, all covered with green slime, betokened the presence of noisome and putrid vapours. Across a raised stone table, with his throat cut and otherwise dreadfully marked, lay the body of a dead man, and around were 3 or four ghastly ruffians engaged in the taking up of a flag from the blood-covered floor.

I cannot go through all the particular events which happened to the hero of my tale during the period of five years which he stayed in this

[2]Probably the notorious 'Pigtail'; see *Characters of the Celebrated Men of the Present Time.*

tavern, but at the end of that time, when he had become perfectly initiated in all the ways of Paris, the following adventure happened to him.

One evening, about dusk, as he was walking in the outskirts of the city among the ruined towers of an ancient feudal castle, he heard a loud yell, somewhat resembling the cry of a mountain vulture but even more strange and savage, and at the same instant a dull rustling sound fell on his ear and the likeness of a cloud passed before him, in the midst of which he perceived a monstrous black giant girded with a blue flame and having hair of speckled and fiery serpents. He now felt himself whirled upwards with the quickness of thought and in a few minutes lost sight of the earth and found himself among a set of beings of whose existence he before had no notion. Mighty aërial creatures swept noiselessly past him on wings of light [and] slowly glided away into nothingness, leaving a track of luminous clouds as they vanished.

Having passed along many millions of miles of space, he came to a place where he beheld four beings of immeasurable height[3] standing upon suns whose rays shot upwards and enveloped them in mantles of fire. Their arms were outstretched and their hands clasped in token of unity. As De Crack and the giant approached, the latter fell down on the bright pavement now spread beneath them, and immediately, with a sound louder than ten thousand peals of thunder, the spirits' wings were unfurled. With infinite majesty they rose aloft, and the glorious apparitions, amid voices of articulate and solemn harmony, disappeared like the melting of a rainbow. At this sight, too terrible and awful for the eyes of mortal man to behold without injury, De Crack fell down insensible, and, when he recovered from his swoon, he found himself lying in a wood under a tall elm whose branches were just lit up with the first sunbeams. The wild flowers around him were beginning to open to the touch of light, and the fresh morning wind was perfumed with their sweet offered incense.

As he was gazing in rapture at the lovely scene, he suddenly heard a voice, singing in soft and rather agreeable accents the following words to the shrill response of a rural pipe:

> O blessed, mildly rising morn,
> I feel thy sweet fresh breeze,
> I see thee wave the springing corn
> And the tops of the green, young trees.

[3]The four Chief Genii, the Brontë children themselves.

When thou com'st stately from the hills,
  Thy flowery mantle o'er thee,
Thy praise is sung by a hundred rills
  And all the woods adore thee.

They bend their mighty branches low
  To kiss the sparkling dews,
Or dip them in the streams which flow
  'Mong flowrets of all hues.

Thou art welcomed by the fields and plains
  And the lark with gladsome song,
And joy pours gentle his matin strains
  On the soft clouds borne along.

The heavens rejoice at thy approach,
  The blue arch with fresh glory
Spans the earth spread beneath, like an emerald couch,
  And brightens the mountains hoary.

Here the voice ceased and Edouard beheld, advancing from the gloom of the forest, a young man habited in a green mantle, his head crowned with a garland of wild laurel and blue everlasting flowers, and a shepherd's pipe in his hand.

Edouard immediately accosted him and demanded his name. The young man replied, 'Eugene Beauchamp'. De Crack then asked if he could show him the way to some city. To this Eugene answered that he could, and, after giving him directions, they parted.

De Crack pursued his way till he came to the brow of a very tall hill which looked down into an immense valley, so admirably cultivated and so exceedingly fertile and so remarkably beautiful that it appeared like a delightful garden. Vineyards, almond trees, orange groves, corn and rice fields, savannahs and olive woods mingling in gay paradisical confusion, the beauty of which was freshened and heightened by a very wide and deep river calmly gliding through the whole. But however much De Crack was astonished by the exquisite loveliness of the valley, he was ten thousand times more so at the sight of a city which stood in the midst and to which it formed only an embroidered belt.

This city,[4] of a wonderful size, was fortified by walls of 3 hundred feet in height, with towers of 9 hundred at every interval of one mile. In the midst was a tower 6,000 feet high situated in an area 3 miles broad. The king's palaces were of radiant white marble, richly ornamented

---

[4]The Glass Town.

with massive silver imagery and the architecture was the soul of nobleness, grandeur, magnificence and elegance combined, and all the other dwellings were majestic and beautiful likewise. The public buildings were resplendent with grace, symmetry, majesty and proportion, and an immense bridge which gloriously spanned the [?Dronooke], like streams of a river, was a perfect model of bold, light, simple architecture. In short, De Crack would have been in doubt as to whether this city was the abode of mortals if it was not for observing certain narrow, black lines winding among the splendid palaces and squares which he but too well knew the meaning of.

Having viewed this scene for some time, he proceeded on his way and arrived at the city about sunset, a little while before the gates were shut. He entered by the large brazen gate and proceeded along the great bridge, stopping every instant to gaze at the wonderful objects which presented themselves to his view. All along the high bank of the river, which rushed in an impetuous and dark brown torrent with a thunderous noise under the massive iron arches of the bridge, were lofty mills and warehouses piled up storey above storey to the very clouds, surmounted by high tower-like chimneys vomiting forth huge columns of thick black smoke, while from their walls the clanking, mighty din of machinery sounded and resounded till all that quarter of the city rang again with the tumult. Down in the river below, a little distance from the swell and rush of the water, were hundreds of huge steam-vessels and merchant ships, all sombre and dark with the smoke of the mills, lying proudly on the heaving waters among the little boats which flitted lightly about them; and, to complete the picture of commercial activity, thousands of human beings, all redolent of fragrant and rancid train-oil, were ceaselessly hurrying to and fro over the wearied and groaning bridge with a bold independent look and step, which told that they descended from the Dukes of York and Lancaster.

While De Crack was standing on the bridge gazing stupidly about, a tall, stout and upright old man with ruddy face, white hair and a brutish aspect, came swaggering up and accosted him with, 'Well Lad, now you've looked so hard at the land, I'll let you have a peep at the water', at the same time making an attempt to throw him overboard. But as De Crack was an active man he escaped from him, screaming out 'murder'.

The brute sprang at him again, and, while they were struggling together, a military officer who was standing by commanded him to leave off. He refused, and the officer, without speaking another word, quietly unslung his carbine and shot him dead upon the spot.

De Crack, thus released from the danger which threatened him, went up to his deliverer in order to express his gratitude. He was a tall and handsome young man and apparently had been much chafed in his mind, which caused him to perpetrate so hasty a deed as that above related. He answered shortly to the protestations of De Crack and was turning to go away when suddenly, as if recollecting himself, he came back and asked De Crack his name and where he came from. Edouard answered both these questions satisfactorily and added that he was without any friend in this city and did not know where to go. The young officer then turned to a stout red-faced man who stood by him and said, 'Dr Badey, I order you to take Naughty,'[5] pointing to the person whom he had killed, 'and cure him, then convey De Crack to the factory of Captain Mourout and say that I wish him to be taken into his employ.'

So saying, he walked off and the doctor prepared to execute his orders. After placing the dead man on the back of one of his assistants, he commanded De Crack to follow him, and this he did till they came to one of the factories, which they entered. The doctor requested to see Captain Mourout who soon made his appearance. He communicated the desire of the young officer to him, whom he called the Marquis of Douro. Captain Mourout immediately placed De Crack in the situation of head-overseer, where he now continues, contented and happy.

THIRD VOLUME OF TALES OF THE ISLANDERS[1]

Third Volume of Tales of the Islanders
[Chapter 1 The Duke of Wellington's Adventure in the Cavern][2]

One evening the Duke of Wellington was writing in his room at Downing Street.[3] Eldon reposed at his ease in an ample, easy chair,

[5]Young Man Naughty, a Glass Town villain.

[1]Cover of *Tales of the Islanders*, vol. III, in NYPL: Berg Collection, formerly a hand-sewn booklet of sixteen pages (9.9 × 6.3 cm). The pages have since been separated, mounted and bound with those of vols I, II and IV.
[2]The chapter titles in brackets are those given by Charlotte Brontë in her *Catalogue of my Books*, 3 August 1830.
[3]Wellington was Tory prime minister from January 1828 to November 1830. Of the following characters mentioned in this scene, only Sir Henry Hardinge (who lost an arm at

140

smoking a homely tobacco pipe (for he disdained all the modern frippery of cigars, etc., etc.) beside a blazing fire whose flames Left[4] had just been feeding by a fresh supply of Londonderry's black diamonds. One-armed Hardinge stood at his desk awkwardly scrawling an army estimate on a gilt-edged sheet of Bath-post.[5] Coxcomical Rosslyn lounged against the polished green marble mantlepiece, eyeing with ineffable contempt the quizzical old pekin who sat opposite, and occasionally casting a sidelong glance at his own dandy figure reflected in a magnificent mirror suspended against the wall, which was hung with purple-figured velvet. Castlereagh, seated on a Turkish ottoman, whined and yawned incessantly; while Mr Secretary Peel, perched upon a treasury tripod close beside His Grace, kept whispering and wheedling in the Duke's ear until at length, happening to interrupt him in the midst of an abstruse calculation, he saw his master's eye suddenly flash on him and without further warning was at the other end of the room in a twinkling.

At this tragical catastrophe, Rosslyn slank back to his desk which he had quitted without leave from headquarters. Hardinge just gave a keck[6] over his shoulder at the prostrate civilian. Eldon ceased puffing, holding up his withered hands half in fear and half in wonder. Castlereagh crawled off [to] the cushion under the table where he lay quietly down, and the Duke of Wellington, without noticing the general consternation, relapsed into his former occupation of unravelling a confused mass of Exchequer-like figures, left by poor Vesey in a sad state of disorder when he was seized with the sickness which superannuated him.[7]

While they were thus employed, a heavy footstep was heard without.

Ligny fighting under Wellington in 1815), Lord Rosslyn (a Whig) and Robert Peel (home secretary) were actual members of Wellington's Cabinet in May 1830 when this manuscript was written. Lord Eldon (an 'Ultra Tory' and fiercely anti-Catholic) had been Lord High Chancellor for the greater time since 1801 and was disappointed when he was not asked to take office again under Wellington. Lord Castlereagh, a distinguished British statesman, especially in foreign affairs, had tragically committed suicide in August 1822; he had been born in Ireland in the same year as Wellington and constantly promoted his friend Arthur Wellesley's career.

[4]Mrs Left Seringapatan, wife of the veteran Seringapatan (see n. 9 below).

[5]A variety of highly glazed letter paper, used by the fashionable visitors to Bath when the spa was in its prime.

[6]Northern dialect, 'to make a sound as if about to vomit' (*OED*); expressing disgust.

[7]William Vesey Fitzgerald was chosen by Wellington in 1828 as president of the Board of Trade, but, although a 'Catholic' Tory, he lost his re-election to the seat of County Clare in June of the same year to the 'illegal' Catholic candidate Daniel O'Connell.

The door opened and a little shrunk old woman, wrapped up and wholly concealed, except her face, entered. Her appearance excited no surprise, for this was one of the famous Little Queens. She advanced up to the Duke and presented him a letter, written with blood and sealed with a seal on which was the motto 'le message d'un revenant'. He took it respectfully and read it. While he was doing this, he changed colour several times, evincing an uncontrollable emotion. When he had finished, he rose and walked about as if trying to calm his mind. Suddenly he stopped and commanded all present to depart. They immediately obeyed. Then, after a pause, he demanded of the fairy if that letter was true or a forgery. She made a sign with her hand and immediately the King and the 2 other Queens appeared.[8] They all knelt down. Each drew out a wand wreathed with ivory. They kissed them and said, 'It is by virtue of these wands we rule the hearts of mortals. We will forfeit them and our spiritual power if what we say is false. That letter is true.' When they had uttered these words they vanished.

His Grace immediately rang a bell and ordered the attendant who answered the summons to get ready the swiftest horse in his stables. His mandates were presently obeyed and the Duke, clad in a Georgian mantle with a broad military belt, brass helmet and high black plumes, mounted the spirited animal, spurred him to full gallop, and in a short time left London and its suburbs far behind.

He rode with such speed that when the sun rose he beheld the towers of Strathfieldsay rearing their proud heads, ruddy with the first beams of morning, from the ancient oak forests which surrounded them. All his wide domains were stretched before his eyes: the peaceful village nestling among venerable woods, the wide fruitful fields extending to the verge of the horizon, the stately trees darkening the scene with their shadow, the white cottages looking out from the bowery retreat of their orchards, and the great river refreshing everything as it passed. All were his own, won by his invincible sword, the monuments of England's gratitude to her glorious preserver.

He passed quickly on and in a short time arrived at the dark gate. The old soldiers' cottages, removed a little way from the narrow path, could hardly be distinguished by reason of the large trees on each side, whose thick drooping branches, now in full verdure, had shot out and increased to such a degree as wholly to surround them with a fresh, verdant barrier, and their situation was only marked by the tall, round, grey chimneys, one of which – that on the right hand – belonging to

[8]Little King and Queens: Branwell, Emily and Anne; Charlotte, also a 'Little Queen', is presumably the fairy who summons them.

Seringapatan,[9] was just breathing a light dun smoke on the stainless ether. The other stood in motionless silence for the inhabitants thereof, to wit Jack-of-all-trades, Orderly-man and Gamekeeper, were for the present tarrying at the more noisy, and, to their dispositions (unlike that of their bookish neighbour), more congenial, Horse Guards.[10]

His Grace was just in the act of raising a huge bough, which guarded the right-hand doorway, for the purpose of entering, when he heard a light buoyant step and a sweet voice at a distance carolling the following words:

> O where has Arthur been this night?
> Why did he not come home?
> For long the sun's fair orb of light
> Hath shone in heaven's dome.
> Beneath the greenwood tree he's slept,
> His tester was the sky;
> O'er him the midnight stars have wept
> Bright dewdrops from on high.
> And when the first faint streak of day
> Did in the east appear,
> His eyes touched by the morning's ray
> Shone out with lustre clear.
> He rose, and from his dark brown hair
> He shook the glit'ring gems,
> Which nature's hand had scattered there
> As on the forest stems.
> The flowers sent up an odour sweet,
> As forth he stately stept;
> The stag sprang past more light and fleet,
> The hare through brushwood crept.

Here the voice suddenly stopped. All the trees which bordered the path rustled and Lord Charles Wellesley bounded by with so much buoyancy, merriment and elasticity that he hardly seemed to touch the ground. His rosy face was radiant with smiles, his large, bright, sparkling blue eyes seemed the transparent palaces of cheerfulness. His parted ruby lips mantling with mirth displayed a row of teeth whiter than the finest oriental pearl. His forehead, fair as ivory, was shaded by

---

[9] An old military retainer, named after Seringapatam, the stronghold of Tipoo Sultan in India; Wellington, then Colonel Wellesley, took part in its capture in 1799.

[10] A building in Whitehall, headquarters of the cavalry brigade of English Household troops. It is described and illustrated in Branwell Brontë's book *Description of London* (London, 1824), signed and dated 'PB Brontë. aged 10 years and 9 months. March 21 – 1828–' (BPM: 141).

ringlets of gold, which hung in beautiful clusters over his temples, and his form was the very emblem [of] aerial symmetry. He passed the Duke without observing him as he was hid by a tall black cypress. His Grace stepped forward and called him by his name. Immediately the light, gay being arrested his swift course, or rather flight, as soon as he heard his father's voice and turned round.

'Good morning, my son, where are you going?' said the Duke.

'Oh, dear, dear father,' exclaimed he, 'I'm so glad to see you! I'm going to seek Arthur, who has never been home since last evening.'

'Never been home since last evening? It is true then, they have not deceived me,' replied His Grace, and the dark sorrowful cloud, which for a moment had been dissipated by the presence of his cheerful son, shadowed his noble brow more gloomily than before. 'Charles, your brother is in danger of death,' he said solemnly.

'In danger of death?' repeated Charles, and immediately all gladness forsook his face and dim tears veiled his lustrous eyes. His face turned pale as ashes, and sinking on the ground, he exclaimed as well as agonizing grief would permit him, 'Oh, Arthur must not die! Little Queens can and shall save him. I will find Mystery wherever he lives. Where is Arthur, father? Where is he? I'll die if he dies, for I cannot live without him.'

'Hush Charles, hush,' said His Grace raising him from the earth, 'come with me into Seringapatan's cottage. I will try to save Arthur.'

By this time Seringapatan, hearing the moans and sobs of Lord Wellesley, had come out of his house. When he saw the Duke supporting his son, who was weeping incessantly, he was somewhat alarmed and exclaimed. 'Poor thing, he seems faintish. What's matter, my lord? Has a pekin been hurting him? Where is the wretch? Let me scald him in boiling lead. But stop, I'd better fetch a drink of something, for he's rather white in the face.'

'No, no, Seringapatan, take him into your house a little while, I wish to speak to you.'

'Oh, pray come in, my lord,' replied the old veteran, rearing himself proudly at the thought of a secret and flinging the door wider open. 'There's nought new to listen at people's keyholes for them 'at lived over the way as at London.'

When they had entered he put two chairs by the fire, wiping them with a dish-cloth and spreading a piece of carpet over the hearth. He then pulled a pillow from the bed-head and placed it in one chair, saying that if Lord Charles felt weakly he might lean on it. When they were in he closed the door, bolted and locked it, and then sat down on a three-legged stool at his master's feet.

'Seringapatan,' said His Grace, 'I believe you to be an honourable and upright man, faithful to my interests and grateful for the favours I have done you. Therefore I will now trust you with a secret of great importance. Last night I received a mysterious letter purporting to be from the spirit of my dead father. It stated that Arthur, the eldest of my children and your future lord, having in the course of his melancholy wanderings been drawn by the power of a secret fascination into the abode of supernatural beings, is at this moment suffering all the torments which they can devise, and that if you did not go with me to a particular place which I am acquainted with, certain death will befall him. And I now require you by your allegiance to me and mine to obey my commands in everything.' Here the Duke stopped, and Seringapatan, falling on his knees, solemnly promised to follow all his orders, not only at the present time but until he should draw his last breath. The Duke then turned to Charles and asked him if he would go also.

'I would willingly die to save Arthur's life,' replied the young lord ardently, while a beam of hope lighted his glistening eyes. His father patted his curly head and smiled on him approvingly.

In a few moments they were ready and when Seringapatan had locked his cottage door they set out at a quick pace on their journey. In a little while they had emerged from the forest, and after crossing several hay and cornfields together with a large belt of meadow-land and orchards that surrounded the village, they entered a very wide plain on which only a few scattered sheep were visible, and even these in a short time ceased to present themselves to the eye. As they went on, the towers and woods of Strathfieldsay gradually sank beneath the horizon, the high church steeple lessened and receded till it became invisible, the enclosed fields and orchards vanished in the distance, and at length only the flat plain beneath and the arched sky above remained for the iris to rest upon. On this plain they continued till evening, when they arrived at [a] place where were huge rocks rising perpendicularly to an immense height; a vast cataract rolling thunderously down the precipices hollowed for itself a basin in the solid stone beneath, and the waters rushing over dashed furiously onwards for some time, until at length, smoothing and widening, they glided peacefully along a lovely valley which opened by degrees to the right hand. It was shaded with sycamore trees and young oaks, through which the rays of the setting sun now beamed with a rich lustre on the subsiding wavelets of the river, imparting to it the beautiful appearance of liquid gold. They proceeded to mount [a] narrow rugged sheep-path winding up one of the rocks till they came to a kind of plateau covered with herbage, above which the rocks rising to a dizzy height appeared wholly inaccessible.

Here the Duke suddenly stopped and commanded Seringapatan and Lord Wellesley to halt as it was not necessary for them to proceed further. This he said in a tone which both his son and servant understood: it was not angry, nor hardly stern, but it had a decisive sound in it which showed that no entreaties would prevail with him to let them go on. They accordingly sat down on the grass without speaking and watched him with earnest eyes, for they saw it was impossible for any mortal man unassisted by supernatural power to scale the perpendicular wall of even stone which they beheld. About 5 yards distant from the plateau was a projecting fragment that hung over the valley beneath. It was, however, exceedingly narrow and such a tremendous height from the ground that this, together with its distance from the little plain where they were, made it perfectly improbable that any living being should dare the horrible leap which must be made before they could reach it.

The Duke stood for a moment gazing eagerly around as if searching for some means to attain his end. At length, fixing his eyes on the fragment, he quickly threw off his dark mantle, which till now he had kept closely wrapped about him, and, advancing to the border of the plateau, sprang from it to the ledge in an instant, as if the spirit of an izard[11] or chamois had been suddenly granted to him. When Lord Wellesley saw his father perform his daring action to which he was prompted and encouraged by the desire to save his eldest son, a smothered scream burst from his lips. The Duke turned round, not withstanding his perilous situation, and looking on him with compassion, he said, 'My dear Charles, do not fear for me. In a short time I shall return with Arthur perfectly safe and well.' Then, turning a corner of the rock, he disappeared from their sight.

Continuing on his course, which became more dangerous at every step, he at length arrived at a vast cavern, the entrance of which was closed with iron doors. These rolled back as he advanced and admitted him into an immense hall of stone. He entered. The doors closed after him, and he found himself alone in this strange apartment, dimly lighted by a blue flame in the middle. Huge massive pillars rose to the vaulted roof. Their capitals were ornamented with human skulls and cross-bones; their shafts were in the form of grisly skeletons, and their bases were shaped like tombstones. The hall was so long that he was unable to see the end, and as he walked to and fro, he heard the echoing of his footsteps at a distance as if the sound was reflected by vaults or cells. After a considerable time, the noise of an opening door

[11]Capriform antelope of the Pyrenees, allied to chamois (*OED*).

was heard. Light, well-known footsteps fell on his ear, and in another moment, he embraced his beloved son.

Almost at the same instant, they found themselves on the plateau where Seringapatan and Lord Wellesley anxiously waited for them. The meeting between the two brothers was joyful in the extreme, and after a short time spent in tears of gladness and affectionate congratulating, the whole party returned in safety to Strathfieldsay. To all the questions put to the Marquis respecting his sufferings while in that cave, his invariable answer has been that they were indescribable.

CB   May 5, 1830

Chapter the II
May 6, 1830
[The Duke of Wellington and the little King's and Queens'
Visit to the Horse Guards]

It was a bright afternoon in August 1829, when the Duke of Wellington rose from the dry, wearisome occupation of composing and copying state documents (better fitted for the mind of a John Herries or a P. Courtenay[12] than his lofty and energetic spirit), which employment he had constantly followed for above 3 months without any relaxation whatsoever. After locking his writing desk and placing all the papers in order, he determined forthwith to proceed to the Horse Guards, for tired of the tedious dull society of gentlemen in office and creeping crawling clerks, ready and even ambitious to lick the dust beneath his feet, he longed once more to breathe the fresh, free, military air of that privileged retreat of all the great field marshals, generals, staff officers and colonels now alive.

Just as he had formed his resolution, the door of his apartment opened and Little King and Queens entered in their usual form. They accosted him with, 'Duke of Wellington, come and see the Horse Guards. We are going there and we wish you to accompany us in order that you may point out all that is worth seeing.'

'I was just about to proceed thither,' replied His Grace, 'and shall be much honoured by your society.'

In a few moments they set out and after a quarter of an hour's walk reached the place of their destination. The gate was closed, but a soldier who stood by immediately hastened to open it as soon as he saw

---

[12]John Charles Herries: see *Tales of the Islanders*, vol. 1, n. 5; Thomas Peregrine Courtenay (1782–1841), statesman and author, secretary to the Commissioners for Affairs of India, 1812 to 1828, when he was promoted to vice-president of the Board of Trade.

His Grace approach, presenting arms and making a low bow. They entered and it was shut after them. The yard of the Horse Guards was covered with rough stones and gravel. 2 or 3 sentinels were pacing about, occasionally turning their eyes towards a lofty triangle, and fixed at one end on which a poor soldier was undergoing the lash of the cat-o'-nine-tails, inflicted by the merciless hand of Orderly-man, who stood with his shirt sleeves rolled up exerting every sinew in the cause of cruelty.

'What crime has that fellow been guilty of to bring on his head, or rather his back, such a bloody punishment?' exclaimed the Duke as he walked towards the instrument of torture.

'He's been making faces at Lord Hill[13] when he told him to lick the dust off his shoes,' replied Orderly-man, halting for a moment.

'Lord Hill's a scoundrel,' replied His Grace. 'In the first place for flogging a man because he refused [to] commit a crime (which that he commanded him to do would have been), and in the second place for ordering you to triangle him, which none but I have a right to. Take that wretch down instantly Orderly-man. Bring Lord Hill and set him in his place.'

For the first time in his life Orderly-man hesitated to obey his master's mandates. Casting the whip on the ground he sighed deeply. Tears came into his glittering grey eyes, and marks of evident grief and disappointment appeared on his rugged countenance.

'What is the matter?' said the Duke, in the utmost surprise. 'I should think the fellow was absolutely under the influence of witchcraft. Why don't you fly like lightning to execute my command?'

For a few moments he was unable to reply. At length a flood of tears came to his relief, and then the following words, intermixed with sobs and moans, made their way: 'Well, my lord, it's baking day today and I was just beginning to make a [?good] currant cake when Lord Hill called me off to triangle this beast, and now when I've done that I'm forced to triangle him too and my cake will be eaten by Seringapatan or some other horrid glutton in the baking room, while I shall have none at all, though I bought the stuff it's made of.' Here, as if touched by the recital of his own misfortune, he wept anew. The Duke of Wellington laughed aloud, and, placing his hand on his shoulder, told him not to break his heart, as he would give him something better than a piece of bread. Orderly-man, consoled by this assurance, hastened to obey his lord, and in a few minutes Hill, suspended from the triangle, suffered the penalty of his crime.

[13]See *A Romantic Tale*, n. 10.

Little King and Queens, understanding from the previous conversation that it was baking day [in] the Horse Guards, expressed a wish to go into the room where the bread was prepared and made ready.

'Your majesties are perfectly at liberty to do so if you please,' said His Grace, 'provided my attendance can be dispensed with, as I never frequent the apartments where the soldiers cook their food.'

'Very well, Duke of Wellington, we can do without you,' replied the fairies angrily and immediately quitting him in an abrupt manner, they entered the Horse Guards and proceeded to the bakehouse.

It was a large room built of brick without any ceiling, so that all the great beams and rafters that formed the roof were exposed to the eye and paved after the fashion of streets and thoroughfares. A fire of a sufficient size and fierceness to roast an ox was blazing at one end. A long table ran down the centre, at which 2 or 3 hundred soldiers were standing busily employed in the manufacture of coarse loaves and cakes. At the head, on a high rustic tripod, sat a very old man, apparently more than 6 feet in height,[14] with muscles as strong and supple as those of Hercules, and bones as big as a mammoth's. His grizzled, grey hairs were drawn all together, tied with a piece of a rope and plaited into a long queue behind. His nose was like an eagle's beak when, by reason of its age, the upper mandible has pierced through the under and the venerable possessor, unable either to eat or drink, lies in its inaccessible eyrie, made like a charnel-house by the blanched bones of those which in its vigorous youth it has slain, now— I was going on but I find that the metaphor is too diffuse already.

Seringapatan's nose, then (for the old man was no other), was exceedingly aquiline and his mouth a scarlet thread stretching from ear to ear and, together with his fine large, dark, expressive eye, betokened him of true Milesian origin.[15] He sat on his exalted throne in an attitude of extreme dignity and imperial majesty. His head, gently inclined to one side, leaned on a hand whose colour the snow might have envied, it being of a dark tawny red. One foot lay on the far of the table and the other on the head of a horrible wretch, who had ventured to rebel against his high power but who, at length having succumbed from a gentle intimation that tomorrow at drill-time he should suffer for his impudence, was now doing penance for his black crime. When Seringapatan spoke, he invariably stretched out his right arm in

[14]Seringapatan's height and bird-like features are reminiscent of the giants in 'Our Fellows' Play' and the huge bird-like creatures in *Tales of the Islanders*, vol. IV.

[15]An early example of Charlotte Brontë's characterization of 'Irish'. (Milesius was a fabulous Spanish king whose sons are said to have conquered Ireland *c.*1300 BC.) Later in the juvenilia, 'Irish' or 'Western' characteristics are synonymous with passion and decadence.

[?tukrds] imitating the elegant action of all the great Grecian, Roman, British and Hibernian orators.

After Little King and Queens had viewed this scene for some time, they left the room and proceeded to find out the Duke of Wellington. They found him in the public apartment of the officers. It was an ample rotunda, carpeted with green cloth. A large brass lustre, suspended from the roof, was covered with the accumulated dust of several years. A billiard table stood in the middle about which a number [of] officers sat playing or talking. The Duke was standing at one end of the room surrounded by Lords Rosslyn, Beresford, Somerset and Arthur Hill together with Generals Murray, Hardinge, Londonderry, Fitzroy,[16] etc., etc. Rosslyn was just delivering an encomium upon His Grace in the following words:

'My lord, when you appear a mist seems withdrawn from my eyes. You are as the clear splendour of the sun shining after rain. The dark clouds hasten at your approach to mingle with the swelling waves of the deep, from whence they came and to whence they will return. A hundred flowers, whose beautiful heads drooped beneath the fury of the storm and whose radiant colours waned as it beat upon them, raise again their slender stems, unfurl their emerald leaflets and hold up their golden crowns towards the first beam of light which heralds your appearance, that they may be filled with loveliness and joy, for lo, you have already glorified the last drops of the departing shower into a faint but fast-brightening rainbow. As I gaze on that mighty apparition spanning the whole earth and heaven, a solemn sign that the victorious waters shall never again roar triumphantly over the world's highest mountains, which clave[17] the clouds with their summits or roll in her pleasant valleys, the palaces of beauty and silence. I think, by a

[16]Friends and colleagues of the real Duke of Wellington: James St Clair Erskine, Lord Rosslyn, a member of Wellington's Reform Cabinet; becomes Earl St Clair of the later juvenilia. Lord Fitzroy Somerset, 1st Lord Raglan, Wellington's military secretary and married to his niece. Arthur Hill: probably based on Lord Dungannon, Wellington's maternal grandfather; not to be confused with Lord Hill (General Sir Roland Hill), who also appears in this story and in *Tales of the Islanders*, volume I, chapter 4. General Sir George Murray and Sir Henry Hardinge were old Peninsular War officers of Wellington and members of his Cabinet from 1828 to 1830. Charles Stewart, 3rd Marquis of Londonderry, served as adjutant-general under Wellington in the Peninsula; he was half-brother to Castlereagh whom he succeeded as 3rd Marquis of Londonderry. Fitzroy: probably Robert Fitzroy, vice-admiral, hydrographer and meteorologist; in 1828 he surveyed the coasts of Patagonia and Tierra del Fuego in the *Beagle*, returning to England in 1830. Charlotte Brontë would have read of his exploits but, unlike the above characters, he seems to have had no connection with Wellington. It is possible that she was referring instead to Henry Fitzroy, son of Lord Southampton, who married Wellington's sister, Anne, in 1790.

[17]An archaism from the Bible; the use of 'clave' as the past tense of 'to cleave', common

mysterious connection of the humble snowdrop, both the arch of the sky and the first blossom of spring are alike in their origin, though one be a child of heaven and the other of earth, for each is 'rocked by the storm and cradled by the blast'. Eh? My lord, is not that very pretty?' said he, and at that moment he certainly bore a much greater resemblance to a monkey than a man.

'Rosslyn,' replied the Duke smiling sarcastically, 'you have certainly not done yourself [proud] today though I am afraid if a [?tick] or a mandrill, a pinch[18] or a pigmy could be brought to speak it would still surpass you in giving utterance to all that is conceited and devoid of sense in the compass of apish phraseology. But sir, and I am now serious, if you bother me again with such language, more resembling the watery scum of a weak, whining poetaster's brains than the conversation of an officer of sense and spirit or even of a civilian, whose capacities are but mediocre in every respect, I shall certainly allow you the privilege of showing off some elegant French attitudes, scrapes and bows, whether of the head or the back will, I presume, be perfectly immaterial, on a triangle formed of deserter's halberts,[19] exposed to the view and derision of the whole regiment of the Guards. You will likewise, sir, be expected to attend drill every day to officiate as caller of the muster roll, to clean your own arms and accoutrements without the aid of any menial attendant, to associate with the common shoeblacks, valets and squatters of the army in order that you may teach them the polite art of elocution besides improving their general manners by your elegant example, and finally, you will be cashiered for a few months, to the end that you may enjoy your favourite solitude, which will perhaps enable you to produce more masterly specimens of rhyming than you have hitherto favoured us with.' Here His Grace stopped.

All the generals around stood staring contemptuously at Rosslyn and when he happened to come near any of them, they shrank from his touch as if he was infectious, not deigning to speak to him for a moment. Seeing their strange conduct and hearing the words of his

---

especially among northern writers until the seventeenth century, was no longer in use in the nineteenth century (*OED*).

[18]Probably refers to a 'pincher', a rogue who, in changing money, by dexterity of hand, secreted two or three shillings out of the change of a guinea (*1811 Dictionary of the Vulgar Tongue*, reprinted with foreword by Robert Cromie, Chicago, 1971).

[19]A weapon carried by an infantry sergeant and used to denote the rank of sergeant. 'To be brought to the halberts; to be flogged *à la militaire*: soldiers of the infantry, when flogged, being commonly tied to three halberts, set up in a triangle, with a fourth fastened across them' (*1811 Dictionary of the Vulgar Tongue*).

master, the poor wretch burst into a flood of tears, sobbed aloud, and then, as if unable to contain himself, he ran out of the room as fast he was able, and a few minutes after he was heard at a distance singing the following verses:

To the forest, to the wilderness,
Ah, let me hasten now.
Where ere I go, I still shall see
My master's lowering brow.

The wood' black shade won't hide my grief,
No influence now I have;
But th' stream will give more quick relief,
I'll seek a wat'ry grave.

Unto the shore I'll swiftly fly,
I'll plunge into the sea;
The foam bells will ascend on high,
When drowning sets me free.

Drown all the ills which life doth give,
O mis'ry in me dwells.
When no longer shall I live,
The tide of sorrow swells.

Suspended from an elm tree tall,
I'll end my mournful life,
My soul more bitter is than gall,
My heart is full of strife.

I'll cut my neck with some sharp blade,
I'll swallow poison dire;
No, now my resolution's made:
I'll set myself on fire!

Just then a loud noise was heard in an adjoining apartment and Gamekeeper came rushing into the room, exclaiming that Lord Rosslyn had thrown himself into the fire but that he had been pulled out before he was hurt.

'Take him,' replied the Duke of Wellington, 'to the lowest dungeon. Keep him there and feed him on nothing but bread and water for a month.' His Grace then quitted the room and little King and Queens followed him.

'Where are you going?' said they.

'To Arthur's apartment,' he replied. 'Will Your Majesties honour me by your company?'

'Yes,' they answered shortly and in a few minutes, after mounting a flight of stone steps, they arrived at the end of a long gallery terminated by a door, which when opened discovered a small antechamber, where was an arched entrance veiled by a curtain of thick, green baize. The Duke undrew the curtain, and a most elegant but rather small saloon presented itself. The floor was spread with a rich Persian carpet. Low sofas surrounded the room covered with green satin, elegantly embroidered in needlework. A dome, tastefully painted in the arabesque style, formed the roof. Several stands of beautiful white marble supported alabaster vases of the finest and most fragrant flowers. On the Parian mantelpiece stood a number of images classically designed and well-executed in Japan china, and on a hearth slab of costly [?Pabruz] marble were ranged magnificent porphyry, lapis lazuli and agate vessels filled with the most exquisite perfumes the East can supply. All the windows were shaded with orange and myrtle trees which grew in large pots of Seville china. At one of these were seated the Marquis of Douro and Lord Wellesley. The former was habited in the uniform of his regiment, imperial blue and gold. The latter in white silk, lightly bordered with green, and a purple mantle fastened on one shoulder by an ornament of sapphire and emerald.

As soon as His Grace entered they both started up joyfully, welcoming him to their peaceful retreat from the noisy and turbulent Rotunda. In a few minutes he sat down, and then, after a short silence, he observed, 'What a luxurious place this is Arthur! Quite unfitted, I assure you, my son, to prepare a man for those hardships which everyone has to encounter during some part of his life.'

'Oh, father,' exclaimed Lord Charles, 'Arthur will always make hardships if [he] has not them ready at hand. Ever since he has been here (that is, 3 hours) I have not observed a single smile on his countenance and after tiring myself to no purpose with trying to make him speak, I was forced to open the window and amuse myself by talking to every person who passed in the court below. At last that resource failed me for no living creature showed its head, and therefore shutting the sash I sat down, remained again silent for half an hour, and then finding that hypochondrism was fast approaching upon me I got up, smelt at every flower and perfume in the apartment, danced, shook the orange branches, sung merry songs, stamped, raged, wept, mimicked Arthur, screamed, smiled, became hysterical, fainted, and at last, finding all my efforts fruitless to provoke him to utter the smallest monosyllable, I flung myself exhausted on a seat and remained staring frantically at Arthur till you entered, when to my inexpressible joy I saw him rise and open his lips to welcome you.'

The Duke of Wellington remained for about an hour at the Horse Guards and then returned to Downing Street, where he found a bundle of official documents awaiting his arrival. These he immediately sat down to decipher, and at this employment I shall for the present leave him.

C. Brontë   May the 8th 1830

THIRD VOLUME OF
THE TALES OF THE ISLANDERS

I began this volume on Monday
May the third 1830 and finished it
on Saturday May the 8, 1830.

C. Brontë   May the 8, 1830

====

The Adventures of Ernest
Alembert. A Tale by C.
Brontë. May 25, 1830[1]

Chapter the 1

Many years ago there lived in a certain country a youth named Ernest Alembert. He came of an ancient and noble race; but one of his ancestors having been beheaded in consequence of a suspicion of high treason, the family since that time had gradually decayed, until at length the only remaining branch of it was this young man of whom I write.

His abode was a small cottage situated in the midst of a little garden and overshadowed by the majestic ruins of his ancestral castle. The porch of his hut, adorned by the twisting clematis and jessamine, fronted the rising sun, and here in the cool summer mornings he would

---

[1]Title on brown paper cover of manuscript, in The Carl H. Pforzheimer Library: Misc. MS. 187, hand-sewn booklet of fifteen pages (18.4 × 11.1 cm.) in cursive script.

often sit and watch its broad orb slowly appearing above the blue distant mountains. The eminence on which his cottage was built formed one side of a wide valley, watered by a stream whose hoarse voice was softened into a gentle murmur ere it reached the summit of the hill. The opposing rocks which guarded the vale on the other side were covered by a wood of young ash and sycamore trees, whose branching foliage, clothing them in a robe of living green, hid their rugged aspect, save where some huge fragment, all grey and moss-grown, jutted far over the valley, affording a fine contrast to the leafy luxuriant branch which perhaps rested on the projection, and imparting an appearance of picturesque wildness and variety to the scene. The valley itself was sprinkled with tall, shady elms and poplars that sheltered the soft verdant turf ornamented by cowslips, violets, daisies, golden cups and a thousand other sweet flowers, which shed abroad their perfumes when the morning and evening summer dews or the rains of spring descend softly and silently on the earth. On the borders of the stream a few weeping willows stood dipping their long branches into the water, where their graceful forms were clearly reflected. Through an opening in the vale this noisy river was observed gradually expanding and smoothing until at last it became a wide lake, in calm weather a glassy unruffled mirror for all the clouds and stars of heaven to behold themselves as they sailed through the spangled or dappled firmament. Beyond this lake arose high hills, at noonday almost undistinguishable from the blue sky, but at sunset glowing in the richest purple, like a sapphire barrier to the dim horizon.

One evening in autumn as Ernest sat by his blazing fire and listened to the wind which moaned past his dwelling, shaking the little casement till the leaves of the wild vine which curled around it fell rustling to the earth, he heard suddenly the latchet of his door raised and a man clothed in a dark mantle, with long hair, and beard of raven blackness, entered. At sight of this singular figure he started up, and the man immediately accosted him as follows: 'My name is Rufus Warner.[2] I come from a great distance, and having been overtaken by darkness in the valley I looked about for some roof where I might pass the night. At length I espied a light streaming through this window. I made the best of my way up to it, and I now request shelter from you.'

Ernest, after gazing a moment at him, complied with his demand. He closed the door and they both seated themselves by the fire. They sat

---

[2]This is the first occurrence of the name Warner; it reappears in the later juvenilia as Warner Howard Warner, the Duke of Zamorna's trusted prime minister of Angria, who is said to be gifted with the supernatural quality of second sight, a possible link with this early fairy character.

thus for some time without interchanging a word. The man with his eyes intently fixed on the ascending flame, apparently quite inattentive to every other object, and Ernest as intently viewing him and revolving in his mind who he might be – the cause of his strange attire, his long beard, his unbroken taciturnity – not unmixed with a feeling of awe allied to fear at the presence of a being of whose nature he was totally ignorant, and who, for aught he knew, might be the harbinger of no good to his humble dwelling. Dim, dream-like reminiscences passed slowly across his mind concerning tales of spirits who, in various shapes, had appeared to men shortly before their deaths, as if to prepare them for the ghostly society which they would soon have to mingle with.

At length, to relieve himself from these almost insupportable thoughts, he ventured to accost his mysterious guest by enquiring whence he came.

'From a rich and fruitful land,' replied the man, 'where the trees bear without ceasing, the earth casts up flowers which sparkle like jewels, the sun shines for ever, and the moon and stars are not quenched even at noonday; where the rocks lose themselves in the skies and the tops of the mountains are invisible by reason of the firmament which rests upon them.'

The answer, uttered in a hollow and hoarse voice, convinced Ernest of the truth of his surmises; but a charm seemed to have been cast upon him which prevented him from being overcome by terror, and he replied as follows: 'If what you say is true, I should like exceedingly to follow you into your country instead of stopping here, where I am often chilled by frost and cold winds, in the absence of the cheering warmth of the sun.'

'If thou wilt go, thou mayst,' replied the other, and Ernest, under the influence of a secret fascination, consented.

'Tomorrow, by daybreak, we will set out,' said his guest. And then, as the night was far advanced, they both retired to their straw couches, after partaking of a simple supper which Ernest had hastily provided.

Chapter the 2

The next rising dawn found Ernest and his unknown guide on their way down the long valley. It was a chill, gloomy October morning. The sky was obscured by grey clouds and the cold wind, which whistled among the yellow withered leaves of the wood that covered the rocks, blew occasionally as a strong breeze arose some mizzling drops of rain in the faces of the two travellers. The distant prospect of the lake and mountains was hidden by a veil of mist, and when the sun rose above them his presence was only revealed by a whitish light gleaming through the thin, watery covering. The only sounds which fell on the ear were the howling of the blast in the caverned sides of the valley and the melancholy murmuring of the stream as its waves beat against the rugged stones which obstructed its passage.

They proceeded along in a straight course till they came to the borders of the lake, where the guide stopped, saying, 'We must now cross this water.'

Ernest gazed at him a moment, and then said, 'How can we? We have no boat, and I am unable to swim for such a length of time as it would require.'

He had no sooner said these words than a brisk gale arose which ruffled and agitated the before stagnant surface of the lake. Presently a light skiff appeared gliding over the waves, and in a few minutes it reached them. The man instantly sprang into the bark and Ernest, though filled with terror at the certain knowledge that he was now in the hands of a supernatural being, felt himself compelled by a strong impulse to follow him. No sooner were they seated than a large, white sail unfurled of its own accord, and in an instant they found themselves at the opposite shore, so lightly and swiftly this fairy boat had borne them.

When they had touched the bank with their feet a huge billow like a mountain overwhelmed it and immediately all the swelling waves disappeared, the rising foam vanished and a great calm fell on the whole lake. At the same time Ernest felt his fear pass away and it was succeeded by a feeling of courage against danger, mixed with a certain curiosity to see what was to come.

When they had travelled a long time, they came to a very wide moor that stretched to the verge of the horizon which was perfectly level, except in one part where tall black rocks were seen raising their heads to the sky. About evening they reached these rocks, when they stopped and sat down to rest themselves. The scene was now grand and awful in the extreme: around lay the dark desert heath, unenlivened by a single streak of verdure; its beautiful pink flowers were withered, and their fragrance had vanished. The mellow hum of the bee was no longer heard humming about them, for he had gathered their honey and was gone. Above rose the tremendous precipices whose vast shadow blackened all the moor and increased the frown on the unpropitious face of nature. At intervals from their summits a shrill scream, uttered by some bird of prey which had built its nest there,

157

swept through the whole arch of heaven in which wild clouds were careering to and fro as if wrecked by a horrible tempest. The sun, shrouded in vapours, had long sunk to rest, and the full moon, like a broad shield dyed with blood, now ascended the stormy sky. A mournful halo surrounded her and through that warning veil she looked from her place in the firmament, with her glorious light dimmed and obscured, till the earth only knew by a faint, ruddy tint that her white-robed handmaid beheld her. All the attending train of stars shone solemnly among the clouds, by their abated splendour acknowledging the presence of their peerless queen.

After they had viewed this scene some time, the guide rose and beckoned Ernest to follow him, which he did, till they came to a particular part of the rocks where was a profound cavern. This the man entered and Ernest was compelled to go after. The way seemed to incline downwards, and as they went deeper and deeper, they soon lost sight of the upper world, and not a ray of light [was] now seen to illumine the thick darkness around them. At length a faint, grey dawn became visible, and at the same time a gentle, warm wind stole past which softened the cold, raw air of the cave. Now they saw branches of trees waving over them and began to perceive that they trod on a velvety turf. In a short time by the increased light, they beheld that they were in a dense, gloomy forest which, as they advanced, gradually changed into a pleasant, shady wood, becoming more beautiful as they went on, until at last it assumed the appearance of a delightful grove. From this they soon emerged into an open country of which the description is as follows.

A wide plain was stretched out before them, covered with the most enchanting verdure: graceful trees sprung out of the earth bearing delicious fruits of a perfect transparency intermingled with others which rose to a great height, casting down their branches all laden with white blossoms and dark flourishing leaves; crystal fountains, that fell with a murmuring noise, were seen glittering through bowers of roses and tall lilies; the melodies of a hundred birds was heard from myrtle and laurel groves bordering a river which glided through the plain; arching rocks of diamond and purple amethyst, up which plants of immortal verdure crept, sparkled in the light and variegated the lovely prospect. This plain was bounded by hills, some of which rose majestically to the heavens, covered with vines and pomegranates, while others only gently swelled upon the sight and then sunk into calm and peaceful valleys. Over all this scene hung an atmosphere of crystalline clearness. Not one fleecy cloud sullied the radiant dome of sky, not one wreath of mist floated over the brows of the distant mountains, but in stainless purity lay the whole land, arrayed in a robe of spiritual and unearthly light.

When Ernest came out of the wood, this view, bursting at once on his eyes, completely overpowered him. For a long time he stood speechless, gazing intently upon it. His mind seemed to be elevated and enlarged by the resplendency of the vision. All his senses were delighted: his hearing by combination of sweet sound which poured in upon it, his sight by the harmonious blending of every colour and scene, his smell by the fragrant perfume of each plant and flower which bloomed in these everlasting fields. At length, in ecstatic admiration, he turned round to thank his conductor for bringing him hither, but when he turned he was gone. The forest by which he came had vanished also, and instead of it a vast ocean appeared in the distance whose extent seemed altogether boundless. Ernest, now more filled with astonishment than before, remained a while suspended between fear and wonder; then, rousing himself, he uttered the name of his guide aloud but his voice was only answered by a faint echo. After this he walked a considerable way into the country without meeting with one visible being either human or supernatural. In a few hours he traversed the plain and the acclivities which bordered it and then entered a wide, mountainous land totally different from that which he had left. He wandered among the rocks unconscious where he went till twilight, when he wished to return, but was unable to find his way back. No signs appeared of the plain he had quitted, except that on the southern horizon a beautiful light lingered long after sunset, and occasionally, as the wind rose, faintly melodious sounds were heard floating fitfully by.

After a while, when the night had closed in, Ernest came to the brow of a lofty precipice. Overcome with fatigue he cast himself on the ground and began to gaze into the profound depth beneath him. As he lay, a death-like stillness was on the earth. No voice was heard in that gloomy region; the air was untracked by any wing. No footstep crushed the desolate sands, echo whispered not in the caverned rocks, and even the winds seemed to have held their breath. At last he saw in the tremendous gulf a thick vapour slowly rising on his sight. It gradually expanded, till the chasm was filled with a cloud swaying to and fro as if moved by an invisible power. Then he heard a dull hollow noise, like water roaring in subterraneous caves. By degrees the cloud rose and enlarged, sweeping round him till all things vanished from his sight, and he found himself encircled by curling mist. Then he heard music, subdued and harmonious, resembling the soft breathings of flutes and dulcimers. This was suddenly broken by a flood of war-like melody rolling from golden trumpets and great harps of silver, which now suddenly gleamed upon him as the curtain of clouds rent and the whole

159

scene was revealed. A pavement of sapphire sparkled below, from which flashes of radiant purple light proceeded, mingled with the glory of an emerald dome that proudly arched a palace whose pillars were the purest diamond. Vases of agate and porphyry sent up wreaths of refined incense formed of the united fragrance of a thousand flowers. Beings of immortal beauty and splendour stood in shining ranks around a throne of ruby guarded by golden lions, and sounds so sweet and enchanting swelled on the ear of Ernest that, overwhelmed with the too powerful magnificence, he sank senseless on the bright pavement. When he recovered from his swoon, he found himself no longer surrounded by the gorgeous splendour of the fairy palace, but reposing in a wood whose branches were just moved by a fresh, moaning wind. The first sunbeams penetrating the green umbrage lighted up all the dewdrops which glistened on tender blades of grass, or trembled in the cups of wild flowers which bordered a little woodland well. When Ernest opened his eyes, he beheld standing close to him a man whom he presently recognized to be his guide. He started up, and the man addressed him as follows: 'I am a fairy. You have been, and still are, in the land of fairies. Some wonders you have seen and shall see more if you follow me.'

Ernest consented. The fairy immediately stepped into the well and he felt compelled to do the same. They sunk gradually downwards. By degrees the water changed into mists and vapours; the forms of clouds were dimly seen floating around. These increased until at length they were wholly enveloped in them. In a short time they seemed to land and Ernest felt his feet resting on a solid substance. Suddenly the clouds were dissipated and he found himself in a lovely and enchanting island encircled by a boundless expanse of water. The trees in the island were beautiful rose laurels[3] and flowering myrtles, creeping pomegranates, clematis and vines, intermixed with majestic cypresses and groves of young elms and poplars. The fairy led him to a natural bower of lofty trees whose thick branches mingling above formed a shady retreat from the sun, which now glowed in meridian splendour. This bower was on a green bank of the isle, embroidered with every kind of sweet and refreshing flower. The sky was perfectly free from clouds, but a milky haze softened the intense brilliancy of its blue and gave a more unbroken calmness to the air. The lake lay in glassy smoothness. From its depths arose a sound of subdued music, a breath of harmony which just waved the blue water-lilies lying among their dark green leaves upon its surface. While Ernest reposed on the green turf and viewed

[3]Oleanders.

this delightful prospect, he saw a vision of beauty pass before him. First he heard the melody of a horn, which seemed to come from dim mountains that appeared to the east. It rose again nearer, and a majestic stag of radiant whiteness, with branching and beaming golden horns, bounded suddenly into sight, pursued by a train of fairies mounted upon winged steeds, caparisoned so magnificently that rays of light shot from them and the whole air was illumined with glory. They flew across the lake swifter than wind. The water rose sparkling and foaming about them, agitated and roaring as if a storm darkened the sky.

When they had disappeared Ernest turned towards the fairy, who still continued with him, and expressed his admiration of the beautiful scene which had just vanished. The fairy replied that it was but a shadow compared with the things infinitely more grand and magnificent which were still reserved from him to behold. Ernest, at these words, replied that he felt extremely impatient for the time to come when he might see them. His conductor arose and commanded Alembert to follow him. This he did and they proceeded to enter a very dark and thick wood which grew on the banks of the island. They journeyed here for several days and at length emerged into an open glade of the forest, where was a rock formed like a small temple, on the summit of which, covered with grass and various kinds of flowers, grew several young poplars and other trees. This curious edifice the fairy entered alone. After continuing some time, he came out and approaching Ernest bade him look up. Alembert instantly complied and, as he did so, beheld a chariot, which shone as the clouds that the sun glorifies at his setting, descending from the sky. It was conducted by two swans, larger than the fabulous roe, whose magnificent necks, arched like a rainbow, were surrounded by a bright halo reflected from the intense radiancy and whiteness of their plumage. Their expanded wings lightened the earth under them and, as they drew nearer, their insufferable splendour so dazzled the senses of Ernest that he sank in a state of utter exhaustion to the ground.

His conductor then touched him with a small silver wand and immediately a strange stupor came over him, which in a few minutes rendered him perfectly insensible. When he awoke from this condition, he found himself in an exceedingly wide and lofty apartment, whose vast walls were formed of black marble. Its huge, gloomy dome was illumined by pale lamps that glimmered like stars through a curtain of watery clouds. Only one window was visible, and that, of an immense size and arched like those of an ancient Gothic cathedral, was veiled by ample, black drapery. In the midst arose a colossal statue, whose lifted hands were clasped in strong supplication and whose upraised eyes and fixed features betokened excessive anguish. It could be distinctly seen by the lighted tapers which burnt around. As Ernest gazed on this mysterious room he felt a sensation of extreme awe, which he had never before experienced. He now knew that he was in a world of spirits. The scene before him appeared like a dim dream. Nothing was clear, but a visionary mist hovered over all things, that imparted a sense of impenetrable obscurity to his mental as well as his bodily eyesight.

After continuing in this state for some time amidst the most profound silence, he heard the sweet soft tones of an æolian harp stealing through the tall, pillared arches. This mournful melody rose and filled the air with wild music as the wind began to moan around the dome. By degrees these sounds sank to rest and the death-like stillness returned with a more chilling and oppressive power than before. It continued for a long period till its unbroken solemnity became supernatural and insupportable. Ernest struck the ground with his foot but this effort produced no sound. He strove to speak, but was unable to make his voice utter any noise. At that instant a horrible, crashing peal of thunder burst the frozen air and roared around the mighty building, which shook and trembled to its centre. Then the wind arose and the music swelled again, mingling its majestic floods of sound with the thunder that now pealed. The unearthly tones that rolled along the blast exceeded everything which any mortal had before heard and Ernest was nearly overwhelmed by the awe which they inspired, when suddenly the fairy who had been his conductor appeared, and, approaching the window above mentioned, he beckoned him to come near. Ernest obeyed, and on looking out his eyes were bewildered by the scene which presented itself to his view. Nothing was visible beneath but billowy clouds, black as midnight, rolling around a tower six thousand feet in height, on whose terrible summit he stood. For a long time he gazed intensely on the wild vapours tossed to and fro like waves in a storm. Sometimes they lay in dense gloom and darkness, then globes or flashes of fire illumined them with sudden light.

At length the thunder and the wind ceased, the clouds slowly disparted and a glorious brightness shone upon them. Through the dismal piles of mist passing away beyond the horizon, a fair vision gleamed which filled Alembert with wonder and delight. A beautiful city appeared, girding the tower far below, whose lovely hues charmed the eye with their mild attractive splendour. Its palaces, arches, pillars and temples all smiled in their own gentle radiance, and a clear wide stream (transformed by the distance into a silver thread) which circled its crystal walls was spanned by a bright rainbow, through whose arch it flowed into a broad expanse of green hills, woods and valleys,

162

enamelled by a thousand flowers that sent up their united fragrance so high that even the atmosphere around the summit of this lofty tower was faintly perfumed by it.

'That city,' said the conductor, 'is the abode of our fairy king, whose palace you may see rising above those long groves near the south gates.'

Ernest looking in that direction, but beheld only a star of light, for the palace was formed of certain materials too brilliant for any but fairies to behold distinctly. Ernest continued for some time at the window, until the prospect beneath began to fade away as twilight shed her dim influence over it. Slowly the stars looked forth one by one from the sky's deepening azure, and the full moon as she ascended the east gradually paled the bright orange dye which glowed in the western heavens. The murmur of the aerial city died away. The voice of the giant harp was heard only at intervals to break the stillness of eventide, and its wild, mournful melody as it floated on the balmy breeze served but to enhance the calm, sacred and mysterious feeling of that peaceful hour.

'We must now depart,' said the fairy, turning suddenly to Alembert, and at the same instant he found himself upon the very summit of the tower. His conductor then, without warning pushed him from the tremendous and dizzy eminence into the immense void beneath.

Ernest gave a loud shriek of terror, but that was dissipated instantly by a delightful sensation which followed. He seemed to sink gently and slowly downwards, borne on a soft gale which now fanned his cheek and guided by invisible beings who appeared to moderate the velocity of his fall into a quiet, easy transition to the lower regions of the earth.

After a while he alighted in the fairy city, still attended by his conductor. They proceeded along a magnificent street, formed of the rarest gems gorgeously sparkling in the moonlight, until they arrived at a majestic palace of lapis lazuli, whose golden gates rolled back at their approach and admitted them to a wide hall paved with the purest alabaster, richly carved and figured, and lighted by great silver lamps perfumed with the most costly odours.

Ernest was now exceedingly weary, and the fairy led him into another apartment more beautiful than the first where was a splendid couch overhung by a canopy adorned with emeralds, diamonds, sapphires and rubies, whose excessive brilliancy illuminated all the room. Here he flung himself joyfully down to rest. In a few minutes a profound slumber closed his eyelids, which continued undisturbed till break of day, when he was awakened by the sweet singing of birds. He arose, and on looking forth from his crystal casement beheld an immense garden full of the sweetest flowers and plants, unknown among mortals, spread beneath. Lofty rows of trees bearing fruits that sparkled like precious stones, shaded long green walks strewn with fallen blossoms. On their fresh, verdant branches sat innumerable birds of the most rich and resplendent plumage, who now filled the air with delightful and harmonious warbling. Ernest was astonished at beholding no appearance of the city, but continued for some time listening to the enchanting music of the birds, enjoying the fragrant perfume of the blossoms and the dark grandeur of the majestic trees that surrounded him.

This contemplation was at length interrupted by his conductor, who now appeared in the apartment and, without speaking, led him into the open air, and, when he had done so, he made him a sign to turn round. Ernest obeyed, and instead of the palace he saw a high bower formed of trees whose flowers were more lovely than the finest roses, lilies or camellias. The prospect then suddenly changed and a deep glen, embosomed in hills, woods and rocks took the place of the garden. A clear and profound stream meandered past them. Into this the fairy plunged, and Ernest, forced by an overmastering spell, followed. For a long time they sank slowly down and nothing was visible save the vast expanse of waters that encompassed them.

At length, leagues beneath, a new realm dawned on Ernest's astonished sight. Their speed now accelerated and in a few hours they arrived at the fairy king's abode. It was a palace of liquid diamond. A great fountain rushing upwards from the earth parted into a thousand arches and pillars, through whose transparent surfaces appeared an immense quantity of emeralds, rubies, amethysts, topazes, opals, pearls and other gems which the fountain continually cast up. The palace roof was formed of the humid vapour that proceeded from the living arches ever in motion. These, congealed into round, lucid drops, assumed the appearance of a lofty dome, from which descended other pillars of a larger size that seemed to support it. Over the summit of the dome was suspended in the air a sun of insufferable brightness and from within gleamed hundreds of stars sparkling with supernatural splendour.

From the translucent nature of the edifice the interior was perfectly visible, and Ernest saw the fairy king seated in his glittering and moving palace, surrounded by attendants, one of whom held a diamond cup filled with the honeydew of wild flowers. The others played sweetly on silver harps and lutes, or sang in more melodious tones than the nightingale or skylark. I cannot relate all the marvellous adventures that befell Ernest Alembert while he abode in the land of Faery. He saw their midnight revels in many a wild glen and wood, when they feasted beneath the solemn moon, and the spells by which they drew the lonely traveller into their enchanted circlet. He often watched their sports on the 'beached margin of the sea'[4] and saw the rolling billows fall calm under the magic influence of their muttered incantations. He heard and felt the sweet witchery of their songs chanted at unearthly banquets, and when the sound swelled to a starlit, lofty sky, all the revolving worlds arrested their mighty course and stood still in the charmed heavens to listen. But this life in time grew insupportable. He longed once more to dwell among human beings, to hear the language of mortals again and to tread on green grass-covered turf, under the shade of earthly trees. The fairies, who were acquainted with his desire, at length determined to grant it, which they did in the following manner.

It was a fair and mild evening in the decline of summer, when all the elfin court assembled within a dell, one of those privileged spots which the pinching frosts and snows of winter are unable to deprive of their everlasting green array. The soft velvet turf served them for seats, and the profusion of sweet flowers with which it was embroidered shed a refreshing perfume. The lily canopy was raised and the glittering table was covered with crystal goblets brimming with nectarous dew. The song of a lark now hymning his vespers in the cloud-wrapped dome was all their music, and as its tones fell on the silent earth they diffused a holy calm around. Before the festival began, a fairy approached towards Ernest, who reposed on the ground a little apart, and, presenting him a goblet, bade him drink the contents. Ernest obeyed, and when he had done so, a strange stupor seized him, which soon overpowered all his senses and in a short time he sank into a profound swoon.

When he recovered from this he found himself at the entrance to a very wide green vale, bounded by pleasant woods and romantic rocks together with high hills clothed in dark groves, that descended to their feet and advanced a considerable way into the valley. It was sunset and not one purple cloud was visible in all the radiant sky. The west swam in an ocean of golden light that bathed the heavens in glory and poured its reflected splendour over half the world. Eastward a long of brilliant red appeared, gradually growing softer and paler towards the point of sunrise. Above, all was a clear, bright, silvery blue, deepening at the zenith and faintly tinged with grey as it receded from the gorgeous west. Beneath this sky the earth glowed with tints whose warm and mellow richness would have honoured the loveliest scenes in Italy. Hills, rocks and trees shone, invested in a lustrous halo of beauty. The vale flowed with light, and a hundred flowers stirred among their leaves as the sun shed its last beams over them. For a long time Ernest lingered, gazing entranced on the sight. He knew that this was not a

---

[4] *A Midsummer Night's Dream*, II, i, 85.

delusive vision and no mystery hung upon it. As he stood a sound stole past him like the music of a harp. He trembled, thinking he was still in the power of supernatural beings. It swelled and swept solemnly down the long wild glen, awakening low, sweet echoes among the frowning rocks and pleasant woods in which it was embosomed.

Soon, however, Ernest's fear was dissipated, for he heard a human voice accompanying the music. He moved a step or two and bent eagerly towards the spot whence the tones issued, striving to catch the sense of what was uttered. This he at length did, and it was as follows:

> Proudly the sun has sunk to rest
>   Behind yon dim and distant hill;
> The busy noise of day has ceased,
>   A holy calm the air doth fill.
>
> That softening haze which veils the light
>   Of sunset in the gorgeous sky,
> Is dusk, grey harbinger of night,
>   Now gliding onward silently.
>
> No sound rings through this solemn vale
>   Save murmurs of those tall, dark trees,
> Who raise eternally their wail,
>   Bending beneath the twilight breeze.
>
> And my harp peals the woods among
>   When vesper lifts its quiet eye,
> Comingling with each night-bird's song
>   That chants its vigils pensively.
>
> And here I sit, until night's moon
>   Hath gemmed the heavens with many a star,
> And sing beneath the wandering moon
>   Who comes, high journeying, from afar.
>
> O sweet to me is that still hour
>   When frown the shades of night around,
> Deepening the gloom of forest bower,
>   Filling the air with awe profound.
>
> I hush my harp and hush my song,
>   Low kneeling neath the lofty sky,
> I hark the nightingale prolong
>   Her strain of wondrous melody,

Forth gushing like a mountain rill,
  So rich, so deep, so clear and free;
She pours it forth o'er dale and hill,
  O'er rock and river, lake and tree,

Till morn comes and with rosy hand,
  Unbars the golden gates of day;
Then, as at touch of magic wand,
  The earth is clad in fair array.

Then from its nest the skylark springs,
  The trembling drops of glittering dew
Are scattered, as with vigorous wings
  It mounts the glorious arch of blue.

Before the strain ceased the hues of sunset had begun to fade away, yet sufficient light remained for Ernest to behold a man of a very ancient and venerable aspect seated at the mouth of a deep cavern, under the shade of an immense oak, whose massive limbs and foliage stood in dark relief against the sky. Every leaf and twig was clearly pencilled on the silvery blue, the outline of the trunk and larger branches only being visible. He was clad in a long white robe and dark mantle which partly enveloped his person and then, falling downwards, swept the ground in picturesque and magnificent folds. His robe was confined by a black girdle, down to which his snowy beard flowed and formed a fine contrast to his mantle and belt. His right hand rested on a harp, whose chords he now and then swept with his left, causing a few, sweet transitory notes to issue therefrom, which rose and swelled in an uncertain cadence and then died away at the distance.

As Ernest approached, he raised his hand, and demanded his name. When Alembert had satisfied this question he requested permission to sit beside him for a few moments that he might rest himself. The old man instantly complied and, after a short pause, asked him whence he came and the reason of his being in so unfrequented and lonely a place. Ernest related then all his adventures and by the time he had finished night had closed in, and the moon was risen. His host now arose and invited him to lodge for the night in his cave. Alembert gladly consented and they proceeded together to enter it. When they were seated at their frugal supper of roots, Ernest in his turn asked the old man to recount the circumstances of his life, which he did in the following manner.

'You have told me that your latter years have been spent among

167

fairies. I likewise abode for a short time with supernatural beings, but they were of a less gentle nature than those you have described. When very young, I determined to go and seek my fortune in the world. The [?portion] of the globe which I fixed upon as the first scene of my wanderings was Asia, and, accordingly, I embarked myself on board a ship bound for Odessa. In a few days we set sail and, after a prosperous voyage, arrived at that part of the Russian dominions. From thence I proceeded to Tcherkask,[5] where I halted a few days, and then went on to Good-Gard, a mountain in the Caucasus. Here I decided upon crossing that stupendous range alone, and, upon communicating my intentions to some of the natives, they solemnly warned me against such an enterprise, assuring me that many powerful genii held their courts among the snows of Elbruz and Kasbek.[6] These words I disregarded, and as soon as extreme fatigue would permit me I began to ascend the Good-Gard road, which with great difficulty I proceeded along for several days until I reached the towering Elbruz. During the whole of my journey this mountain had been partly hidden from me by the subject hills that surrounded it, but, on passing a gorge of the last of these, a full view of its tremendous magnitude burst upon my sight. It was a fair and sunny afternoon in autumn when I beheld the sublime vision, only separated from me by a lovely green vale, through which a branch of the Aragva wound its silent course. Never shall I forget that awful scene. The grandeur of its radiant summit majestically cleaving the skies; its yawning abysses and clefts sufficiently wide to engulf the world; and its immovable aspect, as if the base were fixed below the seas. As I gazed, suddenly the mountain trembled, the top rent asunder and an immense spirit arose from the horrible chasm thus produced. He raised his hand to heaven and uttered a cry which shook all Georgia. At this appearance I sank to the ground insensible, and when I recovered from my swoon I found myself in a vast cave, illuminated by an opening at the top through which a ray of light streamed. On looking round I perceived an iron door in the side of the cave, which I opened, and within there was a narrow passage tending downwards. I entered it and continued for several days, journeying as it led. At length I heard a dull noise like the roaring of the sea at a distance, and after a while found myself surrounded with green rushing waves. I went on among

[5]Tcherkesses, an autonomous region in the northern Caucasian area.
[6]Mt Elbruz (18,465 ft) and Mt Kasbek (16,545 ft), spelt 'Elborus' and 'Kasibeck' in manuscript. The Caucasus form the setting of several of Charlotte Brontë's tales of supernatural beings written about this time: see *Tales of the Islanders*, vol. 4, n. 10.
[7]A fabulous sea-monster, said to have been seen off the coast of Norway and to be capable of sucking down large vessels by the whirlpool it created.

them without fear or injury, but some strange and ghastly scenes saluted my eyes, for I was walking at the bottom of the ocean. Thousands of huge monsters lay there, glaring with fixed, solemn eyes through the tenebrous gloom. I saw the kraken fish[7] with its hundred arms, the great whale, the sea bear and others unknown on the earth. Voiceless they glided through the regions of eternal thunder and the black billows broke around them in the midst of loneliness and solitude. Unutterable were the feelings with which I viewed the foundation of the everlasting hills and beheld the trackless pathways of the sea. Useless gems glittered on every side, groves of coral begirt the rocks, myriads of pearls gleamed constantly around, and the most beautiful shells shone below my feet. As I walked onward a cavern opened before me, which I entered. At that instant a wave rose beneath and swept me swiftly down the abyss under the arches of a magnificent palace, larger than all the land which floats on the ocean's surface. There I saw [?coiled], in his own vast halls, that tremendous snake known among ancient Scalds[8] by the name of Jormandugar, who holds the earth girded in his coils. For many days I remained here and beheld sights which no mortal tongue can depict. Afterwards I returned to the cave in Elbruz, whence I was taken by the spirit who had brought me there. Since that time I have wandered in many regions of the earth and seen many wonderful things, and at length I retired to this valley, where I have now abode happily for twenty years.'

Here he stopped and Ernest thanked him for his narration, adding that he likewise wished to spend the remainder of his life in that lovely glen. The old man approved of his resolution and for many years they lived together in perfect tranquillity and peace.

C. BRONTË
May the 25, 1830

The Adventures of Ernest
Alembert, A Tale
By Charlotte Brontë
May the 25
1830

———

[8]Scandinavian poets, usually of the Viking period.

169

AN INTERESTING
PASSAGE IN THE LIVES
Of Some Eminent Men of the
PRESENT Time
BY LORD
Charles Wellesley
JUNE THE 18
1830
BY CHARLOTTE
BRONTË[1]

June the 17, 1830

I believe that in great houses few know more of family concerns than servants, and even in middling establishments the case is the same. As I am generally kind to grooms, valets, footmen, lackeys, etc., etc., they often make me their confidant, entrusting me with many important secrets, which by degrees has enabled me to amass such a quantity of information respecting almost every grandee in the Glass Town that if I chose I could unveil a scene of murders, thefts, hypocrisy, perjury and so forth which can scarcely be paralleled in the annals of any other city.

There are also many who have not waded so far or deep in the slough of criminality[2] but are nevertheless filthily bespattered with more petty sins such as deceit, meanness, toadism, underhand dealings, evil speaking, envy, etc. Of this latter class I purpose to make a selection, reserving the remainder for some future period, when I shall no doubt avail myself of the wonderfully extensive miscellaneous information I possess to enlighten the public mind still further on this pleasant subject.

I am aware (to use a cant phrase) that my disclosures will cause a

---

[1]Title on blue paper cover of manuscript, in HCL: Lowell 1(1); hand-sewn booklet of sixteen pages (5.3 × 3.7 cm.). Charlotte Brontë gives this manuscript a variant title in her *Catalogue of my Books*: 'An Interesting Incident in the Lives of Some of the Most Eminent Persons of the Age'.

[2]Compare *Macbeth*, III, iv, 136, and the slough of despond in *Pilgrim's Progress*: phrases of the juvenilia often echo Shakespeare and Bunyan.

very considerable sensation among those who are implicated in the various transactions to which I shall allude, but as I care about them, their views and actions just as much as my monkey, all their censures will pass by me with as little effect as the zephyrs in a hot summer's day fanning a sea-surrounded rock. I shall now proceed to the subject of my present volume.

Chapter the first

One warm and sunny afternoon in August 1829, I was reposing in one of the orange groves that adorn the luxuriant vale by which Babylon the Great is girdled. Oppressed by broiling heat, I plucked listlessly the golden fruit from a graceful bough which shaded me, and flinging the bright oranges into a cool artificial rivulent flowing past, I watched their course till intervening branches hid the crystal stream from my sight. Tringia lay at my feet, dissolved in peaceful slumber, dreaming no doubt that he was in his native shades of Chile gathering rich wild grapes clustered on every vine, or sporting with his hairy brethren among the old umbrage through which no glimpse of sky disturbs the profound twilight reigning for aye beneath the forest's shadow.

As I fried with heat under an African summer's sun, I continued casting up my eyes to a zenith more intensely brilliantly blue than the most flowless sapphire that ever sparkled in Golconda,[3] like a duck in thunder wishing for some cloud even though charged with a tropical tempest to variegate the monotonous azure. While thus I lay, I heard someone enter the grove and at the same instant perceived a gentleman in livery advancing towards me. On a nearer approach he raised his hat and addressed me familiarly as follows: 'Well, my lord, what is your opinion of the day? For my part, I'm on the point of being reduced to ashes with heat.'

'Oh,' said I, not wishing to coincide with him, 'it's tolerably cool, I think. You see I've been obliged to retire within this little close grove to keep myself even moderately warm.'

'Well,' returned he with a chuckling laugh, 'that's odd, and I've come here with the directly opposite purpose of shielding my head from the fervid sunbeams.'

Disgusted at his flippancy, I was on the point of ordering him to quit the place, but then, thinking that his presence might be productive of amusement, I ordered him to sit down at some distance from me. This

---

[3]Golconda: an ancient kingdom and city in India; famous for its great wealth, especially for the diamonds which were cut and polished there.

fellow was valet de chambre to the well-known author Captain T—,[4] and, as I had shown him kindness when in a destitute condition, he thought himself privileged to speak freely. He was, however, not of an ill disposition but, on the contrary, possessed a slight tincture of good nature and intelligence, for which latter reason he sometimes proved rather useful to me.

I asked him how his master was.

'Pretty well,' he answered, and then added slyly, 'If your lordship pleases, I could relate two or three little incidents respecting him which might entertain you for half an hour.'

I consented, and the substance of his narrative is as follows. I do not give his words but merely the sense attired in the garb that I conceive fittest.

Chapter the second

One morning last May as I was standing behind a tree in the avenue of my master's country house, a gentleman came riding up the road on horseback at a smart pace. When he drew nigh I perceived that it was Lieutenant B—,[5] Chief Librarian of the city. I stepped from my hiding place and did him obeisance. He asked if Captain T— was at home. I replied in the affirmative and at that instant my master appeared. They shook hands and appeared glad to see each other but I thought there was a thing in the librarian's squint eye (for he has but one) that showed harm in his head.

They both went into the house after ordering me to cover the horse. I did so and led it up and down the avenue afterwards, till Lieutenant B— returned. When I heard them coming I slipped over the hedge and laid flat down on the other side to listen what they would say, for I could not conjecture the reason of his coming here, which he had never been accustomed to do. They talked very low and nothing reached me but these words, which my master spoke as they parted: 'At the square at twelve at night? Very well, goodbye.' He then went back to the house and B— cantered away.

When it was 8 o'clock in the evening, I was sent for to Captain T—. I found him in his library. He ordered me to prepare in all haste for a journey to the Glass Town, where he was to go to attend a funeral that would take place there at midnight. I thought that an uncommon time

---

[4]Captain Tree (a pseudonym of Charlotte) is a famous Glass Town prose writer. In this manuscript especially, Charlotte Brontë has adopted the nineteenth-century practice of using capital letters only for people's names when referring to scandalous material.

[5]Lieutenant Brock.

for an honest man to be buried and my curiosity quickened me. In half an hour all was ready. We set off (for I went with him) and arrived at the city before eleven. He got out of his carriage at the Fetish Inn and there he left it with all his servants except me, whom he ordered to accompany him.

We proceeded through many narrow darksome streets till all at once emerging from these we came to a wide square surrounded by decayed houses, none of which seemed to be inhabited save one. In an upper chamber of that a light was burning. We went into it and passing up a ruined staircase entered a low garret where – behold! – the librarian was standing dressed in a cloak and mask. He whispered to my master and gave him the same sort of habiliments wherewith the Captain presently arrayed himself.

Then he said in a low voice, 'I dread to pass through the Great Square.'

'But it must be done,' replied Lieutenant B—. 'There is no other way to the cemetery.'

After this they both quickly descended the stair and I followed.

When they got out of the house, [?6] men came, all masked (but among whom I could plainly distinguish by their gait Sergeant T— and Sergeant B—, one of whom is a lawyer and the other a bookseller).[6] They bore with great difficulty a very long, wide and seemingly heavy coffin. Following this as mourners, we all proceeded at a slow pace toward the Great Square. In a short time we arrived at it. About 20 or 30 noblemen and generals were standing around the image laughing and conversing gaily. Among these I could easily distinguish your father, my lord, the Duke of Wellington. None of the others appeared to mind the funeral, which stole softly along in the shade of a lofty range of houses. He, however, without discontinuing a conversation he was then holding with a dark, tall, ugly man in uniform (whose name I afterwards learnt is General Bobadill[7]) cast a keen glance towards it, which after wandering over all the figures fully concentrated on T—. He shrank and trembled, but the Duke quickly withdrew his gaze and we moved onward. I cannot tell how many streets and lanes the procession traversed till it stopped at a house in Charles Row. There Sergeant B— rung a bell and in a few minutes his father, the great

---

[6]Sergeant Tree, son of Captain Tree, is the Glass Town's chief bookseller and publisher of the second series of *The Young Men's Magazine*. Sergeant Bud, son of Captain John Bud, the eminent political writer, is an unscrupulous lawyer.

[7]General Bobadill is based on the boasting, cowardly soldier Bobadilla in Ben Jonson's play *Every Man in His Humour* (1598); he also appears in Charlotte Brontë's following manuscript *The Poetaster*.

political writer,[8] came out. As he joined us I heard him say to the librarian, 'Magrass has taken the bribe.' Then all was silence.

We quickened our pace and, by the time St Andrew's clock struck one, had arrived at a huge black marble wall where was a brass gate, strongly locked and barred. This they knocked at several times without anyone appearing. Captain B— became impatient. He stamped and muttered, 'Has the scoundrel betrayed us?'

Just then the door of a little tower built in the wall opened and a man came forth. He ran down some steps and disappeared on the other side. Presently the gate was unbolted and we beheld a vast enclosed plain full of tombs and monuments. One of the graves were open. This we proceeded towards. It was a very deep vault full of chests. The coffin being let down and covered with earth, all went away except I and my master who stopped behind as watchers. We continued till daybreak without any disturbance and then quitted the yard also. A carriage which waited at the gate conveyed us to T—'s residence. When we arrived there, he commanded me to go to bed immediately. I obeyed but was unable to sleep, though very much fatigued, with thinking of what had occurred.

Next night we proceeded again to the cemetery. For about 2 hours no noise reached us and we were thinking of going home, but then we perceived 3 men sliding down the wall. One was Doctor H— B—, the other Young Man N— and the third Ned L—.[9] At this Captain T—, who is a great coward, turned pale and though he had sworn to defend the grave, slinked off, cowering behind a monument. I followed his example, not wishing to hazard my skin for what did not concern me.

As his myrmidons approached I heard N— say, 'The lad was buried here. I think he'll be middling fresh to some that you get doctor.'

They then began to uncover the vault and in a little time turned up the coffin. T— gave an involuntary squeal at the sight which startled the resurrectionists. They turned round and spied him trembling behind a stone. Ned dragged him out by the collar, while I crawled off unobserved to a more secure hiding place.

'How did you come here?' said H—. 'Speak or I'll dash this spade through your skull.'

'Never.'

'Hold him!' bawled N—. 'But look at this coffin! If I don't declare

---

[8]Lord Charles Wellesley (Charlotte Brontë's chief pseudonym) rarely passes up the opportunity of including his rival Captain John Bud (Branwell Brontë's pseudonym) in one of his scandalous tales.

[9]Doctor Hume Badey, Young Man Naughty and Ned Laury, Glass Town compatriots in body-snatching and dissection.

it's full of books instead of bones, and here's ever so many chests crammed with the same kind of traffic.'

'They're mine!' cried T——. 'And I've buried them here for safety.'

'That's a lie,' replied H——, after glancing over them. 'These books belong to the Public Library; you've stole them and buried them here for secrecy. I'll inform against you!'

'Oh don't!' exclaimed the Captain. 'If you will never tell anybody of this, I promise to procure you a living subject every week. Besides, Captain B——, Sergeant B——, Lieutenant B——, Sergeant T—— and Magrass the gatekeeper are all concerned as well as me in the affair and they'll have to be executed likewise.'

'Humph, I don't much care for that', answered H——. 'But as you say you'll get me a living subject once a week, I'll not tell. The first time however that you fail in the performance of that promise or in any way displease me your life is in my hands. Now be off.'

'I shall certainly mind,' rejoined T——, 'But remember, Doctor H——, that I also have found you engaged in not the most legal work. I have a tongue which can speak too.'

'It's safest to clap you sideway then,' said H——, and he struck him dead on the spot. Ned and N—— flung the books again into the grave and covered it up and they all quitted the yard carrying T—— along with them.

After this tragical scene had been acted, I emerged from my concealed situation and returned home, which my master did also in a few days; but I have since heard him say that he spent 2 days and 2 nights in Doctor H—— B——'s macerating tub.

Here my garrulous informant stopped, and after I had expressed my approbation of the ability with which he had related the affair, I left him to the solitary enjoyment of the sylvan shade within which he reclined.

After walking about a mile, I reached one of the green refreshing alleys bordered with majestic elms, limes or aloes which form public promenades for the highest circles of the metropolis. Here I beheld an assemblage of noblemen and gentlemen conversing together with great earnestness: Young Rogue, with the body of a male mandrill, the head of a jack and the dress of a buffoon; Old Rogue, the image of a hopeless insolvent; Young Bud, like walking parchment stuffed with straw or law, which you will; Old Bud, a bottle of [?elixir]; Sergeant Tree, an absolute ape; Captain Tree, conceit personified; Lord Lofty, a buck;[10] Old Rogue's youngest son, a promising youth; etc., etc. This motley throng with bent brows and self-important looks were evidently discussing no trifling topic. I perceived the Marquis of Douro, my brother, in the midst and overheard the following conversation between him and Lord Lofty.

Lofty: Well, my lord Marquis, have you heard of this little affair concerning the robbery of the Public Library?

Douro: Yes, it has surprised me, I own.

Lofty: Brock is taken and will, I hope, be put to the torture.

Douro: That would be most unjustifiable cruelty in his case. No blood ought to be shed, in my opinion.

Lofty: Well, but they might rack him. That instrument leaves a man whole as before though a little stretched. Ha, ha, ha, ha!

Here Arthur turned from him to Captain Tree, whom he accosted thus.

Duoro: Tree, you are, I think, more merciful; what would be your mode of procedure?

Tree: Kill the wretch outright without trial or question. He may accuse innocent persons as his accomplices in his crime.

I now stept forward and said, 'Aye, Tree! Kill him and all like him outright without trial or question. They might accuse such an innocent person as you, for instance, and witnesses are easily to be got who could swear to seeing you in company with him on a certain night going after a black coffin not filled with flesh and blood.'

Tree (reddening): What do you mean, sir?

Me: Many a thing.

I was going on but Arthur restrained me with, 'Charles, Charles, hush love.' He then took hold of my hand and hurried me away from the walk.

It was now evening and by the time we reached the palace, a flaming South African occident cast a transcendency of light over all the vast city that resounded with a loud murmur, and gloriously irradiated its stupendous tower, which rose encompassed with magnificent oaks now standing in undefined masses of darkness against a sky of gold. Far off the broad harbour lay dotted by innumerable white-sailed vessels. The ocean heaved in terrible beauty. Its mighty voice deepened with the hush of evening. A hundred streams of the vale pouring forth their emulous song were unheard amid that awful thunder, which rolled over the fading earth through an atmosphere of balm and fragrance. My brother and I stood on the terrace for a long time wholly absorbed in

---

[10]Probably Lord Macara Lofty, friend of Lord Charles Wellesley and Glass Town scoundrel who later becomes a leader of the Republican Rebellion.

admiration, till at length Finic[11] came to remind us that the dew was falling and colds abroad in the air.

Charles Wellesley

June the 18, 1830   C. Brontë

'The following strange occurrence'[1]

The following strange occurrence happened on the 22 of June 1830. At that time papa was very ill, confined to his bed and so weak that he could not rise without assistance. Tabby and I were alone in the kitchen, about half past 9 ante-meridian.

Suddenly we heard a knock at the door. Tabby rose and opened it. An old man appeared standing without, who accosted her thus:

Old Man: Does the parson live here?

Tabby: Yes.

Old Man: I wish to see him.

Tabby: He is poorly in bed.

Old Man: Indeed. I have [a] message for him.

Tabby: Who from?

Old Man: From the LORD.

Tabby: Who?

Old Man: The LORD. He desires me to say that the bridegroom is coming and that he must prepare to meet him; that the cords are about to be loosed and the golden bowl broken; the pitcher broken at the fountain and the wheel stopped at the cistern.[2]

Here he concluded his discourse and abruptly went away. As Tabby closed the door I asked her if she knew him. Her reply was that she had never seen him before nor anyone like him.

Though I am fully persuaded that he was some fanatical enthusiast, well-meaning, perhaps, but utterly ignorant of true piety, yet I could not forbear weeping at his words, spoken so unexpectedly at that particular period.

Charlotte Brontë
June the 22, 1830
6 o'clock pm
Haworth near Bradford

---

[11]The Marquis of Douro's elusive dwarf servant, said to be the offspring of a liaison between the young Douro and Sofala, a Mooress.

[1]Untitled manuscript fragment in HCL: Eng. 35.3; one page (9.4 × 4.2 cm).
[2]Ecclesiastes, xii, 6.

Charlotte Brontë

Leisure Hours[1]

I once knew a man who said he had been caught by fairies one night as he was travelling on a lonely moor, and that he had lived 5 years among them. He used often to relate his adventures to me, and some of them I yet remember though it is long, long since I heard them, being a mere child at the time. When I am sad and solitary without any cause, these and similar stories come into my mind, affording pleasant food for meditation, far pleasanter than any other sort in such moods. I am so now and therefore will set down on paper the first of his tales that comes into my head. Here is one.

A while after I was caught, all the fairies assembled among some wild hags to feast. 3 lambs they stole from a poor shepherd's flock as they were feeding beside him while he slept. These being slain served for the repast, and when it was finished they filled their cups from the rills of blood which had streamed from the lambs. Each drank; then they all seemed intoxicated with blood, dancing in the strangest attitudes and sending forth such terrible yells that I felt my heart tremble with fear.

Suddenly they flew at me, cast me to the earth and bound me with invisible chains, for though I felt a galling tightness round my limbs which restrained me from the smallest exertion of them, yet I could not perceive any link or band. When that was done, they delivered me to one particular fairy as his servant and slave forever. He accepted me. The rest, changing into a flock of crows, flew away. Then my master unbound me and commanded that I should follow him. But lo! at that instant, instead of a bright aerial creature with wings and robes of a dazzling splendour (not dazzling, at least, but fascinating, for the emerald never injures our eyesight), I saw an old man with a long brown ragged coat, crownless hat and stockingless feet.

I nevertheless obeyed in silence and we journeyed along a lonely path till sunset. Then a cottage chimney appeared over a green hill, and two or three tall trees were seen shaking their tresses over the thatched roof. At a turn of the road we came in sight of the door, before which was a little rustic girl and a boy, who held in his hand a bird's nest with four young ones. She was earnestly imploring him not to harm them, and he, deaf to her entreaties and tears, was just about to dash them on

---

[1]Manuscript fragment in BPM: B83; two pages (9.3 × 4.5 cm). The previous day, Charlotte Brontë wrote a long poem entitled 'The Evening Walk A Poem by The Marquis of Douro' (*Poems*, p. 99); in the preface Douro mocks his brother's 'emanations of leisure hours' and scorns his appeal to the reading public for their indulgence.

the ground when the girl prayed him to stop one moment, and running into the house presently came back with a piece of money. She offered it to him for the birds and, after a moment's reflection, he consented and then went away. Her eyes glistened with joy at the exchange and sitting down she said, 'It was all I had, but not too much to save your lives.'

After a few moments a woman came out of the house carrying a small bowl of lentils. She gave it to the child, and after bidding her to eat her supper went in again.

Then the fairy approached at a slow pace and said in a faint tone that he had eaten nothing that day and was ready to swoon with hunger. Tears started into the compassionate little cottager's eyes. She instantly presented him her untasted supper, which the fairy received thankfully, bowing at the same time. When he had devoured his homely meal, he appeared much revived, and rising prepared to go; but first he drew forth a large bag, heavy with gold, which he flung at her feet saying, 'Charity and mercy shall have their reward.' After this he disappeared with me, leaving her motionless as a statue with surprise.

Charlotte Brontë

June 29th 1830
I wrote this in the space of one hour.
Charlotte Brontë. June the twenty-ninth, eighteen hundred and thirty.

Charles Wellesley   CB

===

THE POETASTER

A DRAMA

IN

TWO VOLUMES

VOL

I

BY LORD CHARLES

WELLESLEY[1]

[1]On yellow paper cover of manuscript, in HCL: Lowell I(2); the following list of characters appears on the verso; hand-sewn booklet of sixteen pages (5.1 × 3.2 cm).

179

Characters

Duke of Wellington 1
Marquis of Douro 2
Lord Charles Wellesley 3
Henry Rhymer 4
Captain Tree 5
Jailer 6
Executioner 7
Sheriff 8
Crowd 9
[Bobadill] 10
[Finic] 11
[Tree's servant] 12

Volume
First
July 3, 1830

Scene the first

Rhymer[2] alone in a garret with a skylight at the top surrounded by shreds of paper and a few old books. Time: half past 11 at night.
Rhymer. How solitary is the scene! How sublime likewise! For does not the tenement take its attributes from that which abideth therein? Though this be a garret yet methinks one now holds lonely communion with his own gentle, nay, in some degree poetical, thoughts whose name will not decay with the frail shrine that it designates. Meek merit may pine awhile in obscurity, yes, and die, but from the grave of genius shall arise a fixed star ascending to the heaven of literature and there establishing its glory, in the midst of poets which are its fellows, to all

---

The Poetaster is Charlotte Brontë's only original full-scale play. (She translated Voltaire's *Henriade* on 11 August 1830.) It is based on Ben Jonson's *The Poetaster, or His Arraignment* (1601), in which he attacks the poetry of Thomas Dekker and John Maston. Jonson identifies himself with Horace at the top of a hierarchy of poets; so too, Charlotte Brontë identifies with the respected Glass Town writers Captain Tree and Lord Charles Wellesley (her pseudonyms) and satirizes the Romantic cliches and posturing of Henry Rhymer, who is actually the Glass Town poet Young Soult (pseudonym of Branwell Brontë). See Melodie Monahan, ed., 'Charlotte Brontë's *The Poetaster*: Text and Notes' (*Studies in Romanticism* 20, Winter, 1981, pp. 475–8), for a detailed discussion of the play's literary allusions.

[2]Probably based on Thomas Rhymer (1641–1713), poet and critic, known especially for his *Short View of Tragedy* (1692) in which he condemned *Othello*.

eternity. This delicate frame was not formed to bide all blasts. Soon must the feeble texture be rent under the proud swellings of that keen and sensitive spirit which it enwraps. Yet let me not now think on the neglect and scorn which has stung me too deeply. Rather would I contemplate yon pale moon, so softly shedding her silver light through my exalted casement. Would that I were laid in sweet forgetfulness of sordid mankind and their oppressive dealing, beneath the shade of some churchyard yew.[3]

Starting.

What's that? Oh! 'twas but the wind, mournfully serenading me on its passage through the sky. Methinks I will apostrophize it. Yea, the thoughts are crowding into my mind. Dost though, oh wind, look from thy ever resounding halls with pity on me, the Forsaken? Dost thou send forth thy blasts to moan thy compassion in my disconsolate ear? I will believe that thou dost, though no articulate response comes on the winged breeze. Let me see. That's good poetry. I'll versify it.

Thinks.

No, it'll not do. The thoughts should come spontaneously as I write[4] or they're not the inspirations of genius. But I'll try again.

Seizes a bit of paper, pen and ink.

How my hand trembled. I'm certainly in a consumption brought on by excessive drinki— study, I mean. Or was it only the effect of those fervid flashes from one of the Muses' lamps that just then passed through my mind?

Writes for some time. Then reads aloud.

    Silver moon how sweet thou shinest

    In the midnight sky;

    Hollow wind how wild thou whinest

    Through the vault on high.

Very pretty, especially the third line, I declare!

Writes again. Seems puzzled. Reads.

    The heavens, how beautiful they are,

    Majestically dark.

---

[3] Charlotte Brontë has recently read Edward Young's *The Complaint, or Night Thoughts on Life, Death, and Immortality*, a copy of which Mr Brontë owned (BPM: 526); she satirizes this and the Graveyard School of poetry in Rhymer's speeches. Rhymer also adopts the attitudes of the Romantic poet: compare, for example, Keats's attraction to death and fascination for the cold moon; and the following apostrophe to the wind recalls Shelley's 'Ode to the West Wind' and Coleridge's association of the wind with the imagination or poetic inspiration in such poems as 'The Eolian Harp'.

[4] Compare Wordsworth's definition of poetic composition in his Preface to *Lyrical Ballads*: 'the spontaneous overflow of powerful feelings'.

They are bedecked with many a star.
Oh, dear! I can't get on.
  Stamps and seems in a passion.
Shark, clark, bark, stark, mark, lark. Ah, that'll do.
  Writes again. Then reads.
    Fit sojourn for the lark.
Capital. How lucky to find it out. It came quite apropos.
  Writes for about half an hour. Then reads again.

When he comes to the realms on high,
Like wandering Savoyard,
To teach the people of the sky
The music of nature's bard,
How lightly sail the clouds along,
While he continues there
Electrified by his sweet song,
He even charms the air.
Presumptuous it would be of me
To tell his magic deeds,
For he enchants the very sea
  And spell-binds even reeds.
And th' nightingale, he has his powers,
  When singing 'neath the moon
In those soft melancholy hours
  Held sacred to night's noon.

Now that's really beautiful. The ideas are quite poetical. There is a sort
of tender softness about them, perfectly delightful. The Marquis of
Douro would like them,[5] I am certain. He shall see them, however, and
then I can judge if he is like the rest of human beings, selfish and
tasteless. Perhaps, too, I might see Lord Charles, whom they talk so
much about. And who knows, even in the end, whether if I could get
favour in the eyes of the two young princes, the Duke might not be
induced to condescend to an interview. Yes, yes. The thing is settled,
and by tomorrow's dawn— We shall see. We shall see. I am a good-
looking young man. The fire of genius lights up my eye and my whole
appearance will, I think, tend to interest them in my favour. That is, if
they have one particle of feeling or sense. I hope they will not be jealous
for my verses are every bit as good as theirs. And now, the pensive
moonbeams invite me to repose and to dream of the future greatness
that still awaits Henry Rhymer. I obey your gentle call, ye pearly

---

[5]The Marquis is known for his Romantic poems; 'he delights to dwell among pensive
thoughts and ideas' (see *Characters of the Celebrated Men of the Present Time*).

threads of light, and oh, like guardian spirits, watch by my couch this night!
Exit.

Scene the second

One of the private apartments in Waterloo Palace. Duke of Wellington. Marquis of Douro. Lord Charles Wellesley.
Duke of Wellington: Charley, what's the matter with you?
Lord Charles Wellesley: Trill has scratched my cheek with one of his paws, father, while I had him in my arms.
Duke of Wellington: Come here, kitten.
Taking it in his hands.
Now, Charles, I'll throttle it. Listen, how it squeaks!
Lord Charles Wellesley: Oh, don't, father! Pray, don't!
Duke of Wellington: Well, I'll let it live a little longer if it amuses you, Charles. And now Arthur, what are you looking so thoughtful about?
Marquis of Douro: Nothing, father.
Lord Charles Wellesley: Oh, father, I dreamt such an odd dream last night. Do you believe in dreams?
Duke of Wellington: No. Yes. No. Sometimes, Charley.
Lord Charles Wellesley: Badey believes in them so implicitly that I think if he were to dream that he ought to stop without a subject[6] 3 weeks together, he would do it. Indeed, I remember once—
Duke of Wellington:
Interrupting him.
You little wandering, giddy creature! I thought you were going to tell me your own vision and not Badey's.
Lord Charles Wellesley: So I was, father, but it has disordered my mind to such a degree that I can remember nothing. I dreamt I was walking in a large and pleasant garden, full of fruit trees and many fine flowers. As I was wandering about, I lost Tringia, who [was] with me, and proceeded to seek him. To this end, I entered a long green alley, shaded by high umbrageous trees. Then I continued, still advancing onwards while the trees grew thicker and darker. On looking up, I perceived the sky covered with very dark clouds. Large drops of rain began to patter among the branches, and the wind blew so furiously that the sound of rustling leaves resembled distinct thunder. On observing these signs of approaching tempest, I thought I called aloud for Tringia. And, just then, a little squirrel fell from a bough above my

[6]A body for dissection: see *Blackwood's Young Men's Magazine*, November 1829, n. 5.

head. It opened its mouth and spoke to me in a human tongue thus: 'Lord Charles, you want your brother? Follow me.' I did not feel astonished or afraid but did as the animal bade me. After walking about a couple of miles, we reached a little strong tower built in the very heart of the forest. At the gate an enormous dog lay couched. It had an iron collar on which was engraven: 'Surgeon. A bloody rascal.' At our approach, it gave a tremendous inward growl then suddenly calmed itself, while the portcullis of the castle was drawn up. We now entered a hall and, quickly passing through that, arrived at a parlour of unpretending pretensions and dimensions. The floor was covered with an English carpet. The chairs were of cane with chintz cushions. On a carved oak stand were some pots of wild flowers. A cheerful fire blazed in a polished brass grate, and in one corner of the room stood a harp with some sheets of music. But the objects which most attracted my attention were first a young lady whose figure I remember as well as if I now saw her before my eyes. She was about the middle size, not deformed, had a fair complexion, tolerably glossy brown hair—

Marquis of Douro: Charles, hold your tongue! Father, do make him be quiet.

Duke of Wellington: Go on, Charles.

Lord Charles Wellesley: Her eyes were largish, hazel-coloured and not wholly devoid of expression. Her nose, neither Roman nor Grecian but something between the two. Her mouth, small and smirking. Her chin, oval. Her cheeks, red, and her face, egg-shaped. Have I ever seen Miss Hume,[7] I wonder? She had a green frock on, a white silk scarf and white satin sandals. She was seated at a work-table busily engaged in the tedious manufacture of a point-lace veil. The other object that interested me was a shadowy form which, as well as I could discern it through the cloud of surrounding mist, something resembled you, Arthur. It stood with folded arms leaning on a window sill, ever and anon casting its eyes, which shone with still serenity through the vapour, on the other figure. All at once the door opened, and a little child entered that had wings on his shoulders and a bow and arrow at

---

[7]The first appearance in the prose manuscripts of Marian Hume, daughter of Sir Alexander Hume Badey and, later, second wife of the Marquis of Douro and mother of Arthur Julius Wellesley, Lord Almeida. Several days earlier on 29 June 1830, Charlotte Brontë wrote the poem 'Miss Hume's Dream' (*Poems*, p. 261) in which she describes Marian embroidering the same lace veil mentioned here and dreaming of the Marquis of Douro – in this case, of his death. At this stage in the juvenilia, Marian is depicted as Douro's first love, a gentle 'angel' always clothed in green and white; Lord Charles's tale here has been invented to embarrass his brother. Marian is based on Elizabeth Hume (eldest daughter of Dr John Robert Hume, surgeon to the real Duke of Wellington) with whom the real Douro fell in love at the age of fourteen; the secret romance continued for several years until the Duke abruptly terminated it.

his back. He had also an arrow in his hand, the point of which was thrust through a bleeding heart. He flew towards Miss Hume, the young lady I mean, and gave it [to] her, saying, 'Here is the Marquis of Douro's heart which I promised thee.' She smilingly accepted it and the child vanished. Then she took a pair of very fine scissors and began to cut and lacerate the heart dreadfully, smiling all the time, while the other form wept and sighed and moaned so pitifully that I awoke in the greatest trepidation. Now, father, wasn't it a strange dream, as I said?

Duke of Wellington: Yes, it was, love, and the effects of your relating it are still stranger. Look at Arthur, biting his lips, mumping his cheeks, pursing up his mouth and playing the fool.

Marquis of Douro: Charles, what nonsense you have been spending your breath about!

Lord Charles Wellesley: Arthur, what a charming book that was you spent your money about the other day. That I mean which you wrapped in the finest silk paper you could get, then in blue embossed, hot pressed satin paper, sealed in green sealing wax, with the motto, 'L'amour jamais'. But, who's this coming?

Enter General Bobadill.[8]

Duke of Wellington: Bobadill, what's the reason of your coming here without orders?

General Bobadill: May it please you, my lord, Sir Alexander Hume Badey has with the most consummate insolence horse-whipped me while in the discharge of my duty.

Duke of Wellington: Well, it certainly does please me, Bobadill. But what am I to do in the case?

General Bobadill: If Your Grace would just condescend to examine into the true merits of the circumstance, I should be satisfied.

Duke of Wellington: I have no objection to do that. Come along, then.

Exeunt Duke of Wellington and General Bobadill.

Marquis of Douro: Charles, why do you take such delight in tormenting me?

Lord Charles Wellesley: I don't take delight in tormenting you, Arthur, but then— somebody else is coming to interrupt us.

Enter Finic.[9]

Finic: I've been watching ever so long for your father to go out, my lords, as I want to speak with you, and I do dread appearing before him. His eyes are so constantly fixed upon me. He seems as if he wished to scrutinize my very heart!

[8]See *An Interesting Passage in the Lives of Some Eminent Men of the Present Time*, n. 7.
[9]See *An Interesting Passage*, n. 11.

Marquis of Douro: Well, Finic, what is it you wish to tell us?

Finic: There is a young man in the Servants' Hall who has a great desire to see you. He has been twice today and I can't get rid of him by any means.

Marquis of Douro: Do you know him?

Finic: I never saw him before.

Lord Charles Wellesley: What is he like?

Finic: He's a little man, very thin and pale, and has such a whining tone of voice, I can hardly bear to listen to him. He talked something about dedicating himself to the Muses.

Lord Charles Wellesley: A poetaster, I declare! Let's have him up to this room directly, Arthur.

Marquis of Douro: No. No, Charley. Suppose my father was to come in while he was here.

Lord Charles Wellesley: That would be an awkward accident certainly, but then I am sure he would not be angry if we were to tell the truth, namely, that he was here merely for our amusement and not instruction or example.

Marquis of Douro: Well, that may be, but still I have no inclination to enter into conversation with such a person. Besides Charles, you are not ignorant of the methods people of his grade use so that they may worm themselves into the favour of those they consider above them.

Lord Charles Wellesley: It's better that they should worm than snail themselves in, as in the latter case we should both run a chance of being marked with the slime of their hatred, brother. Now, do consent to let him come up!

Marquis of Douro: I can't, Charles. My father would not approve of it, I'm sure.

Lord Charles Wellesley: I'll go and ask him.

   Exit.

Marquis of Douro: What a foolish young being! I believe he wishes the poetaster to come only to hear himself flattered.

Finic: Please you, my lord Marquis, Lord Lofty wished me to tell you that he would feel much obliged if you would meet him on the Grand Terrace after parade tomorrow.

Marquis of Douro: Do you know what for, Finic?

Finic: I can't exactly say, but I believe it's as a friend. Your lordship, perhaps, hasn't heard of the quarrel between him and Earl Ryder.

Marquis of Douro: Yes, I have.

   Aside.

Now I shall be concerned in some duel. But, however, I'm determined not to go before I've spoken to my father about it.

Re-enter Lord Charles Wellesley.
Lord Charles Wellesley: My father says, Arthur, that he's not to come here, but we may grant him an audience in the antechamber.
Marquis of Douro: Very well. Now, Finic, show him up there. Stop a minute – if Lord Lofty asks you respecting the success of his message, say you know nothing about it.
Finic: Your orders shall be obeyed, my lord.
Lord Charles Wellesley: What message, Arthur?
Marquis of Douro: I'll tell you some other time, love, and now let us go to meet this dedicatee of the Muses.
    Exeunt

End of the first volume
of The Poet-
aster, a Drama
By C. Brontë
July 6th, 1830
CB

═══════

THE POETASTER

A DRAMA

IN

TWO VOLUMES

VOL

II

BY LORD CHARLES

WELLESLEY[1]

THE POETASTER

A DRAMA

BY

Lord Charles Wellesley

CHARLOTTE BRONTË

[1]On yellow paper cover of manuscript, in PML: Bonnell Collection; hand-sewn booklet of sixteen pages (4.9 × 3.2 cm).

187

RELATING TO THE
YOUNG MEN PLAY
in two volumes
PUBLISHED
BY NO
ONE
Published by Sergeant Tree
POSSESSED BY EVERY
ONE
Sold by all other booksellers
JUNE THE EIGHTH
1830
in the Chief Glass Town, etc., etc.[2]

Characters

Duke of Wellington 1
Marquis of Douro 2
Lord Charles Wellesley 3
Henry Rhymer 4
Captain Tree 5
Jailer 6
Executioner 7
Sheriff 8
Crowd 9

Volume
II
July 8, 1830

[2]Title-page, followed by list of characters on verso.

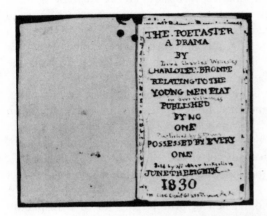

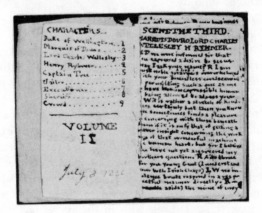

Plate 4 The initial pages of *The Poetaster*, volume II, a drama written by Charlotte
Brontë at the age of fourteen

Scene the third

Marquis [of] Douro. Lord Charles Wellesley. Henry Rhymer.

Marquis of Douro: We were informed, sir, that you expressed a desire to see us. May I ask your name?

Rhymer: I am, most noble Marquis and lord, overwhelmed with your boundless condescension in permitting such a one as me to have the inexpressible honour of being allowed to address you.

Lord Charles Wellesley: It is rather a stretch of kindness, certainly, but then, you know, one sometimes finds a pleasure in conversing with those beneath him, if it is only that of getting a better insight concerning the workings of that wonderful machine, the human heart. But, sir, I believe you have not yet answered my brother's question.

Rhymer: And it's [?true] for you, young gent. I understand you're both Irish chaps.

Lord Charles Wellesley: No insolence, brute! Respond in a respectful manner directly.

Rhymer:

 Aside.

The mine of envy is already sprung,[3] I perceive; but I'd better not irritate them too much. I'll withhold my cutting sarcasms for a time, until they are dumbfounded by the sublimity of what's coming.

 Aloud.

Prince, forgive me. The wings of poesy are ever expanded, and they often bear this unbending spirit by a sudden involuntary flight afar into the wild realms of imagination, and there, for a while, I bask amid the shadows of unearthly groves or the lights of superhuman vales, utterly forgetful of all that belongs to this external workaday world, till some biped's voice calls me again to these darksome regions to converse among those I dwell with in the body, not the mind. And now, most noble Marquis, I will reply to your interrogatory. My name is Henry Reaumier corrupted into Rhymer.

Marquis of Douro: Have you any particular business with me, Mr Rhymer?

Rhymer: My business, sir, is that you will hearken to the midnight emanations of a mind not, I trust, wholly unendued with the dew of that delightfully pensive genius which distinguishes yourself and the crystal drops are also faintly lit up by the joyous rays of heart-gladdening splendour that render Lord Charles Wellesley conspicuous among his fellow authors.

Lord Charles Wellesley: You'll excuse me, sir, but I've got a tremendous

---

[3]Compare Jonson's *Poetaster*; this image is common in Jonson.

headache, which makes the sound of a man's voice long continued extremely painful. Therefore, I would beg of you to cut the tails of your orations as short as possible.

Rhymer:
Aside.
The mine's exploding. He can't bear to hear of the grandeur of my ideas. I must be careful, however.
Aloud.
Your wishes shall be obeyed, my prince.

Marquis of Douro: Perhaps, sir, I could read the documents you speak of myself.

Rhymer:
Drawing some papers from his pocket.
There they are! Read and be electrified!
The Marquis of Douro and Lord Charles Wellesley take each of them a paper and commence the perusal of it, during which Lord Wellesley breaks into suppressed laughter several times and the Marquis of Douro bites his lip to prevent himself from doing the same.
Meanwhile Rhymer watches them in silence, and at length, as they lay down the papers, says thus:

Rhymer: There, you are astonished! What is your opinion?

Marquis of Douro: That you had better, sir, sit quietly down to some honest employment and think no more of writing poetry.

Lord Charles Wellesley: That you had better, sir, sit or stand down to any employment, whether honest or dishonest, and think no more of blotting white paper with unmeaning hieroglyphics by which a wicked taste of a useful article is incurred and much guilt laid to your account.

Rhymer: Envious rattlesnakes! How your two hearts are boiling in a black flood of jealousy! But genius will guard his cherished favourite. I fear not that filthy vomit you have just cast upon me. No, the dirt has fallen off and the robes of my innocence are whiter than before. Ay, wince, wince under my lash, like whipped turnspits as you are! But now I go, I go to try whether [?candour] has yet its abode with mortals. If this time I fail, then revenge, revenge! Ay, quiver, quail, quirk, but you shan't escape!

Exit with a rush.

Lord Charles Wellesley: There, Arthur, the wrath of a poetaster, terrible, terrific. I shall not be able to sleep tonight with the thoughts thereof. Hard adamant, why don't you weep, Arthur? It's dreadful to behold your tearless, stony agony. Weep, brother, weep. But listen, I hear the supper bell. We go, we go to try whether food has yet its abode with mortals. If this time we fail, why then revenge, revenge on the cook.

Exeunt.

191

Scene [the] fourth

Captain Tree alone in his study.

Captain Tree: How most people in general are deceived in their ideas of great authors. Every sentence is by them thought the outpourings of a mind overflowing with the sublime and beautiful. Alas, did they but know the trouble it often costs me for me to bring some exquisite passage neatly to a close, to avoid the too frequent repetition of the same word, to polish and round the period and to do many other things. They would soon lower the high standard at which our reputation is fixed. But still the true poet and proser have many moments of unalloyed delight while preparing their lucubrations for the press and the public. Witness my – who's this?

Enter a servant.

Servant: A gentleman wants to see you, sir.

Captain Tree: Show him up.

Servant: Yes, sir.

Exit.

Captain Tree: Who can it be, I wonder? Perhaps my brother, Swivel. He wrote me in his last letter from England that he intended to pay the incredible Glass Town a visit. Well if it is him, I could easily dispense with his presence. But he's coming, however.

Re-enter the servant with Rhymer.

Rhymer: May I be permitted to behold the greatest author of this or any other age?

Captain Tree: Yes, if you please, but first what do they call you and what's your will with me?

Rhymer: My name, sir, is Henry Reaumier; my business, to request your patronage and support. I am a friendless poet. Here are a few of the productions of my mind.

Captain Tree: Indeed, and am I to read them?

Rhymer: If so it pleases the king of all writers.

Tree takes the poems and begins to read. When he has finished he lays his hands on Rhymer's shoulders and says:

Captain Tree: Get along out of my sight, lad. You're the grandest poet I ever saw! What could induce you, a linen-draper's apprentice, to think of writing? Be off directly, I say!

Kicks Rhymer out of the room and slaps to the door.

Oh, how that noble profession is dishonoured! I could weep for very misery. Alas, alas, that those days would come again, when no one had even a transitory dream of putting pen to paper except a few choice spirits set apart from and revered by all the rest of the world; but it

cannot be hoped for, it cannot be hoped for. And some years hence, perhaps, these eyes will see, through the mists of age, every child that walks along the streets, bearing its manuscripts in its hand, going to the printers for publication. I am unable to abide these thoughts. But I will go to my friend Cowal's house and we will both drown our manifold sorrows in a glass of wine.
Exit half crying, half laughing.

Scene the fifth

A dungeon lighted only by a dim lamp. Rhymer stretched on a bed of straw in one corner.
Rhymer: Here, then, I am, a martyr to the cause of honour. By an unjust judge and jury I have been found guilty of the murder of one who had insulted me past all human sufferance. I should not have been worthy the name of man, if I had tamely submitted to such treatment, much less that of poet. But my heart's blood boiled high, and with the cold steel I slaked that raging fire of revenge. Yes, Tree's dying groans went like delicious music to the insatiate depths of my dark, unfathomable soul. The soft breathings of a harp hath not such power over the might of winds and seas howling, eddying, whirling, gulphing, roaring, thundering, crashing and dashing in the affrighted vast of earth and air, as had that harsh death-rattle and shriek over my mysterious spirit. It calmed it, and I felt that inexpressible thrill of delight which once, and only once before, have I experienced, when on a tempestuous night I stood all alone in the midst of a mighty desert, entranced, enwrapped, enfolded with the mantle of my own glorious thoughts and broodings. The yellings of a hundred ghosts arose on each successive blast that swept over the heath with wild, maniacal moaning. Oh, in that sublime solitude, how my heart beat and my brain throbbed, while I felt the blackness and ghastliness of midnight draw round me like a wall. I looked up. A dark, thick shroud wrapped the blue dome from mortal sight. I looked down. A tenebrious gloom concealed all objects with an impalpable but impenetrable veil. I heard the roar of unseen torrents and the hushed murmur of invisible groves. My strained eyeballs strove in vain to pierce this mist. A sense of suffocation came over me; I shook and trembled like a poplar in a wind-shaken wood. At that moment, a sudden silver light shone on the earth and revealed its features. Again I looked upward. The clouds were split asunder and the moon was shining from out a deep blue, star-spangled abyss in the heavens. Hark! There is the sepulchral bell tolling the dead hour of night. Now will my fate soon be decided: whether I am to live or die. If it should be to die—

193

Oh, that thought 'tis unendurable. 'The knell, the shrowd, the mattock, and the grave.'[4] To mount the scaffold, to feel the adjustment of the rope, the withdrawal of the bolt – I cannot bear the idea! Hark, again. He comes. He comes, the pronouncer of my destiny.

Enter the jailer.

Jailer: Now, lad, come along with me.

Rhymer: To life or death?

Jailer: To be hung. Tree shows no sign of life and the time is expired.

Rhymer:

With a shriek.

Then my doom is fixed!

Jailer: Aye, to be sure.

Rhymer: And to complete the tragedy, it is to be acted at midnight.

Jailer: At midnight! What are you talking of? It's just struck twelve at noon. Most people are taking their lunches now, I reckon, while you are lying in bed. Get up, lazysides, and take your swing. It'll be good exercise!

Rhymer: Iron-hearted man, is it thus you talk? But I must now prepare to meet my fate. Hitherto I have supported myself like the great Socrates and let me not fall off at the end.

Jailer: Yes, when the scaffolds draw you'll fall a good many feet, lad. But what can induce me to stand shilly-shallying with you here so long? Come, I say, this minute.

Exeunt together.

Scene the sixth

The execution yard. Rhymer on the scaffold. The hangman and a crowd of people.

Rhymer: Gentlemen, I have now related to you my innumerable wrongs. Pity, I know, is overshadowing you with her wings and taking up her abode in your hearts. I desire not vengeance on my relentless persecutors. All I ask is sympathy and compassion. If you will grant me that, then shall I die in peace. If not, my own injured innocence shall still be a rich reward for the tribulation I have gone through in this life. Gentlemen, fare you well. I leave you, as a legacy, my writings.

Voice [from the crowd]:[5] Thank you lad. They'll do to light our pipes.

Rhymer:

Enraged.

[4]Edward Young, *Night Thoughts*, Night IV, 1.10.
[5]'Voice' cancelled in manuscript and speech in brackets.

Have I still enemies? Wretches, take my curse and malediction on your guilty heads, and Thou, oh Geni—
Executioner: Stop, lad. Here's the rope.
Rhymer: Have mercy on me, for one instant!
Executioner: Nay, I won't. You shall have it now.
Rhymer:
Falling on his knees.
Mercy! Mercy! Save me, but for a little—
Executioner: Not I, marry.
Rhymer: I cannot die! I cannot die! Oh, pardon and compassion! I'll be Tree's slave forever, if you will but save me from death.
A sheriff stepping forward.
[Sheriff]: Mr Executioner, do your duty.
Executioner: I'm going to. Do you think I care for the squeaking of such a ratton as him?
Crowd: Huzza! Huzza!
Rhymer: I'm wicked. I am wretched. I am whatever ye will, but then, ye hard hearts, am I not a human being still?
Sheriff: Mr Executioner, make haste and let the drop fall. I never had to do with such a restive criminal in my life!
Executioner fastens the noose round his neck and draws the nightcap over his eyes, amidst great struggles and resistance from Rhymer.
Executioner: Now, then, must I draw away the bolt?
Sheriff: Yes— but, stop, stop a minute! Somebody approaches.
Voice from the crowd: Let the poor being loose.
Sheriff: It's Lord Wellesley. Hold, Mr Executioner.
Lord Charles Wellesley:
Springing from among the people.
Tree has at length been brought to life again[6] and Rhymer's pardoned. Unchain him quickly, hangman.
Executioner: He's hardly worth it, my lord.
Takes the rope from Rhymer's neck, who instantly flings himself at the feet of Lord Charles.
Rhymer: Thanks! Thanks! Thanks, generous prince.
Lord Charles Wellesley: Arthur and I have obtained your pardon on condition that you should write no more but immediately take to some useful employment.
Rhymer: That condition shall be, on my part, punctually fulfilled for this poetizing has brought me nothing except misery and mortification.

[6]No doubt as a result of Dr Hume Badey's 'macerating tub': see *An Interesting Passage in the Lives of Some Eminent Men of the Present Time.*

But what shall I take to?

Lord Charles Wellesley: If you like, you may be my under-secretary, which post is a perfect sinecure with a salary of £200 a year.

Rhymer:
  Kissing Lord Charles Wellesley's feet
My gratitude has no tongue.

Lord Charles Wellesley: Now, come. Follow me.

  Curtain falls.

July 12, 1830

FOURTH VOLUME OF TALES OF THE ISLANDERS[1]

FOURTH VOLUME OF THE TALES OF THE ISLANDERS

CHAPTER THE FIRST. VOLUME 4
[The Three Old Washerwomen of Strathfieldsay][2]

One fine autumnal evening the Duke of Wellington was on his way from London to Strathfieldsay. He had just passed through the village and had entered a narrow bridle-path leading to the park gate. Here he dismounted from his horse and, leading old Blanco-White[3] by the reins, proceeded at a leisurely pace onwards. It was, as I have said, a fine evening in autumn: the air was warm and breezeless, the sky covered with high light clouds except where here and there a few pale, soft, blue streaks appeared on the hazy horizon. The sun had just set. The snails were crawling forth from the hedge-side to enjoy that refreshing dampness which immediately precedes dusk at this period of the year. Scarcely a leaf fell from the oaks and hawthorns bordering the

---

[1]Cover of *Tales of the Islanders*, vol. IV, in NYPL: Berg Collection; formerly a hand-sewn booklet of sixteen pages (9.9 × 6.3 cm). The pages have since been separated, mounted and bound with those of vols I, II and III.

[2]The chapter titles in brackets are those given by Charlotte Brontë in her *Catalogue of my Books*, 3 August 1830.

[3]The historical Duke's famous charger, which he rode at the Battle of Waterloo and which is buried at Stratfield Saye, was called Copenhagen.

path, for the dark hue of their foliage had hardly begun to mellow with the waning season. The only sounds audible were the noise of an occasional lady-clock[4] humming by the trickle of a rill, as it flowed invisibly down [an] ancient cart rut (now unused) hid by dock leaves, wild vetch grass and other hedge plants with which the road was completely overgrown. A hill rising on one hand concealed from view the Hall with its extensive parks, pleasure grounds, gardens, woods, etc., situated in a broad and delightful valley sloping far down on the other side.

As the Duke walked quietly forward, he suddenly heard a murmuring sound, like the voices of several people conversing in an under-tone, a little in advance of him. He stopped and listened, but was unable to understand what they said. At a few paces farther on, a turn in the path brought in sight the figures of 3 old women seated on a green bank under a holly, knitting with the utmost rapidity and keeping their tongues in constant motion all the while. Stretched in a lounging posture beside them lay Little King, languidly gathering the violets and cuckoo-meat which grew around. At the Duke's approach he started up, as likewise did the old women. They courtesied and he bowed much after the fashion of a dip-tail on a stone. He then, after a sharp peal of laughter from his companions, addressed the Duke thus.

'Well, Duke of Wellington, here are three friends of mine, whom I wish to introduce to you. They lived for some time as washerwomen in the family of the late Sir Robert Peel, Bart, who respected them so much that in his will he remembered them each for twenty guineas. After his death, however, the present Bart[5] turned them away, together with several other antiquated but faithful servants of his deceased parent, to make room for the modern trash of fopish varlets that now constitute every gentleman's establishment. Thus they are now cast on the wide world without shelter or home, and if you would consent to take them into your service it would be conferring a great obligation on me as well as them.'

'I am not much accustomed to engage servants,' replied His Grace, 'but you may take them to my housekeeper, and if their characters will bear the old lady's scrutiny, I have no objection.'

---

[4]Lady-bird. Charlotte Brontë's description here of oaks, hawthorns, docks, violets and cuckoo-meat (wood sorrel) is more reminiscent of Shakespeare's lyrics than of Hampshire in autumn.

[5]Sir Robert Peel, at this time a prominent member of Wellington's Cabinet, inherited his baronetcy on the death of his father, a wealthy cotton manufacturer, on 3 May 1830. Peel was often at loggerheads with Wellington, and Charlotte Brontë's criticism here probably reflects her dislike of Peel's antagonism towards her hero.

'Very well, that's right, Duke of Wellington,' replied Little King, much pleased.

The Duke then remounted his horse and proceeded at a smart trot onward, wishing to escape from the company of his new acquaintance. They, however, stuck close to him and continued by his side, talking and laughing and trying to draw him into conversation incessantly. In a short time they turned the hill and, going rapidly down a long inclined lane, entered the vast wood which forms a boundary to one side of Strathfieldsay Park.

After threading the puzzling mazes of the labyrinth which leads to Seringapatan's, Orderly-man's, Jack-of-all-trades' and Gamekeeper's cottages, they stopped at the door of Seringapatan's and the Duke, stooping his head to avoid the huge, thick branches waving around, lifted the latchet. Seringapatan instantly sprang out and, bowing low, without waiting for his master's orders flung open the park gate. His Grace then bent aside and whispered something in the old man's ear, commanding him to detain Little King and his comrades until he reached the Hall. Seringapatan bowed again, lower than before, and the Duke, tickling Blanco's flanks, galloped swiftly off.

'If you please, will you step into my kitchen a minute and rest you?' said Seringapatan.

They thanked him and without further ceremony walked in. It was a small apartment, neatly whitewashed. An oaken dresser, furnished with the brightest pewter and Delfware, covered one end. Above it was suspended a highly polished musket and sword. Several ancient books were carefully piled in a black oak kist. Two substantial armchairs stood at each end of a hot, blazing fire and, opposite the window seat, a number of stout 3-legged stools were ranged in a row. The floor and hearth were as clean and white as scouring could make them. Mrs Left Seringapatan sat mending her husband's stockings by a round deal table. She was clad in a dark-green stuff gown, with snow-white cap and apron, and looked as sedate as if she had been 60 instead of 25.

When Little King and the old women entered, she rose and begged and them to be seated. They complied. After chatting a while, she got up again and went out, but in a short time returned with a plateful of rich currant cake and a bottle of perry.[6] These dainties she invited her guests to partake of, which they did, of course, and then prepared to depart. Seringapatan, knowing that by this time his master had arrived at his seat, opened the door and permitted them to go. They pursued their way up the park without stopping, for night was fast coming on,

[6]Drink from the juice of fermented pears (*OED*).

198

and the moon, pouring her light on the long groves and alleys which in dark, obscure lines stretched far over the undulating prospect, was climbing the mild, autumnal heavens amid freckled, downy clouds and dimly visible stars.

It happened that Lord Charles Wellesley had that day been taking one of his wild rambles over his father's domains and he was now returning homewards. At a distance he saw the three old women with their conductor. Being fond of company, he made haste to overtake them, but, as he approached, his volatile mind changed and he determined to walk close behind and remain a concealed listener to their conversation, promising himself much amusement from the scheme. In this, however, he was deceived, for voluble as they had been while in Seringapatan's cottage, they now became perfectly silent.

In about a quarter of an hour, they reached the deep, rapid stream which runs through the grounds. Its banks are shaded by willows and larches, and the long rays of moonlight trembling through the high boughs fell with sweet serenity on the turbulent waves, producing a soothing contrast to their impetuous and dark ridges following each other in quick succession down the waters. A grassy mile extending to the opposite bank formed a kind of natural bridge and over this Lord Charles supposed they would go, so he halted a while to observe them. They, however, to his utmost astonishment, glided noiselessly into the midst of the river and there, turning three times round amidst the shivered fragments of brilliant light in which the moon was reflected, were swallowed up in a whirlpool of raging surges and foam. He stood a moment powerless with horror, then springing over the mound dashed through the trees on the other side and, gaining the open path, beheld Little King and the three old women walking whole and sound a few yards before him. More surprised than before, he viewed them in silence for an instant and then concluded that they were other fairies whom Little King had brought with him to this earth. He strove to satisfy himself with this conjecture, but, notwithstanding his endeavours, he still felt an uneasy, vague, and by no means pleasant, sensation when he looked at their little sharp faces and heard the shrill, disagreeable tones of their voices (for they were now chatting away as merrily as before) for which he was unable to account.

At length they arrived at the mansion. Little King knocked at the Great Gate, the folding doors rolled back, and a blaze of red light burst forth, illuminating the grand flight of broad, sculptured steps and the dark avenue for a great distance off. A huge fire was burning in the wide hall chimney and every branch of the brass lustre bore a flame. The servants were gathered together at supper. Gamekeeper sat at the head of the table, Jack-of-all-trades officiated as waiter and Orderly-man as vice-president. Peels of laughter rose every instant to the lofty roof, and the oaken rafters trembled.

Little King and his companions entered. The doors were shut again and Lord Charles was left to the darkness and solitude of night, which formed a wide difference to the revels he had just caught a glimpse of. After a moment's thought, he cleared the steps with a bound, and springing along the path came to a door in the wall, which he opened with a key he took from his pocket, and then entered a small, green plain, delightfully planted with many beautiful shrubs and trees and watered by a fountain in the midst. This he presently crossed, and ascending a high flight of balustraded, marble steps, reached a terrace that led to an arched, glass door. He opened this also and a small, elegantly furnished room became apparent, which was his own and his brother's private apartment.

Arthur was sitting by the fire with his head resting on his hand, lost in deep abstraction. The moment Lord Wellesley entered he started up exclaiming, 'Oh! Charles, I have been listening and wishing for you a long time and now I am rejoiced at your arrival! Come, sit down, and let us have our usual pleasant conversazione before retiring to rest.'

Charles met his brother's welcome with equal cordiality and, flinging himself on the warm Persian rug, began to relate his adventures of that day, in which employment I must for the present leave him and return to Little King and the 3 old women.

After supper was over, he requested leave to speak with the housekeeper and was informed by one of the maids that she had withdrawn for the night and they dared not now disturb her, but that tomorrow he might procure an interview for himself and friends. This answer by no means pleased the dames, who were beginning in a loud shrill cadence to express their dissatisfaction, when Old Man Cockney coming in, they, together with the servants, were driven off to bed.

The next morning they rose with the sun and were only prevented from breaking in upon Mrs Daura Dovelike's[7] rest by a chamber-maid, who met them at the door and warned them of the consequence of their intrusion, namely instant dismissal without an audience. It was with difficulty they were persuaded to wait till nine o'clock, so great was their anxiety to have the affair of engagement settled. At that time Mrs Daura sent word that she was ready to receive them. On proceeding to her apartment, they found her seated at breakfast in an armchair, with

[7]Thought to be modelled on Miss Elizabeth Branwell, the Brontë children's aunt who came to live with them after their mother's death.

her feet on a cushioned footstool. Her stiff figure was invested in an old-fashioned, bustling, black silk gown, with cap and ruff starched to the consistence of buckram. As kind Fortune would have it, she happened this morning to be in good temper, so after bidding them sit down and asking a few questions, she agreed to take them before her lady, the Duchess of Wellington.

When they had passed through a long corridor, gallery and antechamber, they came to her private sitting-room. It was ornamented after a most splendid but nevertheless simple and unostentatious style. The Duchess was engaged at her usual charitable employment of working for the poor.[8] She was attired in a rich robe of dark crimson velvet, almost entirely unadorned except one bright diamond which fastened the belt. The redundant tresses of her fine, brown hair were confined in a silken net, over which gracefully waved a single white ostrich feather. Her face and figure were extremely beautiful and her large, hazel eyes beamed with expression. But the principal charm about her was the gentleness and sweetness ever visible in her countenance. It seemed, and it was, impossible for her to storm and frown or even be angry, for if anything wrong was committed by her servants or dependants, she only looked grieved and sad and not dark or lowering.

When they entered, the Duke was also in the room conversing with his lady, and the housekeeper, on seeing him, courtesied respectfully and was going away when he called her back and, quitting the apartment, left them to transact business without being under the embarrassment of his awe-inspiring-minister-general-and-clerk-confusing presence. After a short conversation, it was settled that the 3 old dames should act for one month on trial as washerwomen and laundry-maids and that if during the prescribed time they behaved well, they should then be taken into permanent service at wages of 10 guineas per annum each. When this was fixed they left her ladyship's, equally delighted with the mild condescension of her manner, the enchanting benignity of her smiles and the unexpected success of their application.

The next day they commenced the performance of the duties of their office, which they continued for some weeks to execute with equal punctuality, diligence and sobriety, but not without many quarrels

---

[8]Kitty Pakenham, the real Duchess of Wellington, was known for her charitable works, her simple dress and lack of ornamentation. Lord William Lennox described her as 'amiable, unaffected and simple-minded ... generous and charitable', *Three Years with the Duke, or Wellington in Private Life*, by an ex-aide-de-camp (London, 1853) p. 270. As mistress of Stratfield Saye, her chief concern was for her servants and the poor.

among themselves, often ending in ferocious fights where tooth, nail, feet and hands were employed with equal fury. In these fracas Little King (who always continued with them) was observed to be exceedingly active, inciting them by every means in his power to maul and mangle each other in the most horrible way. This circumstance, however, was not much wondered at, as his constant disposition to all kinds of mischief was well-known, and he was considered by every member of the House of Strathfieldsay, not excepting the Duke himself, more as an evil brownie than a legitimate fairy.

Lord Charles had not revealed to anyone the strange incident, of which he was witness, that happened on the first night of their arrival. His curiosity, of which he naturally possessed a considerable share, strengthened. He watched them narrowly, but nothing occurred further to warrant the suspicion of their being supernatural creatures. One afternoon, he went alone to that part of the river's banks whence he saw them walking on the waves. After wandering some time among the trees gathering wild roses, blue-bells and other field flowers, he lay down on the green turf and fixed his eyes on the blue sky, peering at intervals through the thick masses of overhanging foliage. The sounds that saluted his ear were all of a lulling, soothing character: only the soft murmuring of the water flowing, the distant cooing of turtle-doves from the groves or the whispering of wind in the trees. By degrees his eyes closed, a pleasing sensation of secluded rest glided through him, and he was gradually passing away into a profound, balmy slumber when suddenly an articulate voice came up on the breeze, which said, 'Meet us at midnight in the corridor.' He started up and listened. The sound had died off and no trace or tone of it remained in the wild, woodland music breathing around.

'I am bewitched,' he exclaimed aloud. 'Those beings have certainly cast a spell over me, but I will keep the assignation notwithstanding for I can do so without anyone being acquainted with it as Arthur is at London.' He then rose and walked home.

During the remainder of the day a most unusual expression of thought appeared on his countenance, and at night he retired early to his chamber. He sat pensively alone, reading by a table, till every noise ceased and not a voice or footstep was heard to break the dead hush reigning throughout the whole house. Then the dull, heavy toll of the great hall clock fell on his ear: twelve times the hammer resounded. He got up and extinguished his taper and quitted the room by a secret outlet opening to the corridor. His eyes glanced with an involuntary shudder down the long vista; all was veiled in impenetrable darkness. At length a bright light appeared moving among the pillars. He advanced onwards. It receded slowly from him, but he still followed. After a while he saw it ascending a stair which wound up the great round tower. There he bent his course till he gained a huge door where the light vanished and left him alone. The door, with a harsh jawing din, opened, and a vast, lofty chamber became visible, faintly illumined by long, glimmering rows of torches, which cast on all sides a bloody and terrific light. It had no roof, but the sky above seemed as if a starlit and cloudy dome. A huge, black canopy in the midst swayed to and fro in the wind that rushed through the open top, and underneath were set 3 coffins, each of which held a shrouded corpse.

Lord Charles advanced towards them, and turning aside the winding sheets perceived that they were the 3 old washerwomen. He trembled with dread, and at that instant a loud laugh rang in his ears. He looked up and beheld Little King and Queens standing beside him. One of them gave him a hearty slap on the shoulder saying, 'Charles, don't be frightened, they were only our enchantments.'

He opened his eyes at this salute, stared around, wondered [and] became bewildered, for lo! he was lying in the pale moonlight on the river's bank and no living creature near. He immediately ran with all haste to the house, and, when he had arrived there, repeated his tale with eagerness to his father, mother and brother, whom he found together in the private parlour. They laughed at it, of course, but on enquiry it was found that the old women had been absent from Strathfieldsay since the morning. Investigation was set on foot, but no clue by which they could be traced was discovered. One country-man said that he had observed them about noon on the moor with Little King, but that he had occasion to turn away his eyes for an instant, and, when he looked again, he saw Little King and Queens standing in the same place, but not the smallest mark of them. This was all that could, after the strictest search, be gathered, and they have never been seen or heard of from that time to this.

Charlotte Brontë   July 14, 1830

CHAPTER THE SECOND. VOLUME 4TH
[Lord C. Wellesley's Tale to His Brother]

It was a sweet July evening when the Marquis of Douro and Lord Charles Wellesley lay stretched on the verge of a lofty precipice, silently beholding the prospect around. Majestic forest trees, waving above their heads, formed with woven, intermingled boughs, a sylvan roof to the natural carpet of grass and flowers spread beneath. Far down, hundreds of green oaks and sycamores clothed the rocky and almost perpendicular shelving abyss, in the dark super-verdure with which their branches were now arrayed, and from the profound depth below arose the voice of a concealed torrent, hid by the gathering obscurity of dusk, which was there heightened because of the gulph into which the sides of the precipice sloped that lay beyond the reach of the uncertain light lingering on the horizon after sunset. No sound, save that, dissipated the twilight sensation of stillness with which every passing breath of wind was charged, until the Marquis, taking a guitar that lay by his side, swept its chords till every string vibrated in unison and then played an old, mournful air which, sweeping over the broad landscape, was answered from a great distance by the same tune.

'There, listen to Marian's[9] reply,' exclaimed Lord Charles.

Arthur listened attentively, but the music and its echoes in a little while died softly away. They both remained silent for some time again. Their eyes were fixed on the east where a pale light, spreading over the sky, began to herald the moon's advent. At length, like a silver shield, she heaved slowly up among stars and clouds and sat like Empress of the Night on a throne of blue hills which bounded the orient expanse of scenery.

'It is surely impossible for that orb of light to be a world like ours,' said Arthur, as the splendour of its beams shone around him.

'Not at all, my dear brother,' replied Lord Charles laughing. 'If you like, I'll tell you a tale concerning it, while we sit idly here.'

'Do, Charles, you know I always enjoy your stories, particularly when I'm melancholy, as I happen to be just now. Begin, love, I am ready.'

'Well, I will directly, but first, where's my ape? Tringia! Tringia! Oh, here he comes. Now, Tringia, sit down under that branch of underwood. There are some nuts and blackberries to amuse yourself with, and you must be more quiet than a dove while I divert Arthur's attention from the inhabitant of that pretty house which you may see yonder, Tringia, surrounded by a garden and plantation and— lo! What do I see stooping amid the flowery parterres of that garden? An object clothed all in white! It cannot be, yes, it is Marian Hume! And now that I look better through this small opera-glass, she is watering the very rose-tree that Arthur gave her from the greenhouse and planted there with his own hands, kind youth that he was. Yet, and there is her harp, standing by the bower, from which a few minutes ago she played that enchanting air.'

'Charles, are you going to tell me this story or not?' said Arthur,

[9]Marian Hume: see *The Poetaster*, vol. 1, n. 7.

apparently wishing to draw off his attention.
'Yes, I am, brother,' replied Lord Wellesley, and he began as follows.

Once upon a time, there lived in Georgia upon the banks of Silver Aragva, which washes the feet of mighty Elbrus, an old man named Mirza Abduliemah. He abode all alone in a solitary hut far from the habitations of men, the nearest hamlet being twelve miles distant. His occupation was that of a woodcutter, an easy business was for one who lived in the heart of Georgia's forests, and he likewise gathered and sold the fruit of chestnut-trees. Accustomed from his youth to the vast solitudes of Caucasus's giant mountains, he needed not the society of human beings, but loved rather to walk in the vales of young vines and lindens which smile round the boarders of Aragva, to gaze at the wonderous ravines rent in the stupendous sides of icy Kasbek or to view in mute astonishment the awful form of good Gara,[10] towering aloft and raising its snow-crowned head afar into the deep azure of his native skies.

One evening, as he returned homewards, weighed down under the burden of sticks which he had gathered in a wood 3 miles distant from his hut, he sat him down in a little, green glen between two rocks. The sky overhead was bright, cloudless and beautiful. The horizon round about was clear as liquid amber and the light which streamed from it was of the purest golden hue, enriching the summits of the coniform hills with a faint glow of orange that divested the snow of that cold, deadly aspect which would ill have harmonized with the transparency of warmth that tinted every other object. The aged Mirza felt himself touched with the beauteous prospect, and, kneeling, he turned towards Mecca, said his sunset prayers to Mahomet, and then thanked the one Almighty God for his goodness in creating such a profusion of fair and lovely scenes merely for ungrateful man's pleasure and recreation. When he had finished, he rose, resumed his bundle of faggots, and casting a last look at the glorious horizon he prepared to quit the glen. But what was his surprise on beholding a black, even line drawn around the pellucid heavens like a zone. It rose slowly up, coiled itself in rings

[10]Probably Shkara, 17,040 ft; with Mt Elbruz and Mt Kasbek (which Charlotte Brontë spells 'Elborus' and 'Kasibeck'), it is one of the highest peaks of the Caucasus and of Europe. Charlotte also spells the River Aragva, which flows south of Kasbek, incorrectly (namely 'Aragua'). Her spelling indicates that she is probably working from memory, recalling a geography lesson, newspaper article or old atlas; compare *A Description of the Duke of Wellington's Small Palace on the Banks of the Indiva*, n. 3. Gara, Elbruz and Kasbek are again mentioned in the following *Young Men's Magazine* for August 1830 ('Lines to the River Aragva'); see also *The Adventures of Ernest Alembert*.

and unfurled, with a noise like the concentrated winds of heaven, two dark dragon pinions, which shadowed the west as if the obscurity of thunder clouds hung over it. For a few moments it wavered between the vault of heaven and the globe of earth, then gradually descended. Mirza shook like one palsy-stricken, but how was his fear heightened when he felt himself drawn powerless towards it. He prayed, he shrieked, he called on the name of Mahomet in vain; still, like iron before the magnet, he continued his charmed course upward. Swifter than light he fled to the sky. On, on, for days and nights, till the moon grew larger than the earth to his eyes.

At length, overwhelmed with dread, he fell into a long swoon, and, when his orbs of vision were released from the bondage by which they were held fast closed and sealed, he was in a land the like of which no man ever before saw. Nothing was to be seen but black mountains, higher than the highest on earth, vomiting forth floods of fire and clouds of smoke, nothing to be heard but the roaring of internal flames. The ground quaked constantly under him and was continually rending in every direction, and from the ravines fresh streams of red, burning liquid burst boiling forth and overwhelmed everything near.

'I must die, I cannot live,' he exclaimed aloud, while the cold sweat of terror fell in large drops from his writhing visage. 'O Mahomet! O Allah! Save thy servant! What horrid crime has he committed thus to die the death of an infidel!'

'Squilish squilli keriwes Nevilah!' exclaimed a sharp, shrill voice above him.

He looked up and beheld a creature standing on the point of a rock surrounded by several others of a similar form. But how shall I describe its shape? To what being shall I liken it? It was seven feet in height, stood on legs that resembled branches of trees, its eyes were two holes in a square block that formed its head. Its mouth was invisible, except by a pucker in the rugged skin when shut, but when open it was an oblong hole displaying 3 rows of brown teeth as sharp and slender as pins. Its arms were so long that from the elbows downward they rested on the ground. It, with the others, cleared the rock at one leap and alighted near Mirza. They seized and bound him with long scarfs that hung on their heads and afterwards remained for about half an hour examining him closely and showing every sign of extreme astonishment. At the end of that time Mirza heard a great hissing, bubbling noise. He looked up and beheld a vast volume of lava rolling impetuously towards him. They saw it likewise and, catching him up in their arms, fled with incredible swiftness in an opposite direction; it, however, followed and would presently have overtaken [them] if a steep rock had not come to their relief. In a moment they sprang from it to one which stood opposite and the lava, when it reached the brink, was precipitated with a noise like the tremendous crash and rattle of approximate thunder down the declivity where, in a short time, it assumed the appearance of a black mass, undistinguishable from the dense gloom of the ravine where it lay.

When this was over, they hastened on without halting till day began to wane. At that time they reached a narrow vale, irrigated by a branch from a neighbouring river and planted by several high trees of a kind unknown on the earth. One, which far outdid the rest in loftiness and beauty, spreading its huge branches for a vast extent around, bore among thickly clustered leaves and blossoms hundreds of strange appearances like the nests of great birds. To this the beings, who still carried Mirza with them, directed their steps and, quickly ascending the trunk and boughs, took possession of the topmost of these nests and snugly ensconced themselves there, behind an entrenchment of rich purple- and golden-streaked fruit growing luxuriantly on one side of their circular habitation. When they had plucked and eaten themselves, they offered some to Mirza. He tasted it at first warily, but finding that it proved gratefully refreshing to his palate, though the flavour was different from any he had ever before known, he ate freely and without restraint. When the repast was concluded, they all sat perfectly silent having their eyes fixed on a certain point of the sky which was azure like that which canopies our world. Mirza looked in that direction also and began mentally to repeat his evening prayers.

Scarcely had he commenced, when a light appeared over the hills. It slowly rose, and when all was revealed Mirza saw his earth in the form of a great luminary, 15 times larger than the moon seems to us. He bowed his head and thanked God in silent ejaculations. Then all his companions turned away as the earth rose, and coiling themselves round in the nest presently gave Mirza notice by loud snores that sleep had closed their eyelids. Somnus also soon asserted his empire over him and in the oblivion of deep sleep he buried his woes for the space of one lunar night, which is, I believe, Arthur, much about the length of a terrene.[11]

How long he continued with these strange creatures I cannot say, for I never heard, but his deliverance from them happened thus. One day when they were all gone down from the tree in search of fruits and had left him alone, he knelt and earnestly implored for liberty at the hands of Mahomet who it seems heard and accepted his petitions, for before

[11]That is, an earthly (night).

he had finished he was startled by the sound of wings, and ere he could look up, an immense, feathered and pinioned animal of marvellous form and dimensions had him safely secured in its great brazen claws. He calmly resigned himself to his fate without one shriek or struggle, imagining that these judgements coming so thick and fast upon him, one at another's back, were for some dreadful crime that his fathers had committed. The moon eagle, for it was nothing else, quivered for a while over the valley and then rose perpendicularly to an immense altitude. Mirza feared that it was mounting to the sun and in that case he knew that the eternal torment of fire was certain to be his portion. Again his fervid though inward prayers were sent up to the Great Prophet; the eagle waved its wing, loosened the strong grasp of its talons, and Mirza found himself whirling at rather an uncomfortable rate downward.

Of the particulars of his descent I am ignorant, as long before he arrived at a landing place sense had fled his skull. When, however, it returned, he was reposing on the ground and two gigantic forms were bending over him.[12] Their countenances and figures were majestically beautiful, shaped like those of human beings. Instead of ears, they had long flaps of flesh hanging gracefully down on their shoulders. Their hair was soft and glossy as unspun silk, in colour a pale blue, arranged in artful wreaths and curls upon their heads. From their foreheads projected a long taper horn, white and polished as the finest ivory, and a string of gold beads was wound spirally about it. Their attire was a long robe of white lawn, bound at the waist with a richly embroidered belt and falling thence in the [?softest] and most elegant folds. Their arms and ankles were adorned with bracelets of gold and their feet with sandals of down, ornamented by silver bands and fastened with jewels. From their necks also hung several strings of precious stones and gold or silver. They were gazing at Mirza in smiling astonishment, turning him over and examining him with the utmost gentleness and care, and conversing to each other meantime in a strange but harmonious language. After some time spent thus they rose and, wrapping him in the leaf of a huge plant that grew near, they conveyed him towards a great plain where was a very large and magnificent tent surrounded by several meaner ones. This they entered, passing through formidable ranks of armed giants between thirty and forty feet in height, all of whom showed them the greatest respect. In the midst of the tent sat

[12]Compare Gulliver's experience in Brobdingnag; Charlotte Brontë has probably read *Gulliver's Travels* by now, since she mentions it in the Advertisements of *Blackwood's Young Men's Magazine*, August 1829. Mirza's experiences with the huge flying creatures also recall the story of 'Sinbad the Sailor' from the *Arabian Nights*.

one who appeared to be the chief, in a thoughtful attitude: his right hand supported his monstrous head and his left a dagger. They advanced and unfolding the leaf placed poor little unfortunate Mirza before him. He gave an exclamation apparently of delight, snatched him up and, rising hastily, quitted the tent, making a sign that none should follow. For about the space of an hour he walked, or rather strode, on over hills, plains and rivers, till there appeared a valley full of tents that encompassed a palace-like edifice constructed of a species of variegated marble, not in the best architectural taste but from its enormous bulk inspiring an idea of sublimity and grandeur. This was the metropolis of the country where Mirza was and that building was its King's residence. The giant directed his course thither.

It would be needless for me to give an account of the odd ceremonies that took place on his introduction to the King which, besides being tedious, would make my tale even drier than it now is, Arthur. But when they were over, he showed Mirza with a joyful countenance to His Majesty, who lept from his throne in a transport and on resuming his seat poured forth an energetic speech expressive of his joy. Then Mirza was consigned to a golden box enriched with gems, where he lay, a miserable captive, till next day. At that time he was taken out and food was offered to him. Being extremely hungry he ate, though with great loathing and disgust, as he knew what animal it was the flesh of and the taste was coarse and disagreeable. Just when he had concluded his repast, he heard a tremendous sound of shouting, instruments and music, etc. He was then placed in his box and hurried off. After many hours of marching, he was again let out and found himself in the midst of a vast army of giants, who were ranged at a respectful distance from an altar where he stood in the hands of a venerable old priest clothed in wide, flowing garments, with a snow-white beard hanging lower than his girdle and long, grey hair, dishevelled in the wind. A great fire burnt on the altar, and, as he sprinkled perfumes thereon and anointed Mirza with fragrant oils and essences, he uttered these words: 'Here is the sacrifice which Thou didst demand, O Mountain! Here we our warriors assembled to do thee homage. Accept our offering and spare us.' By these words Mirza knew his doom, for though spoken in a strange tongue, they were supernaturally understood by him. He trembled and quaked with horror as the idea of being burnt alive flashed through his mind, but no shriek or supplication burst from his whitened lips, and, after some inward strife, he resigned himself to his inevitable fate hoping that the joys of Paradise would be his subsequent reward. The priest now poured the last libation over his devoted head and bathed him in the blood of a newly slain beast, and more fuel was added to the fire, whose flames were already ascending with intense fierceness and heat. Mirza was on the point of being dropped headlong in, when a cry of horror broke from those around. The priest with-held his arm and looked up. A huge black mountain appeared in the sky wavering over their heads and slowly descending on them. Suddenly a flood of fire burst from the summit, and a terrible voice was heard to say, 'Have ye, O wretches, provided the offering?'

'We have,' they all exclaimed in an agony of dread. With a dull, rumbling sound it went up again, while they watched it in breathless silence till every trace vanished from the heavens.

The priest then turned to Mirza and said, 'Creature, whoever thou may be, thou art doomed to die for our safety. We for a length of time have been tormented by that vision which thou sawst. It threatened to destroy us if a being like thee was not procured to appease it by death. At length some good spirit has placed thee in our power. Thou wert found by the daughters of our chief warrior asleep and defenceless in a field. They brought thee to their father and by him thou wast delivered to our King. Hitherto thou hast behaved with becoming resignation. Let not thy heart fail thee in the hour of death.'

With these words Mirza was committed to the flames and the tortures he endured were hard and indescribable, for as the fire seized his feet and legs, he felt all the sinews crack, the calcined bones started through his blackened, cindery flesh, by degrees his extremities crumbled to ashes, and he fell prostrate amid their ruins. A short time now sufficed to extinguish his insupportable agony. The rising smoke presently suffocated him and he died amid shouts and cries of gladness from his sacrificers.

The remnant of my parched tale is clad in a veil of mystery. This same Mirza who suffered the extreme rigour of the law among those giants was, I know not how, long subsequent to that event, wakened from his sleep of death by a shake on the shoulder, which brought life again into him. He looked about and discovered that he was standing upright against the door-cheek of his hut with a bundle of faggots lying before him. His surprise and joy I will not attempt to depict, but on examining his hands and feet he found that they were all marked with long seams and scars of burning. This staggered him a little, but after some consideration he concluded that it was all the machinations of those evil spirits who haunt the Caucasian range. For my part, I do not agree with him but think that these circumstances I have related really occurred. Mirza never knew whether the giants were inhabited of the sun, moon, stars or earth. I believe the latter.

'Well, my sons, what witch- or wizard-craft is going on between you that you have need to do it under the midnight (or thereabouts) moon and sky? Come home, my young scapegraces,' exclaimed a voice close behind them. They started to their feet and saw their father standing near.

'I'll come directly,' replied Lord Wellesley. 'Tringia, Tringia, where are you?'

Tringia sprang from under his branch of brushwood and in a short time was seated in softer and warmer quarters with Trill, Philomel and Pol on the rug of the private parlour before a warm, blazing fire.

4 volume of the Plays of Islands.
That is Emily's, Branwell's, Anne's and my lands.
And now I bid a kind and glad goodbye
To those who o'er my book cast an indulgent eye.

July the 30, 1830   C Brontë

Catalogue of my Books

with the periods of their completion

up to August 3, 1830[1]

Two Romantic Tales, in one volume, viz. The 12 Adventurers and The Adventure in Ireland, April 28, 1829.

The Search After Happiness, a Tale, Aug. 17, 1829.

---

[1] Two page manuscript (10.2 × 5.7 cm), in PML: Bonnell Collection. Many of the dates and titles in this catalogue are incorrect; Charlotte Brontë was probably working from memory, especially in the case of the earlier manuscripts. The contents of the later manuscripts also vary from the originals, and appear to have been hastily copied. Eight fragmentary manuscripts written before August 1830 are not listed here: namely 'There was once a little girl', *The History of the Year*, *The Enfant*, *The Keep of the Bridge*, 'Sir – it is well known that the Genii', *Anecdotes of the Duke of Wellington*, *Description of the Duke of Wellington's Small Palace*, and 'The following strange occurrence'.

211

Leisure Hours, a Tale; and two fragments, July 6, 1829.[2]

The Adventures of [Mon] Edouard de Crack, a Tale, February 22, 1830.

The Adventures of Ernest Alembert, a Tale, May 26, 1830.

An Interesting Incident in the Lives of Some of the Most Eminent Persons of the Age, a Tale, June 18, 1830.[3]

Tales of the Islanders, in four volumes.
Contents of 1st vol: 1 An Account of their Origin.
    2 A Description of Vision Island.
    3 Ratten's Attempt.
    4 Lord C. Wellesley's and the Marquis of Douro's Adventure.
Completed June 31, 1829.

2 vol: 1 The School Rebellion.
    2 A Strange Incident in the Duke of Wellington's Family.
    3 The Duke of Wellington's Tale to his Sons.
    4 The Marquis of Douro and Lord C. Wellesley's Tale to Little King and Queens, etc., etc.
Completed Dec. 2, 1829.

3 vol: 1 The Duke of Wellingon's Adventure of the Cavern.
    2 The Duke of Wellington and Little King and Queens' Visit to the Horse Guards.
Completed July 30, 1830.

---

[2]The manuscript of *Leisure Hours* is dated 29 June 1830; the two fragments may refer to *A Fragment August the 7, 1829* and *Fragment August the 8, 1829*. Charlotte Brontë was working from memory here. She probably grouped these manuscripts together for convenience; it is unlikely that they were part of the same hand-sewn volume, since *Leisure Hours* was written a year later on different size paper. It is also possible that 'two fragments' refers instead to *The Enfant* and *The Keep of the Bridge*, both written on 13 July 1829.

[3]See *An Interesting Passage in the Lives of Some Eminent Men of the Present Time*, n. 1.

4 vol: 1   The 3 Old Washerwomen of Strathfieldsay.
      2   Lord C. Wellesley's Tale to his Brother.
      Completed July 30, 1830.

Characters of the Great Men of the Present Age, December the seventeenth, 1829.[4]

The Young Men's Magazines, in six numbers from August to December (the latter month a double number), completed December the 12, 1829 General Index to their Contents:

1   A True Story.
2   Causes of the Late War.
3   A Song.
4   Conversations.
5   A True Story continued.
6   The Spirit of Cawdor.
7   Interior of a Pothouse, a Poem.
8   The Glass Town, a Song.
9   The Silver Cup, a Tale.
10   The Statue and Vase in the Desert, a Song.
11   Conversations.
12   Scene on the Great Bridge.
13   Song of the Ancient Britons.
14   Scene in my Inn, a Tale.
15   An American Tale.
16   Lines on Seeing the Garden of a Genius.
17   The Bay of the Glass Town.
18   The Swiss Artist, a Tale.
19   Lines on the Transfer of this Magazine.
20   On the Same by a Different Hand.
21   The Chief Genii in Council.
22   Harvest in Spain.
23   The Swiss Artist continued.
24   Conversations.

The Poetaster, A Drama in 2 volumes, July 12, 1830.

---

[4]The title of the actual manuscript is *Characters of the Celebrated Men of the Present Time.*

A Book of Rhymes, finished December 17, 1829.[5]
Contents: 1 The Beauty of Nature.
2 A Short Poem.
3 Meditations while Journeying in a Canadian Forest.
4 Song of an Exile.
5 On Seeing the Ruins of the Tower of Babel.
6 A Thing of 14 Lines.
7 A Rhyme.
8 Lines Written on the Bank of a River One Fine Summer Evening.
9 Spring, a Song.
10 Autumn, a Song.

Miscellaneous Poems, finished May 31st 1830.[6]
Contents: 1 The Churchyard.
2 Descriptions of the Duke of Wellington's Palace on the Pleasant Banks of Indiva. This article is a small prose tale or incident.
3 Pleasure.
4 Lines Written on the Summit of a High Mountain in the North of England.
5 Winter.
6 A Fragment.
7 The Vision.
8 A Short Untitled Poem.

The Evening Walk, A Poem, June 28, 1830.[7]

Making in the whole 22 volumes
C Brontë   August 3, 1830

August the 3,   Charlotte

---

[5]Manuscript untraceable: see Christine Alexander, *A Bibliography of the Manuscripts of Charlotte Brontë* (Haworth and USA: The Brontë Society in association with Meckler Publishing, 1982), p. 7. In the manuscript of *Catalogue of my Books* contents 5 and 6 are both numbered '5'; and so Charlotte Brontë mistakenly totals 9 contents only here.

[6]Manuscript in PML: Bonnell Collection MA 2538; hand-sewn booklet of 12 pages (18.4 × 11.2) in brown paper cover.

[7]Manuscript in BPM: 11; hand-sewn booklet of 16 pages (5 × 3.4 cm) in blue paper cover.

SECOND SERIES OF THE
YOUNG MEN'S
MAGAZINES

NUMBER
FIRST
FOR AUGUST 1830
Edited by Charlotte Brontë
SOLD
BY
SERGEANT TREE, ETC.
AND ALL
OTHER
Booksellers in the Chief Glass Town,
Duke of Wellington's Glass Town,
Paris, Ross's Glass Town, Parry's
Glass Town, etc., etc., etc.
Finished August 18, 1830[1]

This Second Series of magazines
will be conducted on like
principles with the first.
The same eminent authors
are also engaged to
contribute for it.
Charlotte Brontë

[1]Title-page of manuscript, in BPM: B84; the following editorial note and contents on verso. The manuscript is a hand-sewn booklet of twenty pages (5.3 × 3.2 cm), in brown paper cover, dated on front 'AUGUST 1830'.

CONTENTS

Liffey Castle, a Tale by Lord Wellesley I
Lines to the River Aragva, by Marquis [of] Douro II
Journal of a Frenchman, by Tree III
Conversations IV

NO. FIRST: FOR
AUGUST 1830

Finished August the 13th 1830
1830
CHARLOTTE
BRONTË

August 13th 1830

Liffey Castle,[2] a Tale by C. Wellesley

In the summer of the year [?1832], being at that time on a tour in the south of Ireland, I one lovely morning of June set out on a pedestrian excursion to the small but romantically situated village of Liffey. In the yellow light of sunrise, I crossed a green, dewy meadow and spruce fir plantation, which intervened between the cabin of my sojourn and the high road.

The most sequestered and beautiful walk, amid hills, woods or fields, is not in my opinion superior to an airing on the public pathway early in a fine summer morning. No human being disturbs your quiet ramble, not even a wreath of blue smoke curls up from the distant cottage chimneys. Snails and worms luxuriate in dampness under the heath and hawthorn hedges, glittering with dew or white with blossoms, and star-eyed robin-flowers and stately fairy-caps are seen gleaming from trailing underwood by the roadside, or crowning with crimson bells the sloping green banks. Music at that happy hour is above, below and around: larks warble in the sky, thrushes sing in the hedge and grasshoppers chirp in the fields. After some time you hear also the voices of human being chanting their son in the morning, and a merry

---

[2]No record exists of an actual castle; the River Liffey rises in the south-east of Ireland and flows through Dublin to the Irish Sea.

village maid trips past with her pail and milking stool. You are constrained to feel happy, whether you will or not, amid the general cheerfulness.

Such, at least, was my case; but in about 3 hours the sun grew intolerably hot and I grew intolerably miserable. Cloud or mist there was none to soften the fervour of his beams. I looked for a shady tree or some patch of verdure to rest my eyes on. Stone walls occupied the place of the hedge and not a blade of grass was suffered to intrude on the broad smooth mail-road; so I toiled along, sweating and complaining of the heat to everyone I met, till about 4 in the afternoon, when according to the directions I had received previously to setting off I turned down a cool green lane, where I joyfully rested and refreshed myself on such fare as I had brought with me. The rest of my way lay through fields, except 2 miles of bad ditch road.

I reached the village before sunset. It was merely a cluster of mud cabins, most of which had a piece of garden ground planted with cabbages and potatoes, and some few a rose bush or two. One, larger than the rest but every whit as ill-conditioned or rather more so, was distinguished as an public house by a bench at the door, on which sat a man regaling himself with a noggin of the 'crathur'.[3] I placed myself beside him and called for some refreshment. While I was taking it, he asked me in the broad Irish tongue where I wid be coming from this fine day. I answered that I was a stranger who wished to examine the various features of that beautiful scenery in which this village lay. He said he could perceive as much, and if my honour liked he could take me that very evening to some of the fine parts. I agreed, knowing of course that a proper consideration was an understood part of the compact.

In a few minutes we left the village behind, and in a few more found ourselves in the heart of a beautiful glen, smiling in the shade of a dark forest over-spreading its almost perpendicular boundaries. This glen was singularly deep and narrow. Consequently the lowest depths were shrouded in almost continual gloom. The ground rose in sometimes gentle undulations, sometimes abrupt projections. The low hillocks were sprinkled with cowslips, and from the receding obscurity under the projections glinted out clusters of violets and primrose buds, half sunk in soft mossy verdure.

We ascended the surrounding rocks with toil, but when at length we reached the summit of the highest an unexpected scene of beauty, bursting suddenly into life, fully compensated me for the labour. A vast

[3]A small mug of whiskey: 'crathur' represents the Irish pronunciation of 'creature', a humorous term for intoxicating liquor, especially whiskey (*OED*).

lake lay mirror-like at our feet, calm and unruffled as the sky it reflected. Its shores were indented with still, azure bays, lying like crystal drops in the relief of frowning woods, 'Whose long-long groves eternal murmur made'.[4] The bold outlines of distant mountains wrapt in golden mist arose to the west. Southward, green meadows inclined upwards to the horizon, and in the middle of the nether heavens an emerald island seemed suspended in the air, so faithfully its image was pictured in the liquid plains from whose pellucid bosom it rose. Yet, as if even in the fairest scenes something must be visible to remind man of his frailty, the grey, ruined turrets of some ancient and now decaying structure appeared, towering joy-clad from the isle.

'That castle is finely situated,' said I, addressing my guide.

He answered that it was and then, after a pause, remarked that many supposed it to be more than three hundred years old.

'Who were the last inhabitants?' I asked.

'A wiser man than I am must tell you that,' he said.

'Why, is there any mystery about them?'

'Yes, I think there is.'

That rejoiced me and I begged him to explain himself, which he briefly did as follows.

Hundreds of years since, there came to live at that castle a rich lord and his daughter. None knew either them or the place whence they came, so that everyone's curiosity was constantly on the stretch respecting them. The lord was proud and fierce. He seldom spoke to any and his aspect was so forbidding that it scared all men from him. His daughter's name was Lady Mabel. She was one of the most beautiful creatures that ever appeared on earth. Her condescending kindness could not be surpassed and her compassionate charity could not be equalled; in the lowest shieling she might be found kneeling by the bed of age or sickness, comforting and relieving the poor inmates like an angel. No servants were ever in the castle and no visitors were ever observed to enter the gates. Yet often at night every window blazed with light, while sounds of merriment and dancing were heard to ring from the walls.

'Once, a poor peasant's curiosity tempted him so far that he went to the island in a boat to try if he could unravel the strange mystery. None expected to see him come back but to the joy of the whole village he did. They flocked round him immediately and asked him a hundred

---

[4]Many quotations in the early manuscripts either appear to be of Charlotte Brontë's own invention or are difficult to identify since she usually quotes from memory.

questions. He said that all the way as he went he kept his eyes steadfastly fixed on the castle, and that the lights seemed to burn clearer and the singing and music became more sweet and distinct as he approached. Yet when he landed on the island, without having observed the act of vanishing, every light was gone, and though he had not been sensible when the sound ceased, all around was as silent and dark as if the place had been wholly uninhabited.

'Ten years after this, there appeared one morning in the eastern sky, the apparition of a land whose beauty cannot be described by mortal tongue. Every soul in the village saw it while they stood on the top of these very rocks where we now are. After a while a great black cloud like a mountain rolled over the scene, and when it had passed away only blue sky remained. That night all the dogs in the countryside howled as if the Gitrash[5] was abroad, and a sound like a funeral cry was heard at midnight in every house. The next day Lady Mabel was nowhere to be found. She was sought for a whole month without effect, and at the end of that time the Lord went distracted with sorrow and died. He was shrouded and laid out in the great chamber, but when they came to bury him, the body had disappeared and was never afterwards seen. When my grandfather was a little boy, there happened one summer a great drought. The lake sunk 20 yards and in a cavern at the side thus exposed, the corpse of a lady was found, fresh and beautiful, arrayed in long white robes, with a golden cross on its forehead on which was engraven "Mabel".'

August the 12, Lord C. Wellesley, 1830

Lines to the Aragva,* a River of the Caucasian Mountains[6]
by Douro

Mighty river, bold gushing
From the mountains snowclad height;
Wildly furious onward rushing,
As nought could thy wrath abey.

---

[5]An ill-omened spectre of local belief. In *Jane Eyre*, vol. I, chapter 12, she describes it as 'a North-of-England spirit . . . which, in the form of horse, mule, or large dog, haunted solitary ways, and sometimes came upon belated travellers'. According to Branwell, it also appeared as 'a black dog dragging a chain, a dusky calf, nay, even a rolling stone or a self-impelled cartwheel' ('Percy' fragment, 30 December 1837: BPM).

[6]See *Tales of the Islanders*, vol. 4, n. 10. Following Branwell Brontë's example, Charlotte provides her own footnote at the bottom of the manuscript page (i.e. after verse 2 in manuscript but placed at the end of the poem in this edition).

Soon shall thy anger cease:
Soon thy waves in peace,
Soft subsiding, still and slow,
Calmly gliding, gently flow.

Lovely valleys sleeping mildly
In the frozen hills embrace;
Ice rocks round them soaring wildly,
Give their beauty fairer grace.
There let thy waters glide,
Verdure on each side
Shall brighten, as the azure waves
Peacefully its green banks doth lave.

When the soft moonbeams are playing
On thy deep and rapid stream,
All in web of light arraying,
Dyed with their own pearly gleam,
Dost see Elbruz' ghosts
Flit forth in winged hosts,
While with [?hoarse] tumults might
Trembles the ebon ear of night.

Or doth music breathed from heaven
Serenade each giant hill,
Pierce the yawning chasm's rivers,
E'en stern rocks with sweetness,
Till solemnly and slow
Hark the melodies flow,
See awful Gara listening bends
And Kasibec on high attends?

Now in storms of grandeur pealing,
Faintly now it dies away.
Then again terrific swelling,
Listen to the music play,
On this foamy tide
The last calm robe hath died,
Like the strain of skylark [?loud],
The sounds are into silence gone.

August 13, 1830   Douro

---

* The Aragva rushes at times with violence amid masses of ice and snow, and then glides gently through the green vales of Georgia. *Note by Charlotte Brontë.*

JOURNAL OF A FRENCHMAN

February 3, 1820

This day my father died and left me a fortune of 600,000Ls, 30,000 a year. Now I begin to be master of myself, and though I shall be obliged to pretend sorrow for the loss, or rather gain, I have sustained yet, en vérité, je suis bien aise. I will, however, send orders to bury the old hunks decently, though not by any means expensively. I did not shed a tear over the good news of his death. Some people will blame my want of feeling. Yet did I owe him any? No! He, for a little youthful frolic, sent me here to this Convent of Monserrat,[7] forcing me to spend my best days among old pride-swollen monks and friars over dusty worm-eaten books, starving on an allowance of 3 Louis d'or per annum. Stingy old miser! But peace be to his bones. I will restrain my unreverential pen. Tomorrow I quit these woods and mountains for – Paris! What a transporting change! Oh Paris! Toi, Reine de la terre! How I love thy name! Je suis ravi si je pense a tes murs, rues et chateaux; everything there is certain to be delightful: court in the morning; balls, routs, concerts in the afternoon; and theatre – that charming, that entrancing place – in the evening and greater part of the night. What a life have I planned out! What a continued unbroken course of pleasure! How happy shall I be! No individual in France will be happier. But now, ye scenes of my youth, adieu. How much lies in that little word! Adieu! Adieu!

Feb. 9th

Yesterday I left Monserrat and already I begin to feel the joys of freedom. I had a pleasant journey in the diligence. One of my companions was a pale, pensive-looking young man, with a certain indescribable air of grace and gentility about him that quite charmed me. Sighs came from him like gusts of wind from a cavern, and as I watched him narrowly I could perceive crystal tears at intervals straying down his cheek, on which bright bloom of youth had faded to a faint pinky hue that betokened the greatest delicacy of health and constitution. His appearance affected me so much that I wept aloud. He turned to me and said in a tone of dolour, 'Quelle[8] vous fait

---

[7]A town south-west of Valencia in Spain.

[8]Presumably Charlotte Brontë means 'Qu'est ce qui' here. Minor mistakes in Charlotte's French grammar and spelling have been corrected in this edition; but an exact transcription of her French from the manuscript may be found in the textual notes at the back.

larmoyer, monsieur? Êtes vous malheureux pour moi?'

'No, my cher monsieur,' I replied, 'but it afflicts me to see you so miserable. What is the cause of your unhappiness?'

'Ask me not,' he said solemnly.

I, however, persisted and after much solicitation he favoured me with the following brief recital.

'My father was a rich and influential courtier of Louis 15th, but when that monarch and his noble queen were beheaded, he, with all that remained faithful to the royal family, fled to England. Here he married a young native of that island, who died half a year after my birth so that I never knew my mother: une douloureuse pensée, monsieur. I grew up under my father's eye, being taught by him in a school which he kept and thereby earned his livelihood. Of course he strove constantly to instil a love for the Capets[9] into my mind, and I pretended to feel the greatest reverence for them, but secretly my heart was captivated by Napoleon's glory, and the greatest contempt for the House of Bourbon influenced me.

'One day, I remember my father took me to the Marquis of Buckingham's villa, where [the] royal family of France were hospitably sheltered. I was presented to them. The haughty Duchess of Angoulême[10] deigned to notice me. She said, "I know when thou art a man thou wilt fiercely fight against the vile usurper Bonaparte, mere son of a scrivener." In saying this she stroked me over the face. I could have bitten her hand off.

'When I was fifteen years of age, I one morning rose early and taking all my little store of goods, amounting to 30 shillings in cash and a suit of clothes, I stole out of the house and set off for Gravesend with a determination to take ship for France and there immediately join Napoleon's army. I arrived safely at Calais and thence took the route to Paris on foot, asking as I went (to save the 10 of my 30s that remained) with these words, "Donnez-moi du pain pour l'honneur de la France", meaning that I was an advocate for the honour of France and therefore

[9]The family name of the kings of France for nearly nine centuries, until the last great Capetian family, the Bourbons, lost the throne.

[10]Duchess d'Angoulême (1778–1851), daughter of the guillotined Louis XVI and only member of her immediate family to survive the revolutionary Terror. She married her cousin, Duc d'Angoulême, son of Comte d'Artois who, as Charles X (see *Blackwood's Young Men's Magazine*, December (second issue) 1829, n. 9), succeeded Louis XVIII in 1824. All were disliked by the French who saw them simply as puppets of foreign powers. They had survived the Republic and Empire in exile and, like many other French emigrés, were settled by the Buckinghams (friends of Wellington) in London or at their estate of Stowe.

they ought to keep me from starvation.

'After innumerable hardships I arrived at Paris. Of the first man I met, I enquired like a simpleton where the army was.

'"If you mean the French army, it is where I wish the perfidious Island was." So saying, he passed on.

'I walked forward through a great number of streets till I came to a very wide one full of soldiers. This rejoiced me.

'While I was gazing at them in delight, they suddenly fell back in regular ranks and presented arms to a person that then passed through them, whose appearance perfectly charmed me. He was middle-sized, attired in regimentals and possessed the noblest countenance that the sun ever looked upon. In short, he was the personification of my idea of Bonaparte. In a transport, I threw myself at his feet and begged to be allowed to serve him. Smiling, he ordered me to rise and asked my name. I told him and said, "Are you not Napoleon?"

'He frowned, and an old man who now came up struck me down saying, "Wellington, let us exterminate all these French rascals."

'The other held his arm as he was about to redouble the blow, with, "No, no, Blucher,[11] they are now harmless, let them live." They then walked away.

'This incident confounded me. But in a short time, I learnt that the allies had taken Paris and heard all the particulars of my favourite hero's defeat and flight.

'The sequel of the story is soon told. After the Bourbons had reascended the throne of their fathers', all the exiles' confiscated estates were restored to them and my father became, from a poor schoolmaster in England, a wealthy nobleman of France. I wandered about Paris for 3 weeks, living all that time on alms before I could discover my father's above. When I at last did, he refused to own me, and I was again sent forlorn into the street. A compassionate individual took me under his care and I lived happy with him till about a month ago, when he died without a will and, all his property devolving on a near relation, I was left entirely unprovided for. Again I appealed to my father's compassion. He remained immovable, and I am now on my way to Switzerland, where in the canton of Zurich I have some relatives who may perhaps take pity on me. That, at least, is my forlorn hope.'

Captain Tree. To be continued.

August 13, 1830

[11]Gebhard Leberecht von Blucher (1742–1819), Prussian general, field marshal, Prince of Wahlstadt in Silesia. Instrumental in the defeat of Napoleon and the overthrow of the First Empire. With the return of Napoleon, he took command of the Army of the Lower Rhine,

Charlotte Brontë

CONVERSATIONS

A parlour in Bravey's Inn.[12] 7 o'clock pm. Captain Bud, Captain Tree, Marquis of Douro, Lord Charles Wellesley and Stumps.

Finished August 13, 1830

Captain Bud: It's a long, long while since you were at the Glass Town, Stumps. Do you see any alteration in its appearance?
Stumps: Aye, that I do. My sensations on seeing the old lady again were— but you could not enter into their spirit so I will not describe them.
Marquis of Douro: If you would favour us with the account, sir, it would give me great pleasure and I can answer for these gentlemen.
Stumps: Since you desire it, my dear Douro, I shall certainly comply. Well then, I lay awake for the whole night on the morrow of which I might expect to catch the first glimpse of Babel.[13] It dawned; sunlight gleamed through the windows of my travelling carriage. I looked forth with the same feelings as a child returning from school to its mother, but instead of the peerless tower I saw a veil of mist. Disappointed, I fell back and soon snored myself into oblivion. My valet told me that I slept for forty-eight hours. Whether this be true I cannot say, but when I awoke it was in the heart of the world's metropolis. I had stopped at the gate of a splendid palace and outside my carriage I heard a silvery voice say, 'Is this Stumps's equipage?' The door opened and in an instant Lord Wellesley was at my side.
Captain Tree: Do you think he is less childish in his manners and appearance than when you last saw him?
Stumps: Childish he never was, but he certainly is not less sugarish and beautiful than when I last saw him, a little cherub with ringlets of gold, from which – when the sun shone on them – I have often marked a

---

and, after a severe defeat and injury at Ligny (June 1815), he came to the assistance of Wellington and led the Prussian Army with decisive effect in the battle of Waterloo, enabling the allies to re-enter Paris on July 7.

[12]Later called Bravey's Hotel: meeting place for the Young Men and Glass Town literati. 'Conversations' is obviously a continuation of 'Military Conversations', featured in the *Blackwood's Young Men's Magazines* for 1829 and presumably also held in Bravey's Inn, which is named after its corpulent landlord, Bravey, one of the original 'Twelves'. See *The Foundling*, 31 May – 27 June 1833, for a detailed description of Bravey's Hotel; Charlotte's poem 'Written upon the occasion of the dinner given to the literati of the Glass Town', 8 January 1830 (*Poems*, p. 80), was probably also held in the great hall of Bravey's Hotel.

[13]Tower of Babel, later called 'Tower of All Nations': see *Blackwood's Young Men's Magazine*, October 1829, n. 10.

reflected halo playing round his temples.

Captain Tree: Poo, all stuff! Vanity will turn the poor young thing inside out if he is puffed up in that manner constantly; and pray, may I ask the meaning of that elegant expression 'sugarish', which you made use of, sir?

Stumps: By that word I meant, sir, to express that indescribable sweetness and light, innocent gaiety, which everyone but an ass (another word for some kinds of Trees) must instantly be struck with.

Captain Tree: What do you mean, sir? I demand an explanation and that immediately too!

Captain Bud:
  Rising.
Gentlemen, you have constituted me your president or chairman, with full powers to repress any disturbance that may arise. I, therefore, in legal exercise of the duties of mine office, do insist and command that this disturbance between Stumps and Tree do cease, and while I am upon my legs I may at the same time request Lord Charles Wellesley to pay more attention and respect to the gentlemen around him and leave off noticing the pranks of that ape.

Lord C. Wellesley: Bud, Bud, the richest haunch of venison is in my possession at present that was ever laid upon a table. Tomorrow I shall be much obliged by your company to a snug dinner at which only you and I will be present at Waterloo Palace.

Bud: I am extremely much obliged to you, my lord; your kind request shall not be disregarded. And now Captain Tree, I command you to utter no more insolent insinuations respecting this admirable young nobleman.

Captain Tree:
  Muttering.
Some folks like good eating better than justice, methinks.

Lord C. Wellesley: Tree, have a care what you do, my lad. Who was it that got into a spunging house t'other day? I wonder?

Captain Tree: Lord Wellesley, what do you mean? I say, what do you mean?

Marquis of Douro: Charles, be silent, love.[14]

Lord C. Wellesley:
  Laughing.
I'll tell you what I mean as you don't know, Tree. A certain gentleman

---

[14]The following text (2 manuscript pages) has been mistakenly inserted into the *Young Men's Magazine* for December, second issue, 1830 (in BPM: B86). There was probably a page of advertisements, similar to the other miniature magazines, which also became detached and subsequently lost.

of this city, brother to an eminent though rather doltish bookseller,[15] one day took it into his wise head to go to a certain shop where fancy articles were sold, intending to purchase largely on the strength of certain sums of money which that same gentleman had swindled from a ward of his, then in her tenth year, the only daughter and child of a worthy and wealthy merchant deceased. Well, he purchased the articles consisting of an elegant epergne, table-lamp, diamond brooch, silver urn, 3 gold rings: one set with a ruby, another with an amethyst and the third with a sapphire. Well, after this he told the shop man to make out his bill and direct it 'Captain Tree, No. 5 Branch Street, Connaught Square', where it would be settled to his satisfaction.

Then he went to the house of one Monsieur le Tocsin, a well-known fashionable tailor, whom he directed to measure him for a suit of handsome dress-clothes. From this he went to Private Curry, the hat-maker, of whom he bought an expensive hat and then returned home.

The Wednesday evening of next week saw him step into his carriage, attired in the new suit consisting of a pink kerseymere[16] coat, white satin waistcoat and inexpressibles, white cloak, adorned silk stockings and small pink slippers wth white ribbon. Thus charmingly arrayed, he was proceeding on his way to a ball given that eve by Lady Serena Clarinette Rose Chubby but, mournful to tell, 3 potent bailiffs came up in a dark, oil-lighted street and dragged him from his chariot to a prison.

There he was informed that Colonel Travis, uncle to the young lady above mentioned, had been informed of the whole transaction, and that he was now in his hands. Tree wept and prayed and wept again with the most abject importunity. He implored the Colonel to pardon him, promising to return all the money and deliver up the ward without further delay. On these conditions he was set at large.

But a new misery yet awaited him. One little month after, his creditors came to have their bills liquidated. Of course he was unable to comply with their wishes and they accordingly committed him to jail. This circumstance, coming to the knowledge of my dear brother the Marquis of Douro, he immediately hastened to his relief. On examining the state of Tree's accounts, it was found that he had in various ways greatly exceeded his income and that bankruptcy was inevitable. Arthur then generously, in conjunction with someone else whom perhaps it would be deemed egotistical in me to mention, satisfied all his creditors

[15]Elsewhere in the juvenilia, Captain Tree is generally referred to as the father of Sergeant Tree, publisher and bookseller in the Chief Glass Town.

[16]A twilled, fine, woollen cloth of a peculiar texture. The word is a corruption of cassimere or cashmere, due to erroneous association with kersey, a coarse, narrow, woollen cloth (*OED*).

and set Tree at liberty. I should never have related this incident if it had not been that Tree still [?continues] his system of tormenting me, which is very ungrateful.

Curtain falls. [?continued]

SECOND SERIES OF THE
YOUNG MEN'S MAGAZINE
NO. SECOND
FOR SEPTEMBER 1830

Edited by Charlotte Brontë

SOLD

BY

SERGEANT TREE

AND ALL

OTHER

Booksellers in the Chief Glass Town,

Duke of Wellington's Glass Town,

Paris, Ross's Glass Town,

Parry's Glass Town, etc., etc.

Finished [?21] August 1830

CONTENTS

A Letter from Lord Charles Wellesley I
A Midnight Song, by the Marquis of Douro II
A Frenchman's Journal Continued, by Captain Tree .... III[1]

---

[1]Miniature hand-sewn booklet; manuscript lost, title-page reconstructed here. The contents are listed in the 'General Index' at the end of the *Young Men's Magazine* for December, second issue, 1830; the manuscript was obviously written between 18 and 21 August. The *Young Men's Magazine* for October 1830 describes the evening 'after that delightful evening I spent at Madame le Comtess d'Ouvert', which is probably the subject of this missing episode of 'A Frenchman's Journal Continued'.

SECOND SERIES OF THE
YOUNG MEN'S MAGAZINE NO
THIRD
FOR OCTOBER 1830
Edited by Charlotte Brontë
SOLD
BY
SERGEANT TREE
AND ALL
OTHER
Booksellers in the Glass Town,
Paris, Ross's Glass Town,
Parry's Glass Town and the Duke of
Wellington's Glass Town.
Finished August 23, 1830
Charlotte Brontë
August 23
1830[1]

This second series of magazines is conducted on like
principles with the first. The
same eminent authors are
also engaged to contribute for it.

[1]Title-page of manuscript, in BPM: B85; the following editorial note and contents on vero. The manuscript is a hand-sewn booklet of twenty pages (5.4 × 3.3 cm), with brown paper cover dated on front at top 'OCTOBER 1830'.

CONTENTS

A Day at Parry's Palace, by C. W. I
Morning, by the Marquis [of] Douro II
Conversations III
Advertisements IV

NO. THIRD FOR
OCTOBER 1830
Finished August 23, 1830
1830
CHARLOTTE
BRONTË
August 23, 1830
Charlotte Brontë

A DAY AT PARRY'S PALACE
BY LORD CHARLES WELLESLEY

'Oh Arthur!' said I, one morning last May. 'How dull this Glass Town is. I am positively dying of ennui. Can you suggest anything likely to relieve my disconsolate situation?'

'Indeed, Charles, I should think you might find some pleasant employment in reading or conversing with those that are wiser than yourself. Surely you are not so empty-headed and brainless as to be driven to the extremity of not knowing what to do!' Such was the reply to my civil question, uttered with the prettiest air of gravity imaginable.

'Oh, yes! I am, brother! So you must furnish me with some amusement.'

'Well then, Charles, you have often spoken of a visit to Captain Parry's Palace as a thing to be desired. You have now time for the accomplishment of your wish.'

'Very true, Arthur, and you deserve your weight in gold for reminding me of it.'

Next morning, I was on my way at an early hour in the direction of William Edward's country.[2] In less than a week I crossed the borders

[2]Parry's Land (later, Parrisland), one of the four Glass Town kingdoms; controlled by Captain Sir William Edward Parry, originally Emily Brontë's chief man in the Young Men's

and was immediately struck with the changed aspect of everything. Instead of tall, strong muscular men going about seeking whom they may devour, with guns on their shoulders or in their hands, I saw none but little shiftless milk-and-water-beings, in clean, blue linen jackets and white aprons. All the houses were ranged in formal rows. They contained four rooms, each with a little garden in front. No proud castle or splendid palace towers insultingly over the cottages around. No high-born noble claimed allegiance of his vassals or surveyed his broad lands with hereditary pride. Every inch of ground was enclosed with stone walls. Here and there a few regularly planted rows of trees, generally poplars, appeared; but no hoary woods or nodding groves were suffered to intrude on the scene. Rivers rushed not with foam and thunder through meads and mountains, but glided canal-like along, walled on each side that no sportive child might therein find a watery grave. Nasty factories, with their tall black chimneys breathing thick columns of almost tangible smoke, discoloured not that sky of dull hazy colourless hue. Every woman wore a brown stuff gown with white cap and handkerchief; glossy satin, rich velvet, costly silk or soft muslin broke not in on the fair uniformity.

Well, 'on I travelled many a mile',[3] till I reached Parry's Palace. It was a square building of stone, surmounted by blue slates and some round stone pumpkins. The garden around it was of moderate dimensions, laid out in round, oval or square flower beds, [with] rows of peas, gooseberry bushes, black, red and white currant trees, some few common flowering shrubs, and a grass place to dry clothes on. All the convenient offices, such as wash-house, back-kitchen, stable and coalhouse, were built in a line and backed by a row of trees. In a paddock behind the house were feeding one cow, to give milk for the family and butter for the dairy and cheese for the table; one horse, to draw the gig, carry Their Majesties and bring home provisions from market; together with a calf and foal as companions for both.

As the wheels of my carriage were heard on the stone pavement of the courtyard, the kitchen door opened and a little oldish maun and waman[4] made their appearance. They immediately ran back again at

---

Play. Lord Charles Wellesley's disparagement of Parry's Land reflects Charlotte's scorn for the unromantic, realistic characters and setting of her sister's early writings.

[3]Compare Wordsworth, 'The Sailor's Mother', l. 23.

[4]'Man and woman' in the original Young Men's language, invented by Branwell Brontë and spoken with fingers 'applied to' the nose, a possible early attempt to reproduce the local dialect (see Christine Alexander, *The Early Writings of Charlotte Brontë*, Oxford: Basil Blackwell, 1983, p. 35). The following conversations between Parry and Ross are again part of

sight of my splendid (for so it must have seemed to them) equipage. A slight bustle now became audible inside the house and in a few moments Sir Edward and Lady Emily Parry came out to welcome their newly arrived guest. They too were a little frightened at first, but I soon quitted their fears by telling them who I was.

After this explanation I was ushered into a small parlour. Tea was on the table and they invited me to partake of it. But before sitting down, Parry took from the cupboard a napkin which he directed me to pin before my clothes lest I should dirty them, saying in a scarcely intelligible jargon that he supposed they were my best as I had come on a visit and that perhaps my mama would be angry if they got stained. I thanked him but politely declined the offer. During tea a complete silence was preserved; not a word escaped the lips of my host or hostess. When it was over little Eater was brought in, habited in a most dirty and greasy pinafore which Lady Emily presently stripped him of and substituted a clean one in its stead, muttering a cross tone that she wondered how Amy could think of sending the child into the parlour with such a filthy slip on.

Parry now withdrew to his study and Lady Aumly[5] to her work room, so that I was left alone with Eater. He stood for more than half an hour on the rug before me with his finger in his mouth staring idiot-like full in my face, uttering every now and then an odd grumbling noise, which I suppose denoted the creature's surprise. I ordered him to sit down. He laughed but did not obey. This incensed me, and heaving the poker I struck him to the ground. The scream that he set up was tremendous, but it only increased my anger. I kicked him several times and dashed his head against the floor, hoping to stun him. This failed. He only roared the louder. By this time the whole household was alarmed: master, mistress and servants came running into the room. I looked about for some means of escape but could fine none.

'What hauve dou beinn douing tou de child?' asked Parry, advancing towards me with an aspect of defiance.

As I wished to stop a day longer at this palace, I was forced to coin a lie. 'Nothing [at] all,' I replied. 'The sweet little boy fell down as I was playing with him and hurt hisself.'

Charlotte's attempt to ridicule the provincial nature of Emily and Anne's chief characters. The earlier description of the inhabitants of Parry's Land, in blue jackets and white aprons, corresponds to the inhabitants of 'Mons and Wamons Islands' described in *Branwell's Blackwood's Magazines* for January and June 1829 (in HCL: MSS. Lowell I (7 and 8)).

[5] Parry's pronunciation of 'Emily'; 'Emily' is cancelled in the manuscript and replaced by 'Aumly'.

This satisfied the good easy man and they all retired, carrying the hateful brat still squalling and bawling along with them.

In about an hour afterwards, supper was brought in. It consisted of coffee and a very few thin slices of bread and butter. This meal, like the former, was eaten in silence, and when it was concluded we went to bed.

I rose next morning at 9 o'clock and came down just in time for breakfast, after which I took a walk through the fields. In the yard I saw Eater, surrounded by three cats, two dogs, five rabbits and six pigs, all of whom he was feeding. On my return I found a new guest had arrived in the shape of Captain John Ross.[6] He and Parry were conversing together but I could understand very little of what they said. It was, however, something about 'Aun having moide Trahl a nou clouk of flouered muslin waud punk rubun ot de bottom and faul saulk belt', which he liked very much. Parry said that 'the laust dress Aumy haud moide haum wauss a boutiful pale craumson, traumed waud yaullow, groin and purple, and a fadher aun hid caup of a rauch lilac cauler'.

Dinner was set on the table precisely at twelve o'clock. The dishes were roast-beef, Yorkshire pudding, mashed potatoes, apple pie and preserved cucumbers. Ross wore a white apron during dinner. I observed that he took not the smallest notice of me, though I must necessarily have been a different object from what he was in the habit of seeing. All ate as if they had not seen a meal for three weeks, while 'The solemn hush of twilight lay/On every tongue around'. I felt a strong inclination to set the house on fire and consume the senseless gluttons. At the dessert each drank a single glass of wine, not a drop more, and ate a plateful of strawberries with a few sweet cakes. I expected some blow-up after the surfeit which Ross, if I might judge from his continued grunting and puffing, had evidently got, and was not disappointed. An hour subsequent to dinner, he was taken extremely sick. No doctor being at hand, death was momentarily expected and would certainly have ensued, had not the Genius Emily arrived at a most opportune period; and when the disorder had reached its crisis, she cured with an incantation and vanished.[7]

I only remained at Parry's Palace till the morrow, for I found my visit

---

[6] Captain John Ross, King of Ross's Land (later, Rossesland) and Anne Brontë's chief man in the Young Men's Play.

[7] Although Ross is usually protected by 'Chief Genius Annii' (Anne Brontë), Emily Brontë obviously assumes control of events in her kingdom. Few Glass Town characters remain ill or dead for long: the four Chief Genii have a habit of intervening in their 'play' and restoring life with 'a single incantation'.

intolerably dull, as much so as I fear the reader will find this account of it. But the journey had given me some notion of things as they are, and for that reason I did not regret it. For many days after I had returned to the Glass Town, my life was a very brisk one, as persons were constantly coming to hear my account of the place where I had been. I happened at that time to be in an exceedingly taciturn disposition of mind, which circumstance prevented my satisfying their curiosity by word of mouth. I have therefore had recourse to the only way of obviating the inconvenience, namely by sending this brief narrative for insertion in the *Young Men's Magazine*.

August 22, 1830   Farewell, Genius CW

MORNING
BY MARQUIS [OF] DOURO[8]

Lo! The light of the morning is flowing
  Through radiant portals of gold,
Which Aurora, in crimson robes glowing,
  For the horses of fire doth unfold.

See Apollo's burnished car
Glorifies the East afar;
As it draws the horizon nigher,
As it climbs the heavens higher,
Richer grows the amber light,
Fairer, more intensely bright,
Till floods of liquid splendour roll
O'er all the earth from pole to pole.

Hark! The birds in the green forest bowers
  Have beheld the sun's chariot arise;
And the humblest, the stateliest flowers
  Are arrayed in more beautiful dyes.

Now, while the woodland choirs are singing,
Opening buds fresh odours flinging;
And while nature's tuneful voice
Calls on all things to rejoice.

---

[8]This is a typical poem of the Marquis of Douro: melancholy, pensive and full of Classical allusions. Sunrise and sunset are favourite subjects of Douro; later, as King of Angria, he chooses the rising sun as his emblem and he himself is constantly compared to Apollo.

I cannot join the common gladness:
'Tis to me a time of sadness:
All these sounds of mirth impart
Nought but sorrow to my heart.

But I love evening's still quiet hour,
The whispering twilight breeze,
The damp dew's invisible shower
Conglobing in drops on the trees.

Then is heard no sound or tone
But the night-bird singing lone;
Peacefully adown the vale
It passes on the balmy gale;
Ceases oft the pensive strain,
Solemn sinking, and again
Philomela sends her song
To wander the night-winds along.

While silver-robed Luna is beaming
Afar in the heavens on high,
And her bright train of planets are gleaming
Like gems in the dome of the sky.

From the firmament above,
Down they gaze with looks of love
On the minstrel, all unheeding,
Still their ears entranced feeding
With the notes of sweetest sound
Gushing forth on all around:
Music not unfit for Heaven
But to earth in mercy given;
Thou dost charm the mourner's heart
Thou dost pensive joy impart:
Peerless Queen of Harmony,
How I love thy melody!

August 22, 1830   Marquis of Douro

CONVERSATIONS

Marquis of Douro, Young Soult, Lord Wellesley, Sergeant Bud, De
Lisle. Parlour in Bravey's Inn.

Lord Wellesley: Well, De Lisle, this is the first time you have been present at our conversations and right glad I am to see a gentleman of such genius among us.

De Lisle: My lord, one of the chief pleasures which such an honour gives me is that of being made acquainted with such distinguished personages as yourself, my lord, and your noble brother.

Marquis of Douro: I do not know, sir, that I have had the happiness of seeing you before, but often have I seen your mind displayed in the peerless productions of your pencil, where the sublime and beautiful are set forth with a supreme mastery of execution and elevation of feeling that none but a genius of the highest order could ever hope to attain.

Lord Wellesley: Arthur, have you seen his view from the summit of the Tower of All Nations?

Marquis of Douro: I have, Charles, and my admiration of it is unbounded. Who can conceive the thoughts and sensations of such a man, while from that aerial altitude he traced the grand lineaments of nature? None. How was he then raised above all sublunary concerns? How must his already gigantic spirit have dilated, as he saw the farthest isles and coasts drawn into the vast circle of an horizon, more extensive than that beheld from Chimborazo or Teneriffe?[9] De Lisle, you are already among those consecrated names that form the boast and glory of Britannia, Empress of the Waves.

De Lisle: My lord Marquis, I cannot deserve your eulogium. Painting is but the younger sister of Poetry, that divine art which is yours.

Marquis of Douro: Mine, De Lisle? She belongs to none. She is confined to no realm, shore or empire: alike she reigns in the heart of peasant or king; painter and statuary, as well as poet, live, breathe, think, act under the celestial influence of her inspiration.

Lord Wellesley: Och! No Arthur! One would think Marian Hume was Poetry in disguise.

Sergeant Bud: Well, well, the lawyer is happily free. Pray, young gentlemen, have not you lately taken a jaunt of some hundred miles into the country?

Lord Wellesley: Yes, parchment, we have. What then?

Sergeant Bud: Why, I should like to hear an account of it.

Lord Wellesley: Which I am in no humour for giving.

Young Soult: But I am and I will. We saw Nature in her fairest dress. Art has not yet built a palace in the dark hills of Jibbel Kumri, the wide desert of Sahara, the palmy plains of Fezzan, or the mountain vales

---

[9]Mountains in Ecuador and the Canary Islands respectively.

which no eye but the lone travellers hath seen.[10] Oh! Oft as I wandered, in a delightful kind of insanity, far from the caravan, I have tout a la coup in the midst of mountains that clave the whirlwind-swept heaven, in stern and naked grandeur, beheld glens reposing in supernatural loveliness, in the arms of circling rocks that seemed unwilling for any to seek their beauty, which was [?wildered] and enhanced by the accompaniment of unearthly objects. Strange trees grimly shook their long dark tresses over the grassy ground where stars, instead of flowers, gleamed. Clouds ever hung over them. The sun was screened by jealous hills frowning in majesty above—

> O spirits of the sky were there,
> Strange enchantment filled the air:
> I have seen from each dark cloud,
> Which in gloom those vales did shroud,
> White-robed beings glance and fly
> And rend the curtain from the sky.
> I have seen their wings of light
> Streaming o'er the heavens' height;
> I have seen them bend and kiss
> Those eternal vales of bliss;
> And I've seen them fast enshroud
> Those Edens of unfading bloom.
> O, the darkness of that night!
> O, the grandeur of that sight!
> None can speak it, none can tell.
> Hark! I hear the thunder swell,
> Crashing through the firmament;
> 'Tis by wrothful spirits sent
> Warning me to say no more.
> Now hath ceased the dreadful roar,
> Now a calm is all around;
> Not a breath and not a sound
> That frozen stillness durst break:
> This is Nature's silent sleep.
> Sudden music round me rings;
> Now again the spirits dance,
> And again the sunbeams glance.
> This is light and this is mirth,
> All of heaven, not of earth.

[10]Landscape north of the Glass Town and home of the Genii; described in the early manuscripts (see *A Romantic Tale*).

Up hath risen purple morn,
Love and joy and life are born.
I veil my eyes with holy fear,
For the coming visions no mortal
May bear!
*Sinks down in a fainting fit and the Marquis of Douro, who is sitting by,
catches him in his arms and reinstates him in a chair.*
Lord Wellesley: Ring! Ring the bell! Be quick! Bring hartshorn, cold
water, vinegar, salvolatic, [?salzaikaling] and sal everything else! The
poet has fallen into an inspiration dream! Haste, haste, if you mean to
save his life![11]
Sergeant Bud: What's the matter with him? Nobody touched him that I
saw of, but I suppose he is mad. Alack-a-day to be a poet!
De Lisle: His excited feelings have overcome him.
Young Soult:
  Opening his eyes.
Where am I? Who is this so kindly bending over me? Is it you, Douro,
my friend, patron, benefactor, to whom I owe more than to all the
world beside?
Marquis of Douro: Be composed, my dear Soult; it is me. You should
not allow your genius to gain so much ascendancy over your reason, for
it exposes you more to ridicule than admiration.
Young Soult: I will try to follow your advice, my dear Douro, since I
know the motives that induce you to give it.
Sergeant Bud: What ailed you? May I ask?
Young Soult: I cannot tell. My sensations at the moment of swooning
were inexpressible; they were indeed 'all of heaven and not of earth'.
Sergeant Bud: Humph!
  Turning to Lord Wellesley.
You look very fresh and rosy somehow; your journey seems to have
done you good.
Lord Wellesley: So it has. I never feel well in this dismal unwholesome
Glass Town.
De Lisle: For several months before you went, it much concerned me to
see your white countenance and cheeks without a streak of vermeil.
Now the fairest leaf of the wild rose could not surpass their bloom.
Your eyes also are more radiant and your hair more glossy than ever.
Lord Wellesley: Nonsense, I hope I'm rather tawny.
De Lisle: No, of a purer white than before.

---

[11]Charlotte Brontë is again mocking the romantic excesses and posturing of Branwell by
ridiculing his character (and pseudonym) Young Soult.

Lord Wellesley: That's a flat lie! I'm not fair. Do you think I use cosmetics, pray?

De Lisle: Yes, one: that of an incomparably sweet temper.

Lord Wellesley: You're out again, sir. Was there ever a more malignant being than I am, Arthur? Now, speak truth, honestly.

Marquis of Douro:
  Laughing.

What! Always appealing to me? As I do not know tout le monde, it is a useless question, Charles: but I believe if what it implies was a veritable maxim, I should not love you as well as I do.

Lord Wellesley: De Lisle, you've disturbed my happiness and made me angry with Arthur, so get along, don't sit so near me!

De Lisle:
  Aside to the Marquis of Douro.

Have I displeased him, do you think?

Marquis of Douro:
  Aside to De Lisle.

No, no, sir, he loves flattery. You can't lay it on too thick. Butter away! The more there is, the better he will be pleased. Watch his eye: when it glares his wrath has risen, then beware; but while it sparkles, fear not: he is delighted. Never mind the knit brow, pouting lip and raging tongue; they are but so many marks of pleasure.

De Lisle: Is he as charming in private as in public?

Marquis [of] Douro: Infinitely more so. When he and I are alone, his sweetness of manner would force the merest misanthrope to love mankind. Among strangers, he wishes to be thought less amiable than he really is.

De Lisle: That is strange. What a wayward disposition.

Lord Charles Wellesley: Young Soult and Sergeant Bud, behold those two whispering together. Ill-bred rustics! Turn about, sirs, and face the company, I say!

De Lisle: We were talking of you.

Lord Wellesley: Of me! I demand an explanation.

  Enter a servant.

What do you want?

Servant: A messenger has arrived from Waterloo Palace, whom His Grace the Duke of Wellington has sent to command the Marquis of Douro's and Lord Wellesley's immediate attendance.

Lord Wellesley: Be off ape! Come, brother, we must go. What can my father want, I wonder?

Young Soult: We'll go too.

De Lisle: May I be allowed the honour of an introduction to His

Grace's august presence?

Marquis of Douro: Certainly, if you desire it, and I will present you.

De Lisle: By so doing, your lordship will confer on me a great obligation.

Sergeant Bud: It is time for me to return home.

Lord Wellesley: Come with us then. Come, come, come.

Exeunt omnes. Curtain falls.

> August the 23, 1830
> Finished August 23, 1830
> C Brontë   Charlotte

ADVERTISEMENTS

BOOKS
PUBLISHED BY SERGEANT TREE

The Elements of LYING
BY LORD CHARLES WEL-
LESLEY in one vol., duodecimo
PRICE 2s 6d
With some account of those
who practice it.

SOGAST, a Romance. By
CAPTAIN TREE
in 2 volumes, oct. price 20d

Orion and Arcturus,[12] a POEM
LORD WELLESLEY
Recommendation: 'this is the
most beautiful poem that ever
flowed from the pen of man. The
sentiments are wholly original;
nothing is borrowed.'
Glass Town Review

---

[12]Orion, giant and hunter of Boeotia, who, after his death, was placed among the stars; and Arcturus (bear's tail), star in the first magnitude in the tail of Bootes.

An Essay on Conversation, by
THE MARQUIS [OF] DOURO
1 vol., price 5s

Solitude, by the same. price 10d

The Proud MAN, by Captain
TREE. PRICE 30s, 3 vol.

ADVERTISEMENTS: SALES
TO BE SOLD: a rat-trap, by
MONSIEUR it-can-catch-nothing-
FOR-it's-BROKEN.

THE ART OF BLOWING
One's Nose, is taught by
Monsieur Pretty-foot at his
house, No. 105 Blue Rose Street,
Glass TOWN.

LORD CHARLES WELLESLEY
hereby challenges that impudent
braggadocio, who boasted of being
able to manage forty such as
the above whom he denominated 'a slender weed that ought
to be rooted up'. The Advertiser
was then incognito, at a small
tavern, named The Flame of Fire,
and he requests his insulter to
meet him in the great croft
behind Corporal Rare-lad's barn,
thirty miles east of the Glass
Town, with seconds, etc., to try
a match at fisty-cuffs. LCW.

A Feather will take an aerial
excursion, from the ale house
Sulky Boys, Dec. 9, 1830. The price
of admission will be payment for
a tankard of ale.

===

SECOND SERIES OF THE
YOUNG MEN'S
MAGAZINE NO
FOURTH
FOR November 1830
SOLD
BY
SERGEANT TREE
AND ALL
OTHER
Booksellers in the Chief Glass
Town, Wellington's Glass Town,
Paris, Parry's Glass Town,
Ross's Glass Town, etc., etc.
FINISHED
August 28, 1830
Charlotte Brontë[1]

---

[1]Title-page of manuscript, in BPM: No. 12; following editorial note and contents on verso. The manuscript is a hand-sewn booklet of twenty pages (5.3 × 3.5 cm), with brown paper cover dated on front at top 'NOVEMBER 1830'.

This Second Series of magazines is conducted on like
principles with [the] first. The
same eminent authors are
also engaged to contribute
for it. Charlotte Brontë.

CONTENTS

Silence, by the Marquis [of] Douro I
A Song, by Lord Wellesley II
Frenchman's Journal III
Advertisements IV

NO. FOURTH FOR
NOVEMBER 1830
Finished August 22, 1830
1830
CHARLOTTE
BRONTË
Finished August 28, 1830
Charlotte Brontë

SILENCE

'The ability to keep silence well is, in my opinion, far superior to the ability of conversing well, and much more difficult of attainment,' said I to my friend Alexander,[2] as we were sitting together one December evening, by a warm cheering fire, before which – on a sofa – [he] lay stretched in a deep slumber.

'It may be so,' he replied, 'I shall not combat that axiom, but nevertheless I think you will allow that it requires a mind more expansive and better stored with the gifts of nature to excel in the mighty art of eloquence than merely to know when one should hold his tongue.'

'No,' was my answer, 'I cannot agree with you: the wisest of

[2]Alexander Soult, or Young Soult, 'The Rhymer' (Branwell's pseudonym); see *The Enfant*, n. 6.

242

mankind, have both valued and practised silence more than either the graces of rhetoric or the more solid principles of logic.'

'What, then, do you mean that we should all condemn ourselves to a voluntary dumbness, and sit forever mute as statues?'

'No, you quite mistake me. My fundamental laws for the organ of speech are, firstly, that they should restrain their sounding when a wiser or more experienced person than him to whom they belong speaks. Secondly, that when upon any occasion some grand phenomena, beauty or sublimity of Nature or Art is visible, they should invariably leave the eyes and spirit to feast upon it without interruption. Thirdly, that except in rare and special cases their assistance is not requisite to decide a disputed question: action should there act and the tongue be still; its motion but inflames the opposing and overthrow party in a higher degree.'

'That is strange, but at present I leave it untouched to revert to the second law which is still stranger. If a man stood by a cataract of Niagara, on the summit of Etna, the top of Mont Blanc, in the vale of Arno, the plains of my own dear France, [or] saw for the first time ocean in a tempest, a thunderstorm under the Equator, beheld an eclipse of the sun or a hundred other prospects which I cannot now mention, would you not allow him to express his admiration?'

'Certainly not. Indeed, if he felt it sufficiently he could not express it. How? Because his soul, his faculties, his being, would be swallowed up in the glorious scene. No more would a true poet, a Milton or a Shakespeare for instance, utter ejaculations of delight by the falls of Niagara than laugh beneath the hand of Death! Ask yourself Alexander,' I continued, 'you are a poet en vérite and have drunk deeply of the fountain which Pegasus created; also inspiration from Helicon has tuned your lips.[3] Could you exclaim, 'How grand!' or 'How awful!' while the world around was darkened and a bloody circle marked the sun's place in heaven?'

'No, I don't think I could, my lord Marquis, but can you relate me any instance of a man being benefited by his silence amid such appearances?'

'Yes, one, and that is it which has induced me to the opinion I hold.'

'Well, pray favour me with the narration.'

---

[3]When the Muses contended with the daughters of Pieros, Helicon (home of the Muses in Parnassus) rose heavenward with delight, but Pegasus (the winged horse) gave it a kick, stopped its ascent, and brought out of the mountain the soul-inspiring waters of Hippocrene; hence, both Helicon and Pegasus are used allusively of poetic inspiration (Brewer's *Dictionary of Phrase and Fable*).

'I will if you desire it. More than some hundred and eighty years ago, an old man dwelt in Ispahan,[4] who was beloved of a genius for his wisdom. He had more riches than twenty of the most opulent noblemen in Persia together and lived in a style of the utmost magnificence, but in the midst of his splendour, always remembering that those who languished in poverty were members of the same great family of human beings equally with himself, he fed 100 poor men at his house daily and bestowed large donations to the hospitals, charitable asylums, etc.

'He had, however, no heir to inherit his greatness, which circumstance caused him many hours of sorrowful reflection. At length he determined to leave his property to some stranger whom he might judge excellent in wisdom, learning and piety. (Note: I use the word "excellent" here according to its genuine etymology. It comes from the verb "to excell". The accent ought therefore to be placed on the second syllable, as there is reason to believe was the usage in old time, whence the new word-sellers of our language have wrongfully wrested it.) But being unable to find a criterion on which he could depend to try them, he almost despaired of discovering one sufficiently qualified for the happiness and honour meant to be bestowed.

'One evening, he walked out for the purpose of enjoying the cool air. Wholly occupied with these thoughts, he drew near a mosque. It was the hour of sunset prayers. He entered, and, prostrating himself towards Mecca, raised mental supplications to God for direction. Upon rising he felt much comforted and went from the mosque to a public cemetery, where was the tomb of a Persian poet renowned over the world for his wisdom. It was situated under an immense cypress. He lay down beneath its shade and, taking a steel dagger with a sharp, bright point like adamant, carved upon the monument some characters understood only by those that hold commerce with elves, fairies or other inhabitants of the invisible world. Presently a mist began to darken the horizon. It thickened as it rose, and when it reached the zenith assumed the form of a great eagle, which rapidly descended upon the bough of the cypress tree. The old man lifted up his head and thus addressed it:

' "Genius, hear me. I am of a great age. When I die (and the day of that event cannot be far distant), strangers unknown to me will inherit my riches, unless I can find one deserving of them whom I may adopt as my son. Hitherto my efforts to do so have been unsuccessful. I require thy assistance; give it as thou hast done at other times. But first,

---

[4]Esfahan, a principal city of Iran (then Persia). The Brontës' *Grammar of General Geography*, by the Rev. J. Goldsmith (BPM: B45) includes an illustration of Ispahan.

change thy hostile shape and stand obediently before me."

'At these words the eagle became a man. He held in his hand a silver tube, which he presented to Houssain[5] (for that was the old man's name) saying, "Take this, and let him that looks through it without uttering a sentence be thy heir." Then he vanished, and Houssain returned home.

'Shortly after, as he was sitting in a chamber of his palace alone, a slave entered and, kneeling down in token of respect, said that a traveller had arrived who wished to see him, having heard much of his great virtues. Houssain directed the slave to provide him with a repast in one of the chief rooms, to bathe his feet in perfumed water, to show him all the palace and then, after attiring him in a dress taken from his wardrobe, to bring him there. The slave obeyed and in an hour's time he came. Houssain welcomed him kindly; he directed him to sit in the place of honour and asked his name. He replied, "Ibraham".[6]

'When they had conversed awhile, Houssain produced the silver tube and requested him to look through it. He took it with a salaam and applied his eye to one end. Houssain watched with intense anxiety as marks of the most extreme astonishment appeared on the traveller's countenance. At last he broke out with, "I can see Paradise! The glories of heaven! Structures built by angels and beings of imortal beauty! The divine Houris! And lo! Mahomet, our Lord, on the Borak with the golden saddle! Oh! Those mountains, majestic, grand! Those valleys lovely with delights of spring! More enchanting than all that the poets have conceived! That grove where pleasure reposes and where spirits— But what is this? A darkness! A mist has come over the scene. Take it old man, there is magic. You deal with things that are forbidden. Commercing with creatures that the shaster[7] allows no man to think of. Wretch! I leave you; but for the kindness which has been shown me, may our divine Prophet reward you. Farewell." Then he rushed from the apartment and left Houssain perfectly astounded with his vehemence.

'Many others were shown the tube but none, on looking through it,

---

[5]Brother of Prince Ahmed and owner of the magic carpet in the *Arabian Nights*; this story is obviously influenced by the *Arabian Nights*.

[6]Charlotte Brontë was probably aware that the name 'Ibraham' is the Koran's version of Abraham. Her Persian character has all the trappings of his culture: he gives a salaam (the oriental salutation 'Peace'), refers to the Houris (nymphs of the Mohammedan Paradise), and mentions Mohammed's (or Mahomet's) ascent to heaven on the fabulous animal Al Borak (spelt 'Borac' by Charlotte).

[7]Possibly Charlotte Brontë is thinking here of the Shastra, one of the sacred Hindu writings.

could restrain the loudest ejaculations of surprise and pleasure. At length he gave up all hopes of the accomplishment of what he so ardently desired, and for more than a year the tube lay by neglected. One day, however, he was informed that a Frank was in Ispahan at the [?caravan camp] for travellers, whom everyone admired for his knowledge and goodness. Houssain sent a servant with an invitation to his palace, though scarcely hoping that he would prove adequate to the trial.

'The Frank accepted it and came that evening. When Houssain saw him, he was struck with delight at his appearance: exceedingly tall, but so well proportioned that at first sight the tall height of his stature was hardly observed. His countenance and features were noble and handsome; in his large black eye there was a deep scrutinous glance, an intense – almost superhuman – spirit of expression, fire attempered by gentleness, that instantaneously awed beholders. His thick raven hair (contrary to the fashion of his country) waved in wreathed locks over his broad majestic shoulders. With a stately gait he advanced and gracefully knelt. But Houssain hastened to raise him. As soon as they were seated, he gave him the tube and showed the proper end to look through. The Frank continued for a long time gazing in silence. At last he seemed about to speak, but seeing Houssain's perturbed visage, he put it aside without having uttered a word. The old man sprung up and cordially embraced him.

'"My son," he exclaimed at length, "I have attained my wish. Thou art he whom I have so long desired for the inheritor of my fortune." Then after relating the tube's history and the circumstances connected with it, he asked the Frank how he had been able to refrain from speaking.

'"Father," he replied, "what I saw was too glorious for the tongue of man to do justice to in any degree, therefore I was silent. But when the obscurity came over it, I was about to utter an expression of surprise if I had not seen your countenance after when I attempted to speak. This held the words escaping from me, and so I was reserved for the honour I felt unmerited, which you intend to bestow."

'"I shall now die happily," answered Houssain, "for I have found the wisest man on earth. I no longer desire to live; death will be a release from the clay which clogs my soul, and the joys of Paradise will come thereafter."

'Next morning, when his slaves entered the apartment, they beheld him stretched on a couch dead. His countenance was peaceful and serene. His eyes and mouth closed, and all his features settled. Fragrant flowers and spices were strewed over the corpse, which was enveloped in a fine white sheet and, in short, every duty had been performed by an unseen hand. When he was buried all the poor of Ispahan followed his bier to the grave with weeping and lamentation. As for the strange Frank, he – after disposing of his riches in purposes of charity – quitted the city and was never more heard of.'

'Well,' said my friend, when I had finished, 'your story is certainly a curious one; but can you vouch for the truth of it?'

'I can, for I heard it from the identical Frank himself.'

'You said it happened one hundred and eighty years ago!'

'Well, so it did.'

'Then how could you, a person only twenty-three years of age, have heard it from him? Who was he?'

'Guess.'

'I cannot. Pray inform me.'

'He was then Crashie! The perfection of wisdom and our great progenitor!'[8]

August 16, 1830   Marquis of Douro

SONG
By Lord Wellesley

Some love Sorrow's dismal howls,
Write verses on her sighs and scowls,
    And rant about her mourning dress,
Her long black funeral array,
Her veil which shuts out light and day,
    And love her not the less;

Although she sits with woeful face
On some old monumental tomb,
Where yellow skulls and bones have place,
Where corpses rot in churchyard gloom.

I wish some eve as thus she's weeping,
While sober men are soundly sleeping,

---

[8]Crashie (Crashey or Crashi), captain of the original 'Twelves', founders of the Glass Town kingdom. Since *A Romantic Tale*, he seems to have acquired supernatural powers and now resides in the Tower of All Nations. In subsequent manuscripts he is 'the divine Crashie', chief Glass Town arbiter, a venerable old man with long white beard and hair, usually seated on a throne, and possessed of the 'purest benevolence' blended with 'more than mortal wisdom' (*The Foundling*, 31 May – 27 June 1833).

Amid the obscurity of night,
From out its grave a ghost would start
And make her throat receive her heart
  And give her sore afright.

Or catch her by the long black gown,
No matter how the lady screams,
Into the damp vault drag her down
Where sun or moonlight never beam.

But Cheerfulness full well I know,
And oft I've seen her ruddy face,
Her lips, whence streams of pleasure flow,
And where tones of joy have place.

One morn as the skylark tuned his song
Afar in the heavens on high,
I walked forth, the green fields and upland [?throng],
I list the sweet tones from the sky.

  Onward I sprung,
  While light music rung
Above and below and around:
For the blackbird, the linnet, the dove and the thrush
Filled the air with a warbling sound.

The fresh breeze of dawn passed over the hills
  Laden with incense of flowers;
It sung with the fountain and rippled the rills
  And sighed softly through the green bowers.

Joy was in earth and joy was in heaven,
  And joy was also in me;
I felt gladness and strength, health and strong might, given
  By the wind of the morning [?free].

While I brushed the dew with hasty feet
From golden cups and clover sweet,
I felt on my arm a touch like light,
Or the downy wing of some gentle sprite,
And e're I could turn myself around,
I heard the sweet tones and the silvery sound
  Of an oft-heard, well-known voice:

And one stood by, in a robe that shone
As the soft fair clouds which array the moon;
Her radiant eyes were of lucid blue
And her crown of flowers rich odours threw.
   It was her whom all lands and nations bless
   And her welcome name is 'Cheerfulness'.

She gave me a sign with winning grace,
While dimpled smiles illumed her face.
   I followed as she led:
On we passed by moor and lea
Plain and vale and stream and tree,
Over hills where torrents rushed,
Down deep glens where whirlwinds gushed,
   Nought could stop our way.

Now Apollo reached the west,
   Diving in the ocean's wave;
Thetis'[9] bowers afford him rest,
Billows vast his coursers lave.

When we gained a mighty plain
   Stretching to the horizon's bound,
Verdant as the robe of Spring,
Flowers of Summer strowed the ground;
Gloomy silence held her reign,
And the sky's exalted dome
Shone with glory of the stars,
Beauteous gems of twilight's throne.

Suddenly a song arose
Through the obscurity of night;
O'er my sight fair visions grew,
Lovely fawns all swiftly flew,
Upsprang a golden light.

Then merry music rang
And bright lamps radiance flung[10]
On thousand burning gems,
Who sent back the dazzling streams;
And the green grassy earth and the mild ambient air
Glowed with the strong insufferable glare.

[9]Chief of the Nereids, wife of Peleus and mother of Achilles.
[10]'flang' in manuscript.

I viewed it for an instant, then night in double gloom
Fell around on the world, with the silence of the tomb.

The moon no more her pale light shed,
No glimmering stars were o'er my head,
  For I lay asleep in a curtained bed;
  And when I had wakened
  The apparitions all were fled.

Instead of the music's heavenly strain,
I heard the fast-descending rain
Rattle against my window pane;
I tossed about and strove in vain
To sleep or slumber once again.

So, at length I rose
And put on my clothes.
The whole house slept
So I softly crept
Down the long, winding stair,
And passed the gate by bribing the guard,
And I bent my steps to the poultry yard;
  When who should I meet
  At the turn of the street
But Tree, with a cock and hen!

I collared the thief and bade him say
Why he was [there] at this time of day;
But Tree got free and skulked away
  And I never caught him again.[11]

August 27, 1830   Charles Wellesley

A FRENCHMAN'S JOURNAL
CONTINUED, by Tree

May the 12th

The night after that delightful evening I spent at Madame le Comtesse
d'Ouvert was passed at the theatre. I cannot give any adequate

---

[11]Crude as the execution of this poem is, its change in metre and subject matter from
feigned melancholy to blunt, mundane cheerfulness illustrates Lord Charles Wellesley's
ridicule of his brother Douro's plaintive pieces at this time, such as Douro's song in the
previous magazine (and probably Branwell's equally morbid romantic verses).

description of what I saw and felt, but however I will try. Our party consisted of six ladies: Madame Civette, her two daughters Matilde et Louise, La Duchess [de] Rouselle, Madame Crontene and Mademoiselle Cecile Cinolin; and three gentlemen: Le Duc de Rouselle, Le Marquis de Graves and Monsieur le Baron Dupont.

When we entered our box (a front one, handsomely furnished), the prompter's bell was heard to tinkle for the first time. I placed myself in the attitude of eager attention: my eyes fixed towards the stage and my body gracefully bent in the same direction. The bell sounded again, the curtain was gathered up with the celerity of magic, and a general burst of applause announced the actress's appearance. She advanced to the lights and dropped an elegant courtesy to the admiring spectators.

If I might judge from her look, she was about twenty-five years of age. Her dark hair was simply bound with a garland of flowers, her cheeks bloomed with a rouge – I mean, rose hue, and though I heard a vulgar, unpolished Anglais in the next box say broadly out, sans qualification, that she squinted, yet to my mind her harmonious features shone with added lustre from the brilliancy of her eyes. The white robe which she wore swept the ground in the softest folds. In short, she was une perfect beauté.

After an impassioned soliloquy she sung a song, in the midst of which a demoiselle burst from the side scenes and exclaiming, 'Notre père est mort!' sunk senseless on the ground. The curtain descended amid loud weeping – loud weeping and lamentation from the sister!

When it rose again, a vast church was discovered, illuminated by moonlight. Round a tomb in the centre stood a band of nuns chanting masses for him that lay therein, and kneeling at the head and foot were two veiled female figures. In a little time the song for the dead died away, the nuns all slowly retired, a noise like closing doors was heard, and they were left alone. My flesh shuddered at the sight pour c'est une vraisemblance of reality. Presently they rose from the attitude of devotion. Throwing themselves on the tomb, they wept and embraced each other. The veils which had hitherto concealed their faces fell back and I recognized them as those who had formerly appeared. The moon was now hid by gathering clouds, the light faded away, a perfect darkness ensued.

'Soeur,' said one, 'Allons.'

'Non, Henriette,' replied the other. 'Je ne peux pas quitter le tombeau de mon père.'

Their voices came with thrilling power from the impenetrable obscurity in which they were involved.

'Ah, quelle est cette lumière?' they exclaimed, as a faint halo shone round, partially revealing their forms, 'C'est la lune.'

'Non, elle est dérobée—' she was going on, when an apparition rose out of the earth before them.

They shrieked, but in a hollow, sepulchral tone it commanded silence and said, 'Je suis le revenant de votre père: je vous aimais quand j'étais vivant et je vous aime quand je suis mort mon enfant.' The ghost then went on to warn them not to look into a certain small gold box which they would find in his cabinet, for the reason that he was not permitted to disclose. They both solemnly promised to obey him and he vanished. And the curtain dropped.

In ten minutes it was again drawn up, and there appeared a small but splendid room, apparently un boudoir, on a sofa in which sat the youngest of the sisters with the gold box on a table before her. She was silent for some time, but at length this expression escaped her lips, 'Je peux l'ouvir. I will try! But stay, my father's spirit conjured me not to! Yet still, I cannot resist. That sight which I saw might have been an illusion. Oh heavens! What shall I do? Open it? Yes, courage, courage, I may find riches.'

With these words she burst the box and after gazing for a moment said, 'There is nothing! I am disappointed. Ah! yes, here is a paper with writing.' Here she read aloud as follows: 'When next the black hour of midnight wraps the world in darkness, Amraphael (i.e. the angel of death)[12] will guide thee on that far journey whence no traveller returns. Miserable wretch, at the price of life hast thou purchased satisfaction for thy unholy curiosity.'

When she had finished, a long, loud scream announced her late repentance and she sank from the seat in a profound swoon, while a voice exclaimed in mournful accents, 'Oh, my daughter! My daughter! Why hast thou despised the warning?'[13]

Then the usual manoeuvres passed with the curtain, and on its rising for the fourth time a chamber was revealed, all hung with the purest white. In the middle stood a table, likewise covered with white drapery, on which was a coffin that contained a corpse, sheeted and swathed and strewn over with evergreens. It was night; a single lamp shed pale light on the fixed marble countenance of the dead body. No sound disturbed the scene of frozen stillness. The whole theatre hushed at that ghastly spectacle. In a few moments a woman in deep mourning entered noiselessly. She advanced to the coffin and knelt. I felt my heart

[12]Literally, Amraphael means one that speaks of judgement or of ruin. Charlotte Brontë is also possibly thinking here of Azrael, the angel of death, and the subject of one of Branwell Brontë's later poems.

[13]Compare opening lines of Psalm xxii; later quoted by Christ on the cross.

throbbing violently, while involuntary tears trickled down my checks. She raised her voice and sang in low sweet tones the following words:

Death is here, I feel his power,
Here are trophies of his might;
Ruthless warrior, that fair flower
Hath fallen beneath thy blight.

He hath cast his dart at thee,
Sister, thou art gone for aye;
He hath set thy spirit free
And it hath fled away.

Soon the grave will be thy bed,
Tears no more shall dim thine eye;
Thou wilt rest that weary head,
All calm and peacefully.

Undisturbed will be thy sleep,
Nought can break its still repose;
Though the worm may o'er thee creep
It cannot raise thy woes.

I have shut thy glazed eye,
I have heard thy funeral knell,
Now I hush the struggling sigh:
Sister, fare thee well![14]

At the conclusion of this song she rose and burst into a flood of passionate tears, then suddenly flinging herself on the corpse she [did so] again and again for twenty times. After some time she appeared calmer, but her face had assumed an expression of heroic resolution. Presently she cried out, 'Sister, I will not survive thee!' and drawing a sharp bright dagger, which she had hitherto concealed, stabbed herself to the heart and fell dead across the coffin.

At this catastrophe the curtain once more fell. When it rose for the fifth and last time a funeral procession was displayed accompanied by solemn music; but I could not much attend to the final scene for my feelings, together with those of everyone else who was present, were raised to such a pitch by the dreadful denouement, that nothing but sobs and weeping were heard.

When I got home I immediately retired to bed, but was unable to

[14]A year earlier Charlotte Brontë wrote 'The Churchyard A Poem', 24 December 1829, which contains a similar description of a mourner lamenting her dead sister: see *Poems*, p. 83.

sleep a wink the whole night from thinking of the tragedy I had seen. The next morning I was somewhat relieved and went out to walk about the city, and found that the whole talk at cafés, hotels and private houses was concerning the admirable manner in which the two actresses had acquitted themselves the previous night. I cordially joined with everything I heard in their praise, and indeed a better written and better acted tragedy was never produced on any stage.

August the 28, 1830   Tree

ADVERTISEMENTS
BOOKS

The Thief's Dream, A TALE
BY
LORD CHARLES WELLESLEY
Price 10 shillings and 6d

THE CARROT, BY
Private Slingo
Price 6s

[?Colderdenda] of Silverglad, by
CAPTAIN TREE
Price 30s

Clouds and Stars, a Philosoph-
ical Essay, BY THE
MARQUIS DOURO
Price 40 shillings, in 2 vols.

The Bookseller and His Dwarf,
By Lord Wellesley
Price 20s and 4d

ADVERTISEMENTS

Private CRINKLE has the honour of informing his FRIENDS
that he has at length accomplished the WONDERFUL

ACHIEVEMENT
OF Teaching GEESE TO
SPEAK!!!
Six who have learnt that
art, hitherto supposed to belong
exclusively to the human race,
are exhibited by him at his
HOUSE
Known by the name of the
CUT-THROAT
Prices of admission: three s.
grown-up people; 1 and 6d children

NOTICE!!!!
Rare Lads hear me:
If you don't mind I'll kill ye
YOUNG-MAN-NAUGHTY
Inn Ned Laury!!!
August 28, 1830

SECOND SERIES OF THE

YOUNG MEN'S

MAGAZINES. NO.

FIFTH

FOR DECEMBER 1830

Edited by Charlotte Brontë

Sold

by

SERGEANT TREE

AND ALL

OTHER

Booksellers in the Great Glass

Town, Wellington's G T, Paris,
Parry's G T, Ross's G T, etc., etc.
finished September the 1, 1830[1]

This second series of magazines
is conducted on the like principles
with the first. The same eminent
Authors are also engaged to
contribute for it
CHARLOTTE BRONTË

CONTENTS

Strange Events, by Lord Wellesley I
On Seeing an Ancient Dirk, etc. II
A Frenchman's Journal III
Conversations IV

NO FIFTH: FOR DECEMBER
1830
Finished September 1, 1830
1830
CHARLOTTE
BRONTË
1830
September 1, 1830

STRANGE EVENTS
BY LORD CHARLES WELLESLEY

It is the fashion nowadays to put no faith whatsoever in supernatural
appearances or warnings. I am, however, a happy exception to the

---

[1]Title-page of manuscript, formerly in Law Collection, now lost; following editorial note
and contents on verso. The manuscript is a hand-sewn booklet of twenty pages (5 × 3.5 cm)
in brown paper cover. Fortunately a transcript of the manuscript, made by Davidson Cook
when he examined the Law Collection in 1925, survives in the BPM. The following text has
been printed from this source, although several of the contents have been published,
presumably also from Davidson Cook's transcription (or from C. W. Hatfield's copy of Cook's
work): see Christine Alexander, *A Bibliography of the Manuscripts of Charlotte Brontë* (Haworth
and USA: The Brontë Society in association with Meckler Publishing, 1982), pp. 30, 62, 132.

general rule, and firmly believe in everything of the kind. Instances of the good foundation I have for this obsolete belief often meet my observation, tending to confirm me in it. For the present I shall content myself with mentioning a few.

One day last June happening to be extremely wet and foggy, I felt, as is usual with Englishmen, very dull.[2] The common remedies – razor, rope and arsenic – presented themselves in series, but as is unusual with Englishmen, I did not relish any of them. At last the expedient of repairing to the Public Library for diversion entered my head. Thither I accordingly went, taking care to avoid crossing the great bridge lest the calm aspect of the liquid world beneath it might induce me to make a summary descent.

When I entered the room a bright fire flickering against the polished sienna hearth somewhat cheered my drooping spirits. No one was there, so I shut the door. Taking down Brandart's *Finished Lawyer*,[3] I placed myself on a sofa in the ingle-cheek. Whilst I was listlessly turning over the huge leaves of that most ponderous volume, I fell into the strangest train of thought that ever visited even my mind, eccentric and unstable as it is said by some insolent puppies to be.

It seemed as if I was a non-existent shadow, that I neither spoke, eat, imagined or lived of myself, but I was the mere idea of some other creature's brain. The Glass Town seemed so likewise. My father, Arthur and everyone with whom I am acquainted, passed into a state of annihilation; but suddenly I thought again that I and my relatives did exist, and yet not us but our minds and our bodies without ourselves. Then this supposition – the oddest of any – followed the former quickly, namely, that WE without US[4] were shadows; also, but at the end of a long vista, as it were, appeared dimly and indistinctly, beings that really lived in a tangible shape, that were called by our names and were US from whom WE had been copied by something – I could not tell what.

Another world formed part of this reverie in which was no Glass Town or British Realm in Africa except Hindoustan, India, Calcutta. England was there but totally different in manners, laws, customs, and inhabitants – governed by a sailor – my father Prime Minister – I and

[2]The inhabitants of Glass Town have a general dislike for Englishmen, whom they see as sallow, bilious, 'whey-faced whiners'.

[3]No record has been found of this book.

[4]A curiously sophisticated concept of the symbiotic relationship between the creator and the created (and the latter's historical counterpart) for a fourteen-year-old. This discussion may also throw some light on the origins of Charlotte Brontë's signatures 'UT' and 'WT' ('us two' and 'we two'): see textual introduction.

Arthur young noblemen living at Strathaye, or something with a name like that – visionary fairies, elves, brownies, the East Wind, and wild Arab-broken horses – shooting in moors with a fat man who was a great book. But I am lost, I cannot get on.

For hours I continued in this state, striving to fathom a bottomless ocean of Mystery, till at length I was roused by a loud noise above my head. I looked up and thick obscurity was before my eyes. Voices, one like my own but larger and dimmer (if sound may be characterized by such epithets) and another which sounded familiar, yet I had never, that I could remember, heard it before, murmuring unceasingly in my ears.

I saw books removing from the top shelves and returning, apparently of their own accord. By degrees the mistiness cleared off. I felt myself raised suddenly to the ceiling, and ere I was aware, behold two immense, sparkling, bright blue globes within a few yards of me. I was in [a] hand wide enough almost to grasp the Tower of All Nations, and when it lowered me to the floor I saw a huge personification of myself – hundreds of feet high – standing against the great Oriel.[5]

This filled me with a weight of astonishment greater than the mind of man ever before had to endure, and I was now perfectly convinced of my non-existence except in another corporeal frame which dwelt in the real world, for ours, I thought, was nothing but idea.

After I had gazed for an unconscionable time at this vision, the door opened and Colonel Crumps entered. The apparition immediately vanished away like smoke, the voices ceased, and I am left in dismal uncertainty as to whether I am or am not for the remnant of my doubting days.

Can anybody account for this that I have related? And is it not the height, depth, breadth of metaphysical insight, enquiry, illumination, science, knowledge, profundity, unsatisfactoriness or whatever else you choose? I think it is. Who after this will disbelieve in Ghosts? None but sceptics, deists, atheists, infidels; or if any else do, here is another proof of my creed's verity.

A year or two ago I went one fine morning in summer to the residence of a respected friend of mine. On my arrival I was told that he had not yet risen! It was ten o'clock and I knew that one of his favourite and most practised maxims was

> Early to bed and early to rise
> Is the way to be healthy, wealthy and wise,

so I suspected that something wrong must have occurred. I asked if he was ill: the servant answered, 'No.' I demanded to see him and was

[5]Note the influence of *Gulliver's Travels*.

shown upstairs into the antechamber of his apartment where the valet left me.

Being on very intimate terms, I entered the room sans cérémonie. To my surprise it was completely darkened by thick curtains let down over the windows. Everything stood in deep shade, only the white towel over the washstand gleamed like a sprite through the gloom. There was a solemn silence unbroken save by deep groans as of one in mortal agony. I advanced to the bed. As I approached, my friend raised himself and threw his arms round my neck. For a few minutes I stood in taciturn sympathy while he wept like a child. When in a pitying tone I ventured to ask what afflicted him so dreadfully, he only redoubled his heart-rending sobs, which caused me to mingle my tears with his. When he became calmer I again enquired the cause of his grief. He replied thus:

'My dear young friend, it is the knowledge that I must now take a long farewell of you, for ere twelve hours are past, Death will have bound with indissoluble chains the tongue which now speaks falteringly, and he will have firmly sealed the eye which weeps bitter tears as it gazes for the last time on the only one whom I have ever found worthy of my friendship.'

'And what do you mean?' said I alarmed. 'You, a hale and strong man, not more than forty years old, talking of dying before twelve hours – I do not understand you.'

'Then I will inform you,' he answered mournfully. 'One night exactly twenty years since, I was with a party of young people at a friend's house. The conversation happening to turn on superstition, many instances of it were brought forward, and among others the following, viz., that if a man went out on a night when the moon was at its full and spoke words to this effect: "Moon, thou knowest all things, number to me my days," a being would appear and tell him the day and hour of his death. Most of the company laughed at this but it affected me strangely. The moon chanced that night to be a full one, and I determined to try the truth of what I had heard. Accordingly I slid out of the house without being observed and took my way to a hill a mile distant. When I reached it my resolution somewhat failed me, and fear, the troubler, took possession of my heart.

'All was so still and silent around. The far off habitations of man were distinguishable only by the brightness of the candles or fires within. No voice or murmur came on the low moaning wind, and in these circumstances I half felt inclined to go back again, leaving my errand unexecuted, but at length, ashamed of my childishness, I summoned courage to pronounce the mysterious phrase, looking steadfastly at the cold bright moon as she held on her appointed course.

'No sooner had I finished than I saw a dim form flitting over towards me from the opposite bank of a river that rolled at my feet. It came swiftly on. I trembled and strove to flee, but could not. Presently it alighted beside me. The shape was a column of mist with a thin mantle through which I could discern trees and other objects, and floating round it I could hear a murmuring sound, inarticulate but perfectly dissimilar from the tone of a human being's voice, come from the spirit, and this was its speech: "Mortal, hear thy doom! At this hour twenty years hence, thy body will be given to the worms." Then it vanished and left me.

'Do not say it was an illusion or imposition. I know to the contrary. Adieu, Lord Charles, I shall never see you in this world. Come again at eight o'clock to close my eyes.

I left him as he desired, supposing that his brain was disordered, and at eight o'clock returned. He was dead, but I saw his corpse stretched out and ready for interment. His eyes were staring wide open; nobody was able to shut them. I laid my fingers on the lids and they fell instantly.

August 29, 1830   C. WELLESLEY

ON SEEING AN ANCIENT DIRK IN THE ARMORY OF THE TOWER OF ALL NATIONS BLOODSTAINED WITH THREE DISTINCT SPOTS WHICH MARKS NONE HAVE YET BEEN ABLE TO ERASE. BY THE M[ARQUIS OF] DOURO.

Dagger, what heart hath quivered neath thy blow?
Whence fell these three dark spots to stain the steel?
All else is bright: was it a human Foe
Who did the rankling of thy strong blade feel?
Or has some ruffian grasped that jewelled hilt
And pierced of innocence the quiet breast?
Hast thou the glorious blood of martyrs spilt,
Or torn the mighty warrior's lofty crest?

Perhaps in gloomy Forest thou has slain
The Tiger or the Lion – horrid King.
Does hot blood from his heart thy brightness stain?
Didst thou from him loud roars of anguish wring?
Why, 'midst each glancing sword and shield and spear
Which dart around insufferable day,
Dost thou alone tarnished and marked appear,
Not sending forth an undefiled ray?

Ages on Ages long have passed away
Since thou wast ruthless in the battle plain,
Since chieftains clad in polished war array
Have with thee triumphed o'er the bloody slain.
Thou hast not yet forgot the purple streams
That slaked of old thy savage thirst for gore.
Black mid the radiance which around it gleams
Appear those remnants of the days of yore.

What spell, pronounced by the unholy tongue
Of wizard or magician, gave command
That those three drops in wrath or treachery wrung,
For rolling years untold would steadfast stand
Irraseable by power of mortal hand?
Dagger, thou knowest not: voiceless is the crowd
Of ancient arms that clothe this spacious wall.
Voiceless and speechless are those nobles grand
Who bore thee once; now each in gloomy pall
Lies deaf even to his own shrill battle call,
Which erst had roused him from the slumber deep
And girt him with a giant's vigorous might,
Sent him like thunder or the whirlwind sweep
To death or victory in the glorious fight,
Vict'ry's reward and death's eternal night.

August 30, 1830   DOURO

A FRENCHMAN'S JOURNAL
CONTINUED BY TREE

June the 19th

A few days after my visit to the theatre, I was sitting in my apartment
meditating on the various things I had seen, when a servant entered and
announced the arrival of Monsieur de Mas-berri, one of my most
intimate friends. I ordered him to be shown up. After we had greeted
each other and conversed on the ordinary topics of the day, a pause
ensued during which his thoughts appeared to be occupied with some
important affair. At length he broke silence with, 'Monsieur le Baron,
mon ami, avez-vous joué au rouge et noir?'
'Non,' I answered.
'Je veux vous l'enseigner, vous voulez venir avec moi?' said he.
I was perfectly ignorant of the danger I ran the risk of encountering

261

and consented out of a foolish curiousity. I was about to order my carriage, but he told me that was unnecessary, as in many portions of the route he intended to take me I should find it useless.

After quitting the square I resided in, we turned down a long street and from thence entered a narrow lane of great length. Knocking at the door of one of the houses, it opened and discovered a passage with an iron gateway at one end which, when my friend touched a concealed spring, in one tick started asunder displaying a wide square, well-swept and sprinkled, surrounded by a range of magnificent buildings, which however were only one storey high, in order I suppose that their summits might not overtop the mean edifices around, thereby proclaiming their existence to the world, 'for evil deeds love darkness'.

In the centre of the building at the farthest side was a splendid mirror covered with brass plates. It unfolded at our approach and admitted us to a saloon, which for grandeur I think can scarcely find a rival in all Paris. The walls were entirely built of highly polished grey marble, as was the roof, supported by fluted pillars of the same, crowned with Corinthian capitals. At one extremity was a little mirror of plate glass in the most massive and costly frame I remember to have seen, reflecting the whole saloon and producing a beautiful effect. The cornices were richly gilt. Low sofas, covered with superfine crimson cloth bordered by a deep fringe of gold twist, ran along each side of this spacious apartment. But the most wonderful adornment and that which chiefly attracted my gaze was the figures of two eagles suspended in mid-air, on the principle of that enterprising ancient[6] who proposed to construct a leaden statue of Cleopatra which would hang between heaven and earth by the influence of two magnets, one above and other below, of equal powers of attracting, that acting against each other should leave the poor statue unable to make choice of either: a spectacle for all the nations of the earth to gaze at. Those eagles were in battle array: they were of iron and most spiritedly moulded, every feather being erect and seeming to shiver with rage, while the fearful talons, vigorously contracted, betokened mortal hatred. In the night time, I was told, the appearance was greatly heightened by a marvellous piece of mechanism which caused continual coruscations of light to emanate from their eyes, thereby illuminating the room, and so bright were these flashes that no candelabras were requisite.

In the midst of all this splendour was a company of about fifty human beings, congregated round a table. The faces of some glowed with joy;

[6]It seems unlikely that Charlotte Brontë derived this idea from an ancient source, since knowledge of magnets attracting ferrous metals only (not lead) was widespread in the ancient world; see Plato (*Ion*) and Lucretius Carus (*De Rerum Natura*).

others had the ashy paleness of despair. A few were with cool but desperate madness persevering steadfastly in a luckless course of gambling (for that was the occupation of these deluded creatures), merely at every fresh loss giving vent to the bitterness of their heart by an energetic grin or gnash of teeth. I need not relate the entreaties, illusions and lies which were used by one of the party to induce me to join him in a single game for a very small sum. Suffice it to say that I complied and risked three games, at all of which I won, and then went home highly delighted at my success.

For a fortnight after, scarcely a day passed that I did not revisit the saloon, sometimes losing and sometimes winning. But now I was a confirmed gamester: that fascinating, enchaining, spell-binding vice had gained full ascendancy over me, for my disposition was of that singular character which is most ready to take the viper to its bosom, and there retain and hold it fast, though the poison may be destroying peace and consuming life.

On Thursday, June the eleventh, I went there in a cheerful temper, having the night previously gained a thousand louis d'or. On my arrival I found only an old grey-headed man reading the *Moniteur* and some other journal with a similar name. (Since my bout at the dinner mentioned in a former chapter, I have taken nothing to do with politics, and do not even know the cognomens of the various Parisian newspapers.) On my entrance he laid it down and, after a little ordinary small-talk, asked me to play a hand with him at whist. I readily agreed. We each staked our separate fortunes. He told me that he was Le Duc de Cassamboul, who I knew was the richest nobleman in France; and I believed him at the word of a friend who accidently dropped in. The desire to possess his riches tempted me to the step. I felt certain of gaining when I glanced at his withered, doting countenance, and palsied, trembling hand. But he was too cunning for me. I lost. Yes, I lost all my fortune!

In truth, it was a sad and an unexpected blow; but there is no use in lamenting that [?enough of that work], and at the time, ay, for many a long day, I fear my eyes were seldom dry. No matter! I have now a merry little tavern, though I've lost my fine palace and estates. True, I was bundled out of them to make room for a scoundrel (for who should this Duc de Cassamboul turn out to be but a dirty swindler). What does that signify? He is perhaps as good as the heir I might have left them to. It is also a fact that nobles no longer honour me with their company. This circumstance, however, troubles me in a very slight degree; pleasanter companions than they are now surround me. My cellar is now oftener cheered by the sought of light feet 'tripping the fantastic toe',[7] while human voices give answer to the music of a viol, which though the strings be cracked may yet have a sweet tone in the ears of the happy.

Aug. 31   To be continued. Tree   1830

CONVERSATIONS

De Lisle and Lord Charles Wellesley.

Lord Wellesley: Well, De Lisle, I'm happy to see you; nous deux can enjoy half an hour's talk before the rest of the company arrive.

De Lisle: Conversation is, I think, the most agreeable mode of passing away time in the absence of books; that is, when one has a pleasant companion to enliven or diversify the talk, and none can possibly be better off in that respect than I am at present. But I thought, Lord Charles, that we would have the honour of your brother's company?

Lord Wellesley: I waited for him nearly an hour, but as he did not make his appearance I sent for his valet, who informed me that the Marquis of Douro had gone that morning to Doctor Hume's residence and was not yet returned. Of course I understood by this that he was retained by important business. I therefore came without him. Indeed I had myself heard the day before that a certain young lady had arrived at the Glass Town, but did not chuse[8] for certain reasons to tell Arthur.

De Lisle: I believe I have seen the person to whom you allude. Is she not Sir A. Hume's daughter?

Lord Wellesley: Yes, do you know her?

De Lisle: I have painted her portrait in the character of Hebe.[9]

Lord Wellesley: A very fit subject (as her father would say) for that character. She's the picture of youth and health, a play upon your painting. By the way, do you think her handsome?

De Lisle: Extremely so. Her face and figure well become the Elysian scenes in which I placed her. I touched off her glossy brown hair well, but it is impossible to do justice [to] fine eyes which hers are in an eminent degree.

[7]Compare Milton, *L'Allegro*, l. 31.

[8]An archaism probably derived from the Bible, Shakespeare or Scott: 'chuse' rather than 'choose' was commonly used in the seventeenth and eighteenth centuries; it was less common in the nineteenth century, although Scott appears to have used it (*OED*).

[9]Greek goddess of youth and cup-bearer to the gods, daughter of Zeus and Hera (Juno); she had the power of restoring youth and vigour to gods and men. On 10 November 1830, Charlotte Brontë wrote the poem 'Lines on seeing the portrait of— [Marian Hume], Painted by De Lisle'. It is signed 'Marquis of Douro' and is related to this discussion; see *Poems*, p. 121.

Lord Wellesley: And who, pray, was it ordered you to paint her as Hebe? It could not surely have been her father; he would never have thought of such a thing.

De Lisle: No, it was my own idea. I thought her cheerful, smiling countenance and juvenile form well adapted to personate Juno's daughter.

Lord Charles Wellesley: So they were. Has Arthur seen the portrait, do you know?

De Lisle: I believe he has, but on that point I cannot be certain. The day after it was carried to Doctor Hume's palace, he paid me a visit in my studio and uttered some fine philippics[10] on the beauty of portrait painting in the hands of a great master who has good models to copy from. And how well many of the ancient Grecian and Roman deities were calculated, when managed with propriety, to be the masks or characters under which beautiful persons of all ages might be represented. He spoke with eloquence and more animation than is usual to him. Before his departure, as we were shaking hands, he placed this ring, the most rich and costly one I have ever seen, on my finger. I shall keep it as a memorial of him for life and take it with me to my grave. When he drew it from his own finger he said, 'De Lisle, take this as a mark of my admiration of your wonderful and unsurpassed talents, not only as an historical but also as a portrait painter. Than you I know no man who has a finer sense of what exquisite beauty is, or a more proper judgement of the positions and situations in which loveliness almost divine should be placed.'

Lord Wellesley: Oh, no doubt he was alluding to Marian's effigy. What attitude did you place her in?

De Lisle:

Holding the silver cup on high
Crowned with the dew wine of the sky.

Lord Wellesley:

In still repose all calmly laid
Under the green embow'ring shade.

De Lisle:

The light of youth illumes her eye,
Cares seem before her smile to fly.

Lord Wellesley:

Peaceful reclined mid heavenly flowers
Unheeded glide the endless hours.
Her crown is immortality,

---

[10]An obvious misuse of the word.

> Therefore swift time may onward fly,
> Her lapsing years will ever roll:
> They have no end, no destined goal.

De Lisle:
Laughing.
We are rhythmical about my poor painting, Lord Charles.

Lord Wellesley: Can you tell the reason why the ancients excelled us in statuary but fell far short in painting?

De Lisle: It might have been so. You know the fine arts are scarce in number. Their names are Poetry, Painting and Statuary (Music I exclude). Well then, in my opinion the ancients reckoned Poetry the highest, Statuary next, and Painting lowest. To the first, lofty and sublime themes were assigned. The second dealt chiefly in the depicture of lovely or majestic forms, either with grace and elegance to please the spectator or strength and dignity to awe him. The third contented itself with expressing subjects generally low and common in their nature with truth and animation. Their chief ambition was to deceive those who saw their pieces into a supposition of their reality: witness the Curtain [of] Parrhasius and the Grapes of Zeuxis,[11] but as there is no rule without some exception, the 'Jupiter on his Throne surrounded by Gods', of the latter artist and also his 'Helen', were I doubt not some of the finest specimens of the art whether ancient or modern.

Lord Wellesley: De Lisle, will you paint my portrait?

De Lisle: Certainly, my lord, if you desire it. When would it please you to commence sitting?

Lord Wellesley: Tomorrow morning at twelve o'clock. I will be portrayed in company with my brother. We can never be separated as long as it is in our power to hold together.

De Lisle:
Closing his eyes.
I see it, visions come fast on 'that inward eye which is the bliss of solitude'.[12] There I behold in the gloom of an ancient forest, two creatures of more than mortal beauty, reposing beside a clear rill creeping through wild woodflowers that love the shade. One with majestic hand sweeps the strings of a harp, whence soft strains that are

---

[11]Zeuxis (late fifth century BC), a Greek painter famous for his ideal portrait of Helen of Troy and for his realistic paintings of still-life. Birds are said to have pecked at his painting of a bunch of grapes, mentioned here. Parrhasius, a contemporary of Zeuxis, is said to have excelled him in illusionistic painting. In a competition between the two, Zeuxis mistook Parrhasius's painting of a curtain for reality and attempted to draw it aside.

[12]Wordsworth, 'I wandered lonely as a cloud', ll.21–2.

consecrated on the altar of endurance and wholly devoted to eternity emanate, and with sweet lingering tones bind the ear of pensiveness to listen, or with louder swell challenge storms and tempests to rival the grandeur of their music. See how these large imperial orbs irradiate the darkness. What symmetry of the ancients can equal that peerless figure? Look at that ray of light streaming through the old world concentrating on his lofty forehead, revealing the sublime intellect visible in every feature. Haughtiness and pride contract not that smooth brow or curl that lip expressive only of benignity.

Now, I turn to the other, to a personification of grace and elegance and beauty, and blue eyes that shame the violets crowding round his feet, bright brown hair streaked with threads of gold flung back from his ivory front in ringlet that the Zephyr delights to play among. Inspiration has breathed into his spirit: his head is uplifted to the sky, his parted lips, the glowing glance, the attitude denoting joy – all show that divine enthusiasm which Genius causes sometimes to overflow the souls of her true sons. Sweeter than the symphony of forest minstrels peeping from the bowery trees are the sounds which flow from that lute – 'murmurs beside the woodland stream and music sweeter than its own'.[13]

[Enter a servant.]
What does the scoundrel want? He has dissipated the apparition.
Servant: The company have arrived; they are in the small rotunda, and supper is served and now waits for you, gentlemen.
Curtain falls.

September 1, 1830

SECOND SERIES OF
THE YOUNG MEN'S
MAGAZINES. NO.
SIXTH
SECOND NO. FOR DEC.
1830
Edited by Charlotte Brontë

[13]Wordsworth, 'A Poet's Epitaph', ll.39–40.

SOLD
BY
SERGEANT TREE
AND ALL
OTHER
Booksellers in the Great
Glass Town, Wellington's
Glass Town, Paris, Parry's
Glass Town, Ross's Glass Town, etc., etc.
Finished September 4
1830[1]

This Second Series of magazines have been conduc-
ted on like principles with
the first. The same eminent
authors have also been engaged to contribute for it.
Charlotte Brontë

CONTENTS

An Extraordinary Dream I
Traveller's Meditations II
A Frenchman's Journal III
Concluding Address IV

[1]Title-page of manuscript, in BPM: B86; editorial note and contents on verso. The manuscript is a hand-sewn booklet of twenty pages (5.3 × 3 cm) with a brown paper cover dated 'NO. II. DECEMBER 1830'.

NO. SIXTH. SECOND
NO. FOR DECEMBER
1830
Finished September 4th
1830
CHARLOTTE
BRONTË
September 4
1830

AN EXTRAORDINARY DREAM
By Lord Charles Wellesley

I understand many were convinced of the truth of supernatural interference with the affairs of men by perusing the article entitled 'Strange Events' in your last number. I therefore take the liberty of inserting the following 'extraordinary dream', as a further and indisputable proof of what I have advanced.

When I was lately in the country, I chanced one afternoon to be alone in my father's library.[2] Arthur had gone out and was not expected to return till eleven or twelve o'clock at night, so I shut and barred the door intending to remain here for the rest of the day. Having been all the morning wandering about the fields, etc., I felt a degree of weariness which induced [me to] lie down on the sofa. Presently my eyes closed and I fell into a slumber.

In this slumber, I thought I was walking on the banks of a river, which murmured over small pebbles at the bottom, gleaming like crystals through the silver stream. A grove was on either side, whose trees were tall, graceful and slender. Their branches were clothed with foliage of a light green hue; the leaves were small and apparently had but just unclosed to greet the arrival of spring. Vernal flowers also peeped[3] here and there, scattered or in rich clusters, from the young grass; and the green buds of the wild rose trees around were unopened; and a mild warmth was shed from the sun then at its height [?in the] blue sky. In the groves on each hand all was light and pleasant. The dark impenetrable shades and obscure recesses of summer, when the

---

[2] At Strathfieldsay, the Duke of Wellington's country estate in Wellington's Land, west of the Glass Town.
[3] 'Pept' in manuscript: a misspelling of the archaic 'peept'?

woods are in full leafage, were not to be seen. Long vistas opening amid the trees gave glimpses of the distant landscape, which appeared rocky and woody like that which really surrounds my father's country palace.

Suddenly, as I was gazing at this scene, I thought the portion of bank under my feet gave way and I fell into the water. By dint of good swimming, however, I reached a tree of the willow kind drooping over. I caught hold of its branches and got out with no other harm than a wet skin. Then I immediately took the way home, as it seemed to me, but was detained on the road by something which I have now entirely forgot.

It appeared evening by the time I arrived. I was very hot, but my clothes clung like damp cloths around me. I thought I crossed the hall and ascended the grand stairs, then went through the north square of the corridor, ascended the other flight, passed the gallery and went into the private parlour. Here I found a large fire and in my dream heard distinctly the roar of the flames ascending the chimney. No one was there and I sat down to dry myself.

In a short time, I thought Doctor Hume entered. After staring at me for a short time he asked if I was well.

'Perfectly so,' was my reply.

He shook his head as if in doubt. I laughed and was going to address him again, when my father came in and I heard his voice say as plainly as ever I have in my life, 'Well, Charles, I never saw you look so pale and miserable before. What is the matter? Where have you been?'

At that moment I felt a cold shivering sensation run through my frame. I told him how I had fallen into the river and he ordered me instantly to retire to rest, lest I should suffer from the accident by fever or some other sickness, which from my appearance he greatly feared. In obedience to his commands, I thought I immediately retired to my own room and got into bed as quickly as possibly.

When there, I was racked by a dull torturing pain in my forehead which prevented me from sleeping. Sometimes my limbs were icy cold, sometimes burning hot; I could hear the violent throbbing of my temples. Thrilling pain ran through my body from head to foot. A knot was in my throat. I felt dreadfully thirsty, my tongue dry as a dusty stick and all my teeth aching as if they were in want of the dentist's instruments and skill. In this extremity, I dreamt I rose and, tottering to the washstand, seized the ewer and drained its contents. Then I reeled back to bed and flung myself almost fainting upon it.

After midnight I fell asleep, and in my dream, dreamt many troubled confused dreams, all of which have faded from my memory except this one. I thought I was sitting myself in the garden, on a fine moonlight night, and enjoying the fine scent of the roses in the bower above me, when I saw four huge black indistinct forms stealing up the alley. I was about to rise and run for it but something caught hold of my hair from behind and held me fast till the four came close. They seized me and hurried off at a swift pace.

The scene shifted to a dark room, where was a very old man of most venerable aspect, seated on a throne before which knelt Captain Tree. I thought the old man was a wizard, and I could perceive his familiar spirit lurking in the form of a hideous beast behind the throne. He took me by the hand and presenting me to Tree said, 'The powers of darkness deliver him into thy hands for life and death, to do with him as thou wilt.' Tree gave a shriek of joy, and with that I awoke from the vision within a vision.

It was morning and a warm golden sun was shining through the chamber window. I tried to get up, but a distracting pain which passed through my head at the moment caused me to fall back again on my pillow; so I lay still till Arthur came out of his dressing-room. I called him to the bedside. When he saw me he retreated a step or two, exclaiming in a tone of horror, 'Charles, you look like death!'

'And I feel like it too,' said I.

He gazed at me for an instant, his lips quivered and the tears gushed into his eyes. Then he dashed them away and hastily quitted the room. In a little time he came back with my father and Doctor Hume.[4] My father asked me how I felt. I described my sensations, and Hume muttered in an undertone, 'He can scarcely live many days.' The burning heat which I had hitherto endured now gave way to a feeling as if blasts of cold wind were constantly blowing over me. I shivered incessantly; a loud thundering noise was in my ears; and the thirstiness which I had felt redoubled. To my dismay, when I tried to ask for water my tongue and the organs of speech refused to obey the impulse. About noon all my limbs stiffened and turned icy cold. I lost the power of motion altogether. Hume held a mirror over my mouth, but not a trace of steam was visible when he looked at it.

Now I dreaded that they would suppose I was dead and tried in vain to give some sign of life. The emotions of horror which filled my mind are unutterable, indescribable, as I heard my father say, 'He is gone,' and both he and Arthur burst into tears. After some time of speechless anguish they left the apartment. Hume now removed my living corpse to a sofa and covered it with a white sheet. He then went out with the attendants. Mortal lips must not attempt the relation of my sufferings as

---

[4]See *Tales of the Islanders*, vol. I, n. 14.

the idea of being buried with dead bodies amid stench and putrefaction, while my soul yet held and animated its tenement, took possession of my mind. I lay alone till the shades of evening began to close around. Then the door opened and I heard Arthur's footsteps; I could not see him. He drew near and knelt down by me. I felt his tears falling like hot rain on my face and he sobbed audibly. He remained with me till dawn, and then again departed.

A few hours after sunrise, one came with a leaden coffin into which I was put. Then that into another and the nails were screwed down. I was taken to a different room where I lay for some days, and every night Arthur watched beside me. On the morning of the fourth day, people were constantly coming in and out to see my coffin. Many wept and cried aloud, but at length silence was commanded. I heard solemn steps approaching. They lifted me and I knew I was going to be carried out to the grave. Excruciating, horrible, is the remembrance of that frightful dream!

After the space of an hour my funeral procession reached the cathedral.[5] The burial service was read over me. I heard millions thronging round my coffin and the sound of kisses on the lid. At length a deep voice exclaimed, 'Keep off!' The ropes were fastened and I was gradually lowered into the vault. The doors were closed, bolted and locked. By degrees the sound of the multitude died away and not a voice or step echoed through the vast aisles at that tremendous moment, which but to think of is unsupportable agony. The bonds which chained me were [?removed]: I could now speak and stir. [?Bakracking] was the thought that none could hear. In this state I lay for what appeared to me a thousand years.

At last the iron gates of the vault were raised. I might take oath that no creature on earth ever before experienced such sincere joy as I did at that moment. I heard footsteps descending the stairs and then my father's voice say, 'The uppermost coffin is his, Catherine. I cannot bear to look at it.'

Another voice, in tones like my mother, answered, 'Why could not I close his eyes? Oh! The thought of his lying here is dreadful. I cannot endure it. Let me go! Let me go!'

'No, mother, stop! I am alive!' exclaimed I.

My father said, 'Alive, my son? Then not long shall you be there!' And with these words the lid of my coffin was strongly wrenched open.

The first object that met my dazzled sight was the flashing of his eyes through the gloom of the vault. My mother had fainted, but she soon

[5]St Michael's Cathedral, burial place of the Glass Town nobility.

recovered. We again ascended to the light of day. Arthur was walking to and fro with troubled step. I sprang to him and clasped my arms round his neck. He gave me one long fervent kiss, and said, 'I know that I am embracing my brother's spirit. Yet except this shroud and winding sheet it is like him.'

'No, Arthur,' said I. 'It was a sort of dream into which I had fallen, and now I am happily recovered from it.'

After a long time his incredulity was convinced, and, getting into our carriage which stood at the east gate of the cathedral, we all drove home. The rattling of the wheels caused me to awake, but – strange to say – I was standing at the door of my bedroom with a candle in my hand (for it was perfectly dark), dressed from head to foot in grave-clothes. I rushed terror-struck into the apartment. Arthur was there and he received me with marks of the greatest astonishment.

'Charles,' cried he, 'what trick is this! Where have you been for the last fortnight?'

'That's more than I can tell, Arthur,' was my answer, and then I gave him the relation of my unparalleled vision. The only information that he could favour me with in return was that about a fortnight ago I had been seen by one of the servants crossing the courtyard with hasty strides and the aspect of a somnambulist, and that, from that time to the present, not the slightest intelligence of me could be procured.

A day or two after, I went [hunting] with two or three men, and, resting in the course of the chase, I was detached from the rest of the party, and, trying to rejoin them, came to a place exactly like that I saw in my dream. Lost in surprise, I stood for a moment on the bank and then attempted to fly. But the ground failed and I fell in. Being an excellent swimmer, I made for a drooping willow (the counterpart of the visionary one) and by its assistance got out. In trying to return home I lost my way. But at length I met a man who set me right again. It was evening before I reached the house. I went into the private parlour. My father and Hume came in. They remarked upon the paleness of my face and I was sent to bed. It was a long while before I could fall asleep, but when I did I dreamt the same dream about Tree and the wizard. On awakening, however, in the morning, I was quite well, and that rejoiced me almost as much as being let out of the coffin did.

Sep. 2, 1830

A TRAVELLER'S MEDITATIONS
By the Marquis of Douro

This wide world I have compassed round:
Beheld each distant[6] shore;
I have been where nought but the sullen sound
  Was heard of ocean's roar;

Where boundless liquid plains were spread
Bright in the tropic solar beam,
Afar from the blue arch overhead
  Rushed down a burning stream.

O, I have lain while twilight's robe
Wrapped the heavens and wrapped the globe;
Stretched on the deck for a lonely pillow
List'ning the wind and the rolling billow;
Watching each wave set, sink and rise
Neath the gold light of the evening skies;
While whispered around me the Zephyr calm
Sweeter than music and softer than balm.
Each breeze seemed the voice of a spirit on high
Speaking of peace in the tones of the sky:
Some went past with rushing swell,
Others more mild on the waters fell,
Scarce heaving with their gentle breath
The rippling wavelets snowy wreath,
Subsiding as the moon arose
And threw her light on their liquid snows,
Which melted away and appeared again
Crested by the restless main,
As if, when they saw her silver beam,
They loved to sport in the pearly gleam.
A ceaseless murmur went up from the ocean
Which told of his never-ending motion,
Of the waves that eternally roll and rage,
War against the solid caverns wage:
  Sinking and swelling
  Like sea-monster yelling,

---

[6]In manuscript, 'distant' written above 'star', which has been left uncancelled.

Unseen in tenebrious night.
Loud roars the dull thunder
That still surface under,
Far hid from the regions of light
That fathomless. tomb,
That kingdom of gloom,
Where darkness aye reigns in his might.

And I have been on the icy hill,
   Awe at the thought my soul doth fill.
Unrivalled mid the Alps it towers,
Sternly its form o'er Gallia lowers.
   Clad in robe of purest white,
   Radiant as the lunar light,
   Rearing its bald head on high
   To a clear unclouded sky.
   Cold and chill immensity,
   Subject giants stand around,
   Wastes of snow its [?summits] bound
   Save where far below is seen
   Golden fields and vineyards green,
   Fair Ausonia's[7] fruitful plains,
   Where all-giving Ceres[8] reigns.

O'er all the earth I've wandered long,
In every land of every tongue,
Now I come to my own loved home,
Ne'er again from its bounds to roam.
What though those I knew are dead,
Though my kin from earth are fled?
Yet the same woods and rills and trees
Murmur and sing in the same sweet breeze;
And I can sit in the forest bower
And solace my heart with some wild flower,
That looks from the green and grassy ground
And the dead leaflets strewn around;
Speaking, though voiceless and empty of sound,
Bidding all gloomy care depart,
Soothing the passions and calming the heart.

September 3, 1830   Douro

[7]An ancient name for Italy; derived from Auson, son of Ulysses and father of Ausones.
[8]Roman name for Mother Earth, corn goddess, protectress of agriculture and of all the fruits of the earth.

Charlotte Brontë

A FRENCHMAN'S JOURNAL
CONCLUDED, BY TREE

Dec. 28

On the third of February 1820, I gained a fortune of six hundred thousand livres, and on the eleventh of June 1820 lost it. For five months in my life I have been a rich man. But Fortune, the fickle, has rid me of my riches. Some jewels I possess, however, which she cannot take away: they are contentment, my title, my high birth and my cheerful disposition. I was happy in affluence and I am so likewise in poverty.

The circumstance most worthy of notice which has taken place in my little tavern is the following. One morning lately, as I was taking my breakfast, an onion and a dry crust, I heard the outer door open and someone descending the steps of my cellar kitchen. Expecting a guest, I rose and stirred the fire, whose flames presently threw a cheerful glare round the apartment, that neither needed or possessed any other light. I then called out, 'Come in!' A person entered of rather interesting appearance. He was about the middle height. His features, though not perfectly regular, were very agreeable: his eye bright, forehead lofty, and the whole expression of his countenance full of intellect.

I welcomed him with the usual salute of 'Bonjour, monsieur', and offered a seat.

He thanked me but declined it saying, 'I am informed, sir, that you are the maitre[9] de cet hotel, n'est-ce pas?'

I answered in the affirmative.

'Well then, monsieur,' said he, 'would you take me as your servant and assistant, without wages?'

I replied that such a proposal called for some consideration and asked if he had any friends to whom I might apply for a character.

'Ah, sir,' he responded. 'You behold before you a miserable individual, utterly destitute of cash and kindred, or at least those that he has of the latter desideratum refuse to own him. For what? – Oh ye sacred Muses, avenge my cause! Come from your holy hill[9] to punish my persecutors! – merely for daring to be a poet!'

'That's strange,' said I. 'Who are you?'

He hesitated for a moment and then replied, 'I am Alexander Soult, surnamed The Rhymer, son of the great Marshal of that name. Have

[9]Presumably Charlotte Brontë means 'le patron' rather than 'le maitre d'hotel' here.

276

you never heard me spoken of?'

'Yes, I have, often. Come in, you are welcome; but remember I cannot afford to give any remuneration beyond board and lodging for your services.'

'I do not demand any other,' said he, and at that instant his countenance brightened.

He remained with me for many days, and certainly a more cheery and agreeable companion has never been seen. He brought a great accession of custom to my house, for besides being able to divert the guests with the most pleasant conversation he could make verses and sing songs to admiration. One of them, I well remember it, was as follows:

> Haste, bring us the wine cup
> And let it be full;
> Fill, fill it to the brim up!
> 'Twill [?nock] even the dull,
> Set his feet a-dancing,
> Twinkling and glancing,
> While the tabor, the pipe and the lute,
> The thundering drum and the flute,
> Are ringing around,
> Hark the merry sound!
> Arise, I say, arise guests!
> Dismiss care from your guests.
> See the wine trembles
>   In purple light,
> Its radiance resembles
>   The amethyst bright.
>   Sip, guests, sip!
>   Raise it to your lip.
> Fear not the harmless cup,
>   Drink the sweet nectar up.
>   List to my song!
> 'Tis like the nightingale's singing among
>   Old forest trees,
>   Where murmurs the breeze
> And bears the rich music the calm air along.
>   Nature is my dearest mother,
>   I will never own another,
>   And I am her child,
>   Untamable, wild;

Like the strong mountain eagle, my royal brother,
I was cradled like him in a cloud;
    And the winds as they rushed or swept
Rocked our cold misty shroud
    Till the two innocents slept.
Hah! His strong beak and talons
    And the golden ring in his eye:
    Methinks I see him now,
A speck in the azure sky.
He is soaring to the thunder,
    As swiftly sweeping under
Arched rocks and mountains
Majestically high,
    Whose bright silver fountains
    Spring up to the sky.
Eagle, farewell, I shall see thee no more.
From my sight thy wings have borne
    Thee to Apollo's chariot soar,
    Unwinking mayst thou gaze,
    Fearlessly aspire,
    Thy circlet of fire
May bear the sun's most sweet blaze.

But though he would sometimes appear in the highest spirits, yet it was evident from the bright, flushed look of his countenance and the sparkling, unnatural brilliancy of his eye that it was the consequence of morbid excitement. Except at these intervals, he was always pale and restless. I saw he was fast wasting away and could not long survive the disgrace of being forced to seek a livelihood as a servant to a tavern-master. At length he was compelled to keep his bed. Though now utterly useless to me, I could not by any means prevail upon myself to turn him friendless into the streets. He was not, however, very expensive, for hardly a morsel or drop would he eat or drink from morning till night.

One tempestuous evening I was sitting by my fire meditating as to whether or not I should send information to his relatives respecting his situation, and every now and then casting a sorrowful glance at him as he lay stretched on a straw pallet in the corner of the cellar, a mere attenuated shadow, when he suddenly interrupted my train of thought by exclaiming wildly, 'Ah! There is Fortune! At last the fickle one has returned to me! Do you see her, monsieur?'

'No,' said I, 'It is a delusion.'

'That cannot be, for I hear her speaking. Hark! What does she say?' Shortly after this fit of delirium he fell into a sound sleep, notwithstanding the violent din of the storm which was raging without. After some time I was thinking of retiring to rest myself, when tout a coup the door flew open and two young men sprang in.

'Sir,' cried the youngest. 'Pray give us a night's shelter. Have dry my cloak, and if you possess food set some without delay before us. I'm desperately hungry and so I dare say is my brother. Make haste!'

While I was hurrying to obey this order, I could not avoid stealing a look now and then at the intruders, for two finer fellows I never in my life have seen. The eldest stretched himself on the settee crying, 'I am uncommonly weary. Your orages francais knock a man up.'

After a time he got up and walked towards the corner. For a moment he bent with a pitying expression of countenance over the poor being that lay there and then turning to me asked, 'Who is this gentleman?'

'Alexander Soult, The Rhymer,' said I.

'Alexander Soult, The Rhymer!' he exclaimed, while the blood rushed indignantly to his face. 'Has France no care of her honour that she should let her great poet lie thus? At least it shall not be said that the Marquis of Douro saw him and had no compassion. Charles, come here!' Charles was already kneeling at the bedside and mercifully weeping over the ghastly counterfeit of humanity.

That very night they sent for one of the most skilful physicians in Paris and some refreshments, which I was surprised to see the patient greedily devour; but I suppose those that I had been able to procure for him were of too coarse a nature to please the fastidious appetite of a sick man. They watched with him by turns all night and, next morning, after paying me an exorbitant price for my trouble and making me beside a present of fifty pounds sterling for, as they said, my disinterested kindness to their friend, departed in a magnificent carriage, taking Alexander Soult with them.

I have since heard that he perfectly recovered from his sickness and has now reached the pinnacle of fame as a poet in the Glass Town; that he lives in Waterloo Palace, a rich man and the Marquis of Douro's confidential friend. Lord Wellesley has since often been to my tavern, and, in truth, he is a blessing whenever he comes. He never leaves me without exciting in my mind a desire for his speedy return.

I must now close my journal, as I find the keeping of it not consistent with the life of a tavern-master and detrimental to his interests, for it employs his thoughts and time about other things than those they should be devoted to.

September 4, 1830   Tree

NB   The reader will perceive that the incidents in the foregoing brief narrative are anticipated. They are, however, perfectly correct, and truly relate the manner in which the intimacy between the Marquis of Douro and Alexander Soult begun. Editor, September 4, 1830.

CONCLUDING ADDRESS

Reader, farewell!
Hark my note of
Triumph swell:
My labour finished,
My trouble diminished,
Though 'twas tedious and long
Here's my last
Concluding
Song!

GENERAL INDEX TO THE CONTENTS

Liffey Castle, a Tale, by Lord Charles Wellesley   I
Lines to the River Aragva, by the Marquis of Douro   II
A Frenchman's Journal, by Captain Tree   III
Conversations   IV
A Letter from Lord Charles Wellesley   V
The Midnight Song, by the Marquis of Douro   VI
A Frenchman's Journal Continued, by Tree   VII
A Day at Parry's Palace, by Lord Charles Wellesley   VIII
Morning, by the Marquis of Douro   IX
Conversations   X
Silence, by the Marquis of Douro   XI
A Song, by Lord Wellesley   XII
A Frenchman's Journal Continued, by Captain Tree   XIII
Strange Events, by Lord Charles Wellesley   XIV
On Seeing an Ancient Dirk in the Armoury of the
Tower of Babylon, etc.   XV
A Frenchman's Journal Continued, by Captain Tree   XVI
Conversations   XVII
An Extraordinary Dream, by Lord Charles Wellesley   XVIII
A Traveller's Meditations, by the Marquis of Douro   XIX

A Frenchman's Journal Concluded, by Captain Tree XX

FAREWELL ADDRESS XXI

The Second Series of the Young Men's Magazine
was begun August 12, 1830, and finished
September the 4, 1830 . . . Charlotte Brontë

CAMPBELL CASTLE[1]
Sculpsit by Goodall. Painted by Arnald.

A fine picture engraved in the first style of the art. The tree, weeds and grass in the foreground are beautifully etched and throw the rest of the landscape into distance. Campbell Castle is situated upon a rock and, with a thick forest that environs it, forms the centrepiece. Both are in deep shade, thereby setting off the lights around. The distant mountains are not very picturesque, but the artist has evidently made the best of his materials. One of them, the highest, is nearly enveloped in mist, which hides all but the summit and a small portion of the base. The pastoral incident of the flock of sheep feeding upon the verdant side of a hill characterizes the picture as being a scene in the Highlands of Scotland, as likewise do the huntsmen in their tartans emerging from the gloom of the wood. Nothing can be more true to nature than the stag turning in the middle of the stream, and as a last resource in its despair butting against its relentless pursuers, a pack of ravenous hounds, who open-mouthed and yelling are rushing in to the death. One of them, stuck fast in a hedge, is represented violently struggling to get loose, with eyes cruelly fixed on the devoted prey. In looking at it one may almost fancy that they hear its short barks and cries of enrage, as it strives to free itself from the entangling thicket. The water trough foaming over and the little cascade in a rocky recess overhung with a cluster of trees are touches equally rural and natural. The sky, seemingly of a clear soft mauve, is variegated by light fleecy clouds that have assumed the form of a grand aerial arch spanning the space above

[1]The manuscript, in HCL: Lowell, includes two pages (9.3 × 5.7 cm) of critiques of three engravings in *Friendship's Offering* 1829, each entitled according to the engraving discussed. The three engravings accompany the following texts: a poem 'Castle Campbell' by Delta; a play 'The Will' by Leitch Ritchie; and a poem 'The Minstrel Boy' by the Ettrick Shepherd (James Hogg).

the castle like an irregular rainbow. Nothing can be more magnificent than this appearance: it is a stroke betokening the most consummate genius in the eminent artist who has produced it, and finishes off the prospect nobly.

Charlotte Brontë   Sept. 30, 1830

THE WILL
Painted by W. Kidd. Sculpt. by Mitchell.

This picture, though the subject is not of the highest kind, possesses, notwithstanding, considerable merit from the truth of detail which it exhibits. Flora, though not very handsome, has still a good-tempered and rather agreeable countenance. Her attitude as she sits curling her hair at the glass is perfectly easy. Grumblethorpe is the very personification of an ill-natured old man, with his scowling brow, furious eyes, thick cravat, black velvet skull-cap, slipshod heels and crutched hand which has roused the indignation of a snarling churlish little lap-dog, who is most naturally represented as barking at the surly intruder into his mistress's dressing-room. Minnikin, with the towel thrown across her arm and a wash-basin in her hand, exactly comes up to the idea of a simpering waiting-maid. The Will lies mutilated on the carpet, and Flora is in the act of using one of the torn fragments as a papillote.[2] All the adjuncts of the piece are quite characteristic of the place where the scene is laid, such as the bonnet and veil lying on an armchair with a bandbox underneath, the vase of flowers, pincushion and necklace on the toilet, the open closet and the keys hanging in its door. The ornaments on the mantelpiece, the wash-hand-stand with the diminutive toothbrush, bottle, glass and ewer, etc., etc. Without this illustration, the annexed tale would be wholly unintelligible, and even with it the reader feels, while ploughing through, or rather skimming over the pages which it occupies, like a man traversing unknown ways in the dark.

Charlotte Brontë   Sept. 30, 1830

THE MINSTREL BOY
Painted by Leslie. Sculp. by Duncan.

This picture possesses beauties and defects almost in equal proportions. The head of the Minstrel Boy is a beauty. The features are admirable.

[2]A curl-paper.

The hair is well arranged, with the exception of one straight lock falling or rather stretching across the forehead in a slanting direction, but how finely expressive are the uplifted eyes, beaming of rapt inspiration! The neck is rather short and has too sturdy an appearance. The arms are not well formed: one of them is thicker than the other and the hands are more like those of a grown-up persons than a childs. A shirt with the sleeves rolled up is an inelegant and preposterous costume, and the broad leathern belt is quite out of place. Would not the plaid,[3] if wrapped round him and disposed in graceful folds, have been better? The position of his legs is miserably ill-judged and, from the failure in that difficult branch of the art, foreshortening, have the appearance of deformity. He is, nevertheless, well situated under the dark shade of the tree which overhangs him, and the vista of trees and mountains closed by blue sky and soft clouds is most beautiful. There is nothing, however, of 'the crystal pool with its sounding linn',[4] spoken of in the Ettrick Shepherd's poem of the same title as this engraving. Neither is there of 'the weeping birch and [the] poplar tall' nor of the 'waterfall' by which the Minstrel Boy is said to be 'singing his lay'. These, if the picture has been suggested to Leslie by reading the poem, are great omissions, as if he had added them they would have greatly contributed to vary the now somewhat monotonous scenery; and if we owe the production of the poem to Hogg's[5] having seen and been delighted by this not very perfect picture, he has impertinently asserted that features were to be seen in the landscape which were invisible to all eyes except his own. Both painter and poet are Scotchmen and one of them must be in the wrong.

C. Brontë   Sept. 30, 1830

---

[3]Long piece of twilled woollen cloth, usually with chequered or tartan pattern, outer article of Highland costume (*OED*). This is lying next to the boy in the etching, as he sits leaning against a rock.

[4]Chiefly Scottish dialect: cascade or waterfall (*OED*).

[5]James Hogg (1770–1835) was born in Ettrick Forest and early became a shepherd, until his poetical gifts were discovered by Scott. Charlotte Brontë would have known of him chiefly as a contributor to *Blackwood's Magazine* and as the model for the 'Ettrick Shepherd' of its 'Noctes Ambrosianae', on which the 'Conversations' of her own magazines are based; see *The History of the Year*.

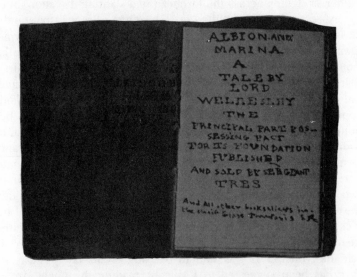

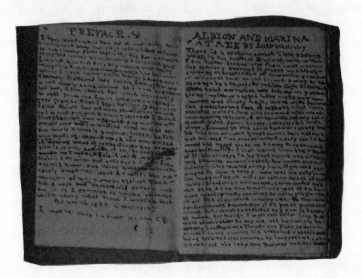

Plate 5 Title-page, preface and first page of *Albion and Marina*, written by Charlotte Brontë at the age of fourteen

ALBION AND MARINA
A TALE BY
LORD Charles Wellesley
October 12, 1830[1]

ALBION AND

MARINA

A

TALE BY

LORD

WELLESLEY

THE

PRINCIPAL PART POS-

SESSING FACT

FOR ITS FOUNDATION

PUBLISHED

AND SOLD BY SERGEANT

TREE

And all other booksellers in

the Chief Glass Town, Paris, etc.

PREFACE

I have written this tale out of malignity for the injuries that have lately
[?been] offered to me. Many parts, especially the former, were

---

[1]Title on blue paper cover, labelled on verso 'Purified Epsom Salts, SOLD BY WEST,
CHEMIST & DRUGGIST, Keighley'; hand-sewn booklet of sixteen pages (5.6 × 3.9 cm) in
Wellesley College Library. The title-page follows with preface on verso. The use of the title
'Albion', the ancient poetical name for Britain, for the Marquis of Douro indicates Charlotte
Brontë's esteem for her hero.

composed under a mysterious influence that I cannot account for. My reader will easily recognize the characters through the thin veil which I have thrown over them. I have considerably flattered Lady Zelzia Ellrington.[2] She is not nearly so handsome as I have represented her, and she strove far more vigorously to oust someone from another person's good graces than I say, but her endeavours failed. Albion has hitherto stood firm. What he will do I cannot pretend to even guess, but I think that Marina's incomparable superiority will prevail over her Frenchified rival who, as all the world knows, is a miller, jockey, tatler, blue-stocking, charioteer and beldame, united in one blazing [?boeus] of perfection. The conclusion is wholly destitute of any foundation in truth, and I did it out of revenge. Albion and Marina are both alive and well for ought I know.[3] One thing, however, will certainly break my heart, and that is the omission of any scandal against Tree,[4] but I hope my readers will pardon me for it, as I promise to make amends with usury next time I write a book.

October 12, 1830   C. Wellesley

I wrote this in four hours, C.B.

[2]Lady Zenobia Ellrington (spelt 'Elrington' here, as in Branwell Brontë's manuscripts); daughter of Lord Ellrington and Lady Paulina Louisada Ellrington. This is the first appearance of this prominent character in the Glass Town Saga: the Marquis of Douro treats her ambiguously (see the poem 'Lines addressed to Lady Z[enobia] E[llrington] sent with my portrait which she had asked me to give her, By Marquis Douro', *Poems*, p. 124), and her frenzied, unrequited love for the Marquis of Douro is a constant theme from now on in the early juvenilia. In later manuscripts she becomes the Countess of Northangerland, the respected friend of Douro (now Zamorna), but neglected wife of Alexander Percy (later created Lord Ellrington and Earl of Northangerland). Zenobia is known for her learning – she is 'the Verdopolitan de Stael' (see n. 21 below) – and for her pride and choler, inherited from her mother, who was a Latin beauty of bad morals. Also from her mother she derives her statuesque figure, raven hair and 'swathy' complexion, which Lord Charles constantly delights to mock. She is usually dressed in rich crimson velvet robes, with dark plumes in her turban headress, and gold bracelets, necklaces and cross, indicative of her decadent background and in contrast to the purity of her rival Marian Hume (see *The Poetaster*, vol. 1, n. 7). She was probably modelled on the historical Zenobia, Queen of Palmyra and the East, described in Edward Gibbon's *The History of the Decline and Fall of the Roman Empire* (see Christine Alexander, *The Early Writings of Charlotte Brontë*, Oxford: Basil Blackwell, 1983, pp. 23–4).

[3]The marriage of Arthur, Lord Douro, and Marian Hume (Albion and Marina) is recorded in the poem and story of *The Bridal*, 14 July – 20 August 1830.

[4]Captain Tree, Lord Charles Wellesley's chief literary rival: see *Blackwood's Young Men's Magazine*, August 1829, n. 2.

ALBION AND MARINA
A TALE BY LORD WELLESLEY

There is a certain sweet little pastoral village in the south of England with which I am better acquainted than most men. The scenery around it possesses no distinguishing characteristic of romantic grandeur or wildness that might figure a way to advantage in a novel, to which high title this brief narrative sets up no pretensions. Neither rugged, lofty rocks nor mountains dimly huge mark with frowns the undisturbed face of nature, but little peaceful valleys, low hills crowned with wood, murmuring cascades and streamlets, richly cultivated fields, farmhouses, cottages and a wide river formed all the scenic features.

Every hamlet has one or more great men. This had one, but he was 'nae sheepshank'.[5] Every ear in the world had heard his fame, and every tongue could bear testimony to it. I shall name him the 'Duke of Strathelleraye',[6] and by that name the village was likewise denominated, for more than thirty miles round every inch of ground belonged to him and every man was his retainer. The magnificent villa, or rather palace, of this noble stood on an eminence surrounded by a vast park and the embowering shade of an ancient wood, proudly seeming to claim allegiance of all the dependent countryside. The mind, achievements and character of its great possessor must not, cannot, be depicted by a pen so feeble as mine, for though I could call filial love and devoted admiration to my aid, yet both would be utterly ineffective.

Though the Duke seldom himself came among his attached vassals, being detained elsewhere by important avocations, yet his lady, the Duchess, resided in the castle constantly. Of her I can only say that she was like an earthly angel. Her mind was composed of charity, beneficence, gentleness and sweetness. All, both old and young, loved her, and the blessings of those that were ready to perish came upon her ever more.[7]

His Grace had also two sons, who often visited Strathelleraye.

Of the youngest, Lord Cornelius,[8] everything is said when I inform the reader that he was seventeen years of age, grave, sententious, stoical, rather haughty and sarcastic; of a fine countenance though

---

[5] 'na sheepshanks' in manuscript. Scots dialect: a person of no small importance (*OED*).

[6] Duke of Strathfieldsay: modelled on the historical Duke of Wellington and his estate of Stratfield Saye in Hampshire.

[7] Closely based on the historical Duchess of Wellington's character: see *Tales of the Islanders*, vol. 4, n. 8.

[8] Lord Charles Wellesley: spelt 'Corneilius' in manuscript.

somewhat swarthy, long thick hair, black as the hoody's[9] wing; and liked nothing so well as to sit alone in moody silence, musing over the vanity of human affairs, or improving and expanding his mind by the abstruse study of the higher branches of mathematics and that sublime science, astronomy.

The eldest, Albion, Marquis of Tagus,[10] is the hero of my present tale. He had entered his nineteenth year; his stature was lofty; his form equal in the magnificence of its proportions to that of Apollo Belvedere.[11] The bright wreath and curls of his rich brown hair waved over a forehead resembling the purest marble in the placidity of its unveiled whiteness. His nose and mouth were cast in the most perfect mould. But saw I never anything to equal his eye! Oh! I could have stood riveted with the chains of admiration, gazing for hours upon it! What clearness, depth and lucid transparency in those large orbs of radiant brown! And the fascination of his smile was irresistible, though seldom did that sunshine of the mind break the thoughtful and almost melancholy expression of his noble features. He was a soldier, captain in the Royal Regiment of Horse Guards, and all his attitudes and actions were full of martial grace. His mental faculties were in exact keeping with such an exterior, being of the highest order, and though not, like his younger brother, wholly given up to study, yet he was well-versed in the ancient languages, and deeply read in the Greek and Roman Classics, in addition to the best works in the British, German and Italian tongues.

Such was my hero. The only blot I was ever able to discover in his character is that of a slight fierceness or impetuosity of temper which sometimes carried him beyond bounds, though at the slightest look or word of command from his father he instantly bridled his passion and became perfectly calm. No wonder the Duke should be, as he was, proud of such a son.

About two miles from the castle there stood a pretty house, entirely hid from view by a thick forest, in a glade of which it was situated. Behind it was a smooth lawn fringed with odoriferous shrubs, and before, a tasteful flower-garden. This was the abode of Sir Alured Angus,[12] a Scotchman who was physician to His Grace, and though of gentlemanly manners and demeanour, yet harsh, stern, and somewhat

[9]Piebald grey and black crow (*OED*).

[10]Named after the River Tagus, which flows through Spain and Portugal and which was defended by Wellington and his troops during the Peninsular Wars.

[11]An ancient statue of Apollo which stands in the Belvedere Gallery in the Vatican; discovered at Antium in 1485.

[12]Sir Alexander Hume Badey: see *Tales of the Islanders*, vol. 1, n. 14.

querulous in countenance and disposition. He was a widower and had but one child, a daughter, whom I shall call Marina, which nearly resembles her true name.

No wild rose blooming in solitude or bluebell peering from an old wall ever equalled in loveliness this flower of the forest. The hue of her cheek would excel the most delicate tint of the former, even when its bud is just opening to the breath of summer, and the clear azure of her eyes would cause the latter to appear dull as a dusky hyacinth. Also, the silken tresses of her hazel hair, straying in light ringlets down a neck and forehead of snow, seemed more elegant than the young tendrils of a vine. Her dress was almost Quaker-like in its simplicity. Pure white or vernal green were the colours she constantly wore, without any jewels, save one row of pearls round her neck. She never stirred beyond the precincts of the wooded and pleasant green lane which skirted a long cornfield near the house. There, on warm summer evenings, she would ramble and linger listening to the woodlark's song, and occasionally joining her own more harmonious voice to its delightful warblings. When the gloomy days and nights of autumn and winter did not permit these walks, she amused herself with drawing (for which she had an exact taste), playing on the harp, reading the best English, French and Italian works (both which languages she understood) in her father's extensive library, and sometimes a little light needlework.

And thus in a state of perfect seclusion (for seldom had she even Sir Alured's company as he generally resided at London) she was quite happy, and reflected with innocent wonder on those who could find pleasure in the noisy delights of what is called 'fashionable society'.

One day, as Lady Strathelleraye was walking in the wood, she met Marina and, on learning who she was, being charmed with her exquisite beauty and sweet manners, invited her to come on the morrow to the castle. She did so and there met the Marquis of Tagus. He was even more surprised and pleased with her than the Duchess and, when she was gone, asked his mother a thousand questions about her, all of which she answered to his satisfaction.

For some time, after, he appeared listless and abstracted. The reader will readily perceive that he had, to use a cant phrase, 'fallen in love'. Lord Cornelius, his brother, warned him of the folly of doing so, but instead of listening to his sage admonitions, he first strove to laugh and then, frowning at him, commanded silence.

In a few days he paid a visit to Oakwood House[13] (Sir Alured's

[13]Charlotte Brontë visited Oakwood Hall, the home of the Walkers, near Birstall, with her friend Ellen Nussey (Mrs Ellis H. Chadwick, *In the Footsteps of the Brontës*, London: Pitman & Sons, Ltd, 1914, p. 368).

mansion), and after that became more gloomy than before. His father observed this, and one day as they were sitting alone remarked it to Albion, adding that he was fully acquainted with the reason. He reddened, but made no answer.

'I am not, my son,' continued the Duke, 'opposed to your wishes, though certainly there is a considerable difference of rank between yourself and Marina Angus; but that difference is compensated by the many admirable qualities she possesses.'

On hearing these words, Arthur – Albion I mean – started up and throwing himself at his father's feet poured forth his thanks in terms of glowing gratitude, while his fine features, flushed with excitation, spoke even more eloquently than his eloquent words.

'Rise, Albion!' said the Duke. 'You are worthy of her and she of you, but both are yet too young. Some years must elapse before your union takes place: therefore exert your patience, my son.'

Albion's joy was slightly damped by this news; but his thankfulness and filial obedience, as well as love, forced him to acquiesce, and, immediately after, he quitted the room with a relieved heart and took his way towards Oakwood House. There he related the circumstance to Marina who, though she blushed incredulously, yet in truth felt as much gladness and as great a relief from doubt, almost amounting to despair, as himself.

A few months afterwards, the Duke of Strathelleraye determined to visit that wonder of the world, the Great City of Africa: the Glass Town, of whose splendour, magnificence and extent, power, strength and riches, occasional tidings came from afar, wafted by the breezes of the ocean to Merry England. But to most of the inhabitants of that little isle it before the character of a dream or gorgeous fiction. They were unable to comprehend how mere human beings could construct fabrics of such a marvellous size and grandeur as many of the public buildings were represented to be; and as to the Tower of All Nations, few believed in its existence. It seemed as the cities of old Nineveh or Babylon with the temples of their gods, Ninus or Jupiter Belus, their halls of Astarte and Semalt.[14] These most people believe to be magnified by the dim haze of intervening ages and the exaggerating

[14]Nineveh and Babylon are great cities of Mesopotamia, called Assyria by the Greek writers such as Herodotus. In the juvenilia, Glass Town is often likened to Babylon, once the magnificent capital of a great empire on the banks of the Euphrates. Its mystical nature in the Apocalypse would also have made it attractive to Charlotte Brontë as a model. Ninus, according to the Greeks, is the founder of Nineveh and second husband of Semiramis (?Semalt), possibly the historical Sammuramat, Queen of Assyria, who ruled as regent for her son for five years. Belus Jupiter is probably Bel, chief god of Babylon. Astarte is the Greek

page of history, through which mediums we behold them.

The Duke, as he had received many invitations from the Glass Townians, who were impatient to behold one whose renown had spread so far and likewise possessed vast dominions near the African coast, informed his lady, the Marquis of Tagus and Lord Cornelius that, in a month's time, he should take his departure with them, and that he should expect them all to be prepared at that period, adding that when they returned Marina Angus should be created Marchioness of Tagus.

Though it was a bitter trial to Albion to part with one to whom he was now entirely devoted, yet, comforted by the last part of his father's speech, he obeyed without murmuring. On the last evening of his stay in Strathelleraye, he took a sad farewell of Marina, who wept as if hopeless, but, suddenly restraining her grief, she looked up, with her beautiful eyes irradiated by a smile that like a ray of light illumined the crystal tears, and whispered: 'I shall be happy when you return.'

Then they parted; and Albion during his voyage over the wide ocean often thought for comfort on her last words. It is a common superstition that the words uttered by a friend on separating are prophetical, and these certainly portended nothing but peace.

In due course of time they arrived at the Glass Town and were welcomed with enthusiastic cordiality. After the Duke had visited his kingdom, he returned to the chief metropolis and established his residence there at Salamanca Palace.[15]

The Marquis of Targus, from the noble beauty of his person, attracted considerable attention wherever he went, and in a short period he had won and attached many faithful friends of the highest rank and abilities. From his love of elegant literature and the fine arts in general, painters and poets were soon among his warmest admirers. He himself possessed a most sublime genius, but as yet its full extent was unknown to him.

One day, as he was meditating alone on the world of waters that rolled between him and the fair Marina, he determined to put his feelings on paper in a tangible shape that he might hereafter show them to her when anticipation had given place to fruition. He took his pen and in about a quarter of an hour had completed a brief poem of exquisite beauty. The attempted pleased him and soothed the anguish that lingered in his heart. It likewise gave him an insight into the

---

name for the Levantine fertility goddess Ashtoreth, who was associated with the Mesopotamian goddess of love, fertility and war, Ishtar (identified with the planet Venus and so also considered a moon goddess).

[15]Known as Waterloo Palace elsewhere in the early manuscripts.

astonishing faculties of his own mind, and a longing for immortality, an ambition of glory, seized him.

He was a devoted worshipper of the divine works that the Grecian tragedians have left for all succeeding ages to marvel at, particularly those of Sophocles the Majestic;[16] and his mind was deeply embued with the spirit of their eagle-like flights into higher regions than that of earth, or even Parnassus.[17] Being now sensible in a degree of his lofty powers, he determined, like Milton, to write somewhat that the [?fractious] Muses should not willingly let die,[18] and accordingly commenced a tragedy entitled 'Necropolis, or the City of the Dead'. Here was set forth in a strain of the grandest mood the mysteries of ancient Egyptian worship, and he has acknowledged to me that he felt his being absorbed while he wrote it, even by the words [he] himself had made.

Sublime is this surprising production! It is, indeed, in the words of an eminent writer, Captain Tree, 'a noble instance of the almost perfectibility of human intellect', but there hovers over it a feeling of tender melancholy, for the image of Marina haunted his thoughts, and Amalthea,[19] his heroine, is but an impersonation of her. This tragedy wreathed the laurels of fame round his brow, and his after-productions, each of which seemed to excel the other, added new wreaths to those which already beautified his temples.

I cannot follow him in the splendour of his literary career, nor even mention so much as the titles of his various works. Suffice it to say he became one of the greatest poets of the age, and one of the chief motives that influenced him in his exertions for renown was to render himself worthy to possess such a treasure as Marina.[20] She, in whatever

[16]One of the three great Attic tragedians and favourite poet of the Athenians. His tragedies are known to be more human, less heroic, than those of Aeschylus; and more dramatically effective than those of Euripides. Charlotte Brontë refers to these and other Classical writers in her poem 'The Violet', 10 November 1830 (*Poems*, p. 113).

[17]A mountain near Delphi, Greece, one of whose summits was consecrated to Apollo and the Muses; and hence regarded as the seat of poetry and music.

[18]Milton, *Reason of Church Government*, Bk. II: 'I might perhaps leave something so written to aftertimes, as they should not willingly let it die'.

[19]A nymph in Greek mythology, the nurse of Zeus; presumably Douro's choice here is indicative of his expectations in a wife.

[20]On 14 November 1830, Charlotte Brontë wrote a miniature volume of poems entitled 'The Violet, A Poem With Several Smaller Pieces, By The Marquis of Douro'. It included seven poems which display Douro's Classical learning (see n. 16 above) and his longing for Marian (see 'Matin', *Poems*, p. 125). For notes on the manuscript volume, which has since been divided, see Christine Alexander, *A Bibliography of the Manuscripts of Charlotte Brontë* (Haworth and USA: The Brontë Society in association with Meckler Publishing, 1982), p. 13.

he was employed, was never out of his thoughts, and none had he yet beheld among all the ladies of the Glass Town – though rich, titled, and handsome strove by innumerable arts to gain his favour – whom he could even compare with her.

One evening he was invited to the house of Earl Cruachan, where was a large party assembled. Among the guests was one lady apparently about twenty-five or -six years of age. In figure she was very tall, and both it and her face were of a perfectly Roman caste. Her features were regular and finely formed; her full and brilliant eyes jetty black, as were the luxuriant tresses of her richly curled hair. Her dark, glowing complexion was set off by a robe of crimson velvet trimmed with ermine, and a nodding plume of black ostrich feathers added to the imposing dignity of her appearance. Albion, notwithstanding her unusual comeliness, hardly noticed her, till Earl Cruachan rose and introduced her to him as the Lady Zelzia Ellrington. She was the most learned and noted woman in the Glass Town, and he was pleased with this opportunity of seeing her.

For some time she entertained him with a discourse of the most lively eloquence, and indeed Madame de Stael[21] herself could not have gone beyond Lady Zelzia in the conversational talent, and on this occasion she exerted herself to the utmost, as she was in the presence of so distinguished a man, and one whom she seemed ambitious to please.

At length one of the guests asked her to favour the company with a song and tune on the grand piano. At first she refused, but, on Albion's seconding the request, rose, and taking from the drawing-room table a small volume of miscellaneous poems, opened it at one by the Marquis of Tagus. She then set it to a fine air and sang as follows, while she skilfully accompanied her voice upon the instrument:

> I think of thee when the moonbeams play
> On the placid water's face;
> For thus thy blue eyes' lustrous ray
> Shone with resembling grace.

---

[21] Anne Louise Germaine Necker, Baronne de Stael-Holstein (1766–1817), referred to by Byron as the greatest mind of her times; a noted intellectual who received, in her Paris salon, on the eve of the Revolution, the most progressive elements in French society. She emigrated to England in 1793, returned to Paris 1795, and was exiled by Napoleon, first from Paris and then from France. She first met Wellington, whom she regarded as a heroic liberator, in 1814 in her reconstituted Parisian salon (he was then ambassador to the reinstated French court of Louis XVIII), and they subsequently became friends and correspondents. Charlotte Brontë often refers to Lady Zenobia Ellrington as the Verdopolitan de Stael.

I think of thee when the snowy swan
  Glides calmly down the stream;
Its plumes the breezes scarcely fan,
  Awed by their radiant gleam.

For thus I've seen the loud winds hush
  To pass thy beauty by,
With soft caress and playful rush
  'Mid thy bright tresses fly.

And I have seen the wild birds sail
  In rings thy head above,
While thou hast stood like lily pale
  Unknowing of their love.

O! for the day when once again
  Mine eyes will gaze on thee;
But an ocean vast, a sounding main,
  An ever-howling sea,
    Roll us between with their billows green,
    High tost tempestuously.

This song had been composed by Albion soon after his arrival at the Glass Town. The person addressed was Marina. The full rich tone of Lady Zelzia's voice did ample justice to the subject, and he expressed his sense of the honour she had done him in appropriate terms. When she had finished the company departed, for it was now rather late.

As Albion pursued his way homewards alone he began insensibly to meditate on her majestic charms and compare them with the gentler ones of Marina Angus. At first he could hardly tell which to give the preference to, for though he still almost idolized Marina, yet an absence of four years had considerably deadened his remembrance of her person.

While he was thus employed he heard a soft but mournful voice whisper, 'Albion!'

He turned hastily round and saw the form of the identical Marina at a little distance, distinctly visible by the moonlight.

'Marina! My dearest Marina!' he exclaimed, springing towards her, while joy unutterable filled his heart. 'How did you come here? Have the angels of Heaven brought you?'

So saying, he stretched out his hand but she eluded his grasp, and slowly gliding away said, 'Do not forget me; I shall be happy when you return.'

Then the apparition vanished. It seemed to have appeared merely to assert her superiority over her rival, and indeed, the moment Albion beheld her beauty, he felt that it was peerless.

But now wonder and perplexity took possession of his mind. He could not account for this vision, except by the common solution of supernatural agency, and that ancient creed his enlightened understanding had hitherto rejected until it was forced upon him by this extraordinary incident.[22] One thing there was, however, the interpretation of which he thought he could not mistake, and that was the repetition of her last words: 'I shall be happy when you return.' It showed that she was still alive, and that which he had seen could not be her wraith. However, he made a memorandum of the day and hour, namely the 18th of June 1815, 12 o'clock at night.[23]

From this time the natural melancholy turn of his disposition increased, for the dread of her death before he should return was constantly [before him] and the ardency of his adoration and desire to see her again redoubled.

At length, not being able any longer to bear his misery, he revealed it to his father, and the Duke, touched with his grief and the fidelity of his attachment, gave him full permission to visit England and bring back Marina with him to Africa.

I need not trouble the reader with a minute detail of the circumstances of Albion's voyage, but shall pass on to what happened after he arrived in England.

It was a fair evening in September 1815[24] when he reached Strathelleraye. Without waiting to enter the halls of his fathers, he proceeded immediately to Oakwood House. As he approached it he almost sickened when, for an instant, the thought that she might be no more passed across his mind, but, summoning Hope to his aid and resting on her golden anchor, he passed up the lawn and gained the glass doors of the drawing-room.

As he drew near a sweet symphony of harp music swelled on his ear. His heart bounded within him at the sound. He knew that no fingers but hers could create those melodious tones with which now blended the harmony of a sweet and sad but well-known voice. He lifted the vine-branch that shaded the door, and beheld Marina, more beautiful he thought than ever, seated at her harp and sweeping with her slender fingers the quivering chords.

Without being observed by her, as she had her face turned from him, he entered, and sitting down, leaned his head on his hand, and closing

---

[22]Compare *Jane Eyre*, vol. III, ch. ix, in which Jane hears Rochester's voice crying out to her although he is many miles away.

[23]The date of the Battle of Waterloo, which probably influenced Charlotte Brontë's use of it.

[24]1817 in manuscript, an obvious error.

his eyes, listened with feelings of overwhelming transport to the
following words:

> Long my anxious ear hath listened
>   For the step that ne'er returned,
> And my tearful eye hath glistened,
>   And my heart hath duly burned,
>   But now I rest.
>
> Nature's self seemed clothed in mourning;
>   Even the star-like woodland flower
> With its leaflets fair, adorning
>   Pathway of the forest-bower,
>   Drooped its head.
>
> From the cavern of the mountain,
>   From the groves that crown'd the hill,
> From the stream and from the fountain,
>   Sounds prophetic murmured still
>   Betokening grief.
>
> Boding winds came fitful, sighing
>   Through the tall and leafy trees;
> Birds of omen, wildly crying,
>   Sent their yells upon the breeze
>   Wailing round me.
>
> At each sound I paled and trembled,
>   At each step I raised my head,
> Harkening if it his resembled,
>   Or if news that he was dead
>   Were come from far.
>
> All my days were days of weeping;
>   Thoughts of grim despair were stirred;
> Time on leaden feet seemed creeping;
>   Long heart sickness, hope deferred
>   Cankered my heart.

Here the music and singing suddenly ceased. Albion raised his head.
All was darkness except the silver moonbeams that showed a desolate
and ruined apartment, instead of the elegant parlour that a few minutes
before had gladdened his sight. No trace of Marina was visible, no harp
or other instrument of harmony, and the cold lunar light streamed
through a void space instead of the glass door.

He sprang up and called aloud, 'Marina! Marina!' But only an echo as of empty rooms answered. Almost distracted he rushed into the open air.

A little child was standing alone at the garden gate. It advanced towards him, and said, 'I will lead you to Marina Angus; she has long removed from that house to another.'

Albion followed it till they came to a long row of tall, dark trees, which led to a churchyard which they entered in and the child vanished leaving Albion beside a white marble tombstone on which was chiselled:

Marina Angus.
She died
18th of June, 1815,
at
12 o'clock pm.

When Albion had read this he felt a pang of horrible anguish [?wring] his heart and convulse his whole frame. With a loud groan he fell across the tomb and lay there senseless for a long time, till at length he was roused from the death-like trance to behold the spirit of Marina which stood beside him, and murmuring, 'Albion, I am happy, for I am at peace', disappeared!

For a few days he lingered around her tomb, and then quitted Strathelleraye, where he was never again heard of.

The reason of Marina's death I shall briefly relate. Four years after Albion's departure tidings came to the village that he was dead. The news broke Marina's faithful heart and the day after, she was no more.

CB   October 12, 1830

VISITS IN VERREOPOLIS

BY

LORD CHARLES WELLESLEY

IN

TWO VOLUMES

VOLUME

FIRST

297

PUBLISHED BY SERGEANT TREE
AND SOLD
BY
ALL OTHER BOOKSELLERS IN
THE
CHIEF GLASS TOWN, THE DUKE
OF WELLING-
TON'S
GLASS TOWN

Parry's Glass Town, Ross's Glass Town, Paris, etc.

I began this volume on the 7th of December
1830 and finished it on the 11th of December 1830
CHARLOTTE
BRONTË
December 11th 1830 Anno Domini[1]

PREFACE

I have nothing to say except that Verreopolis means the Glass Town, being compounded of a Greek and French word to that effect, and that I fear the reader will find this the dullest and driest book I have ever written. With this fair warning I bid him goodbye.

Waterloo Palace, Decbr 11th 1830   Charles Wellesley

CONTENTS

Introduction .... First Chap.
Visit to Lady Ellrington .... Second Chap.

---

[1]Title-page of manuscript, formerly in the Law Collection, now lost; hand-sewn booklet (7.6 × 5.1 cm) in blue paper cover. The following text is from a transcript lent to the editor and now held by Professor Mildred G. Christian.

298

Visit to Captain Bud .... Third Chap.
Visit to Lord Soult .... Fourth Chap.
Visit to Rotunda, Bravey's Inn .... Fifth Chap.

Charlotte Brontë   December 11th 1830

CHAPTER THE FIRST
[Introduction]

'Bene, bene, it is ten o'clock, but, Lord Charles, don't be so impatient to be gone. See! You have thrown down Ovid and the Eclogues![2] The Marquis of Douro desired me last night that I would send you to breakfast in his study when you had finished your lessons. By this time, I dare say, he is up and dressed, so make haste or he will suppose I have neglected his orders. But, stay a moment! His Grace wishes to speak with you first about your conduct yesterday, which was certainly very surprising in a young gentleman that has been so well and carefully brought up. Now you may go; and be quick: don't stop to feed the dogs or quarrel with your brother's valet mind.'

This was the speech of my worthy, learned, ever-to-be-respected and never-to-be-forgotten tutor, Mr Everard Rundell, which I listened to upon tenterhooks, every syllable seeming at lest five yards in length. For what boy of my age (ten years) can receive with complacency a prolix advice administered at the moment when that magical word 'Bene' had set him free to roam wherever his vagrant inclination may lead him?

When the above address was concluded away I darted like an arrow or jet d'eau, and in a few minutes was in my father's presence. He merely wanted to talk to me a little respecting my penchant for roving, which I had given way to rather considerably on the previous evening in the theatre, thereby astonishing and inconveniencing a respectly filled pit and box range, and greatly delighting a no less respectably filled gallery. After a few words he dismissed me with a kiss and blessing which attained the desired end far, far more completely than a thousand thrashings would have done, to say nothing of their rooting still more deeply the principal of filial [love] – not veneration or respect:

[2]Virgil's *Eclogues*; we know also from *The Poetaster*, from *Albion and Marina*, and from Charlotte Brontë's poem 'The Violet' (10 November 1830) that she was familiar with Virgil, Ovid, and other Classical writers by this time, chiefly as a result of her brother's lessons in ancient history and the Classics.

such stiff, cold words do but feebly express the devotional warmth of affection, admiration, confiding love, which I feel towards my most noble father. Whereas, had he flogged me I should perhaps have experienced a chilling sensation of fear whenever I entered his presence, in place of the heartfelt delight with which I now look up to him.

From my father's apartments I proceeded to Arthur's. He was sitting at breakfast and deeply occupied with the perusal of a newspaper (a thing, en passant, which I never touch except it be to glance over the 'Obituary' or the 'List of accidents').

'Good morning, Arthur,' said I.

'Good morning, Charles,' he returned laying down the paper. 'And now make haste and take your breakfast here. Clarissa'[3] (addressing his waiting-maid) 'prepare Lord Wellesley a cup of chocolate. I wish you, Charles, to take this packet to Lord Ellrington's, present my compliments to Lady Zenobia,[4] and inform her that she will greatly oblige me by correcting whatever may appear to need the hand of the polisher in the manuscript it contains.'

'Heigho!' said I. 'It's very odd that you will have your manuscript always corrected by her ladyship when I could do it so much better and have besides so often applied for the honour of rendering you that trifling piece of service.'

'You little, impertinent puppy! How dare you think of comparing yourself with Lady Ellrington? Why, if she heard you, her eyes (which by the by are not so darkly or beautifully blue as her stockings) would flash, and perhaps glare, the most ineffable scorn on your devoted head. I would have you to beware, Charles. It is no very pleasant thing to fall under the hatred of a learned lady. If you continue to throw aspersions on her genius thus, be assured that no lenient punishment will be your lot. And not the most gentle of hands will hers be when they are nerved by wrath.'

As Arthur said this he smiled with an expression of the most biting sarcasm, and, looking at the gold ring on his finger which contains a beautiful enamelled miniature of Marian Hume, went out of the room, singing carelessly:

> The peal within the shell concealed
> Oft sheds a fairer light

---

[3]A possible indication that Charlotte Brontë had read Richardson's *Clarissa* at this early date.

[4]Lady Zenobia Ellrington: see *Albion and Marina*, n. 2.

Than that whose beauties are revealed
To our restricted sight.

So she who sweetly shines at home,
And seldom wanders thence,
Is of her partner's happy dome
The best intelligence.

The highest talents of her mind,
The sunlight of her heart,
Are all to illume her home designed,
And never thence they part.

I only wish Lady Ellrington had been there to hear the tone of his voice
and observe the indescribable nonchalance of his manner.

CHAPTER THE SECOND
[Visit to Lady Ellrington]

When Arthur was gone I put on my cap and forthwith proceeded to
execute the commission he had entrusted me with. After about ten
minutes walk, I arrived at Lord Ellrington's mansion and was shown by
the servant who answered my summons into the entrance hall, while he
went to inform her ladyship of my desire to speak with her. She sent
word that she was ready to receive me in her boudoir, and thither I
accordingly repaired. I found her sitting on a sofa, attired in a morning
costume, reading Herodotus in the original.[5] She hardly deigned to
notice my entrée, not even to the extent of desiring me to be seated,
and so, without asking leave, I took the liberty of planting myself on an
ottoman near the window. On my delivering Arthur's packet and
message she brightened up a little and asked me how the Marquis of
Douro was. I replied that I suspected he had lately been taking large
draughts of blue vitriol as he evinced this morning an unaccountable
dislike for everything. She curled her lip and answered:
    'What! Even your eyes I presume; and, indeed, they are greyish.'[6]
    'My eyes and your stockings, my lady!'
    'No insolence, Lord Charles. I will not hear the Marquis of Douro
spoken saucily of by you. So now silence, I beg, unless you can speak

---

[5]The historical Zenobia, Queen of Palmya, was proficient in Latin, Greek, Syrian and
Egyptian, and familiar with Homer and Plato, having studied under Longinus.
[6]Lord Charles Wellesley is particular proud of his large blue eyes.

something more to the purpose. Answer me this: is Marian Hume now in Verdopolis?'

'Indeed, madam, I can't say with exactness, but I believe she is.'

'What reason have you for thinking so?'

'Why Arthur has been more vivacious and animated for these last few days, and I have likewise observed him of an evening going in the direction of the doctor's palace, with his usual bounding step, when he ought to have been engaged in other business.'

'Pooh! Were those lines which appeared in his last work under the head of "Stanzas on seeing a portrait, etc."[7] addressed to her?'

'Yes. How did you like them?'

'They were pretty enough, but wanted vigour; though, sooth to say in a composition of that kind super-excellence cannot be attained unless the heart is in the matter, and I am persuaded that was not his lordship's case when he indited those very indifferent verses.'

'Why so, my lady?'

'It is not natural that it should be. How could a man of his immense capacity and endowments, both mental and personal, care anything for a silly, trifling girl like Marian Hume!'

'Did you ever see her, madam?'

'Yes, once.'

'And what do you think of her appearance?'

'That she is not even handsome, much less beautiful. Rather pretty she may be, though even that is doubtful.'

'Why her features are regular, her eyes large, blue, bright and expressive, her form perfect, and her manners graceful. What more would you have?'

While I said this her ladyship's brow darkened, and scowling at me she said: 'What a taste is yours which can discover perfection in deformity! But even if what you have said was true, is there a spark of mind visible in that round, rosy face of hers? No! No more than in the faded, blanched countenance of an older lady who is nearly related to you and who might have been pretty in her day too, but is now, alas, a waning flower indeed, fit companion, or rather handmaid, for the imperious lord who domineers over her!'[8]

---

[7]'Lines on Seeing the Portrait of — [Marian Hume] painted by De Lisle', 10 November 1830; signed by the Marquis of Douro (*Poems*, pp. 121). See also 'Conversations', *Young Men's Magazine*, December (first issue) 1830, for a discussion of the portrait.

[8]The historical Duchess of Wellington was very pretty when young, but soon lost her good looks and was well known for her dowdy appearance and unconcern with fashion, a source of constant irritation to the Duke (see Elizabeth Longford, *Wellington: Pillar of State*, London: Weidenfeld & Nicolson, 1972, pp. 112–13).

This sneer at my mother roused my wrath and, starting to my feet, I exclaimed, 'Conceited she-puppy! Do you think that insolence shall go unpunished? No! My father and my brother shall both know of this and, rely on it, sarcasm will be returned for sarcasm! I would advise you not to show that swarthy face in His Grace, the Duke of Wellington's presence for some time henceforth, or it may be forced to blush, bronze though it be!'[9]

So saying, I made for the door. She sprang up in a transport of passion and, raising her dexter-foot, kindly assisted me therewith in my passage downstairs, sending forth at the same time a tremendous yell of ungovernable rage.

CHAPTER THE THIRD
[Visit to Captain Bud]

When I recovered from the state of insensibility into which this novel mode of conveyance had thrown me, I was stretched on a sofa in a small parlour, and near at hand sat my friend Captain Bud. I eagerly enquired where I was and who had brought me there. He answered, smiling significantly, 'Be composed, Lord Charles, you are perfectly safe in my house.'

'And how did I come here?' said I.

'Why,' returned Bud. 'I happened to call this morning at Lord Ellrington's and when I entered found you lying in a swoon at the bottom of the grand staircase. Alsand[10] was kneeling by chafing your temples and weeping. I asked what was the matter. He sobbed out, "Sister has fallen into a terrible rage and kicked Lord Wellesley out of her room down the steps, and I believe he is dead." "What in the name of wonder has she done so for?" said I. "I can't tell," he replied. So, seeing that nothing more was to be got out of him I took you up and carried you hither. It remains for you to inform me of the cause of your summary descent.'

I immediately related the whole of the foregoing conversation, and when I had concluded it he said, after a hearty fit of laughter, 'Ah, she's jealous enough, I believe, of Marian Hume. Talking of that, by the by, I've written a short account of their meeting in the forest, when Lady Zenobia tramped up as far as the Duke's country palace. Of course you know what I allude to?'

[9]Zenobia's complexion, inherited from her Latin mother, is probably also influenced by that of the historical Zenobia, Queen of Palmyra and the East: see *Albion and Marina*, n. 2.
[10]Zenobia has three younger brothers: Alsand, Myrtillus and Surena.

'To be sure,' I replied, 'but pray, Bud, will you oblige me by reading that account while I rest myself, for see it is raining fast and though I've some other visits to pay before night, yet I will wait till this shower is over.'

While I was speaking Bud rose and, unlocking his escritoire, took thence a paper from which he read as follows.

[The Rivals][11]

Scene: a thick forest, under the trees of which Lady Zenobia Ellrington is reposing, dressed in her usual attire of a crimson velvet robe and black plumes. She speaks.

'Tis eve: how that rich sunlight streameth through
The unwoven arches of this sylvan roof!
How their long, lustrous lines of light illume,
With trembling radiance, all the aged boles
Of elms majestic as the lofty columns
That proudly rear their tall forms to the dome
Of old cathedral or imperial palace!
Yea, they are grander than the mightiest shafts
That e'er by hand of man were fashioned forth
Their holy, solemn temples to uphold;
And sweeter far than the harmonious peals
Of choral thunder, that in music roll
Through vaulted aisles, are the low forest sounds
Murmuring around: of wind and stirred leaf,
And warbled song of nightingale or lark
Whose swelling cadences and dying falls
And whelming gushes of rich melody
Attune to meditation, all serene,
The weary spirit; and draw forth still thoughts
Of happy scenes half-veiled by the mists
Of bygone times. Yea, that calm influence
Hath soothed the billowy troubles of my heart
Till scarce one said thought rises, though I sit
Beneath these trees, utterly desolate.
But no, not utterly, for still one friend

[11]Untitled verse drama, previously published as 'The Rivals'. The so-called 'true' account of this drama is described in *The Bridal*.

I fain would hope remains to brighten yet
My mournful journey through this vale of tears;
And, while he shines, all other, lesser lights
May wane and fade unnoticed from the sky.
But more than friend, e'en he can never be.
Heaves a deep sigh.
What thought is sorrowful, but yet I'll hope.
What is my rival? Nought but a weak girl,
Ungifted with the state and majesty
That mark superior minds. Her eyes gleam not
Like windows to a soul of loftiness;
She hath not raven locks that lightly wave
Over a brow whose calm placidity
Might emulate the white and polished marble.
A white dove flutters by.
Ha! What art thou, fair creature? It hath vanished
Down that long vista of low-drooping trees.
How gracefully its pinions waved! Methinks
It was the spirit of this solitude.
List! I hear footsteps, and the rustling leaves
Proclaim the approach of some corporeal being.
A young girl advances up the vista, dressed in green with a garland of flowers wreathed in the curls of her hazel hair. She comes towards Lady Zenobia, and says:
Lady, methinks I erst have seen thy face.
Art thou not that Zenobia, she whose name
Renown hath borne e'en to this far retreat?
Lady Ellrington:
Aye, maiden, thou hast rightly guessed. But how
Didst recognize me?
Girl:
            In Verdopolis
I saw thee walking mid those gardens fair
That like a rich, embroidered belt surround
That mighty city; and one bade me look
At her whose genius had illumined bright
Her age and country, with undying splendour.
The majesty of thy imperial form,
The fire and sweetness of thy radiant eye,
Alike conspired to impress thine image
Upon my memory, and thus it is
That now I know thee as thou sittest there

Queen-like, beneath the over-shadowing boughs
Of that huge oak-tree, monarch of this wood.
Zenobia:
Smiling graciously.
Who art thou, maiden?
Girl:

Marian is my name.
Zenobia:
Starting up: aside.
Ha! My rival!
Sternly:

What dost thou here alone?
Marian:
Aside.
How her tone changed!
Aloud.

My favourite cushat-dove
Whose plumes are whiter than new-fallen snow,
Hath wandered, heedless, from my vigilant care.
I saw it gleaming through these dusky trees,
Fair as a star, while soft it glided by:
So have I come to find and lure it back.
Lady Ellrington:
Are all thy affections centred in a bird?
For thus thou speakest, as though nought were worthy
Of thought or care saving a silly dove!
Marian:
Nay, lady, I've a father, and mayhap
Others whom gratitude or tenderer ties,
If such there be, bind my heart closely to.
Lady Ellrington:
But birds and flowers and such trifles vain
Seem most to attract thy love, if I may form
A judgement from thy locks elaborate curled
And wreathed around with woven garlandry,
And from thy whining speech, all redolent
With tone of most affected sentiment.
She seizes Marian, and exclaims with a violent gesture.
Wretch, I could kill thee!
Marian:

Why, what have I done?
How have I wronged thee? Surely thou'rt distraught!

Lady Ellrington:
How hast thou wronged me? Where didst weave the net
Whose cunning meshes have entangled round
The mightiest heart that e'er in mortal breast
Did beat responsive unto human feeling?
Marian:
The net? What net? I wove no net; she's frantic!
Lady Ellrington:
Dull, simple creature! Canst not understand?
Marian:
Truly, I cannot. 'Tis to me a problem,
An unsolved riddle, an enigma dark.
Lady Ellrington:
I'll tell thee, then. But hark! What voice is that?
Voice from the forest:
Marian, where art thou? I have found a rose
Fair as thyself. Come hither, and I'll place it
With the blue violets on thine ivory brow.
Marian:
He calls me! I must go – restrain me not.
Lady Ellrington:
Nay! I will hold thee firmly as grim death.
Thou need'st not struggle, for my grasp is strong.
Thou shalt not go: Lord Arthur shall come here,
And I will gain the rose despite of thee!
Now for mine hour of triumph: here he comes.
Lord Arthur advances from among the trees, exclaims on seeing Lady
Ellrington.
Lord Arthur:
Zenobia! How cam'st thou here? What ails thee?
Thy cheek is flushed as with a fever glow,
Thine eyes flash strangest radiance, and thy frame
Trembles like to the wind-stirred aspen-tree!
Lady Ellrington:
Give me the rose, Lord Arthur, for methinks
I merit it more than my girlish rival;
I pray thee now grant my request, and place
That rose upon my forehead, not on hers;
Then will I serve thee all my after-days
As thy poor handmaid, as thy humblest slave,
Happy to kiss the dust beneath thy tread,
To kneel submissive in thy lordly presence.

307

Oh! turn thine eyes from her and look on me
As I lie here imploring at thy feet,
Supremely blest if but a single glance
Could tell me that thou art not wholly deaf
To my petition, earnestly preferred.
Lord Arthur:
Lady, thou'rt surely mad! Depart, and hush
These importunate cries. They are not worthy
Of the great name which thou hast fairly earned.
Lady Ellrington:
Give me that rose, or I to thee will cleave
Till death these vigorous sinews has unstrung.
Hear me this once and give it me Lord Arthur.
Lord Arthur:
After a few minutes deliberation.
Here, take the flower, and keep it for my sake.
Marian:
Utters a suppressed scream, and sinks to the ground.
Lady Ellrington:
Assisting her to rise.
Now I have triumphed! But I'll not exult;
Yet I know, henceforth, I'm thy superior.
Farewell, my lord, I thank thee for thy preference!
Plunges into the wood and disappears.
Lord Arthur:
Fear nothing, Marian, for a fading flower
Is not symbolical of constancy.
But take this sign.
Gives her his diamond ring.
                        Enduring adamant
Betokens well affection that will live
Long as life animates my faithful heart.
Now let us go, for see the deepening shades
Of twilight darken our lone forest path;
And, lo! Thy dove comes gliding through the mirk,
Fair wanderer, back to its loved mistress's care!
Luna will light us on our journey home:
For see her lamp shines radiant in the sky,
And her bright beams will pierce the thickest boughs.
Exeunt, curtain falls.

'A very pretty piece, indeed,' said I when Bud had finished reading. 'But pray, as you value the advice of a friend, don't show it to Arthur.'
'I have,' he replied.
'And what did he say?' I asked.
'Say?' returned Bud. 'He only bit his lip till the blood sprang from it, and muttered between his closed teeth, "If you libel my friends thus, sir, again, and prate with such freedom about things which concern me alone, I shall know how to obtain satisfaction." I saw he was roused, and not choosing to irritate him further, I walked off.'

'The most discreet plan,' I answered, 'for you cannot conceive how utterly infatuated he is about Marian Hume. He will allow no one to mention her name in his presence, whether for good or bad. And now I must be going, for the shower has passed away, and look, Bud, at that beautiful rainbow in the north!'

'Aye, the colours are pretty enough,' said he, 'but can't you sit a little longer?'

'No. I have some other visits to pay.'

'Well then, call again in the evening, and take a quiet cup of tea with me.'

I promised to be punctual and then took my departure.

CHAPTER THE FOURTH
[Visit to Young Soult]

It is not generally known that Young Soult, The Rhymer, has quitted Waterloo Palace and set up house for himself. Those who love scandal have attributed this to a quarrel between my brother and him, but from the very best authority, namely Arthur himself, I know this rumour to be totally unfounded. The same fraternal confidence and cordiality exists in all their dealings and feelings with and for each other as there ever did. The only true reason is that Soult found the bustle and ceremony of an imperial palace too great for his poetical propensities and therefore removed to a quieter residence in the suburbs of Verreopolis; and thitherward I went my way after leaving Bud.

In about half an hour I reached it. It is a pretty, rural building, with a pillared portico in front and so overgrown with fragrant creeping plants and vines that scarcely a glimpse of stonework is visible, and very novel and pleasant it looked now that the leaves were all fresh and green after the recent shower. The roses and jasmine gave out such a delightful scent as I approached that one might fancy the air perfumed with incense. Being a privileged guest from my relationship to Arthur, I opened the leaf-draperied door without knocking, and, after passing through a little Gothic hall and ascending a flight of white marble steps, entered the poet's study. He was leaning, with his arms folded, against the sill of an open lattice, gazing earnestly at the fast disappearing rainbow. I accosted him with: 'Well, Alexander, how are you after the rain?'

'Why, how can I be otherwise than refreshed while the influence of that sweet spring shower is diffusing balm and peace over the earth.'

'It will help to bring forward the crops I hope.'

'Aye. I hear the flowers and grass growing! The sound is like the faint sigh of rising zephyrs.'

'Your ears are more acute than mine then, Alexander.'

'It may be so. Poetry refines all the senses in a marvellous degree.'[12]

'Did you notice the rainbow?'

'Did I notice the rainbow! Aye, truly, else should I be unworthy any longer to possess the faulty of seeing. Oh, how gloriously did the apparition front the sun! Beauty created from utter darkness by the vivifying breath of God.

> Now fall the last drops of the shower,
> And sunshine rest on every hill;
> The liquid diamonds in each flower
> Their cups with trembling radiance fill.
>
> Lo! From Apollo's golden light
> The fertilizing vapours fly,
> And reappears in splendour bright
> The calmly lustrous sky.
>
> A clearer azure paints the robe
> Spread gloriously on high;
> A fresher verdure decks the globe
> That far beneath doth lie.
>
> How glad and sweet the murmurings
> That from blue streams ascend,
> While around cool shade the woodland flings
> As its boughs to the waters bend.
>
> But now the clouds with densest gloom
> Have gather'd in the north,

---

[12]Charlotte Brontë continues here the same ridicule of Young Soult's romantic sensibilities (and hence, of Branwell Brontë's poetic pretensions) that she began in *The Poetaster*.

And methinks I hear the thunder's boom
From their dark recess roll forth.

Hushed in heaven and hushed in earth
Every sound of joy and mirth:
For upon that mighty cloud,
Huge and black as Nature's shroud,

Faint appears a vision fair
Pil'd upon the ambient air;
From its darkness breathes a light,
Softly lustrous, dimly bright.

More distant the glory grows:
Lo! A shade of light it throws,
And upon the vaulted skies
Now a second arch doth rise.

And as they span the heavens,
Each gleaming like a star,
They seem as some fair vision
That cometh from afar,

With transitory light
Flashing on our mortal sight,
And upon our slumbers stealing,
Strangest scenes in sleep revealing;

At the dawn of daylight, flies
Swift before the opening eyes,
Scarce leaving memory's shade,
As away they flit and fade.

Never they return again;
Now I close my lightsome strain.'

When Young Soult had concluded this extempore effusion, which was uttered in a strange variety of tones – first speaking, which gradually changed to recitative, then chanting, and last to regular singing – he sat down and said, 'Pray, Lord Charles, forgive my enthusiasm, but really my feelings do sometimes carry me utterly beyond the control of reason and politeness, more especially now as I have not the benefit of your noble brother's admonitions. I hope, by the by, that he is in good health?'

'Yes, very, thank you. He desires to know how you like your suburban residence.'

'Oh, excessively! For now have I always the fresh free air of the country and the most unbroken quiet.'

'In what manner do you divide the time in such a recluse mode of life?'

'I rise at five o'clock, and, as soon as I am dressed, stroll out for the sake of exercise and the enjoyment of Nature's bounties, which are so profusely scattered forth in early dawn when the warbling birds, the dewy flowers, the elastic wind, the trees swayed to and fro as it sweeps among their huge branches and, in short, every feature of creation speaks audibly to the solitary passenger in the heavenly language of song and raise all the latent energies of his soul to praise and thanksgiving. Then refreshed and happy I return home and breakfast upon bread and watercresses, gathered by myself from a neighbouring spring. After this temperate meal, I address myself to study and reading for three hours. Then I have my dinner, at which two dishes of wholesome food suffice for my unsophisticated appetite. The remainder of the day is dedicated to innocent amusements or whatever other harmless employment the impulses of my spirit may suggest, for I do not live entirely by rule and square. In the evening I again wander abroad till dark, sometimes longer, feeding my mind on Nature's own poetry; and then I retire to rest, after a supper of the same materials as my breakfast is composed of.'

After a little more conversation with Young Soult I left him to the enjoyment of his hermit-like existence, not in the least desiring to share it with him, but rather resulting in a quite opposite inclination.

CHAPTER THE FIFTH
[Visit to the Rotunda, Bravey's Inn[13]]

I wandered on through the streets scarcely knowing and not caring whither I went, until I arrived at the magnificent square called —[14] (I love the name) one side of which is formed by that gorgeous and apparently everlasting building, Bravey's Inn. The portals stood open and I entered. Hearing the usual murmurs of conversation, from the

---

[13]Originally a public apartment for officers in Bravey's Hotel (see *Young Men's Magazine*, August 1830, n. 12), it becomes the meeting place for the Young Men and Verdopolitan literati. The following chapter is a continuation of the serial 'Conversations' in the *Young Men's Magazine*.

[14]It is not clear from the transcription whether Charlotte Brontë intended to omit the name or whether Davidson Cook was unable to read the word in the manuscript. Elsewhere in the juvenilia, this square is simply referred to as either the Central Square or the Great Square.

sounds I proceeded there. A group of persons had assembled under the chandelier, among whom I noticed Arthur, De Lisle, Captain Tree, Bobadill, Lord Lofty, Sergeant Bud, Lord Dunsdale, Colonel Grenville, General Ellrington, Captain Flower, Major Goat, etc., etc.[15] My father was there also, but sitting a little apart from the group, watching them with his usual smile. At the moment I entered something had been said which evidently annoyed Arthur, for his forehead was flushed and his manner altogether like a man that had been irritated. During my stay the following conversation, as nearly as I can remember, took place.

Marquis of Douro: No, generally gentlemen, you are too bad. But, in truth, I plainly perceive that envy is a principle and actuating motive in most of your minds. You are certainly jealous because a human being of the feminine gender has displayed such wonderful abilities, the sun of whose genius indeed, when arrived at its meridian splendour, appears likely to pale the ineffectual fires of her male contemporaries.

Captain Tree: That same sun you speak of, my lord Marquis, seems to have burnt her complexion brown, for she's as swarthy as my Martinique scullion! He! he! he! A good joke that!

Marquis of Douro:
Turning rather fiercely to Tree.
As for you, Tree, we all know that you are more of a wren than an eagle. But think not that that magnificent swan will heed your chirping. No! Gracefully she'll glide down the tide of life, her white plumes gleaming with the radiance of an intellect that will leave a glorious and eternal light behind, despite the petty annoyance of such creatures as you.

Duke of Wellington:
Advancing forwards.
Hold there, Arthur! You have likened this lady, Zenobia Ellrington, to a swan. Now, with your leave, I'll pursue the parallel; nay, enlarge it, for I'll liken all womankind to the same bird. We all know that the proper and native element of swans is water, where no creature can equal them in dignity, gracefulness and majestic beauty. There, in short, they are unrivalled. But whenever they presume to set foot on land their unseemly waddle entitles every winged creature, eagle and wren alike,

---

[15]Military associates of the fictitious Duke of Wellington, apart from the Marquis of Douro's friends De Lisle and Lord Lofty. General Ellrington is Zenobia's father; Captain Flower becomes the satiric political author Sir John Flower (later Lord Richton, Verdopolitan ambassador to Angria, and a pseudonym of Branwell Brontë); and Lord Dunsdale and Major Goat are not mentioned again in Charlotte's manuscripts; see also *Blackwood's Young Men's Magazine*, August 1829, n. 2 and 6; *An Interesting Passage in the Lives of Some Eminent Men of the Present Time*, n. 7; and *The Bridal*, n. 11, for other characters.

to laugh till their sides split at the ludicrous spectacle. In like manner the proper and native element of woman is home. That is her kingdom, her undisputed and rightful possession. But when she foolishly wanders thence and forces herself upon the public eye the swan's vagaries are but a type of those she exhibits.

Colonel Grenville: I think what Your Grace says is very true. At least I know that I should not like it if when I went home tired and hungry I found my table heaped with books and papers instead of a good, hot, smoking dinner.

Lord Lofty: And heard that your wife had been taken up for dashing out a little fellow's brains in the streets!

Bobadill: Aye! That was a pretty business! Can you defend Lady Zenobia for that trick, my lord Marquis?

Marquis of Douro: She was not to blame, sir. Repeated insults of the most aggravated nature had stung her to desperation, and she committed the act in a moment of insanity. Besides, knowing as you do the dreadful punishment that my little brother's repentance caused when the faculties of her great mind were restored, I wonder that you should think it necessary to advert to a circumstance now forgotten and forgiven by him whom it chiefly concerned.

Duke of Wellington: Bobadill's allusion seems to have hurt your feeling very much, Arthur. Why are you sore on that particular point?

Marquis of Douro: Because, father, I witnessed the poignancy of her grief subsequently to the act, and I am certain it was unfeigned.

Colonel Grenville: Feigned or unfeigned, I wish I'd been near her when she committed that black deed. Poor Lord Charles! It quite went to my heart when I saw him stretched out dead. He looked so pale and quiet.

Captain Tree: Aye, but did you ever see him quiet before? I am sure I was right glad to hear of his death, for a more mischievous imp never existed. I'll allow that the news of his coming to life again rather troubled me, for to this moment I think the being that now goes by his name is only his spirit!

Captain Flower: I am of much the same opinion, for his eyes instead of sparkling as they used to do have assumed a glazed appearance, and not a flush of red ever tinges his colourless cheeks. What do you think, my lord Marquis?

Marquis of Douro:
   In a rather disturbed manner.
Nonsense! Nonsense! He's as much flesh and blood as any gentleman in the room. These plaints ought to be removed, or they will infect others with their superstitious fears.

Sergeant Bud: Whom did he first appear to after his exhumation?

De Lisle: To me. I was sitting alone in my study at dusk reading by the firelight Tree's horrible romance of *The Incorporeal Watcher*[16] when, at the moment when my mind was prepared for the reception of any supernatural impression, a little, pale, ghastly creature, shrouded in grave-clothes, sprang in through the open window, and fixing on me a pair of large blue glassy eyes exclaimed, 'De Lisle, I have risen from the dead. My spirit has been permitted to revisit Earth from that bourne whence, Shakespeare falsely says, no traveller returns,[17] that I may inflict a terrible punishment on my enemies. And mark my words, De Lisle, though it may not directly fall on their heads, yet sooner or later they must suffer. Adieu, for the present!' And with these words he vanished through the same aperture he had entered at, and when I looked out the moment after not a vestige of him was to be seen.
Omnes: That was strange.
Sergeant Bud:
  Shuddering.
It was about twilight that my father first saw him.
Marquis of Douro: What were the circumstances attending his apparition then?
Sergeant Bud: Why, my father told me he was standing by himself in a walk of one of the public gardens when he felt something colder than ice touch his hand, and, on looking round, saw the figure of Lord Wellesley in the habiliments of the dead. He addressed exactly the same words to him as to De Lisle and then passed away at a pace more like gliding than walking.
Colonel Grenville: It was gloaming or thereabouts when he appeared to me. I was busily engaged in the discussion of my dinner when three slow and distinct raps at the other end of the table caused me to look up, and there was Lord Charles sitting just opposite. He spoke the same speech to me as to De Lisle and Bud, and then went out of the room. I could not distinguish the slightest noise as he advanced towards the door.
Marquis of Douro: These accounts, I must say, agree strongly in substance. Nevertheless, do not suppose that I am convinced by them. What is your opinion, father?
Duke of Wellington: That no nursery-maid could possibly equal De

---

[16]Probably an early manuscript by Charlotte Brontë, now lost; in the texts of different stories she often referred to manuscripts she had written. In the Advertisements of the *Young Men's Magazine*, Charlotte lists several other works by Captain Tree which may also have been early manuscripts: see *Blackwood's Young Men's Magazine*, October 1829, n. 7, and 'Advertisements', *Young Men's Magazine*, October 1830.

[17]*Hamlet*, III, i, 79–80.

Lisle, Bud and Grenville in the important avocation of story-telling. But come, Arthur. Let us return homewards. These old women will certainly persuade you into a belief of your little brother's spirituality. *Marquis of Douro*: I am ready to accompany you, father. Goodnight, gentlemen.

Exeunt Arthur and my father.

When they were gone, this band of wise men gathered closer together and related many more tales of my ghostly propensities. During all this time I had secreted myself behind a curtain in the room. At length, when I saw that they had worked themselves up to the highest pitch of supersitious terror I emerged from my hiding-place and dashing in among them exclaimed, 'Depart without or die!' In an instant the room was cleared and I remained standing alone in my glory. After the space of a few minutes I departed also, remembering my engagement with Captain Bud, which the cathedral bell now told me it was time to fulfil.

Visits

In

VERREOP-

OLIS

By

The Honourable Charles Albert

FLOR-

IAN

Lord Wellesley Aged 10 years.

In Two

Volumes. Volume the Second

Published by

Sergeant Bud, And Sold By All

The Booksellers

In

The Chief Glass Town, the Duke of Wellington's Glass Town, Paris, Parry's Glass Town, Ross's Glass Town, etc., etc., etc., Charlotte Brontë, December the 18th, 1830[1]

CONTENTS

Second Visit to Captain Bud .... Chap. I
The Fairy Gift. A tale .... Chap. II

Charlotte Brontë   December the 18th 1830

CHAPTER THE FIRST
[Second Visit to Captain Bud]

By this time it was perfectly dark. The night had closed in stormily, and as I passed through the miry streets glimmering in gas I hardly recognized a single creature whom I knew, for they were all but deserted. At length I arrived at Bud's large, dark-looking mansion, and after the usual ceremonies of ringing the doorbell, admittance, etc., was shown up to his private parlour. There he sat by the ingle-cheek of as warm a fire as ever cheered an English heart or roasted an English hide. The china cups were ranged on a round baized table, and the sweet music of a silver urn, throwing up columns of blue steam, saluted my ears as I entered.

'Well, Lord Charles,' he exclaimed when he saw me, at the same time drawing closer together the coals of his clear, bright fire, 'so you've come at last. Sit down. I'm glad to see you. 'Tis a wild night and the wind roars in this old-fashioned chimney like thunder.'

I willingly flung myself on the sofa, heartily glad of such a pleasant refuge from the rain that pattered and the blast that howled so dismally without. In two seconds (the tea having been 'weel maskit'[2] before my

---

[1]Title-page of manuscript, formerly in the Law Collection, now lost; hand-sewn booklet (7.6 × 5.1 cm) in blue paper cover. The following text is from a transcript lent to the editor and now held by Professor Mildred G. Christian.

[2]Scots and northern dialect: well infused (Joseph Wright, *The English Dialect Dictionary*, 6 volumes, 1898–1905).

arrival) he had poured me out a cup of excellent gunpowder,[3] which, when mingled with the symbols of sweetness and mildness, to wit, milk and sugar, I drank to the tune of three cups per ten minutes, mingling my libation with hot rolls, muffins and unleavened cakes well saturated with melted butter. At length tea, like all other things from the world to a needleful of thread, came to an end. The things being removed we wheeled the sofa still nearer to the centre of warmth. Then the feast of reason and the flow of soul commenced. Bud set open the sluices of his mind and poured freely his inmost thoughts down my caverned ears. In return I regaled his senses with the sweet incense of flattery and praise. Then the conversation took another turn. Scandal was the principal topic. All our neighours' characters were made to pass through the fiery ordeal of our judgement and not one escaped unscathed. At length, the store of talk being exhausted, a dead silence ensued, which in about a quarter of an hour was broken by my exclaiming, 'Bud, tell me a story. I am just in a humour for hearing one, and unless the music of your voice hinders it this charming fire will assuredly bind me in the chains of sleep and deliver me over summarily to Somnas.'[4]

'Well, Charlie, but what shall I tell you?'

'One of the adventures of your early life would amuse me most.'

'Well, let me see, I'll try to remember one.' (Closing his eyes.) 'Aye, here I behold, gliding from the dimness of the past, an incident that occurred to me more than thirty years ago when I was but a strapping youngster of eighteen years old. How different then from what I am now, wrinkled and with hoary hairs grisling my once raven locks! Ah, Charles, old age will come. Even the light of your blue eyes must wane at its dull, misty breath. The roses will fade from your cheeks and the smiles from your lips when the icy touch of its desecrating finger falls on them. In chill streams will your now full and rich blood creep through withered veins. Trembling and tottering must take the place of lightness and vigour. Heigho! Heigho! I am not now what I once was.'

'I know that, Bud, yet you have scarce passed the meridian of life and are still in the full strength of manhood. Then cease this moralizing strain and give me the story you promised. Lamenting will never bring back your prime of days.'

'That is true, so here's to begin. Now, be attentive and strive to profit by what I am about to relate.'

---

[3]Fine green tea of granular appearance (*OED*).
[4]Roman god of sleep.

CHAPTER THE SECOND
[The Fairy Gift. A Tale]

Hem! Hem! You know, Lord Charles, I was born of poor and humble parents, and you know likewise by what means I rose to my present station. But that is not our business now.

One cold evening in December 17—, while I was yet but a day labourer, though not even at that time wholly without some aspirations after fame and some intimations of future greatness, I was sitting alone by my cottage fire engaged in ambitious reveries of l'avenir, and amusing myself with wild and extravagant imaginations. A thousand evanescent wishes flitted through my mind, one of which was scarcely formed when another succeeded it; then a third, equally transitory, and so on.

While I was thus employed with building castles in the air my frail edifices were suddenly dissipated by an emphatic 'Hem!' I started and raised my head. Nothing was visible, and after a few minutes, supposing it to be only fancy, I resumed my occupation of weaving the web of waking visions. Again the 'Hem!' was heard. Again I looked up, when lo! sitting in the opposite chair I beheld the diminutive figure of a man dressed all in green. With a pretty considerable fluster I demanded his business and how he had contrived to enter the house without my knowledge.

'I am a fairy,' he replied, in a shrill voice, 'but fear nothing, my intentions are not mischievous. On the contrary, I intend to gift you with the power of obtaining four wishes, provided you wish them at different times; and if you should happen to find the fruition of my theme not equal to your anticipations, still you are at liberty to cast it aside, which you must do before another wish is granted.'

When he had concluded this information he gave me a ring, telling me that by the potency of the spell with which it was invested my desires would prove immediately successful.

I expressed my gratitude for this gift in the warmest terms and then enquired how I should dispose of the ring when I had four times arrived at the possession of that which I might wish.

'Come with it at midnight to the little valley in the uplands, a mile hence,' said he, 'and there you will be rid of it when it becomes useless.'

With these words he vanished from my sight. I stood for some minutes half credulous of the reality of what I had witnessed, until at last I was convinced by the green-coloured ring set in gold that sparkled in my hand.

By some strange influence I had been preserved from any feeling of fear during my conversation with the fairy, but now I began to feel certain doubts and misgivings as to the propriety of having any dealings with a supernatural being. These, however, I soon quelled and began forthwith to consider what should be [the] nature of my first wish. After some deliberation, I found the desire for beauty was uppermost in my mind, and therefore formed a wish that next morning when I arose I should find myself possessed of surpassing loveliness.

That night my dreams were filled with anticipations of future grandeur, but the gay visions which my sleeping fancy called into being were dispelled by the first sounds of morning. I awoke lightsome and refreshed, and springing out of bed glanced half-doubtingly into the small looking-glass which decorated the wall of my apartment, to ascertain if any change for the better had been wrought on me since the preceding night.

Never shall I forget the thrill of delighted surprise which passed throught me when I beheld my altered appearance. There I stood, tall, slender, and graceful as a young poplar tree, all my limbs moulded in the most perfect and elegant symmetry, my complexion of the purest red and white, my eyes blue and brilliant, swimming in liquid radiance under the narrow dark arches of two exquisitely formed eyebrows, my mouth of winning sweetness, and lastly, my hair clustering in rich black curls over a forehead smooth as ivory.

In short, I have never yet heard or read of any beauty that could at all equal the splendour of comeliness with which I was at that moment invested. I stood for a long time gazing at myself in a trance of admiration while happiness such as I had never known before or since overflowed my heart.

That day happened to be Sunday, and accordingly I put on my best clothes and proceeded forthwith towards the church. (Breakfast would to me have been altogether superfluous.) The service had just commenced when I arrived, and as I walked up the aisle to my pew I felt that the eyes of the whole assembly were upon me, and that proud consciousness gave a bounding elasticity to my gait, which added stateliness and majesty to my other innumerable graces. Among those who viewed me most attentively was Lady Beatrice Ducie. This personage was the widow of Lord Ducie,[5] owner of the chief part of the village where I resided and nearly all the surrounding land for many miles, who, when he died, left her the whole of his immense estates.

[5]Lord Ducie (1802–1853) was an advocate of free trade and a famous agriculturalist.

She was without children and perfectly at liberty to marry whomsoever she might chance to fix her heart on, and therefore, though her ladyship had passed the meridian of life, was besides fat and ugly, and into the bargain had the reputation of being a witch, I cherished hopes that she might take a liking for me, seeing I was so very handsome, and by making me her spouse raise me at once from indigence and poortith[6] to the highest pitch of luxury and affluence. These were my ambitious meditations as I slowly retraced my steps homeward.

In the afternoon I again attended church and again Lady Ducie favoured me with many smiles and glances expressive of her admiration. At length my approaching good fortune was placed beyond a doubt, for while I was standing in the porch after service was over she happened to pass and, inclining her head towards me, said: 'Come to my house tomorrow at four o'clock.' I only answered by a low bow and then hastened back to my cottage.

On Monday afternoon I re-dressed myself in my best and, putting a Christmas rose in the buttonhole of my waistcoat, hastened to the appointed rendezvous.

When I entered the avenue of Ducie Castle, a footman in rich livery stopped and requested me to follow him. I complied, and we proceeded down a long walk to a bower of evergreens, where sat her ladyship in a pensive posture. Her stout, lusty figure was arrayed in a robe of the purest white muslin, elegantly embroidered. On her head she wore an elaborately curled wig, among whose borrowed tresses was twined a wreath of artificial flowers, and her brawny shoulders were enveloped in a costly Indian shawl. At my approach she arose and saluted me. I returned the compliment, and when we were seated and the footman had withdrawn, business summarily commenced by her tendering me the possession of her hand and heart, both which offers, of course, I willingly accepted.

Three weeks after we were married in the parish church by special licence, amidst the rejoicings of her numerous tenantry, to whom a sumptuous entertainment was that day given.

I now entered upon a new scene of life. Every object which met my eyes spoke of opulence and grandeur. Every meal which I partook of seemed to me a luxurious feast. As I wandered through the vast halls and magnificent apartments of my new residence I felt my heart dilating with gratified pride at the thought that they were my own. Towards the obsequious domestics that thronged around me I behaved with the utmost respect and deference, being compelled thereto by a feeling of

[6]Scots and northern dialect: poverty (*OED*).

awe inspired by their superior breeding and splendid appearance. I was now constantly encompassed by visitors from among those who moved in the highest circles of society. My time was passed in the enjoyment of all sorts of pleasures; balls, concerts and dinners were given almost every day at the castle in honour of our wedding. My evenings were spent in hearing music, or seeing dancing and gormandizing; my days in excursions over the country, either on horseback or in a carriage.

Yet, notwithstanding all this, I was not happy. The rooms were so numerous that I was often lost in my own house and sometimes got into many awkward predicaments in attempting to find some particular apartment. Our high-bred guests despised me for my clownish manners and deportment. I was forced to bear patiently the most humiliating jokes and sneers from noble lips. My own servants insulted me with impunity, and, finally, my wife's temper showed itself every day more and more in the most hideous light. She became terribly jealous and would hardly suffer me to go out of her sight a moment. In short, before the end of three months I sincerely wished myself separated from her and reduced again to the situation of a plain and coarse but honest and contented ploughboy.

This separation was occasioned by the following incident sooner than I expected. At a party which we gave one evening there chanced to be present a young lady named Cecilia Standon. She possessed no mean share of beauty and had besides the most graceful demeanour I ever saw. Her manner was kind, gentle and obliging, without any of that haughty superciliousness which so annoyed me in others of my fashionable acquaintance. If I made a foolish observation or transgressed against the rules of politeness, she did not give vent to her contempt in a laugh or suppressed titter, but informed me in a whisper what I ought to have done and instructed me how to do it. When she was gone I remarked to my wife what a kind and excellent lady Miss Cecilia Standon was. 'Yes,' exclaimed she, reddening, 'everyone can please you but me. Don't think to elude my vigilance. I saw you talking and laughing with her all the time she was here, you low-born creature whom I raised from obscurity to splendour. And yet not one spark of gratitude do you feel towards me. But I will have my revenge.' So saying she left me to meditate alone on what that revenge might be.

The same night, as I lay in bed, wakeful and restless, I heard suddenly a noise as of footsteps outside the chamber door. Impelled by irresistible curiosity, I rose and opened it without making any sound. My surprise was great on beholding the figure of my wife stealing along on tiptoe with her back towards me, and a lighted candle in her hand. Anxious to know what could be her motive for walking about the house at this hour of night I followed softly, taking care to time my steps so as to coincide with hers.

After proceeding along many passages and galleries which I had never before seen, we descended a very long staircase that led us underneath the coal and wine cellars to a damp, subterraneous vault. Here she stopped and deposited the candle on the ground. I shrank instinctively, for the purpose of concealment, behind a massive stone pillar which upheld the arched roof on one side.

The rumours which I had often heard of her being a witch passed with painful distinctness across my mind and I trembled violently. Presently she knelt with folded hands and began to mutter some indistinguishable words in a strange tone. Flames now darted out of the earth, circling her round like fiery snakes, and huge smouldering clouds of smoke rolled over the slimy walls, concealing their hideousness from the eye.

At length the dead silence that had hitherto reigned unbroken was dissipated by a tremendous cry which shook the house to its centre, and I saw six black, indefinable figures gliding through the darkness bearing a funeral bier on which lay arrayed, as I had seen her the previous evening in robes of white satin and tall snowy ostrich plumes, the form of Cecilia Standon. Her dark eyes were closed and their long lashes lay motionless on a cheek pale as marble. She was quite stiff and dead.

At this appalling sight I could restrain myself no longer, but uttering a loud shriek I sprang from behind the pillar. My wife saw me. She started from her kneeling position and rushed furiously towards where I stood, exclaiming in tones rendered tremulous by excessive fury: 'Wretch, wretch, what demon has lured thee hither to thy fate?' With these words she seized me by the throat and attempted to strangle me.

I screamed and struggled in vain. Life was ebbing apace when suddenly she loosened her grasp, tottered, and fell dead.

When I was sufficiently recovered from the effects of her infernal grip to look around I saw by the light of the candle a little man in a green coat striding over her and flourishing a bloody dagger in the air. In his sharp, wild physiognomy I immediately recognized the fairy who six months ago had given me the ring that was the occasion of my present situation. He had stabbed my wife through the heart and thus afforded me opportune relief at the moment when I so much needed it.

After tendering him my most ardent thanks for his kindness to me I ventured to ask what we should do with the dead body.

'Leave that to me,' he replied. 'But now as the day is dawning and I must soon be gone, do you wish to return to your former rank of a happy, honest labourer, being deprived of the beauty which has been the source of so much trouble to you, or will you remain as you are? Decide quickly, for my time is limited.'

I replied hesitatingly, 'Let me return to my former rank,' and no sooner were the words out of my mouth than I found myself standing alone at the porch of my humble cottage, plain and coarse as ever, without any remains of the extreme comeliness with which I had been so lately invested.

I cast a glance at the tall towers of Ducie Castle which appeared in the distance faintly illuminated by the light reflected from rosy clouds hovering over the eastern horizon, and then, stooping as I passed beneath the lowly lintel, once more crossed the threshold of my parental hut.

A day or two after, while I was sitting at breakfast, a neighbour entered and, after enquiring how I did, etc., asked me where I had been for the last half year. Seeing it necessary to dissemble, I answered that I had been on a visit to a relation who lived at a great distance. This satisfied him, and I then enquired if anything had happened in the village since my departure.

'Yes,' said he, 'a little while after you were gone Lady Ducie married the handsomest young man that was ever seen, but nobody knew where he came from, and most people thought he was a fairy; and now about four days ago Lady Ducie, her husband, and Lord Standon's eldest daughter all vanished in the same night and have never been heard of since, though the strictest search has been made after them. Yesterday her ladyship's brother came and took possession of the estate, and he is trying to hush up the matter as much as he can.'

This intelligence gave me no small degree of satisfaction, as I was now certain that none of the villagers had any suspicion of my dealings with the fairy.

But to proceed. I had yet liberty to make three more wishes; and after much consideration, being convinced of the vanity of desiring such transitory things as my first, I fixed upon 'superior talent' as the aim of my second wish, and no sooner had I done so than I immediately felt an expansion, as it were, of soul within me. Everything appeared to my mental vision in a new light. High thoughts elevated my mind, and abstruse meditations racked my brain continually. But you shall presently hear the upshot of this sudden éclaircissement.

One day I was sent to a neighbouring market town, by one Mr Tenderden, a gentleman of some consequence in our village, for the purpose of buying several articles in glass and china. When I had made my purchases I directed them to be packed up in straw and then, with the basket on my back, trudged off homeward. But ere I was half way night overtook me. There was no moon, and the darkness was also much increased by a small mizzling rain. Cold and drenched to the skin, I arrived at the Rising Sun, a little wayside inn, which lay in my route.

On opening the door my eyes were agreeably saluted by the sight of a bright warm fire, round which sat about half a dozen of my acquaintance. After calling for a drop of something to warm me, and carefully depositing the basket of glass on the ground, I seated myself amongst them. They were engaged in a discussion as to whether a monarchical or republican form of government was best. I soon entered deeply into the argument, taking the side of the monarchists. The chief champion of the republicans was Bob Sylvester, a blacksmith by trade, and of the largest loquacity of any man I ever saw. He was proud of his argumentative talents, but by dint of my fairy gift I presently silenced him amid cheers from both sides of the house.

Bob was a man of hot temperament and not calculated for lying down quietly under a defeat. Here therefore rose and challenged me to single combat. I accepted the defiance and a regular battle ensued. After some hard hits and smart peppering, he closed in furiously and dealt me a tremendous left-handed facer. I staggered reeled and fell insensible. The last thing I remember was a horrible crash as if the house was tumbling in about my ears.

When I recovered my senses I was laid in bed at my own house, all cut, bruised and bloody. I was soon given to understand that the basket of glass was broken, and Mr Tenderden, being a miserly, hard-hearted man, made me stand to the loss, which was upwards of five pounds.

When I was able to walk about again, I determined to get rid of my ring forthwith in the manner the fairy had pointed out, seeing that it brought me nothing but ill-luck.

It was a fine clear night in October when I reached the little valley in the uplands before mentioned. There was a gentle frost, and the stars were twinkling with the lustre of diamonds in a sky of deep and cloudless azure. A chill breeze whistled drearily in the gusty passes of the hills that surrounded the vale, but I wrapped my cloak around me and, standing in a sheltered nook, boldly awaited the event.

After about half an hour of dead silence I heard a sound as of many voices weeping and lamenting at a distance. This continued for some time until it was interrupted by another voice, seemingly close at hand. I started at the contiguity of the sound and looked on every side, but nothing was visible. Still the strain kept rising and drawing nearer. At length the following words, sung in a melancholy though harmonious tone, became distinctly audible:

Hearken, O Mortal to the wail
Which round the wandering night-winds fling,
Soft-sighing 'neath the moonbeams pale,
How low, how odd, its murmuring!
No other voice, no other tone,
Disturbs the silence deep;
All saving that prophetic moan.
Are hushed in quiet sleep.

The moon and each small lustrous star.
That journeys through the boundless sky,
Seem, as their radiance from afar
Falls on the still earth silently,
To weep the fresh descending dew
That decks with gems the world:
Sweet teardrops of the glorious blue
Above us wide unfurled.

But, hark! Again the solemn wail
Upon the rising breeze doth swell.
Oh! Hasten from this haunted vale,
Mournful as a funeral knell!
For here, when gloomy midnight reigns
The fairies form their ring,
And, unto wild unearthly strains,
In measured cadence sing.

No human eye their sports may see,
No human tongue their deeds reveal;
The sweetness of their melody
The ear of man may never feel.
But now the elfin horn resounds,
No longer mayst thou stay;
Near and more near the music sounds,
Then, Mortal! Haste away!

Here I certainly heard the music of a very sweet and mellow horn. At that instant the ring which I held in my hand melted and became like a drop of dew, which trickled down my fingers and, falling on the dead leaves spread around, vanished.

Having now no further business I immediately quitted the valley and returned home. Thus, Lord Charles, ended one of the most remarkable adventures of my life.

When Captain Bud had finished, I thanked him for his tale, and then, as it was near eleven o'clock, bade him goodbye. Before twelve I reached Waterloo Palace and, being very sleepy, retired to bed. As I have no doubt my reader is by this time in much the same state, I shall bid him goodbye also.

Lord Charles Florian Wellesley
December the 18th 1830

A Fragment[1]

Overcome with that delightful sensation of lassitude which the perfect repose of nature in the stillness of such an evening occasions, I dropped the oars and, falling listlessly back, allowed my light-winged pinnace to float as chance might lead. For about an hour I lay thus, gazing on the calm, ungemed and unclouded sky above me, from which breathed a sweet balminess that scarcely fanned my temples.

At length my boat lay perfectly motionless, and I raised myself and found that, as if soul-taught, it had wafted itself into a little willow-fringed fairy bay. Disembarking, I fastened it to a decayed larch, and, following a pleasant path embroidered with moss and wild flowers, I presently entered the twilight shadow of a wood. Ere I emerged from the darkness of its impending boughs, the moon and Hesperus[2] had set their watch in heaven. The soft light which fell from them, and was reflected from the calm, fading glories of the west, showed me that I was now in a wild, winding glen, embosomed in lofty precipitous fells, barren of all ornament save the purple heath flower. A chill wind now rose, and as it sighed around or murmured mournfully in the heart of the forest, a sudden burst of sweet, sad music mingled with its wailing. I looked up and saw by the clear moonlight a figure clad in white, sitting on an overhanging cliff and bending over a harp, with whose tones this sorrowful strain was blent.

Lo! stretched beneath the clust'ring palm
The stately noble lies:

[1]Four page manuscript fragment (7.9 × 6.1 cm) in BPM: B82; continued by another four page manuscript (8.4 × 6.3 cm) also in BPM: B87. Both fragments were previously assumed to be separate, incomplete manuscripts; see Christine Alexander, 'Some New Findings in Brontë Bibliography', *Notes and Queries*, June 1983. *A Fragment* was written soon after Charlotte Brontë's return home from Roe Head for her first summer school holidays.

[2]The evening star, which sets in the west.

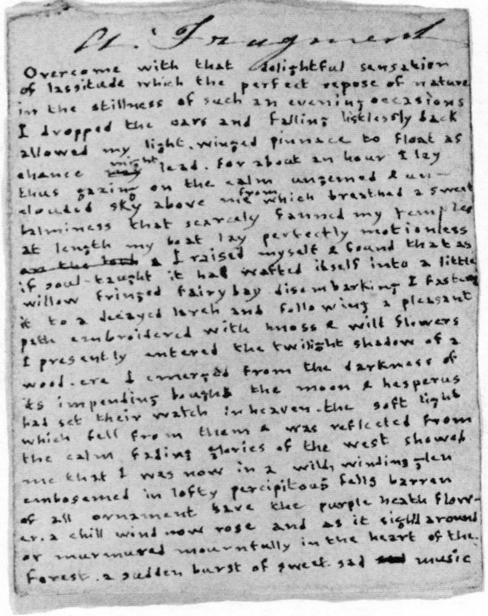

Plate 6 The first and last page of *A Fragment*, written by Charlotte Brontë at the age of fifteen

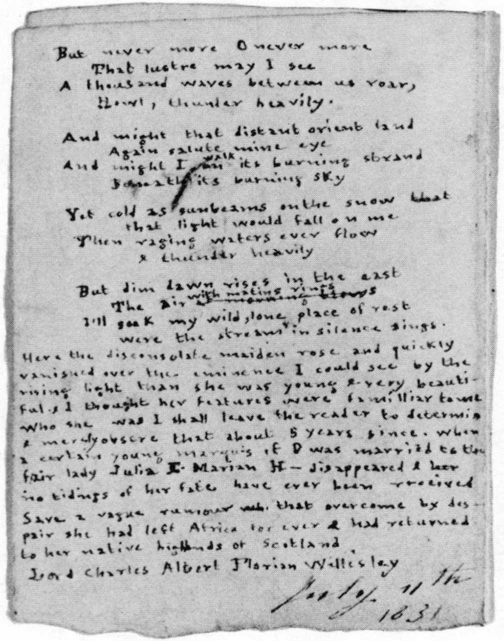

Around him dwells a holy calm
Breathed softly from the skies.

The zephyrs fan with sweet caress
Recumbent majesty.
The loud winds of the wilderness
All silently pass by.

The lion from his desert lair
Comes forth to fierce foray:
His red eyes fired by hunger glare
In eager search of prey.

He spies him in his dreamless sleep
All on the moonlit ground,
And away as with a whirlwind sweep
Behold the monster bound.

For holy, holy, is thy rest,
Though in the desert laid;
A spirit's spell is o'er thee cast
Amid that palmy shade.

O clouds come o'er that vision bright
And soft it fades away,
The witchery of memory's might
Inviting still its stay.

But vainly, where my warrior slept
The cold, sad moonbeams lie,
And where sabean[3] odours wept
The winds of midnight sigh.

But while the ocean wildered spreads
Afar her thund'ring plain,
And while the light of heaven sheds
Still splendour on the main,

I'll ne'er forget that stately form
That eye's entrancing light
Whence oft the wildest passion storm
Flashed forth in sudden might;

Or in those dark orbs lustre lay
Borne from the worlds of thought

---

[3]Arabian; the Sabeans were the ancient people of Yemen.

But brightest shone that wondrous ray
  From holy regions brought

Where spirits of the favoured few
  Alone may ever dwell
Where clearer than Parnassian dew
  A hundred fountains well.

The fountains sweet of poesy,
  That nectar of the sky,
Where wreaths of immortality
  In hallowed beauty lie.

But lo! Diana's silver bow
  Hath quitted human ken,
And the chill night winds coldly blow
  Adown this lonely glen.

O happy may his slumbers be
  This night in lands afar,
Beneath the desert plantain tree
  Beneath the silver star;

Or in his gorgeous Indian home
  On slave-surrounded bed,
And underneath some solemn dome
  Whence lamps their glories shed.

His dreams are of some other world,
  His mighty soul is free;
His spirit's pinions all unfurled
  Rise high in radiancy.[4]

And music all on earth unknown
  Floats solemnly around,
And sweeter swells each following tone
  With clear seraphic sound.

No being of this low earth born
  Is worthy of his love:
Doth the royal rider of the storm
  Ere look upon the dove?

[4]Conclusion of the first manuscript: see n. 1 above.

Then farewell each rebellious thought
And welcome peace again.
Adversity hath wisdom taught;
But who shall break the chain?

The long, long chain of memory
Which leads to other hours,
To other days when happily
I dwelt mid Indian bowers.

And from the dim clouds of the past
Sweet smiles and glances glide;
From those bright lips and dark eyes cast
Where dwells the light of pride.

Smiles faded from his lofty brow,
Sweet glances passed away,
For fell upon another now
Their all desired ray.

And now my rival's hated form
Salutes my mental eye,
And envy's dark unhallowed storm
O'er casts the tranquil sky.

Methinks I see her ringlets play
In the starlight soft and fair;
Methinks I see her eyes still ray
Illume the dusky air.

O, she was fairer than the rose
With morning dew all bright;
She shone among a hundred foes
The central orb of light.

Their spirits were of kindred mould,
From the same sweet fountain sprung,
And melody of heaven rolled
In music when she sung.

How oft beneath the orange grove
By Gambia's rolling tide,[5]

---

[5]River Gambia, in Wellington's Land, where Marian Hume lived while she was in Africa
(see 'About 9 months after my arrival at the Glass Town', n. 4).

While shone on high the star of love
He wandered with his bride.

And while faint light fell on the wave
And fainter music rung.
From the green banks which their waters lave
How sweet that lady sung.

Between each pause so still and calm
The whispering leaflets spoke,
Or wandering zephyrs soft as balm
Her harp's wild echoes woke.

All winged minstrels of the vale
Now silently repose,
And voiceless is the dewy gale
That breathing flower-scents blows.

Slow sailing through the clear wide sky
Earth's handmaid journeys free,
Tracking to all eternity
An ever-shoreless sea.

The solemn airs of evening sigh
Through wood and grove and bower;
Charged with the mystic harmony
Which thrills this hallowed hour.

O, once this happiness was mine
When came still eventide,
How often in that balmy time
I've wandered by his side.

And while I heard his eloquence
And watched his kindling eye,
I saw a lustre beaming thence
Bright as the stars on high.

It was as though his spirit lay
Far in those wells of light;
As though his soul's irradiate day
Shone bright as heaven is bright.

But never more, O never more,
That lustre may I see.
A thousand waves between us roar,
Howl, thunder heavily.

And might that distant orient land
Again salute mine eye,
And might I walk its burning strand
Beneath its burning sky.

Yet cold as sunbeams on the snow
That light would fall on me,
Then raging waters ever flow
And thunder heavily.

But dim dawn rises in the east,
The air with matins rings,
I'll seek my wild, lone place of rest
Where the stream in silence sings.

Here the disconsolate maiden rose and quickly vanished over the eminence. I could see by the rising light that she was young and very beautiful, and I thought her features were familiar to me. Who she was I shall leave the reader to determine and merely observe that about 5 years since, when a certain young Marquis of D— was married to the fair Lady Julia [?I],[6] Marian H— disappeared and no tidings of her fate have ever been received, save a vague rumour that overcome by despair she had left Africa forever and had returned to her native highlands of Scotland.

Lord Charles Albert Florian Wellesley
July 11th
1831

'About 9 months after my arrival at the Glass Town'[1]

About 9 months after my arrival at the Glass Town, I was sitting in a meditative mood at the open window of an upper parlour in the

[6]This probably refers to Lady Julia Wellesley, the Marquis of Douro's cousin; hence the reference to their 'kindred' spirits in stanza 26. Charlotte had intended them to marry but later changed her mind; she planned events well ahead and often wrote fragments that were out of step with the main sequence of events in the saga. Even before Marian Hume married Douro, Charlotte had planned Marian's separation from him and subsequent death.

[1]Two page fragment (9.8 × 6.1 cm) in The King's School Library, Canterbury: Walpole Collection; continued by a fragmentary page (9.6 × 5.6 cm) in BPM: B112. The manuscript is incomplete. The fictitious author is probably Captain Tree, who again describes a journey to Wellington's Land and the Grecian architecture of the Marquis of Douro's country palace in the following manuscript, The Bridal. The similar subject matter and repetition of phrases suggests that this fragment may in fact be an early draft of The Bridal.

Unicorn Hotel where I then lodged. My bodily faculties of eye and ear were absorbed by the contemplation of the quiet sea and the light summer waves that with monotonous murmurs broke on the beach. Languishing and voluptuous music stole through the windless air which proceeded from a small silver-winged pleasure-barge, anchored under the shadow of the willowy banks, and in their passage over the waters its siren tones became so luxuriant sweet and still that, while delighting, they enervated the listener. A low, incessant thundering and the vast harbour whitened by the spread sails of ten thousand vessels of war and merchandise alone told of Babylon's proximity, and cloud alone was visible bounding the Ocean and circling the Pillar of Heaven.[2] This obscurity proceeded from her huge furnaces and great thunder-shaken edifices, misnomered mills.

Lulled by the general calm of earth and sky, I was on the point of falling asleep when a gentle tap at the door roused me.

'Come in,' I exclaimed, starting up.

My friend the Marquis[3] of Douro entered, wrapped in a travelling cloak. 'I am come,' said he, 'to enquire whether I may have the pleasure of your society in a journey I am about to take to my father's palace in the country. Your determination must be prompt: this evening we depart. Night travelling only is practicable under this African sky.'

I gladly availed myself of his invitation and in another minute was jogging behind the Marquis safely seated on my favourite mare Butterboat; while he, mounted on a steed as proud and spirited as its handsome young rider, beguiled our way with a conversation which first was lively and sprightly, the subjects being chariots, horses, hounds, hawks and archery, all of which he seemed to view with enthusiastic admiration. Literature and the drama then succeeded. On these he discoursed most excellent music. Next he rambled for a while among the arts and sciences, displaying almost unconsciously a marvellous fund of knowledge, and lastly, when the moon and stars arose, he fixed on his favourite theme – astronomy. Here he excelled himself. His sweet yet powerful enunciation aided the effect produced by the noblest ideas clothed in the most pure and brilliant language, and as he ever and anon turned round his graceful head and flashed half from his bright eagle eyes and half from his finely moulded smiling lips unanswerable demonstrations and arguments, I thought that a mere human being could scarcely be endowed with beauty and genius so rare and bright.

[2] The Tower of All Nations (see *Blackwood's Young Men's Magazine*, December (first issue) 1829, n. 10) in the centre of Glass Town, which is often referred to as 'Babylon'.

[3] Untypically spelt 'Marquess' in manuscript.

But I must hasten to bring the reader to our journey's end. Arthur's eloquence continued only for that night. As we drew nearer to our destination, his thoughts seemed occupied by something more interesting, to him at least, than all the wonders of nature and art. I could easily guess what this was, knowing that we were approaching the residence of his peerless little inamorata.[4]

Evening had stolen again over the earth ere we entered the vast extent of grounds surrounding the palace. The Marquis conducted me through a deep valley embosomed[5] in green shady hills, looking quietly down on their tree-crested forms reflected in a broad rivulet beneath. Presently light from the windows of the palace began to stream across our path, and, on turning an angle in the glen, the noble edifice burst full upon us. Every part of this beautiful structure is in my opinion perfect, but what struck me most was the regal grandeur of the portico, rising on lofty Ionic columns of dove-hued Italian marble, of which material the whole is composed.

The Bridal[1]

O! There is a wood in a still and deep
And solitary vale,
Where no sound is heard save the wild wind's sweep
And the lay of the nightingale;

And far in the depth of the leafy trees
An elm grows fair and high,
Where ever the voice of the solemn breeze
Sighs with soft harmony;

And far beneath its trembling shade
Soft moss and green grass grow;
There the violet and wild-rose bud and fade,
There the lily and harebell blow.

---

[4]Marian Hume, who lives near the Duke of Wellington's country estate of Strathfieldsay in Wellington's Land, about 500 miles west of Glass Town.

[5]The first manuscript ends here; and the final word although incomplete ('embos') is obviously 'embosomed', a word Charlotte Brontë uses again in her next manuscript.

[1]A fourteen page manuscript (9.2 × 5.7 cm) in PML: Bonnell Collection; hand-sewn booklet with light-brown paper cover. The manuscript of *The Bridal* originally included eighteen pages (see n. 2 below).

A rippling streamlet wanders near,
  Unseen in the flow'r-blent grass,
But a murmur is heard full sweet and clear
  As its silver waters pass.

'Twas night: a pearly lustre fell
  On mountain, wave and tower;
Now spirits wove their magic spell
  In many a hidden bower.

I lay within that calm retreat,
  The greenwood shade among;
And soon I sunk to slumber sweet,
  Lulled by the streamlet's song.

A strange dream o'er my spirit crept,
  As in that shady dell
In silent peace I lay and slept,
  While the balm of heaven fell.

Methought I saw a wild deep sea,
  And heard a sullen roar
As its mighty waves broke heavily
  On the bleak and lonely shore.

I saw two forms of human mould,
  Beneath a tall rock's shade,
Watching the long bright rays of gold
  Far in the bright west fade.

One was a young and noble knight,
  Stately in plumed pride;
The other was a lady bright,
  And she stood by the warrior's side.

I saw the dark light of the noble's eye
  As he leaned on his white war-steed;
But *hers* was as blue as the sapphire sky,
  And frail was her form as the reed.

The young knight made a solemn vow
  Of constancy till death;
Truth's light beamed on his fair marble brow
  While he pledged his knightly faith.

The lady smiled a heavenly smile
  While showed nor doubt, nor fear,
But there stood in her radiant eye the while
  A bright and tender tear.

She took one lock of her golden hair
  From all those clust'ring curls
Bound with a garland of florets fair
  And a string of orient pearls,

Then gave that token tremblingly
  To the soldier by her side,
And he swore again by earth and sea
  That she should be his bride.

Now changed the scene. Upon my sight
  A lofty palace grew;
And a sun-like splendour, a golden light,
  High lamps and torches threw.

The juice of the scorched grape was sparkling bright
With ruby-radiance and blood-red light;
That nectar which lightens the weary soul
Gleamed in the wine-cup and wassail-bowl.

The music of harps and of trumpets rung,
And the strings of the wild guitar were strung;
Full soft were the breathings of viol and lute,
While the clear clarion answered the tones of the flute.

Now white robes fluttered and tall plumes glanced,
While nobles and ladies in bright rings danced,
Gracefully gliding the pillars among
To the sound of the harps and the joyous song.

I knew 'twas a bridal; for under a bower
Of the rose and the myrtle and fair lily flower
Stood that stately noble in plumed pride,
And that sweet, fair lady, his plighted bride.

With the mystic ring on her finger fair,
And the nuptial wreath in her radiant hair,
They are joined; and forever the mingled name
Of Marina and Albion is hallowed to fame.

                              C. Brontë   July 14, 1832

In the autumn of the year 1832, being weary of study and the melancholy solitude of the vast streets and mighty commercial marts of our great Babel; being fatigued with the ever-resounding thunder of the sea, with the din of a thousand self-moving engines, with the dissonant cries of all nations, kindreds and tongues, congregated together in the gigantic emporium of commerce, of arts, of god-like wisdom, of boundless learning and of superhuman knowledge; being dazzled with continually beholding the glory, the power, the riches, dominion and radiant beauty of the city which sitteth like a queen upon the waters; in one word, being tired of Verdopolis and all its magnificence, I determined on a trip into the country.

Accordingly, the day after this resolution was formed, I rose with the sun, collected a few essential articles of dress, etc., packed them neatly in a light knapsack, arranged my apartments, partook of a wholesome repast, and then, after locking the door and delivering the key to my landlady, I set out with a light heart and joyous step.

After three days of continued travel I arrived on the banks of a wide and profound river winding through a vast valley embosomed in hills whose robe of rich and flowery verdure was broken only by the long shadow of groves, and here and there by clustering herds and flocks lying white as snow in the green hollows between mountains. It was the evening of a calm summer day when I reached this enchanting spot. The only sounds now audible were the songs of shepherds, swelling and dying at intervals, and the murmur of gliding waves. I neither knew nor cared where I was. My bodily faculties of eye and ear were absorbed in the contemplation of this delightful scene, and, wandering unheedingly along, I left the guidance of the river and entered a wood, invited by the warbling of a hundred forest minstrels. Soon I perceived the narrow, tangled wood-path to widen, and gradually it assumed the appearance of a green shady alley. Occasionally bowers of roses and myrtles etc. appeared by the pathside, with soft banks of moss for the weary to repose on. Notwithstanding these indications of individual property, curiosity and the allurements of music and cool shade led me forwards.

At length I entered a glade in the wood, in the midst of which was a small but exquisitely beautiful marble edifice of pure and dazzling whiteness. On the broad steps of the portico two figures were reclining, at sight of whom I instantly stepped behind a low, wide-spreading fig-tree, where I could hear and see all that passed without fear and detection. One was a youth of lofty stature and remarkably graceful demeanour, attired in a rich purple vest and mantle, with closely fitting pantaloons of white woven silk, displaying to advantage the magnificent proportions of his form. A richly adorned belt was girt tightly round his waist from which depended a scimitar whose golden hilt, and scabbard of the finest Damascus steel, glittered with gems of inestimable value. His steel-barred cap, crested with tall, snowy plumes, lay beside him, its absence revealing more clearly the rich curls of dark, glossy hair clustering round a countenance distinguished by the noble beauty of its features, but still more by the radiant fire of genius and intellect visible in the intense brightness of his large, dark and lustrous eyes.

The other form was that of a very young and slender girl, whose complexion was delicately, almost transparently, fair. Her cheeks were tinted with a rich, soft crimson, her features moulded in the utmost perfection of loveliness; while the clear light of her brilliant hazel eyes, and the soft waving of her auburn ringlets, gave additional charms to what seemed already infinitely too beautiful for this earth. Her dress was a white robe of the finest texture the Indian loom can produce. The only ornaments she wore were a long chain which encircled her neck twice and hung lower than her waist, composed of alternate beads of the finest emeralds and gold; and a slight gold ring on the third finger of her left hand, which together with a small crescent of pearls glistening on her forehead (which is always worn by the noble matrons of Verdopolis) betokened that she had entered the path of wedded life. With a sweet vivacity in her look and manner the young bride was addressing her lord thus when I first came in sight of the peerless pair:

'No, no, my lord; if I sing the song you shall choose it. Now, once more, what shall I sing? The moon is risen, and if your decision is not prompt I will not sing at all!'

To this he answered, 'Well, if I am threatened with the entire loss of the pleasure if I defer my choice, I will have that sweet song which I overheard you singing the evening[2] before I left Scotland.'

With a smiling blush she took a little ivory lyre, and, in a voice of the most touching melody, sung the following stanzas:

> He is gone and all grandeur has fled from the mountain,
> All beauty departed from stream and from fountain;
>   A dark veil is hung
>   O'er the bright sky of gladness,
>   And where birds sweetly sung
>   There's a murmur of sadness;
> The wind sings with a warning tone
> Through many a shadowy tree;

---

[2]Four pages are missing here from the PML manuscript: they are now part of the Bonnell Collection in the BPM: B88. The following text is from this four page fragment.

339

I hear in every passing moan
The voice of destiny.

Thou O Lord of the Waters! The Great and All-seeing!
Preserve in Thy mercy his safety and being;
May he trust to Thy might
When the dark storm is howling,
And the blackness of night
Over Heaven is scowling;
But may the sea flow glidingly
With gentle summer waves,
And silent may all tempests lie
Chained in vast Æolian caves!³

Yet though ere he returnest long years will have vanished,
Sweet hope from my bosom shall never be banished:
I will think of the time
When his step lightly bounding
Shall be heard on the rock
Where the cat'ract is sounding;
When the banner of his father's host
Shall be unfurled on high,
To welcome back the pride and boast
Of England's chivalry!

Yet tears will flow forth while of hope I am singing,
Still Despair her dark shadow is over me flinging;
But when he's far away,
I will pluck the wild flower
On bank and on brae
At the still moonlight hour;
And I will twine for him a wreath
Low in the fairy's dell;
Methought I heard the night-wind breathe
That solemn word: 'Farewell!'⁴

³Aeolus, in Homeric legend, was appointed ruler of the winds by Zeus, and lived on his Aeolian island.
⁴This poem was probably composed a year earlier, when Charlotte Brontë wrote *A Fragment*, 11 July 1831, in which she also described Marian Hume alone in Scotland, singing of Lord Douro. C. W. Hatfield cites (in *Brontë Society Transactions*, vol. 6 (1922), part 32, p. 111) an earlier manuscript, dated July 1831 and now lost, that was printed in T. J. Wise's edition of *The Red Cross Knight and Other Poems* by Charlotte Brontë (London, 1917). Dr Tom Winnifrith suggests that the early version may simply be a faulty copy by Wise (*Poems*, p. 407),

When the lady had concluded her song I stepped from my place of concealment and was instantly perceived by the noble youth (whom, of course every reader will have recognized as the Marquis of Douro). He gave me a courteous welcome and invited me to proceed with him to his country palace, as it was now wearing late. I willingly accepted the invitation, and in a short time we arrived there.

It is a truly noble structure, built in the purest style of Grecian architecture, situated in the midst of a vast park, embosomed in richly wooded hills, perfumed with orange and citron groves, and watered by a branch of the Gambia, almost equal in size to the parent stream. The magnificence of the interior is equal to that of the outside. There is an air of regal state and splendour throughout all the lofty domed apartments, which strikes the spectator with awe for the lord of so imposing a residence. The Marquis has a particular pride in the knowledge that he is the owner of one of the most splendid, select and extensive libraries now in the possession of any individual. His picture and statue galleries likewise contain many of the finest works, both of the ancient and modern masters, particularly the latter, of whom the Marquis is a most generous and munificent patron. In his cabinet of curiosities I observed a beautiful casket of wrought gold. At my request he opened it and produced the contents, viz. a manuscript copy of that rare work, *Autobiography of Captain Leaf*.[5] It was written on a roll of vellum, but much discoloured and rendered nearly illegible by time. To my eager enquiries respecting the manner in which he had obtained so inestimable a treasure, he replied, with a smile: 'That question I must decline to answer. It is a secret with which I alone am acquainted.'

I likewise noticed a brace of pistols, most exquisitely wrought and highly finished. He told me they were the chef-d'œuvre of Darrow, the best manufacturer of firearms in the universe.[6] I counted 100 gold and

---

but in this case it seems unlikely, since Hatfield's bibliography is fairly reliable, and the subject matter is similar to other manuscripts of the earlier period. Moreover, Charlotte made a habit of incorporating into her stories poems she had written at an earlier date.

[5] Captain Leaf appears to have been part of the original conception of Glass Town, along with such other botanical names as Captain Tree, Captain Arbor, Captain Flower and Captain Bud, although he is not mentioned in any other existing manuscripts. His descendent, General Leaf, features in *The Green Dwarf*, 2 September 1833.

[6] Mr Brontë had a special interest in firearms and warfare, which is reflected in his children's enthusiasm for soldiers and especially the military campaigns of the Duke of Wellington and Napoleon. The whimsical names of General Bayonet, General Ramrod, Corporal Spearman and Captain Cannonball (see 'Military Conversations', *Blackwood's Young Men's Magazine*, August 1829) bear witness to Charlotte's early knowledge of weapons. Since the Luddite riots of 1812, her father – like other householders before the establishment of a

silver medals, which had been presented to this youthful, but all-accomplished nobleman by different literary and scientific establishments. They were all contained in a truly splendid gold vase awarded to him last year by the Academy of Modern Athenians (as that learned body somewhat presumptuously chooses to style itself), as being the composer of the best epigram in Greek. Above this was suspended a silver bow and quiver, the first prize given by the Royal Society of Archers, together with a bit, bridle, spurs and stirrups, all of fine gold, obtained from the Honourable Community of Equestrians. Near these lay several withered wreaths of myrtle, laurel, etc., etc., won by him as conqueror in the great African Biennial Games.[7] On a rich stand of polished ebony were ranged twenty-three beautiful vases of marble, alabaster, etc., all richly carved in basso-relievo, remarkable for classic elegance of form, design and execution. Some of these were filled with cameos, others with ancient coins, and others again bore branches of scarlet and white coral, pearls, gems of various sorts, fossils, etc. But what interested me more than all these trophies of victory and specimens of art and nature, costly, beautiful, and almost invaluable as they were, was a little figure of Apollo, about six inches in height, curiously carved in white agate, holding a lyre in his hand, and placed on a pedestal of the same valuable material, on which was the following inscription:

In our day we beheld the god of Archery, Eloquence, and Verse, shrined in an infinitely fairer form than that worn by the ancient Apollo, and giving far more glorious proofs of his divinity than the day-god ever vouchsafed to the inhabitants of the old pagan world. Zenobia Ellrington implores Arthur Augustus Wellesley to accept this small memorial, and consider it as a token that, though forsaken and despised by him whose good opinion and friendship she valued more than life, she yet bears no malice.

---

regular police force – had possessed his own pistol which he apparently kept loaded and regularly discharged each morning (Ellen Nussey, 'Reminiscences of Charlotte Brontë', *Scribner's Monthly*, May 1871, p. 28). On 15 November 1841, he wrote his only letter to the Duke of Wellington, recommending his novel sighting device for army muskets which, complete with new iron bullets cased in lead, had enabled him to bring down a flying bird. Needless to say, the Iron Duke was not amused by the rector's invention (Elizabeth Longford, *Wellington: Pillar of State*, London: Weidenfeld & Nicolson, 1972, pp. 459–60).

[7]Now a regular occurrence in Verdopolis; see Branwell Brontë's 'Ode on the Celebration of the Great African Games', and *Letters From An Englishman* (*SHCBM*, vol. 1, pp. 165–9 and pp. 123–4 respectively).

There was a secret contained in this inscription which I could not fathom. I had never before heard of any misunderstanding between his lordship and Lady Zenobia, nor did public appearances warrant a suspicion of its existence. Long after, however, the following circumstances came to my knowledge.[8] The channel through which they reached me cannot be doubted, but I am not at liberty to mention names.

One evening about dusk, as the Marquis of Douro was returning from[9] a shooting excursion into the country, he heard suddenly a rustling noise in a deep ditch on the roadside. He was preparing his fowling-piece for a shot when the form of Lady Ellrington started up before him. Her head was bare, her tall person was enveloped in the tattered remnants of a dark velvet mantle. Her dishevelled hair hung in wild elf-locks over her face, neck and shoulders, almost concealing her features, which were emaciated and pale as death. He stepped back a few paces, startled at the sudden and ghastly apparition. She threw herself on her knees before him, exclaiming in wild, maniacal accents: 'My lord, tell me truly, sincerely, ingenuously, where you have been. I heard that you had left Verdopolis, and I followed you on foot five hundred miles. Then my strength failed me, and I lay down in this place, as I thought, to die. But it was doomed I should see you once more before I became an inhabitant of the grave. Answer me, my lord: have you seen that wretch Marian Hume? Have you spoken to her? Viper! Viper! Oh, that I could sheathe this weapon in her heart!'

Here she stopped for want of breath and, drawing a long, sharp, glittering knife from under her cloak, brandished it wildly in the air. The Marquis looked at her steadily and, without attempting to disarm her, answered with great composure: 'You have asked me a strange question, Lady Zenobia, but before I attempt to answer it you had better come with me to our encampment. I will order a tent to be prepared for you where you may pass the night in safety and to-morrow, when you are a little recruited by rest and refreshment, we will discuss this matter soberly.*

Her rage was now exhausted by its own vehemence, and she replied

---

*It is the custom in Verdopolis, where perhaps forty or so noblemen, with their attendants, go to shoot or hunt wild beasts and birds in the desolate and uninhabited Mountains of the Moon, to form a sort of camp for their mutual protection and defence. These camps sometimes contain upwards of a hundred individuals. *Note by Charlotte Brontë.*

[8]The following story is purported to be the 'true' account of Captain Bud's drama in chapter 3 of *Visits in Verreopolis*, volume I.

[9]End of the four page fragment removed from the manuscript: see n. 2 above.

with more calmness than she had hitherto evinced: 'My lord, believe me, I am deputed by Heaven to warn you of a great danger into which you are about to fall. If you persist in your intention of uniting yourself to Marian Hume you will become a murderer and a suicide. I cannot now explain myself more clearly, but ponder carefully on my words until I see you again.'

Then, bowing her forehead to the earth in an attitude of adoration, she kissed his feet, muttering at the same time some unintelligible words. At that moment a loud rushing like the sound of a whirlwind became audible, and Lady Zenobia was swept away by some invisible power before the Marquis could extend his arm to arrest her progress or frame [an] answer to her mysterious address. He paced slowly forward, lost in deep reflection on what he had heard and seen. The moon had risen over the black, barren mountains ere he reached the camp. He gazed for a while on her pure, undimmed lustre, comparing it to that loveliness of one far away, and then, entering the tent, wrapped himself in his hunter's cloak and lay down to unquiet sleep.

Months rolled away, and the mystery remained unravelled. Lady Zenobia Ellrington appeared as usual in that dazzling circle of which she was ever a distinguished ornament. There was no trace of wandering fire in her eyes which might lead a careful observer to imagine that her mind was unsteady. Her voice was more subdued and her looks pale, and it was remarked by some that she avoided all (even the most commonplace) communication with the Marquis.

In the meantime, the Duke of Wellington had consented to his son's union with the beautiful, virtuous and accomplished, but untitled, Marian Hume. Vast and splendid preparations were making for the approaching bridal, when just at this critical juncture news arrived of the Great Rebellion headed by Alexander Rogue.[10] The intelligence fell with the suddenness and violence of a thunderbolt. Unequivocal symptoms of dissatisfaction began to appear at the same time among the lower orders in Verdopolis. The workmen at the principal mills and furnaces struck for an advance of wages, and, the masters refusing to comply with their exorbitant demands, they all turned out simultaneously. Shortly after, Colonel Grenville, one of the great mill-owners,

---

[10]While Charlotte Brontë was away at school at Roe Head, Branwell introduced the Great Rebellion of March 1831, led by Rogue, who sets up in Verdopolis a provisional government on the French model of 1789. Peace is eventually restored by the command of Crashey, the divine arbitrator and progenitor of the early Glass Town (see *Letters From An Englishman*, volumes III–IV, *SHCBM*, vol. 1, pp. 114–58). Under the successive titles of Alexander Percy, Lord Ellrington and Duke of Northangerland, Rogue increasingly becomes Branwell's hero and an important foil to the Marquis of Douro.

was shot.[11] His assassins, being quickly discovered and delivered up to justice, were interrogated by torture, but they remained inflexible, not a single satisfactory answer being elicited from them. The police was now doubled. Bands of soldiers were stationed in the more suspicious parts of the city, and orders were issued that no citizen should walk abroad unarmed. In this state of affairs Parliament was summoned to consult on the best measures to be taken. On the first night of its sitting the house was crowded to excess. All the members attended, and above a thousand ladies of the first rank appeared in the gallery. A settled expression of gloom and anxiety was visible in every countenance. They sat for some time gazing at each other in the silence of seeming despair. At length the Marquis of Douro rose and ascended the tribunal, and it was on this memorable night he pronounced that celebrated oration which will be delivered to farthest posterity as a finished specimen of the sublimest eloquence. The souls of all who heard him were thrilled with conflicting emotions. Some of the ladies in the gallery fainted and were carried out. My limits will not permit me to transcribe the whole of this speech, and to attempt an abridgement would be profanation. I will, however, present the reader with the conclusion. It was as follows:

I call on you, my countrymen, to rouse yourselves to action. There is a latent flame of rebellion smouldering in our city, which blood alone can quench! The hot blood of ourselves and our enemies freely poured forth! We daily see in our streets men whose brows were once open as the day, but which are now wrinkled with dark dissatisfaction, and the light of whose eyes, formerly free as sunshine, is now dimmed by restless suspicion. Our upright merchants are ever threatened with fears of assassination from those dependants who, in time past, loved, honoured, and reverenced them as fathers. Our peaceful citizens cannot pass their thresholds in safety unless laden with weapons of war, the continual dread of death haunting their footsteps wherever they turn. And who has produced this awful change? What agency of hell has affected, what Master-Spirit of Crime, what Prince of

[11]Colonel John Bramham Grenville, one of the wealthiest and most influential of the Verdopolitan merchants; becomes General Grenville in later manuscripts, father of Ellen (Zenobia's protégée and wife of Warner Howard Warner). Probably based on Lord William Grenville (1759–1834), prime minister of the coalition 'Ministery of all the Talents' (1806), who offered Wellington his first seat in Parliament. Charlotte Brontë would have heard stories of the Luddite riots from both her father and Miss Wooler at Roe Head. In nearby Liversedge on 11 April 1812, Rawfold's Mill was attacked by armed cloth-workers. The owner, Mr Cartwright, successfully defended the mill, but soon after another manufacturer was shot. Charlotte uses this same material in *Something about Arthur* (1 May 1833) and later, in *Shirley*.

Sin, what Beelzebub[12] of black iniquity has been at work in this kingdom? I will answer that fearful question: ALEXANDER ROGUE! Arm for the battle, then, fellow-countrymen; be not faint-hearted, but trust in the justice of your cause as your banner of protection, and let your war-shout in the onslaught ever be: 'God defend the right!'

When the Marquis had concluded this harangue he left the house amidst long and loud thunders of applause, and proceeded to one of the shady groves planted on the banks of the Guadiana.[13] Here he walked for some time inhaling the fresh night-wind, which acquired additional coolness as it swept over the broad rapid river, and was just beginning to recover from the strong excitement into which his enthusiasm had thrown him when he felt his arm suddenly grasped from behind, and, turning round, beheld Lady Zenobia Ellrington standing beside him, with the same wild, unnatural expression of countenance had before convulsed her features among the dark hills of Jibbel Kumri.[14]

'My lord,' she muttered in a low, energetic tone, 'your eloquence, your noble genius, has again driven me to desperation. I am no longer mistress of myself, and if you do not consent to be mine and mine alone, I will kill myself where I stand.'

'Lady Ellrington,' said the Marquis coldly, withdrawing his hand from her grasp, 'this conduct is unworthy of your character. I must beg that you will cease to use the language of a madwoman, for I do assure you, my lady, these deep stratagems will have no effect upon me.'

She now threw herself at his feet, exclaiming in a voice almost stifled with ungovernable emotion, 'Oh! Do not kill me with such cold, such cruel disdain. Only consent to follow me, and you will be convinced that you ought not to be united to one so utterly unworthy of you as Marian Hume.'

The Marquis, moved by her tears and entreaties, at length consented to accompany her. She led him a considerable distance from the city to a subterraneous grotto, where was a fire burning on a brazen altar. She threw a certain powder into the flame, and immediately they were transported through the air to an apartment at the summit of a lofty tower. At one end of this room was a vast mirror, and at the other a

[12]In Matthew xii, 24, Beelzebub is prince of the devils. Milton places him next to Satan in power (*Paradise Lost*, i, 79).

[13]See *The Search After Happiness*, n. 5.

[14]Mountains of the Moon, to the north and east of Verdopolis. Spelt 'Gibble Kumri' in this manuscript, although Charlotte Brontë usually uses the alternative spelling 'Jibbel Kumri'.

drawn curtain behind which a most brilliant light was visible.

'You are now,' said Lady Ellrington, 'in the sacred presence of one whose counsel, I am sure, you, my lord, will never slight.'

At this moment the curtain was removed, and the astonished Marquis beheld Crashie, the divine and infallible, seated on his golden throne and surrounded by those mysterious rays of light which ever emanate from him.[15]

'My son,' said he, with an august smile and in a voice of awful harmony, 'fate and inexorable destiny have decreed that in the hour you are united to the maiden of your choice, the angel Azrael[16] shall smite you both and convey your disembodied souls over the swift-flowing and impassable river of death. Hearken to the counsels of wisdom and do not, in the madness of self-will, destroy yourself and Marian Hume by refusing the offered hand of one who, from the moment of your birth, was doomed by the prophetic stars of heaven to be your partner and support through the dark, unexplored wilderness of future life.'

He ceased. The combat betwixt true love and duty raged for a few seconds in the Marquis's heart and sent his life-blood in a tumult of agony and despair burning to his cheek and brow. At length duty prevailed, and with a strong effort he said in a firm, unfaltering voice, 'Son of Wisdom! I will war no longer against the high decree of heaven, and here I swear by the eternal—'

The rash of oath was checked in the moment of its utterance by some friendly spirit who whispered in his ear, 'There is magic. Beware!'

At the same instant, Crashie's venerable form faded away, and in its stead appeared the evil genius, Danhasch,[17] in all the naked hideousness of his real deformity. The demon soon vanished with a wild howl of rage, and the Marquis found himself again in the grove with Lady Ellrington. She implored him on her knees to forgive an attempt which love alone had dictated, but he turned from her with a smile of bitter contempt and disdain, and hastened to his father's palace.

About a week after this event the nuptials of Arthur Augustus, Marquis of Douro, and Marian Hume were solemnized with unprecedent pomp and splendour. Lady Ellrington, when she thus saw that all her hopes were lost, in despair fell into deep melancholy, and while in this state she amused herself with carving the little image before mentioned. After a long time she slowly recovered, and the

---

[15]See *Young Men's Magazine*, November 1830, n. 8.
[16]The Mahommedan angel of death, which both Charlotte and Branwell Brontë often refer to.
[17]Son of Schemhourasch, a geni rebellious to God in the *Arabian Nights*.

Marquis, convinced that her extravagances had arisen from a disordered brain, consented to honour her with his friendship once more.

I continued upwards of two months at the Marquis of Douro's country palace and then returned to Verdopolis, equally delighted with my noble host and his fair, amiable bride.

1832   August 20th

APPENDIX 1

A Visit to the Duke of Wellington's Small Palace
Situated on the Banks of the Indiva[1]

In the summer of the year 18—, circumstances of a very urgent and painful nature compelled me to take a journey from Glasstown northwards along the range of the Jibbel Kumri to the city of Gondar in Abyssinia, where I continued to abide for about a month.

All things being then settled to my satisfaction, I took my departure by the straight route through the kingdom of Nigritra, when I was again forced to alter my course and pass up the River Senegal. From thence I proceeded northward of Timbuctoo and entered the great desert of Sahara.

On the third day of my journeying there I perceived, as the evening was closing in, an object rising out of the sea of sands and just visible on the horizon. This I soon recognized to be one of those oases or green spots of the wilderness, which rejoice the heart of the weary traveller as a friendly isle does that of a despairing mariner after long nights and days of toil and tempest on a fathomless and boundless sea.

The seeming oasis proved, upon nearer approach, to be a broad and fruitful land. On the evening of the fourth day I entered it, but, after walking a little way up the country, I began to question whether or not I should turn back again, for I had often heard that beings of a

---

[1]The text, transcribed by C. W. Hatfield and published in the *Brontë Society Transactions*, vol. 8 (1933), part 43, pp. 78–82, is an alternative to *Description of the Duke of Wellington's Small Palace situated on the Banks of the Indiva*, printed on p. 130. The manuscript has been lost, but the published text provides a unique opportunity to compare a draft with a fair copy. The lost manuscript of *A Visit* was probably written earlier than *Description*, in Charlotte Brontë's typical minuscule hand; whereas *Description* has all the marks of a later fair copy, being written in longhand with fewer cancellations than is usual in Charlotte's manuscripts of this date. I have altered several obvious errors in transcription and checked this published version beside C. W. Hatfield's transcription in the Brontë Parsonage, as well as making several minor editorial changes. (Hatfield reads 'Indirce' for 'Indiva', as did the present editor in earlier publications, but the reading is made clear by Charlotte's listing of the manuscript in her *Catalogue of my Books*.)

supernatural nature, but neither genii nor fairies have their haunts in parts of these deserts, each of which they transform from a barren and dreary waste into a blooming and fragrant paradise. And a paradise indeed did this appear to be. The whole horizon was bounded by gently undulating hills covered with groves and plantations, intermixed with long slopes of green and pleasant verdure.

In the midst of the plain was a palace of the purest white marble, whose simple but most beautiful and noble style of architecture forcibly reminded me of many of the great palaces of Glasstown. Around it lay a wide garden, which stretched over the country to the foot of the range of hills. Here the tufted olive, the fragrant myrtle, the stately palm tree, the graceful almond, the rich vine and the queenly rose mingled their sweet and odorous beauties and shaded the high banks of a clear and murmuring river, over whose waters a fresh breeze played, which cooled delightfully the burning air which swept from the surrounding desert.

After some little reflection, I determined to proceed, and, having walked for about half an hour, I came to a bower of jasmine and lilies. Being exceedingly weary, I laid down beneath its shade and turned my eyes on the bright sky, now glowing in the intense brilliancy of an eastern sunset. The air was filled with soothing balm and wafted on its light wings the gentle rippling of the near stream which flowed softly through this wondrous garden.

I had lain thus for I cannot tell how long, until the moon rose slowly into the wide sky and the quiet evening star was shining in the west. Suddenly I heard a young and merry voice, whose sweet tones carried me back to the metropolis of the world. It brought to my memory many adventures in which a certain young nobleman had played a part. I arose and listened eagerly, and the voice thus proceeded: 'My darling little Tringia and my sweet Trill, I wish you could tell me what and who are the inhabitants of those thousand worlds which roll eternally over your pretty heads! I wonder what were the horrible commotions which split that one star into three, and whether the spirit of the mighty Newton roams in crowned majesty over the glorious plains of the centre of light and life, or whether his disembodied soul soars as far above its sphere as did his sublime and almost superhuman mind above those of the common race of mortals. But now I see that Philomel is pluming and decking himself to commence the concerts which will soon call Arthur, and perhaps my father and mother also, to witness your graceful dancing. Begin.'

At this moment a gush of rich melody began to flood in unison with the sweet tones of a harp-like instrument, and, as I turned the corner of a long green avenue (for I had now arisen from the spot where I had been seated), I beheld the figure of a handsome boy, whom I soon recognized as Lord Charles Wellesley. He was reclining under the shadow of an immense chestnut tree, playing upon a small Spanish guitar, and with a nightingale perched upon his shoulder. A beautiful grey monkey, a small silky spaniel, and a young kitten bounded and danced before him in the brilliant light of the uprisen moon.

In a short time a rustling was heard among the trees, and the Duke of Wellington, Lady Wellington and the Marquis of Douro entered the avenue. They all likewise sat down under the chestnut tree.

I now stept forward. At first they were greatly surprised at the sight of me, but after I had related to them who I was and the cause of my being in that place, His Grace instantly recognized me and gave me a friendly and hearty welcome.

I remained there some days, enjoying the hospitality of the Duke, and then took my departure for Glass Town, at which place I arrived about three months afterwards, as well in health as I could possibly expect after a journey of so many leagues in such a country.

January 16, 1830

APPENDIX 2

Poems written by Charlotte Brontë during the years 1829 to 1832, and not included in this volume

Many of the following poems are referred to in the footnotes of this volume, although not all of the following are related to the Glass Town Saga. Untitled manuscripts are referred to here by their first line, shown in inverted commas. Several untitled manuscripts are known by titles not given by Charlotte Brontë; these are shown in square brackets.

'Highminded Frenchmen love not the Ghost', 17 July 1829
Found in the Inn belonging to E., 28 September 1829
Addressed to the Tower of All Nations, 7 October 1829
Sunset, 8 October 1829
Sunrise, 9 October 1829
'I've been wandering in the greenwoods', 14 December 1829
The Churchyard A Poem, 24 December 1829
Written upon the occasion of the dinner given to the literati of the Glass Town, 8 January 1830
Written on the Summit of a High Mountain in the North of England, 14 January 1830
A Wretch in Prison, by Murry, 1 February 1830
[*Home-sickness*], 'Of College I am tired; I wish to be at home', 1 February 1830
Winter. A Short Poem, 3 February 1830
Pleasure. A Short Poem (or else not, say I), 8 February 1830
Verses by Lord Charles Wellesley, 11 February 1830
The Vision. A Short Poem, 13 April 1830
Fragment, 'Now rolls the sounding ocean', 29 May 1830
[*Reflections*], 'Now sweetly shines the golden sun', 31 May 1830
The Evening Walk. A Poem by the Marquis of Douro in Pindaric Metre, 28 June 1830
Miss Hume's Dream, 29 June 1830

A Translation into English Verse of the First Book of Voltaire's 'Henriade' from the French, 11 August 1830[1]
Young Man Naughty's Adventure, 14 October [?1830]
The Violet, 7 November 1830
Lines on Seeing the Portrait of — [Marian Hume], Painted by De Lisle, 10 November 1830
Vesper, 11 November 1830
Matin, 12 November 1830
Lines addressed to Lady Z[enobia] E[llrington] sent with my portrait which she had asked me to give her. By Marquis Douro, 12 November 1830
Reflections on the Fate of Neglected Genius, 13 November 1830
Serenade, 14 November 1830
'On the bright scenes around them spread', 17 January 1830
[*The Fairies' Farewell*], 'The trumpet hath sounded, its voice is gone forth', 11 December 1831
'O there is a land which the sun loves to lighten', 25 December 1831
St John in the Island of Patmos, 30 August 1832
[*Lines on Bewick*], 'The cloud of recent death is past away', 27 November 1832

[1]This is the only poem in the above list not printed in *Poems*; it can be found in C. K. Shorter's privately printed edition, *Voltaire's 'Henriade' Book I Translated from the French by Charlotte Brontë* (London, 1917).

TEXTUAL NOTES

Page

'There was once a little girl and her name was Anne'

3, l.6 near ⟨the water⟩

3, l.8 ⟨Once Anns⟩ once Anne

The History of the Year

A passage at the beginning of MS. page 1 is cancelled: ⟨Once upon a time there was a king whose name was ⟨Ethelbert⟩ Fleance, who governed all Caledonia. His disposition was warlike and [?what tinged will]⟩

4, l.2 geography ⟨one⟩

4, l.9 upstairs ⟨changing her⟩

5, l.8 ones ⟨the young mens⟩

5, l.11 Following two and a half lines cancelled: indecipherable.

5, l.14 The remainder of this page is cancelled: ⟨Papa bought Branwell some soldiers at Leeds. When papa came home it was night and we were in bed, so next morning Branwell came to our door with a box of soldiers. Emily and me jumped out of bed and I snatched up one and exclaimed, 'This is the Duke of Wellington! It shall be ⟨mine, brother⟩ the Duke!' When I had said this, Emily likewise took one and said it shall be hers, and when Anne came down she said one should be hers. ⟨Branwell likewise took⟩ Mine was the prettiest of the whole and the tallest and perfect in every part. Emily's was a grave looking fellow and we called him Gravey. Anne's was a queer little thing much like herself: he was called Waiting Boy. Branwell chose Bonaparte.⟩

'The origin of the O'Deans' (no cancellations)

'The origin of the Islanders' (no significant cancellations or textual notes)

A Romantic Tale (manuscript missing)

An Adventure in Ireland (manuscript missing)

Tales of the Islanders, volume I

Page two of the manuscript contains the cancelled words ⟨Duke of Wellington⟩. MS. begins on page 3 after cancelled title: ⟨Register of the Islanders⟩ by C Brontë Tales of the Islanders

21, l.15 ⟨damp⟩ dreary

22, l.24 ⟨or splendid reality⟩ than sober reality

22, l.29 ⟨stem⟩ trunk

23, l.8 pure ⟨clear⟩

Textual Notes

23, 1.8 ⟨meadows⟩ plains

23, 1.9 a lovelier verdure, as ⟨smooth lakes whose borders were overhung by the drooping willow, the elegant larch, the venerable oak, the evergreen laurel, seemed the crystal emerald framed mirror of some huge giant. From a beautiful grove of winter roses and twining honeysuckle, towered a magnificent palace of pure white marble, whose tall, fine pillars and turrets seemed the work of mighty genii and not of feeble me.⟩

23, 1.9 borders ⟨were⟩ are

23, 1.12 it ⟨was⟩ is

23, 1.13 all ⟨was⟩ is

23, 1.26 ⟨pours⟩ rushes

24, 1.10 It ⟨is a vaulted⟩ has the appearance

24, 1.11 casts a ⟨revenge like⟩ strange death-like ⟨melancholy⟩

25, 1.16 ⟨wanting⟩ broken

26, 1.8 wandering ⟨in to the wood of Neston⟩; the following two lines are heavily cancelled.

26, 1.12 ⟨nodding⟩ clouds

26, 1.13 ⟨clouds⟩ vapours

26, 1.21 ⟨gained⟩ reached

27, 1.13 ⟨great⟩ white

28, 1.27 chair. ⟨We rang the bell hastily⟩

28, 1.32 vanished ⟨away out of sight. A mystery doth the whole affair remain to this day⟩

29, 1.23 ⟨there's a raven⟩ listen!

32, 1.1 Oh no ⟨replied L⟩

32, 1.6 mirth ⟨which⟩

32, 1.31 ⟨answer⟩ reply

33, 1.4 ⟨was employed⟩ had given

33, 1.7 ⟨place⟩ house

33, 1.12 ⟨great⟩ distance

33, 1.24 ⟨heavens⟩ sky

33, 1.34 edge of the moor ⟨and then all the wild [?5 words]⟩

The Enfant

34, 1.11 ⟨exclaimed⟩ uttered

35, 1.16 ⟨observed⟩ saw

35, 1.18 ⟨away⟩ off

35, 1.23 ⟨about⟩ with such nonsense ⟨H accordingly bent his way towards the Tuilleries⟩

35, 1.26 ⟨Great⟩ mighty

36, 1.15 ⟨returned⟩ entered

The Keep of the Bridge

36, 1.33 ⟨have been⟩ be

38, 1.4 ⟨on a⟩ night

38, 1.8 ⟨it appear like⟩ them appear

38, 1.11 ⟨appear⟩ seem almost as ⟨beautiful⟩ magnificent

38, 1.13 ⟨spending⟩ contemplating

38, 1.22 door ⟨myself⟩

38, 1.23 ⟨might⟩ strength

Textual Notes

'Sir – it is well known that the Genii'
39, l.4 ⟨should⟩ will
39, l.5 ⟨run⟩ roll
39, l.9 ⟨power⟩ might
39, l.9 desert ⟨uninhabited only⟩

A Fragment, August the 7, 1829
40, l.2   dreary ⟨stormy⟩
40, l.24 same ⟨thing⟩
40, l.27 ⟨long⟩ short

Fragment, August the 8, 1829
41, l.15 ⟨the Great D⟩ Arthur
41, l.16 ⟨grave⟩ tomb
41, l.19 ⟨everlasting⟩ celestial
41, l.20 ⟨radiant glory⟩ radiance

The Search After Happiness
44, l.1   resolved ⟨in his own mind⟩
44, l.25 ⟨[?2 words] mighty⟩ great eagle
44, l.27 ⟨your⟩ the mighty
45, l.3   dwelt ⟨a lofty and great⟩
45, l.8   ⟨stark⟩ forests, whose ⟨impenetrable⟩ shade
45, l.27 talked ⟨together⟩
46, l.5   mind ⟨replied⟩
46, l.18 ⟨compulsion⟩ confusion
46, l.19 ⟨such⟩⟨most⟩ tremendous
46, l.31 travelled ⟨for some time⟩
46, l.31 ⟨entered⟩ came
47, l.3   all ⟨things⟩
47, l.5   ⟨followed⟩ wound
47, l.18 ⟨dark⟩ black
47, l.19 ⟨watch⟩ witness
47, l.25 ⟨One morning Alexander Delancy⟩ one evening
47, l.26 ⟨red⟩ its lurid
47, l.29 ⟨of horrible long⟩ fierce
47, l.30 ⟨brow of⟩ heavens
47, l.33 ⟨grew⟩ encircled
48, l.5   vivacity ⟨sparkling wit⟩
48, l.7   army ⟨haughtily [?1 word] viewing the distant ranks of the enemy⟩
48, l.10 voice ⟨penetrating [?1 word]⟩
48, l.12 ⟨sorrow⟩ misery
48, l.20 ⟨silence⟩ tacit thinking
48, l.22 ⟨in⟩ through
48, l.37 fire ⟨again⟩
48, l.38 ⟨relate to⟩ tell
49, l.4   ⟨when⟩ as
49, l.10 we ⟨were⟩ glided

Textual Notes

Page

49, l.16 ⟨immediately⟩ did

49, l.22 ⟨which⟩ like

49, l.23 ⟨oppressive⟩ fearful

49, l.23 ⟨splendour⟩ grandeur

49, l.31 The song is preceded by two heavily cancelled verses; and another heavily cancelled verse occurs before the final chorus.

50, l.21 ⟨thunder⟩ mighty clouds

50, l.23 The lines above and below this line are heavily cancelled.

50, l.35 ⟨face⟩ countenance

51, l.2 temple ⟨of black marble⟩

51, l.23 rest ⟨for the night⟩

51, l.26 ⟨stormy⟩ fiery

51, l.27 ⟨rising⟩ morning

51, l.30 ⟨stormy⟩ gloomy

51, l.33 ⟨which⟩ well-suited

52, l.1 search ⟨after⟩ ⟨for sustenance⟩

52, l.16 ⟨moments⟩ intervals

52, l.18 ⟨moments⟩ little time

52, l.19 ⟨last⟩ words

52, l.20 remember ⟨the [?1 word] of those⟩

52, l.22 ⟨anguish⟩ sorrow

52, l.39 battlements ⟨shone in the⟩

53, l.4 steps ⟨which he had [?c.6 words]⟩

53, l.10 Duke ⟨of Wellington⟩

53, l.12 ⟨Marquis of Douro and Lord Wellesley⟩ young princes

53, l.25 in ⟨the city⟩

Blackwood's Young Men's Magazine, August 1829

55, l.2 ⟨mighty⟩ round

55, l.5 ⟨shade of⟩ palace

55, l.10 ⟨whose⟩ and his

55, l.34 court ⟨of the palace.⟩

56, l.2 by ⟨ Jonathan Adams⟩ the Duke of Wellington

56, l.7 ⟨causes⟩ reasons

56, l.11 Bud ⟨was⟩

56, l.23 ⟨may⟩ might

57, l.21 ⟨mighty⟩ high course ⟨do⟩ doth

59, l.13 ⟨greatest⟩ ⟨first⟩ ⟨best⟩ glorious

61, l.3 ⟨Tale beautiful⟩ Tales of the Tavern

[Blackwood's Young Men's Magazine] September 1829

62, l.13 ⟨delightful⟩ beautiful

62, l.14 ⟨?of seeing⟩ fragrance

62, l.14 air ⟨perfumed by [?6 words]⟩

62, l.27 ⟨glittering⟩ sparkling

62, l.30 ⟨now⟩ silently

62, l.31 ⟨now⟩ changed

62, l.31 ⟨black⟩ masses

63, l.2 ⟨which⟩ who

Textual Notes

Page

63, l.3 ⟨very⟩ huge

63, l.9 ⟨began to⟩ sparkled

63, l.11 ⟨and at last⟩ troops

63, l.14 ⟨entered⟩ came

63, l.21 ⟨sparkling thrones of light⟩ adamantine thrones

64, l.1 ⟨and putting⟩ and blew

64, l.7 black ⟨rolling thu[nder]⟩ clouds

64, l.23 ⟨very⟩ high

64, l.24 ⟨vapours⟩ clouds

64, l.32 ⟨it⟩ both

65, l.7 ⟨lurid glare⟩ ruddy glare

65, l.11 ⟨pewter cups⟩ silver cups

65, l.13 The following two lines have been heavily cancelled and are indecipherable.

65, l.26 The previous line is cancelled: ⟨all is lengthless silence⟩

67, l.2 ⟨US⟩ UT; followed by the cancelled first line: ⟨this evening and the glorious sun⟩.
The title 'The Glass Town' is then repeated and the first four verses are
numbered.

67, l.6 ⟨mountains⟩ evening

67, l.7 ⟨amber⟩ crimson

67, l.11 ⟨while⟩ and

67, l.14 ⟨misty⟩ pale

67, l.18 The following verse is cancelled:
⟨No sound doth break the stillness
Sand [?1 word] every night gale
As [?5 words]
Down the still and lonely vale⟩

67, l.20 ⟨I hear⟩ From

67, l.21 ⟨mighty⟩ cataract

67, l.24 The following line is cancelled: ⟨which guard that glorious city⟩

67, l.25 ⟨roaring⟩ raging

67, l.27 ⟨high⟩ great

67, l.31 ⟨they are a⟩ May he ever

68, l.4 The following eleven lines are heavily cancelled and indecipherable.

68, l.6 ⟨rest⟩ sleep

68, l.9 ⟨pearly⟩ silver

68, l.10 The following line is cancelled: ⟨shed their [?1 word] light⟩

68, l.12 ⟨[?1 word] little⟩ shining; the following line is cancelled and indecipherable.

[Blackwood's Young Men's Magazine], October 1829

70, l.4 ⟨JAR⟩ CUP

70, l.7 in ⟨about⟩

70, l.11 discretion ⟨sometimes⟩

70, l.21 ⟨day⟩ afternoon

70, l.27 ⟨While⟩ As

70, l.30 ⟨jar⟩ cup

71, l.18 ⟨yelling out⟩ saying

71, l.24 ship ⟨which⟩

71, l.32 heart⟨less⟩rending

71, l.36 ⟨that your doing⟩ exclaimed

Textual Notes

Page
72, 1.2 ⟨work⟩ box
72, 1.24 execution ⟨through the exertions⟩
74, 1.4 ⟨dry and barren⟩ wilderness.
74, 1.5 A previous, alternative verse to this has been cancelled:
⟨But see a flash of lightning
Has darted from that cloud
Now listen to that thunder peal
So crashing long and loud.⟩
75, 1.7 one ⟨night⟩
75, 1.10 ⟨along⟩ past
75, 1.13 ⟨reach⟩ came to
76, 1.1 us ⟨and its white deathlike hands⟩
76, 1.2 ⟨suddenly⟩ slowly
76, 1.19 white sun ⟨lane⟩

[Blackwood's Young Men's Magazine] November 1829

79, 1.7 ⟨sweet⟩ breath
79, 1.8 ⟨primrose⟩ wild rose
79, 1.8 ⟨awoke⟩ began
79, 1.9 approach ⟨till the⟩
79, 1.12 ⟨and mighty⟩ city
79, 1.13 ⟨palaces⟩ towers
79, 1.14 ⟨sound of⟩ noise of
80, 1.9 Four words heavily cancelled at the end of the story.
80, 1.18 ⟨wild wilderness⟩ barren desert
80, 1.19 ⟨Soft and propitious is thy clime⟩ And thou wouldst be a pleasant land
81, 1.12 ⟨sw⟩⟨loudly⟩ sweetly; an uncancelled signature and date follow this verse, indicating that Charlotte originally intended her poem to end here. Above this date are four cancelled lines, the title and first lines of an aborted story continuing the theme of the genii: ⟨A CAPTIVE IN ONE OF THE REGIONS of the Genii. Lone in a dismal well, far in the centre of the cavern⟩
81, 1.22 ⟨loud⟩ knocking
83, 1.1 ⟨I was taking a cake of a little flour, cream and brown sugar⟩ sitting
83, 1.26 ⟨Cicero⟩ Scipio
84, 1.22 ⟨because⟩ Clarkson
85, 1.9 ⟨high⟩ scruple
86, 1.9 ⟨with⟩ while
86, 1.18 The two following verses signed and dated 'UT, September 7, 1829' have been cancelled; they are exactly the same as verses seven and eight of the previous poem, 'The Song of the Ancient Britons'. This suggests that Charlotte copied early drafts into her magazines and here copied the wrong poem whose subject and date are similar.
86, 1.20 ⟨purple⟩ yellow
86, 1.25 ⟨ring⟩ sing
86, 1.31 ⟨they may [?1 word]⟩ themselves
87, 1.3 ⟨arise⟩ And throned; the following line is heavily cancelled and indecipherable.
87, 1.5 ⟨bow down to⟩ to wait on them ⟨and⟩
87, 1.6 ⟨will⟩ shall; the following four lines are heavily cancelled and the concluding verse inserted in the manuscript after the contents.

Anecdotes of the Duke of Wellington

89, l.6   90 ⟨years⟩
89, l.12 ⟨moment⟩ instant
89, l.15 ⟨still⟩ yet
89, l.15 ⟨calm⟩⟨quiet⟩ still ⟨dignity⟩ smile
90, l.14 ⟨possessed⟩ had

[Blackwood's Young Men's Magazine] December (first issue) 1829

91, l.9   ⟨town⟩ bay
91, l.21 The following line is heavily cancelled and indecipherable.
91, l.25 ⟨joy⟩ mirth
91, l.29 ⟨upon⟩ tone
92, l.5   ⟨sweep⟩ moan
92, l.19 ⟨scenery⟩ mountains
92, l.22 ⟨grand⟩ mighty
92, l.26 ⟨dark and⟩ stormy
92, l.33 ⟨the⟩ young
93, l.1   ⟨were⟩ hung
93, l.12 ⟨the emperor⟩ Napoleon
93, l.19 ⟨to bed⟩ to rest
93, l.23 ⟨sun⟩ light
93, l.25 ⟨glowing⟩ gliding
93, l.26 ⟨golden⟩ glowing
94, l.2   ⟨his⟩ the
94, l.10 ⟨more⟩ louder, more ⟨joyous⟩ joyful
94, l.22 ⟨written⟩ spoken
94, l.32 ⟨novels⟩ romances
95, l.5   ⟨Happy⟩ Visions of
95, l.11 ⟨tolled⟩ rang
95, l.19 ⟨pleasant⟩ sweet
95, l.23 ⟨toll⟩ sound
96, l.9   ⟨thunder⟩ vapour
96, l.10 Following line cancelled and indecipherable.
96, l.16 Following line cancelled and indecipherable.
97, l.18 ⟨great palace⟩ first court

Tales of the Islanders, volume II

Many pages of this manuscript are heavily blotted with ink which shows through from the previous pages.

100, l.11 ⟨things⟩ [?it]
100, l.16 ⟨times from⟩ 3 months
100, l.19 ⟨sun⟩day
100, l.30 hush: could be read 'rush'
101, l.17 ⟨we are⟩ I am
101, l.18 ⟨and Arthur is lying on a bed. Charles dreadfully wounded⟩ and – but
101, l.35 ⟨Island⟩ Isle
101, l.35 ⟨the vision⟩ a dream
103, l.1   ⟨we⟩ he

Textual Notes

103, l.2 ⟨ravine⟩ glen
103, l.7 ⟨huge dark⟩ rocks
103, l.14 ⟨sharp crevice⟩ aerie; at the bottom of page 1 of this manuscript there are three
    spelling attempts of the word 'aerie': 'eri', 'eire', 'aerie'.
104, l.2 ⟨there⟩ at
104, l.29 ⟨came⟩ went
105, l.10 ⟨unearthly⟩ voices
105, l.11 ⟨cautioning me⟩ supplicating me
105, l.11 ⟨me⟩ them
105, l.18 ⟨him⟩ us
105, l.26 ⟨about 6⟩ many
105, l.33 ⟨light of⟩ glory
107, l.34 aisles ⟨and solemn⟩
107, l.36 ⟨sound⟩ music
107, l.38 ⟨amid⟩ with
107, l.38 ⟨noble⟩ brave
107, l.38 ⟨courage⟩⟨impetuous⟩ noble
108, l.19 ⟨seated⟩ sat
108, l.23 ⟨everything⟩ upon her
108, l.34 ⟨bore⟩ held
109, l.2 ⟨over⟩ whose
109, l.6 ⟨he fe[ll]⟩ The dart
109, l.9 ⟨with a fresh⟩ by a hand
109, l.15 ⟨which⟩ flowing
109, l.22 1829: followed by an indecipherable word: [?Monieulo].
109, l.26 ⟨1828⟩ 1722
109, l.26 ⟨these⟩ four
109, l.31 ⟨a hearing stated their wish and petition⟩ They stated
110, l.2 ⟨which⟩ that
110, l.3 ⟨which⟩ it
110, l.4 ⟨beautiful which⟩ pleasant
110, l.8 ⟨murmuring⟩ rippling
110, l.27 ⟨Alone⟩ Vine
111, l.6 ⟨for⟩ till
112, l.39 ⟨afterwards⟩ became
113, l.2 ⟨snows and frost⟩ frost
113, l.4 ⟨as the⟩ by the

[Blackwood's Young Men's Magazine] December (second issue) 1829

113, l.20 ⟨eminence⟩ merit
114, l.17 ⟨that⟩ which
114, l.29 ⟨where⟩ sweet
115, l.1 ⟨castles of glory⟩ palaces of glory
115, l.2 ⟨beneath⟩ in the midst of
115, l.11 ⟨fair⟩ rich
115, l.16 ⟨pleasant⟩ gentle
115, l.23 ⟨world⟩ land
115, l.28 ⟨C Brontë⟩ U T
116, l.17 ⟨?gleaming⟩ sunlight

Textual Notes

Page

116, l.18 ⟨clouds⟩ purple clouds
116, l.21 west⟨ern sky⟩
116, l.28 ⟨admirable⟩ beautiful
116, l.31 ⟨warm⟩ enthusiastic
117, l.29 ⟨with⟩⟨was shining⟩ shone
117, l.31 ⟨calmness⟩ [?redness]
118, l.19 ⟨winter⟩ spring
118, l.23 ⟨perhaps⟩ if you
118, l.24 ⟨if you are going⟩ you may be going
118, l.35 ⟨dog⟩ greyhound
119, l.1 ⟨clear⟩ silver
119, l.1 ⟨and the glorious round sun⟩ the thin veil
119, l.2 ⟨arises⟩ appears
120, l.4 ⟨ask⟩ said
120, l.21 ⟨May⟩ Joy
120, l.24 ⟨thy pleasant⟩ each
120, l.28 Britan⟨nias⟩s Lion
120, l.29 Following line cancelled: ⟨On to dark and [?2 words] dark shores⟩

Characters of the Celebrated Men of the Present Time (manuscript missing)

Description of the Duke of Wellington's Small Palace Situated on the Banks of the Indiva

130, l.25 ⟨town⟩ city
131, l.7 ⟨there⟩ in
131, l.10 ⟨first⟩ fair
131, l.17 ⟨into⟩ from
131, l.18 ⟨northern⟩ horizon
131, l.19 ⟨with delightful verdure⟩ with groves
131, l.34 ⟨sky⟩ heavens
132, l.2 ⟨wide⟩ pure
132, l.3 ⟨gently⟩ softly
132, l.6 ⟨sweet⟩ young
132, l.12 ⟨was⟩ were
132, l.18 ⟨begin the⟩ air my
132, l.21 ⟨sweet⟩ unison

The Adventures of Mon Edouard de Crack

133, l.8 'Adventure's' in manuscript; the apostrophe also occurs on the title-page
134, l.21 ⟨but wishing so to do. all the little⟩ but
134, l.22 ⟨little⟩ book-knowledge
135, l.13 ⟨after⟩ in a few days
135, l.24 ⟨there⟩ some
135, l.27 ⟨through⟩ from
135, l.37 ⟨numerous⟩ loaves
135, l.41 ⟨who⟩ eating
136, l.10 ⟨loud⟩ wild
136, l.24 ⟨of⟩ which crashed ⟨in⟩
136, l.40 ⟨that⟩ this

Page

137, l.23 ⟨and in⟩ With
137, l.23 ⟨and disappeared in boundless⟩ ⟨like the⟩ and
137, l.25 ⟨glorious⟩ sight
138, l.1 ⟨ever⟩ from
138, l.11 ⟨with⟩ joy ⟨to⟩
138, l.27 ⟨the whole⟩ it
138, l.33 ⟨hundred⟩ thousand
138, l.35 ⟨seemed⟩ was
139, l.11 ⟨But my story becomes too long I must now bring it to a conclusions⟩ Having
139, l.25 ⟨thousand⟩ little
139, l.31 about ⟨him⟩
139, l.35 ⟨cast⟩ throw
139, l.42 ⟨to thank him⟩ to express
140, l.2 ⟨had⟩ caused

Tales of the Islanders, volume III

140, l.23 ⟨Second⟩ Third
140, l.25 One evening ⟨in the beginning of February 1830⟩
140, l.26 repos⟨ing⟩ed
141, l.10 ⟨while⟩ Castlereagh
141, l.19 ⟨Pekin⟩ civilian
142, l.5 ⟨du⟩ d'un
142, l.11 ⟨knelt down⟩ made
142, l.17 ⟨The Duke⟩ His Grace
143, l.11 ⟨has⟩ did
143, l.12 ⟨bri[ght]⟩ fair
143, l.17 ⟨clear⟩ bright
143, l.18 ⟨first bright⟩ first faint
143, l.21 ⟨forth⟩ out
143, l.27 ⟨now⟩ forth
143, l.31 ⟨danced ou[t]⟩ bounded
143, l.31 ⟨past⟩ by with
143, l.31 so ⟨gaily⟩⟨merrily and⟩ much ⟨merri[ment]⟩ buoyancy
143, l.33 ⟨he did not see⟩ his rosy face
144, l.3 black ⟨gloomy⟩
144, l.7 going ⟨so early⟩
144, l.11 ⟨the⟩ His
144, l.13 ⟨returned⟩ shadowed
144, l.14 ⟨dead⟩ in danger
144, l.19 ⟨fetch⟩ find
144, l.23 ⟨go and⟩ try
144, l.34 ⟨widely⟩ wider
144, l.37 ⟨pace[d]⟩ put
145, l.8 ⟨pow[er]⟩ abode
145, l.8 ⟨certain evil gh[osts]⟩ supernatural beings
145, l.10 ⟨be his part⟩ befall
145, l.16 ⟨my bro[ther]⟩ Arthur's
145, l.17 ⟨pierc[ing]⟩ glistening
145, l.18 ⟨placed his hand⟩ patted

Textual Notes

145, 1.19 ⟨after⟩ when
145, 1.22 ⟨medows⟩ hay
146, 1.9 ⟨smooth⟩ even
146, 1.9 ⟨2⟩ 5
146, 1.15 ⟨leap it⟩ reach it
146, 1.18 ⟨flu[ng]⟩ threw
146, 1.22 ⟨Charles⟩ Wellesley
146, 1.23 ⟨his⟩ the
147, 1.1 ⟨the Duke's⟩ his
147, 1.6 ⟨few moments⟩ short time
147, 1.16 ⟨rising⟩⟨rose⟩ ⟨?rising⟩ rose
147, 1.17 John ⟨Charles⟩
147, 1.19 ⟨weeks⟩ months
147, 1.30 ⟨And we wish you to accompany us⟩ We
147, 1.32 thither ⟨myself⟩
148, 1.15 ⟨would not⟩ refused
148, 1.17 right to ⟨do⟩
148, 1.22 ⟨deep gr⟩ glittering
148, 1.24 surprise ⟨for a few minutes⟩
148, 1.26 ⟨dart⟩ fly
149, 1.8 ⟨abrupt⟩ in an abrupt manner
149, 1.21 age ⟨it has⟩
149, 1.21 ⟨grown out⟩ pierced
149, 1.23 ⟨because⟩ by
149, 1.24 ⟨but⟩ now
149, 1.28 ear ⟨betokened him⟩
149, 1.30 ⟨magnificence⟩ majesty
149, 1.34 ⟨had⟩ having
149, 1.35 tomorrow ⟨he should suf[fer]⟩
150, 1.7 ⟨middle⟩ roof
150, 1.8 ⟨round⟩ about
150, 1.16 ⟨join⟩ mingle
150, 1.25 ⟨and duly sign⟩ a solemn sign
151, 1.4 ⟨in⟩ by
151, 1.8 ⟨king⟩ [?tick]
151, 1.13 whining ⟨pek[in]⟩ poetast⟨ing⟩er's ⟨civil lang[uage]⟩
152, 1.28 ⟨I'll jump into the fire⟩ I'll set myself on fire
152, 1.34 ⟨dirty⟩ bread
152, 1.37 going ⟨Duke⟩
153, 1.8 ⟨covered⟩ spread
153, 1.15 costly ⟨velvet⟩
153, 1.16 ⟨odorous⟩ exquisite
153, 1.18 on ⟨at one⟩
153, 1.21 ⟨embroidered⟩ bordered
153, 1.25 ⟨time⟩ silence
153, 1.34 every ⟨body⟩ person

Page

The Adventures of Ernest Alembert

Manuscript has scribbles and trial spelling at the foot of several pages

154, l.20 ⟨family⟩ race
154, l.22 ⟨race⟩ family
155, l.3 ⟨broad⟩ wide
155, l.12 ⟨which⟩ that
155, l.17 ⟨some⟩ a few
155, l.25 ⟨and far⟩ ⟨distant⟩ horizon
155, l.26 ⟨hearth⟩ fire
155, l.27 ⟨around⟩ past
155, l.29 ⟨was abo[ut]⟩ a man
156, l.5 ⟨fear⟩ awe
156, l.9 ⟨ghosts⟩ spirits
156, l.16 ⟨being⟩ man
156, l.16 bear ⟨fruit⟩
156, l.17 ⟨where⟩ the earth
156, l.17 ⟨where⟩ the sun
156, l.20 ⟨not⟩ invisible
156, l.29 ⟨said⟩ replied
156, l.31 ⟨off⟩ out
157, l.7 ⟨narrow⟩ passage
157, l.14 ⟨strong⟩ brisk
157, l.17 ⟨frail⟩ bark
157, l.24 ⟨the then⟩ a huge
157, l.24 ⟨wave⟩ billow
157, l.25 ⟨billows⟩ waves
157, l.31 ⟨in⟩ that
157, l.31 ⟨very⟩ verge
157, l.34 ⟨wild⟩ grand
157, l.35 ⟨all⟩ around
157, l.37 ⟨all⟩ their
157, l.39 ⟨disappeared⟩ and was gone
158, l.9 ⟨black⟩ clouds ⟨and⟩
158, l.22 ⟨wood⟩ forest
158, l.23 more ⟨and m[ore]⟩
158, l.24 ⟨became a delightful⟩ assumed
158, l.29 ⟨rising⟩ which rose
158, l.38 ⟨sky⟩ heavens
158, l.41 ⟨stained⟩ sullied
159, l.2 ⟨scene⟩ view
159, l.5 delighted ⟨by it⟩
159, l.7 ⟨eyes⟩ sight
159, l.7 scene ⟨and⟩
159, l.8 ⟨every⟩ each
159, l.9 fields ⟨that now appeared before him⟩
159, l.11 ⟨disappeared⟩ vanished
159, l.21 ⟨sunset⟩ twilight
159, l.24 ⟨twilight⟩ sunset

Page
159, 1.25 ⟨flitting⟩ floating
159, 1.26 ⟨top of a high hill⟩ brow of a lofty precipice
159, 1.31 ⟨and⟩ echo ⟨never⟩
159, 1.32 ⟨gusty⟩ breath
159, 1.38 ⟨rolling⟩ curling
160, 1.8 ⟨in⟩ overwhelmed
160, 1.13 ⟨rays of the⟩ sunbeams
160, 1.14 ⟨among⟩ on ⟨them⟩
160, 1.14 ⟨opening⟩ cups
160, 1.15 ⟨grew on the borders of⟩ bordered
160, 1.19 ⟨still⟩ more
160, 1.29 ⟨with cl[ematis]⟩ creeping
160, 1.31 ⟨formed⟩ of lofty trees
160, 1.33 ⟨this⟩ a
160, 1.38 ⟨murmuring⟩ breath
161, 1.1 ⟨suddenly⟩ saw
161, 1.3 ⟨sounded⟩ rose
161, 1.23 ⟨And⟩ After
161, 1.25 ⟨like⟩ as
161, 1.39 clouds ⟨and vapours⟩
162, 1.1 ⟨extensive⟩ excessive
162, 1.1 anguish ⟨and misery⟩
162, 1.2 'this lighted' in manuscript
162, 1.6 ⟨over everything⟩ over all things
162, 1.12 returned ⟨covering a⟩
162, 1.21 ⟨roar⟩ rolled
162, 1.22 ⟨succeeded⟩ exceeded
162, 1.27 ⟨to be seen⟩ visible
162, 1.32 ⟨balls⟩ globes
162, 1.32 sudden ⟨and fitful⟩
162, 1.38 ⟨lustre⟩ mild attractive
162, 1.38 ⟨towers⟩ arches
163, 1.7 ⟨them⟩ any
163, 1.15 melody ⟨rose⟩
163, 1.28 ⟨wide⟩ magnificent
163, 1.34 ⟨wearied⟩ weary
163, 1.38 ⟨when⟩ in a few minutes
163, 1.41 ⟨large⟩ immense
164, 1.3 ⟨green⟩ verdant
164, 1.9 ⟨the⟩ his
164, 1.19 ⟨clear⟩ waters
164, 1.20 ⟨appeared to⟩ dawned on
164, 1.26 ⟨roof⟩ palace roof
164, 1.28 ⟨globes⟩ drops
164, 1.29 ⟨proceeded⟩ descended
164, 1.30 ⟨all over⟩ over
164, 1.32 ⟨glory⟩ splendour
164, 1.39 ⟨continued⟩ abode
164, 1.41 ⟨charmed⟩ drew

Textual Notes

164, 1.42 ⟨and drew him⟩ into
165, 1.15 shed ⟨around them⟩
165, 1.21 ⟨a little apart⟩ on the ground
165, 1.27 ⟨long⟩ dark
165, 1.28 ⟨then⟩ advanced
165, 1.32 ⟨fainter⟩ paler
165, 1.33 ⟨as it disappeared⟩ towards
165, 1.34 ⟨towards⟩ at
165, 1.37 ⟨with⟩ in
166, 1.1 ⟨sweet⟩ sound
166, 1.3 ⟨amongst⟩ in the power of
166, 1.3 ⟨stole⟩ swept
166, 1.12 ⟨sounds⟩ noise
166, 1.12 ⟨have⟩ has
166, 1.14 ⟨Yon⟩ That
166, 1.18 ⟨is⟩ rings
166, 1.18 ⟨place⟩ vale
166, 1.22 ⟨steals⟩ peals
166, 1.34 following line deleted as follows: ⟨To listen then ... nightingale⟩
167, 1.1 ⟨str[eam]⟩ rill
167, 1.3 ⟨Her stream⟩ She pours
167, 1.6 ⟨light⟩ day
167, 1.8 ⟨fair⟩ earth
167, 1.12 ⟨soars towards⟩ mounts
167, 1.12 ⟨?rush of⟩ arch of
167, 1.16 oak ⟨stood in dark⟩
167, 1.17 ⟨being⟩ was
167, 1.17 ⟨against⟩ on
167, 1.19 ⟨his⟩ He
167, 1.20 ⟨off one shoulder⟩ downwards
167, 1.21 ⟨A black girdle conf[ined]⟩ His robe
167, 1.27 ⟨?the old man⟩ he
167, 1.31 ⟨a part of the⟩ and lonely
167, 1.32 finished ⟨them⟩
167, 1.34 ⟨Alembert⟩ him
167, 1.37 ⟨why he lived alone⟩ to recount
168, 1.1 ⟨spirits⟩ fairies
168, 1.1 ⟨have⟩ abode
168, 1.1 ⟨long⟩ short
168, 1.2 ⟨kind⟩ nature
168, 1.4 ⟨that part⟩ The [?portion]
168, 1.4 ⟨first⟩ fixed
168, 1.8 ⟨proceeded⟩ went on
168, 1.9 Good-Gard ⟨[?6 words] of the Caspian range [?1 word]⟩
168, 1.10 range ⟨of mountains⟩
168, 1.16 ⟨until then the⟩ During
168, 1.24 wide ⟨enough⟩
168, 1.25 ⟨foundations were⟩ base
168, 1.27 ⟨narrow⟩ chasm

Page

169, 1.1 ⟨sights⟩ scenes
169, 1.3 ⟨?some hundreds⟩ Thousands
169, 1.7 ⟨silence⟩ loneliness
169, 1.12 ⟨Under⟩ below
169, 1.13 ⟨large⟩ wave
169, 1.15 ⟨curled⟩ [?coiled]
169, 1.16 ⟨chambers⟩ halls
169, 1.18 ⟨saw⟩ beheld
169, 1.22 ⟨lived⟩ abode
169, 1.23 years ⟨in perfect happiness⟩

An Interesting Passage in the Lives of Some Eminent Men of the Present Time

170, 1.28 that ⟨if⟩
171, 1.2 ⟨for⟩ about
171, 1.10 ⟨the⟩ broiling
171, 1.15 ⟨the⟩ rich
171, 1.17 ⟨forest⟩ umbrage
171, 1.17 sky ⟨light⟩
171, 1.19 in ⟨with⟩
171, 1.22 ⟨that⟩ for
171, 1.23 ⟨would⟩ to
171, 1.29 him ⟨in opinion⟩
171, 1.35 ⟨place⟩ point
171, 1.37 ⟨some⟩ amusement
172, 1.1 ⟨servant⟩ valet
172, 1.2 ⟨some⟩ kindness
172, 1.9 could ⟨perhaps⟩
173, 1.1 ⟨but⟩ and
173, 1.3 ⟨left⟩ got out
173, 1.9 ⟨one⟩ that
173, 1.9 ⟨this⟩ went
173, 1.9 ⟨that⟩ it
173, 1.9 passing ⟨went⟩
173, 1.18 ⟨then⟩ after
173, 1.19 came ⟨here⟩
173, 1.33 ⟨piercing⟩ gaze
174, 1.4 ⟨tall⟩ huge
174, 1.10 presently ⟨one⟩
174, 1.10 gate ⟨opened and we entered⟩
174, 1.10 ⟨entered⟩ beheld
174, 1.11 ⟨was⟩ were
174, 1.13 all ⟨the men⟩
174, 1.27 approached ⟨the grave⟩
175, 1.14 ⟨your⟩ that promise
175, 1.24 ⟨hid[ing]⟩ concealed
175, 1.35 ⟨wild⟩ buffoon
176, 1.14 Tree ⟨and accosted him⟩
176, 1.21 ⟨easy to⟩ easily

Page
176, l.23 ⟨chest⟩ coffin
176, l.31 ⟨hill⟩ city
176, l.32 ⟨the⟩ which

'The following strange occurrence'
177, l.8 ⟨room⟩ bed
177, l.26 ⟨she⟩ her reply

Leisure Hours
178, l.30 ⟨high⟩ cottage
179, l.2 money ⟨in her hand⟩
179, l.3 ⟨he⟩ after
179, l.7 ⟨big⟩ small
179, l.15 ⟨ga[ve]⟩ flung

The Poetaster, volume I
180, l.27 ⟨all⟩ ⟨of⟩ poets which are
181, l.2 must ⟨it⟩
181, l.2 ⟨rend und[er]⟩ be rent
181, l.6 ⟨rather would I be laid in⟩ would
181, l.13 ⟨and⟩ pity
181, l.32 heavens ⟨are⟩
182, l.1 They ⟨see⟩
182, l.37 ⟨gift⟩ pensive
183, l.1 ⟨keep⟩ watch
183, l.3 ⟨he retires to bed⟩ Exit
183, l.35 ⟨rising⟩ wind
184, l.6 ⟨on⟩ at
184, l.7 ⟨opened it⟩ gave
184, l.8 ⟨and so⟩ while
184, l.11 ⟨coverings⟩ cushions
184, l.15 lady ⟨sitting⟩
184, l.33 ⟨its⟩ his
185, l.1 ⟨its⟩ his
185, l.1 ⟨its⟩ He
185, l.1 ⟨its⟩ his hand
185, l.2 ⟨it⟩ he
185, l.4 ⟨the⟩ she
185, l.23 Badey ⟨while doing⟩
185, l.28 ⟨case⟩ circumstance
186, l.2 ⟨which⟩ who
187, l.13 ⟨Henry Rhymer⟩ The Poetaster

The Poetaster, volume II
190, l.24 flight ⟨in⟩
190, l.25 amid ⟨dim⟩
190, l.28 ⟨earth⟩ regions
191, l.33 ⟨endure⟩ try

Page
191, l.41 ⟨if there's⟩ whether
192, l.1 ⟨second⟩ fourth
192, l.8 ⟨world⟩ word
193, l.4 ⟨cannot⟩ am unable
193, l.12 ⟨him⟩ one
193, l.16 ⟨slaked⟩ slacked
193, l.21 ⟨those⟩ that
193, l.30 ⟨black⟩ dark
194, l.13 ⟨was⟩ it is
194, l.38 ⟨those⟩ that

Tales of the Islanders, volume IV

196, l.25 ⟨season⟩ period
196, l.26 ⟨around⟩ hawthorns
197, l.2 ⟨year⟩ season
197, l.14 brought ⟨him⟩ in sight ⟨of⟩
197, l.30 ⟨house⟩ shelter
198, l.8 ⟨path⟩ lane
198, l.8 ⟨extensive⟩ vast
198, l.22 ⟨after⟩ without
198, l.30 ⟨low⟩ round
198, l.32 ⟨she⟩ looked
198, l.39 door ⟨for them⟩
199, l.2 lines ⟨which in⟩
199, l.21 a while ⟨till⟩ to
199, l.30 ⟨immediately⟩ concluded
199, l.37 ⟨hut⟩ mansion
200, l.13 ⟨which⟩ that
200, l.26 ⟨but⟩ and was
200, l.28 This ⟨satisfied them and⟩
201, l.8 ante(-room) chamber
201, l.8 private ⟨appartment⟩
201, l.15 ⟨countenance⟩ face
201, l.22 Duke ⟨of Wellington⟩
201, l.23 courtesied ⟨when⟩
201, l.32 ⟨enchanted⟩ delighted
202, l.10 ⟨circumstance⟩ incident
202, l.17 ⟨came⟩ lay
202, l.21 flowing ⟨past⟩
202, l.23 ⟨came over⟩ glided through
202, l.24 ⟨falling⟩ passing away
202, l.25 ⟨flew [?1 word]⟩ came up
202, l.26 ⟨at night in⟩ at midnight
203, l.1 ⟨towards it⟩ onwards
203, l.3 door ⟨which sprang⟩
203, l.19 near ⟨him⟩
203, l.26 had ⟨seen⟩ observed
203, l.26 ⟨at⟩ on
204, l.9 ⟨air⟩ wind

Textual Notes

Page
204, l.11 〈ancient〉 old
204, l.16 〈west〉 east
204, l.19 〈occident〉 orient
204, l.37 as 〈that〉
205, l.14 〈raising its〉 the awful form
205, l.32 〈ring〉 line
206, l.1 unfurled 〈two drag[ons]〉
206, l.2 〈earth〉 west
206, l.4 descended 〈towards the [?1 word]〉
206, l.5 one 〈in the〉
206, l.14 〈seen〉 to be seen
206, l.15 〈flames〉 floods
207, l.23 〈heavens〉 sky
207, l.23 〈were〉 was
207, l.27 〈the〉 his
207, l.30 〈bowed〉 turned
207, l.39 〈his〉 for
208, l.15 〈I knew nothing〉 I am ignorant
208, l.26 〈simplest〉 [?softest]
208, l.33 spent 〈in〉
209, l.1 〈on〉 his
209, l.6 follow 〈him〉
209, l.7 〈rivers〉 plains
209, l.8 〈for〉 constructed
209, l.16 〈placed〉 showed
209, l.25 box 〈again〉
209, l.31 〈poured perfumes〉 sprinkled perfumes
210, l.3 〈burst〉 broke
210, l.9 〈with〉 in
210, l.10 〈in〉 from
210, l.27 〈persecutors〉 sacrificers
210, l.31 〈by〉 from
211, l.3 〈you〉 my
211, l.10 〈Strathfieldsay〉 the private parlour

Catalogue of my Books (no significant cancellations or textual notes)

Young Men's Magazine, August 1830

215, l.20 first 〈except that advertisements will be excluded.〉
216, l.15 〈fine〉 lovely
216, l.15 〈in〉 of June
216, l.26 stately 〈caps〉
217, l.10 4 〈?3 hours〉
217, l.16 ground 〈before〉
217, l.18 rest 〈was distinguished〉
217, l.19 〈in[n]〉 public
217, l.22 tongue 〈of which I〉
217, l.24 scenery 〈which〉
218, l.5 west〈wards〉

Page
218, l.6 ⟨sky⟩ heavens
219, l.14 cry ⟨passed thr[ough]⟩
219, l.14 ⟨in⟩ at midnight
219, l.21 ⟨in⟩ at the side
219, l.22 ⟨body⟩ corpse
219, l.25 ⟨13⟩ 12
220, l.6 Following line cancelled: ⟨Flowing of Ice rocks round which wildly⟩
220, l.12 peacefully ⟨there green⟩
220, l.13 ⟨trembling⟩ playing
220, l.18 Following line cancelled: ⟨The air with tumult⟩
220, l.22 each ⟨the⟩
220, l.26 hark ⟨stream⟩
220, l.27 ⟨such⟩ awful
220, l.27 bends ⟨to hear⟩
220, l.33 ⟨Now⟩ On
220, l.36 ⟨in⟩ are
221, l.3 ⟨my⟩ ⟨£⟩ Ls
221, l.10 ⟨to⟩ forcing
221, l.21 ⟨?How happy shall I be Paris⟩ How
222, l.6 following ⟨recital⟩
222, l.7 Louis ⟨the⟩
222, l.29 ⟨my⟩ the
223, l.13 Bonaparte ⟨himself⟩
224, l.2 Tree ⟨Young Soult⟩
225, l.20 venison ⟨in⟩

Exact transcription of French:
221, l.5 en veritè je suis bien aisè.
221, l.12 3 Louis d'ors
221, l.15 Tu Reine d'la terre
221, l.16 Je suis ravis a je pense de ton murs, rues et chateaux
221, l.34 Quelle vous faites larmeyer, Monsieur? Etes vous malheureux a moi? No, my chere Monsieur.
222, l.11 Un dolereuse pensée Monsieur
222, l.31 Donnez moi pain pour le honneur de France

Young Men's Magazine, September 1830 (manuscript missing)
Young Men's Magazine, October 1830
230, l.9 ⟨land⟩ ground
230, l.21 ⟨with⟩ by
230, l.28 cow ⟨one hor[se]⟩
231, l.19 ⟨Emily⟩ Aumly
231, l.24 ⟨I struck⟩ heaving
232, l.7 9 o'clock ⟨just in⟩
232, l.22 ⟨had been⟩ was
233, l.3 ⟨when I remained at the Glass⟩ For many
233, l.26 ⟨Now⟩ Hark!
234, l.12 Following line cancelled: words indecipherable
234, l.13 ⟨Oft doth⟩ Ceases
234, l.24 ⟨his⟩ the

Textual Notes

Page
235, l.10 ⟨excellence⟩ mastery
235, l.27 ⟨peasant's⟩ heart
235, l.30 ⟨we[re]⟩ was
236, l.17 ⟨them soar⟩ their
236, l.22 ⟨the⟩ those
238, l.3 ⟨?immensely⟩ incomparably
239, l.25 Recommendation ⟨for⟩
240, l.3 ⟨price⟩ 1 vol.

Young Men's Magazine, November 1830

241, l.10 ⟨OCTOBER⟩ November
242, l.22 said I ⟨one day⟩
242, l.26 ⟨opinion⟩ axiom
242, l.29 ⟨heart⟩ art
243, l.11 ⟨some⟩ rare
243, l.15 That ⟨see⟩
243, l.16 man ⟨in⟩
243, l.33 ⟨circumstance⟩ instance
244, l.2 man ⟨in Ispahan⟩
244, l.18 qualified ⟨to deserve⟩
244, l.30 ⟨cloud⟩ mist
244, l.31 ⟨and in⟩ as it
245, l.5 ⟨the old man⟩ Houssain
245, l.9 ⟨that⟩ who
245, l.13 obeyed ⟨and in a hours time he brought him⟩
245, l.24 ⟨flow⟩ lovely
246, l.1 ⟨most⟩ loudest
246, l.12 ⟨exceedi[ngly]⟩ noble
246, l.13 ⟨and⟩ an
246, l.19 ⟨produced the tube⟩ gave
246, l.20 ⟨to⟩ gazing
246, l.21 ⟨gave⟩ he put
247, l.30 ⟨day while⟩ eve as
247, l.31 ⟨And to⟩ While
248, l.34 around ⟨to see⟩
249, l.16 ⟨sea god's vast oc[ean]⟩ ocean's wave
250, l.1 ⟨with⟩ in
250, l.2 ⟨and⟩ with
250, l.7 ⟨had⟩ were
250, l.12 ⟨slumber⟩ sleep
250, l.25 ⟨he⟩ Tree
251, l.5 ⟨du⟩ de Graves
251, l.11 ⟨actor's⟩ actress's
252, l.2 dérobée ⟨pour⟩
252, l.6 quand ⟨mort⟩
252, l.14 lips ⟨pere⟩
253, l.12 ⟨thy⟩ thine
253, l.25 ⟨an⟩ twenty
255, l.13 ⟨RARE⟩ NOTICE

Textual Notes

Page

Exact transcription of the French:

250, l.31   Madame le Comtesse De Ouvert
251, l.4   Le Marquis au Graves
251, l.20   un perfect beautè
251, l.30   pour ce'est un vraisemblance
251, l.38   Je ne peut pas a quitter mon père tombeau
251, l.42   c'est le lune
252, l.2   Non, elle est deroha
252, l.5   Je suis le Reverant vos père: Je aimais vous quand Je etais vivant et Je aime vos quand Je suis mort ma enfants
252, l.14   Je peut ouvrir il

Young Men's Magazine, December (first issue) 1830

Exact copy of French in Davidson Cook's transcription (manuscript lost: see p. 256):

261, l.34   Monsieur le Baron ami avez vous le jeux de rage et nôir?
261, l.37   Je vent insignior vous, vivous voulons aller en moi?

Young Men's Magazine, December (second issue) 1830

269, l.20   been ⟨out⟩
269, l.27   ⟨light⟩ tall
272, l.24   ⟨I felt⟩ the bonds
273, l.19   with ⟨was⟩
273, l.22   ⟨got⟩ procured
273, l.25   ⟨the party⟩ them
274, l.3   ⟨I have⟩ This
274, l.4   ⟨star⟩ distant
275, l.20   ⟨places⟩ fields
276, l.3   ⟨July 29th⟩ ⟨August⟩ Dec 28
277, l.25   ⟨purple⟩ wine
277, l.34   ⟨such as⟩ like
278, l.2   ⟨she[ltered]⟩ cradled
278, l.34   ⟨tavern⟩ fire
279, l.32   tavern ⟨since⟩
280, l.35   ⟨A Frenchman's Journal concluded by Captain Tree ... XIX⟩ A Traveller's
281, l.1   ⟨continued by⟩ concluded

Exact transcription of French:

276, l.24   Maitre de ces hotel, est il si?
279, l.4   tout a la coup
279, l.12   francais orarages

Campbell Castle

281, l.9   ⟨elabor[ately]⟩ beautifully
281, l.12   ⟨far⟩ distant
281, l.26   ⟨thicket⟩ entangling
281, l.27   ⟨cascade⟩ recess
281, l.30   ⟨appearance⟩ form
282, l.2   ⟨of most⟩ betokening

Page
282, l.34 ⟨beautiful⟩ admirable
283, l.1 ⟨lock⟩ straight
283, l.20 ⟨they had then⟩ he had
283, l.21 ⟨if the poem has⟩ and if we

Albion and Marina

285, l.21 injuries ⟨I have⟩
286, l.8 ⟨the⟩ her
286, l.11 ⟨truth⟩ in truth
286, l.15 ⟨that⟩ my
287, l.7 has ⟨sets⟩
287, l.20 ⟨To⟩ The
287, l.26 resided ⟨there⟩
288, l.9 ⟨rich ?halo⟩ bright wreath
288, l.14 large ⟨luxuriant⟩
288, l.16 break ⟨through⟩
288, l.22 ⟨versed⟩ read
288, l.24 ⟨lan[guages]⟩ tongues
288, l.33 odoriferous ⟨flow[ers]⟩
289, l.6 ⟨excelled⟩ would excel
289, l.9 ⟨lip⟩ silken
289, l.19 with ⟨her⟩
289, l.24 he ⟨was⟩
289, l.34 ⟨A day or two⟩ For some time
290, l.11 spoke ⟨with⟩
290, l.23 ⟨Two⟩ A few
291, l.11 ⟨Of⟩ On
291, l.12 ⟨the beautiful⟩ Marina
291, l.18 ⟨last⟩ words
291, l.35 in ⟨a short time⟩
292, l.4 ⟨to the⟩ for
292, l.4 ⟨won[der]⟩ marvel
292, l.15 Sublime ⟨and grand⟩
292, l.16 writer ⟨of the people⟩
293, l.2 all ⟨the ladies that strove to gain his favour⟩
293, l.10 ⟨her⟩ the
294, l.23 ⟨most of⟩ the company
294, l.26 ⟨firs[t]⟩ At first
294, l.30 whisper ⟨behind him⟩
294, l.32 visible ⟨at a little distance⟩
294, l.38 vanished ⟨and⟩
295, l.8 showed ⟨her⟩
295, l.12 death ⟨was⟩
295, l.19 I ⟨shall⟩
295, l.30 ⟨none bu[t]⟩ no
297, l.2 as ⟨known⟩
297, l.7 followed ⟨with he⟩
297, l.9 Albion ⟨by [?1 word]⟩
297, l.16 ⟨Arthur⟩ Albion

297, l.23 never ⟨?more⟩
297, l.25 ⟨Albion⟩ he

Visits in Verreopolis, volume I (manuscript missing)

Visit in Verreopolis, volume II (manuscript missing)

A Fragment, 'Overcome with that delightful sensation of lassitude'
327, l.12 ⟨may⟩ might
327, l.15 motionless ⟨on the loch⟩
327, l.26 sad ⟨and⟩
329, l.3 ⟨pure⟩ fan
329, l.7 ⟨den⟩ lair
329, l.27 ⟨through⟩ while
329, l.27 ⟨dimly rolls⟩ wildered spreads
329, l.27 Following line cancelled: ⟨Her liquid main between⟩
329, l.33 ⟨passions⟩ oft the
329, l.33 ⟨darkest⟩ passion
330, l.1 ⟨And⟩ But
330, l.9 ⟨While⟩ Where wreaths of immortality ⟨around⟩
330, l.10 ⟨Around their borders⟩ in hallowed beauty
330, l.18 ⟨And silver evening⟩ Beneath the silver
330, l.22 ⟨star⟩ their
330, l.25 Following line cancelled: ⟨Mount up to victory⟩
331, l.8 ⟨in⟩ mid
331, l.14 ⟨were no more⟩ past away
331, l.15 ⟨They⟩ for
331, l.26 ⟨And⟩⟨All dew⟩ with morning dew all bright ⟨with morning dew⟩
331, l.31 ⟨the sweet tones⟩ melody
331, l.31 ⟨dwelt⟩ rolled
331, l.31 Following line cancelled: ⟨from her harmonious tongue⟩
332, l.2 ⟨hath⟩ wandered
332, l.7 calm ⟨and still⟩
332, l.26 Following verse cancelled:
  ⟨And while his wondrous eloquence
    Made hours like moments fly
  While the spirit of intelligence
    Lit up his radiant eye⟩
332, l.34 ⟨Shone forth as hea[ven]⟩ Shone bright
333, l.3 ⟨on⟩ walk
333, l.10 ⟨at morning blows⟩ with matins rings
333, l.18 ⟨her⟩ no

'About 9 months after my arrival at the Glass Town'
334, l.6 willowy ⟨and [?1 word]⟩
334, l.10 ⟨vast⟩ cloud
334, l.25 ⟨while⟩ beguiled
334, l.28 literature ⟨music⟩
334, l.36 ⟨form⟩ finely
335, l.14 regal ⟨por[tico]⟩

Textual Notes

The Bridal

335, l.25 ⟨round it⟩ with
335, l.26 ⟨the⟩ its
336, l.13 ⟨eyes⟩ ⟨closed⟩ spirit
336, l.27 ⟨And most bea⟩ The other
336, l.33 vow ⟨A [?4 words] the young king⟩
336, l.35 light ⟨shined⟩ beam⟨ing⟩ed
336, l.35 ⟨brig[ht] clear⟩ fair
337, l.4 ⟨One⟩ A bright
337, l.15 ⟨golden glory⟩ sunlike spendour
337, l.15 ⟨sunlike⟩ golden
337, l.23 ⟨And⟩ Full
337, l.28 ⟨tune⟩ sound
337, l.31 ⟨kni[ght]⟩ noble
337, l.36 ⟨honoured⟩ hallowed
338, l.7 ⟨satiated⟩ dazzled
338, l.16 set out ⟨with⟩ ⟨on my excursion⟩
338, l.17 ⟨on the th[ird]⟩ After
338, l.20 ⟨by⟩ here
338, l.21 ⟨lay like⟩ lying
338, l.30 ⟨avenue⟩ alley
338, l.35 ⟨arrived at the confines of the wood⟩ entered
338, l.38 ⟨When⟩ at sight
339, l.4 ⟨long⟩ tall
339, l.4 ⟨on the ground⟩ beside him
339, l.8 ⟨dark⟩ eyes
339, l.11 ⟨formed in the⟩ moulded
339, l.13 ⟨added⟩ gave
339, l.14 ⟨her⟩ what
339, l.14 ⟨handsome⟩ beautiful
339, l.39 ⟨green⟩ shadowy
340, l.3 ⟨May the⟩ Thou
340, l.4 ⟨his⟩ thy
340, l.13 ⟨thou⟩ he
340, l.16 ⟨thy⟩ his
340, l.20 ⟨wave in England's sky⟩ be unfurled
340, l.31 ⟨Hush⟩ Methought
341, l.1 ⟨immediately⟩ stopped
341, l.2 ⟨Marquis⟩ youth
341, l.6 ⟨reached⟩ arrived
341, l.9 ⟨clothed wi[th]⟩ perfumed
341, l.13 awe ⟨into the⟩
341, l.13 ⟨Possessor⟩ Lord
341, l.14 ⟨such⟩ so
341, l.14 ⟨takes⟩ has
341, l.17 ⟨some⟩ many
341, l.19 ⟨great encourager⟩ most generous
341, l.21 ⟨from it⟩ the contents

Page

342, l.11 ⟨Now⟩ On
342, l.11 ⟨another shelf⟩ ⟨one⟩ a rich
342, l.26 ⟨old⟩ inhabitants
342, l.26 ⟨Greece and Rome⟩ the old pagen world
342, l.27 ⟨Lady⟩ Zenobia
342, l.27 ⟨Mar[quis]⟩ Arthur
343, l.13 ⟨cloa[k]⟩ mantle
343, l.15 ⟨fine⟩ features
343, l.16 ⟨and⟩ at
343, l.33 ⟨calmly⟩ soberly
343, l.36 ⟨on⟩ to
344, l.10 ⟨whirled⟩ swept
344, l.12 ⟨his way⟩ slowly
344, l.13 ⟨back to the camp⟩ forward
344, l.15 ⟨loveliness⟩ lustre
344, l.25 ⟨given his⟩ consented
344, l.35 ⟨The⟩ Shortly
345, l.8 attend⟨ing⟩ed
345, l.9 ⟨were⟩ appeared
345, l.21 ⟨sullen fire⟩ latent flame
346, l.9 ⟨public sta⟩ shady groves
346, l.16 ⟨on⟩ among
347, l.1 ⟨hung⟩ visible
347, l.9 ⟨on⟩ in
347, l.9 ⟨day⟩ hour
347, l.10 ⟨of Death⟩ Azael
347, l.14 by ⟨the⟩
347, l.17 Duty ⟨sen[se]⟩
347, l.19 ⟨Sense⟩ Duty

INDEX OF FIRST LINES AND TITLES

Alphabetical arrangement
This is letter-by-letter; punctuation within a title or line has been ignored.
As some titles in this book have been derived from first lines, neither titles nor lines of text in this index have been inverted, so definite and indefinite articles have been treated as keywords in alphabetization and occur at the beginning of lines.
When there are several instalments of one story, these have been placed in chronological order.

Space and format of the index
Titles of manuscript volumes and of stories and poems within these volumes have been indexed. These are printed in italics. First lines of stories and poems, including poems that occur within stories, are printed in roman type in inverted commas. Italic titles with inverted commas indicate story titles derived from the first line of text.
Dates have been included in square brackets where necessary to distinguish two or more stories with the same title.
Cross-references to associated titles are given.
Numbers in italic indicate illustrations of the manuscript.

'About 9 months after my arrival at the Glass Town', 333–5
A Day at Parry's Palace, 229–33
'A few days after my visit to the theatre', 261–4
'A fine picture engraved in the first style', 281–2
A Fragment, August the 7, 1829, 40
A Fragment [1831], 327–33, *328*
A Frenchman's Journal Continued, 250–4
  see also *Journal of a Frenchman*, 221–3
A Frenchman's Journal Continued (manuscript lost), 227
A Frenchman's Journal Continued, 261–4

A Frenchman's Journal Concluded, 276–9
'A large room hung with tapestry', 58–60
Albion and Marina, 284, 285–97
A Letter from Lord Charles Wellesley (manuscript lost), 227
'All soberness is past and gone', 94–5
A Midnight Song (manuscript lost), 227
An Adventure in Ireland, 18–21
An American Tale, 83–5
Anecdotes of the Duke of Wellington, 88–90
An Extraordinary Dream, 269–73
An Interesting Passage in the Lives of Some Eminent Men of the Present Time, 170–7
'A parlour in Bravey's Inn', 224–7

A Romantic Tale, 7–18
A Scene in my Inn, 81–3
A Traveller's Meditations, 274–5
A True Story [August 1829], 54–5
A True Story [September 1829], 62–4
*A Visit to the Duke of Wellington's Small
    Palace Situated on the Banks of the
    Indiva*, 349–51
  see also *Description of the Duke of
    Wellington's Small Palace Situated
    on the Banks of the Indiva*, 130–3

Blackwood's Young Men's Magazine
    August 1829, 54–62
    September 1829, 62–9
    October 1829, 70–8
    November 1829, 78–88
    December 1829, 91–9, *98*
    December 1829 (second issue),
      113–23
    A General Index to the Magazines,
      122
  see also *Young Men's Magazine*
'By this time it was perfectly dark',
    317–27

Campbell Castle, 281–3
*Catalogue of my Books with the periods of
    their completion up to August 3,
    1830*, 211–14
*Characters of the Celebrated Men of the
    Present Time*, 123–30
Concluding Address, 280
Conversations [December 1829],
    118–21
  see also *Military Conversations*,
    58–60, 74–6
Conversations [August 1830], 224–7
Conversations [October 1830], 234–9
Conversations [December 1830],
    264–7

'Dagger, what heart hath quivered
    neath thy blow?', 260–1
'Death is here, I feel his power', 253

'De Lisle and Lord Charles
    Wellesley', 264–7
*Description of the Duke of Wellington's
    Small Palace Situated on the Banks
    of the Indiva*, 130–3
  see also *A Visit to the Duke of
    Wellington's Small Palace Situated
    on the Banks of the Indiva*, 349–51
'During my travels in the south of
    Ireland', 18–21
'Dusk, curtains down, fire blazing
    brightly', 74–6

'Early one beautiful morning', 78–80

'Farewell, O thou pleasant land', 80–1
Fragment. August the 8, 1829, 41

Harvest in Spain, 115
'Haste, bring us the wine cup', 277–8
'Hearken, O Mortal to the wail', 326
'He is gone and all grandeur has fled
    from the mountain', 339–40
'How pleasant is the world', 86–7

'I believe that in great houses', 170–7
'I have before put forth a volume of
    these tales', 99–113
'I have nothing to say', 298–316
'I have written this tale', 285–97
Interior of a Pothouse, 65–6
'In the autumn of the year 1832',
    338–48
'In the Palace of Waterloo, there is a
    secret court', 54–5
'In the summer of the year 18—',
    130–3
'In the summer of the year 18—',
    349–51
'In the summer of the year [?1832]',
    216–19
'In the year 1829', 70–3
'In this fairy land of light', 49–50
'I once knew a man', 178–9
'I think of thee when the moonbeams
    play', 293–4

'I understand many were convinced',
269–73
'It is now many years', 113–15
'It is now, we should suppose', 56
'It is the fashion nowadays', 256–60

Journal of a Frenchman, 221–3
  see also *A Frenchman's Journal
  Continued*, 227, 250–4, 261–4; *A
  Frenchman's Journal Concluded*,
  276–9

Leisure Hours, 178–9
Liffey Castle, 216–19
*Lines by One who was Tired of Dullness
  upon the Same Occasion*, 95–6
*Lines Spoken by a Lawyer on the
  Occasion of the Transfer of this
  Magazine*, 94–5
*Lines to the Aragva, a River of the
  Caucasian Mountains*, 219–20
'Long my anxious ear hath listened',
296
'Lo our mighty chieftains come', 63
'Lo! stretched beneath the clust'ring
  palm', 327–33
'Lo! The light of the morning is
  flowing', 233–4

'Many years ago there lived a man',
92–4
'Many years ago there lived in a
  certain country', 154–69
'Marquis [of] Douro. Lord Charles
  Wellesley. Henry Rhymer',
  190–6
'Marquis of Douro, Young Soult,
  Lord Wellesley, Sergeant Bud,
  De Lisle, Parlour in Bravey's
  Inn', 234–9
'Merry England, land of glory', 120–1
'Mighty river, bold gushing', 219–20
Military Conversations [August 1829],
  58–60
  see also *Conversations*, 118–21,
  224–7, 234–9, 264–7

Military Conversations [October 1829],
  74–6
Morning, 233–4
'My motive for publishing this book',
  134–40

'Night. Captain Tree, Captain Bud,
  Marquis of Douro and Lord
  Charles Wellesley', 118–21
'Now all is joy and gladness, the ripe
  fruits', 115
'Now fall the last drops of the shower',
  310–11

'O blessed, mildly rising morn', 137–8
'"Oh Arthur!" said I', 229–33
'Once papa lent my sister Maria a
  book', 4–5
'One cold, dreary night', 40
'One evening the Duke of
  Wellington', 140–54
'One fine autumnal evening', 196–211
'One fine morning in the month of
  July', 34–6
'One very cold and dark night', 81–3
*On Seeing a Beautiful Statue and a Rich
  Golden Vase full of Wine lying
  beside it in the Desert of Sahara*,
  73–4
*On Seeing an Ancient Dirk in the
  Armory of the Tower of All Nations
  Bloodstained with Three Distinct
  Spots which Marks None have yet
  been Able to Erase*, 260–1
On Seeing the Garden of a Genius, 86–7
On the Great Bay of the Glass Town,
  91–2
'O! There is a wood in a still and
  deep', 335–7
'On the third day I came to a wide
  plain', 41
'On the third of February 1820',
  276–9
'O spirits of the sky were there',
  236–7

381

'Overcome with that delightful
  sensation of lassitude', 327–33
'O when shall our brave land be free',
  57
'O where has Arthur been this night?',
  143

'Proudly the sun has sunk to rest',
  166–7

'Reader, farewell!', 280
*Review of the 'Causes of the Late War' by
  the Duke of Wellington*, 56
*Review of 'The Chief Genii in Council',
  by Edward De Lisle*, 113–15
*Review of the paiting of the Spirit of
  Cawdor Ravine by Dundee, a
  private in the 20th*, 64–5
'Rhymer alone in a garret', 180–7

Scenes on the Great Bridge, 78–80
*Second Scenes of the Young Men's
  Magazine: see Young Men's
  Magazine*
'See that golden goblet shine', 73–4
Silence, 242–7
'*Sir – it is well known that the Genii*, 39
'Some love Sorrow's dismal howls',
  247–50
Song, 247–50
'Soon after the arrival of Alexandre',
  115–17
Strange Events, 256–60
'Sweep the sounding harp string',
  95–6

Tales of the Islanders
  Vol. I, 21–33, *31*
  Vol. II, 99–113
  Vol. III, 140–54
  Vol. IV, 196–211
' "The ability to keep silence well" ',
  242–7
The Adventures of Ernest Alembert,
  154–69

*The Adventures of Mon Edouard de
  Crack*, 133–40
The Bridal, 335–48
'The cheerful fire is blazing bright',
  65–6
'The Duke invariably reposes', 88–90
The Enfant, 34–6
'The first time I saw His Grace',
  123–30
'*The following strange occurrence*', 177
The Glass Town, 67–8
The History of the Year, 4–5
The Keep of the Bridge, 36–8, *37*
'The legend from which this painting
  is taken', 64–5
'The mill-wheel of America is going
  downwards', 83–5
The Minstrel Boy, 282–3
'The night after that delightful
  evening', 250–4
'*The origin of the Islanders*', 6
'*The origin of the O'Deans*', 6
'The peal within the shell concealed',
  300–1
'The persons meant by the Chief of
  the City', 42–53
'The play of the Islanders', 21–33
The Poetaster
  Vol. I, 179–87
  Vol. II, 187–96, *189*
'There is a tradition', 7–18
'*There was once a little girl and her name
  was Anne*', 3
The Search After Happiness, 42–53
The Silver Cup, 70–3
*The Song of the Ancient Britons on
  Leaving the Genii Land*, 80–1
The Swiss Artist, 92–4
The Swiss Artist Continued, 115–17
The Twelve Adventures, 7–18
The Will, 282
'This day my father died', 221–3
'This keep or round tower is
  celebrated in tradition', 36–8
'This picture possesses beauties and
  defects', 282–3

'This picture, though the subject is not of the highest kind', 282
'This wide world I have compassed round', 274–5
''Tis pleasant on some evening fair', 91–2
''Tis sunset and the golden orb', 67–8
'To the forest, to the wilderness', 152
Two Romantic Tales, 7–21
'Two Romantic Tales, in one volume, viz.', 211–14

Visits in Verreopolis
Vol. I, 297–316
Vol. II, 316–27

'What is more glorious in nature or art', 60
'When the young nobles had quitted the city', 62–4

Young Men's Magazine, ii
First, August 1830, 215–27
Second, September 1830 (manuscript missing), 227
Third, October 1830, 228–41
Fourth, November 1830, 241–55
Fifth, December 1830, 255–67
Sixth, December 1830 (second issue), 267–81
General Index to the Contents, 280–1
see also Blackwood's Young Men's Magazine